Stranger in Our Midst is written with such warmth and detail you can feel the strength of every character, especially Pastor Mike, who is the glue in the story. I look forward to the next book.

—Tina Edwards, Festus, Missouri

Very good reading, *Stranger in Our Midst* culminates in a surprise ending that left me hanging and looking forward to reading the sequel.

—Chris Armstrong, Festus, Missouri

Stranger in Our Midst was a great example of how simple and wholesome life can be. Sharon used her characters to remind me of what life is all about: God, family, and friendships. Once again, refreshing to read a book where people stand on their moral, godly convictions no matter the cost, no matter the heartbreak.

—Brandi Gunn, VBS/preschool director,
Faith Baptist Church

Property of Chesterfield
Meadow Little
Library

STRANGER IN OUR MIDST

THE OAK GROVE
CHRONICLES

SHARON TRAVERS

STRANGER IN OUR MIDST

TATE PUBLISHING & *Enterprises*

The Oak Grove Chronicles, Stranger in Our Midst
Copyright © 2010 by Sharon Travers. All rights reserved.

No part of this publication may be reproduced, stored in a retrieval system or transmitted in any way by any means, electronic, mechanical, photocopy, recording or otherwise without the prior permission of the author except as provided by USA copyright law.

This novel is a work of fiction. Names, descriptions, entities, and incidents included in the story are products of the author's imagination. Any resemblance to actual persons, events, and entities is entirely coincidental.

The opinions expressed by the author are not necessarily those of Tate Publishing, LLC.

Published by Tate Publishing & Enterprises, LLC
127 E. Trade Center Terrace | Mustang, Oklahoma 73064 USA
1.888.361.9473 | www.tatepublishing.com

Tate Publishing is committed to excellence in the publishing industry. The company reflects the philosophy established by the founders, based on Psalm 68:11,
"The Lord gave the word and great was the company of those who published it."

Book design copyright © 2010 by Tate Publishing, LLC. All rights reserved.
Cover design by Amber Gulilat
Interior design by Jeff Fisher

Published in the United States of America

ISBN:978-1-61566-792-5
Fiction, Christian, Historical
10.01.25

Dedication

I extend heartfelt gratitude to Reverend Bual Bales and Brother Mike Goodwin, former pastors who touched my life and showed me the way. Both men preached God's Word faithfully, lived what they preached, and exemplified God's love in action, thereby, revealing his love, his truth, and his infinite grace in my own life. Thank you for sowing the seed and watering the plant. You have been and always will be a great inspiration. I love you, Brother Bales and Brother Goodwin.

—Sharon

Those who hope in the LORD will renew their strength. They will soar on wings like eagles, they will run and not grow weary, they will walk and not be faint.

Isaiah 40:31, NIV

Walk with Me to Yesterday

I invite you to stroll along with me down the path and through the years to a time and place I believe everyone longs for at one time or another as they travel this road of life. If this is your first visit to Oak Grove, welcome to yesterday and days that were much simpler than the world we live in today. Perhaps you caught a glimpse of that time in *A Summer Long Remembered*. If so, I welcome your company once again as we return to the quiet, peaceful little town of Oak Grove and the people who lived there.

Stranger in Our Midst continues where *A Summer Long Remembered* ends, and no matter how many twists and turns were encountered along the way, the truth still remains that small things mattered and simple things were enjoyed. I hope you find pleasure in those simpler days, and perhaps if nothing more, may they jog your memory or give you a glimpse of a time that was very special.

If my story warms your heart, brings a smile, or leaves you pleased to have walked this path with me, I am truly happy.

—Sharon

Preface

Summer is quickly coming to an end. The mysterious ringing of the bell in the town square has been solved, and the thief that caused such havoc has been identified, much to everyone's astonishment.

In spite of the confusion and fear that accompanied early summer, doors remain unlocked, and children play Hide and Seek after dark. Trust and faith is as strong as ever, neighbors call back and forth and compare homegrown tomatoes across back fences, and families gather around the supper table at five o'clock on the dot.

The hot, sultry sun bears down across the valley, ushering in long, hazy dog days of summer and, though expected, still catches everyone by surprise. Relief arrives with the night air, and families retreat to front porches to discuss the day's events to the tune of chirping crickets and the sparkle of fireflies.

Young and old lie awake murmuring quietly, and the clock's chime at city hall reassures that all is well. Beyond the window, leaves move slightly, stars twinkle in the night sky, and a full moon's glow illuminates backyards, creating mysterious, dancing shadows around familiar bushes, garages, and trees. Children's imaginations are stirred no small amount as they peer out into the night and wonder what lurks among the rows of tomato vines, beanpoles, and corn stalks. Somewhere a dog barks, and the eleven o'clock train becomes more distinct as it chugs down the ridge and around the bend, blowing its whistle as it passes along the edge of town. Too hot for cover, bed linens are kicked to the foot of the bed, eyes droop, and spinning fan blades lull people to sleep.

Cool morning air slips away too quickly. Everyone is wilted by eleven o'clock, and housewives ponder what to prepare for supper without using their oven. Retreating from the heat, customers linger a little longer in Williams Drugstore; the Cranston Café has reverted to its light summer menu; and old Ben has propped open every door and window in the Blacksmith Shop. No one has any energy, and Melvin, making his milk run earlier than usual, bangs on the door so milk will not be left out to curdle or butter to melt.

Betting on how high the temperature will climb is a daily occurrence wherever two or three are gathered. Cooley claims he has never repaired so many fans in his whole life, and Pastor Mike and Reverend Clark both preached last Sunday without suit coats.

Oh to jump into the cold spring water at Seabaugh Mill, but the insufferable heat and long bicycle ride up the ridge deters that idea. Therefore, hoses are strung across lawns and spray children, dogs, windows, and anyone strolling by.

Children of all ages take refuge beneath shade trees and play marbles, paper dolls, read comics, or take inventory of the color and make of each and every automobile traveling down the street.

Throwing all caution to the wind, Willy is actively seeking Melba's favor, and Pastor Mike takes responsibility for a young mountain boy's education and adjustment to a new way of life.

The St. Louis Cardinals' chance to make it to the World Series and early preparations for Founders Day are topics of conversation all over town. Montgomery Ward and Sears' fall and winter catalogues have arrived, and the Dime Store window advertises, "Everything you need for school."

Edna's Dress Shop heralds its new line of fall clothing and hats, whereas, Baker's Clothier displays a new Kuppenheimer suit—*the choice of men who seek the mark of good breeding in everything they own and wear.*

Of course, some things never change: Sunday dinner, the fragrance of honeysuckle on the square, and Miss Mattie's candy box. The familiar lunch crowd buzz at the Cranston Café, a cork on the end of a fishing line, and the ongoing bickering over checkers in Old Ben's Blacksmith Shop are all but a part of everyday life.

I often long to return to that small town nestled in the plush, green valley of the Ozark Mountains and, on occasion, do so in my mind. Journey with me and discover a time that will capture your heart and make you smile as it did those who shared life, love, and laughter in 1946. They were truly blessed, and I sincerely hope you will be too.

Oak Grove Folks
-1946-

Mike Daniels Family
Pastor, Oak Grove Baptist Church (38), wife: Leah (35)
Children: John (12), Laura (11), Shari (8), and Jimmy (6)

Andrew Baxter (38)
Artist - aka Jonathon Wilkins

Benjamin A. Cook (90) **"Old Ben"**
The Blacksmith Shop

Peter Clark
Pastor, Methodist Church (56), wife: Sarah (53)

Thomas Cooley "Cooley"
Janitor at Oak Grove Public School (30), wife: Alice (29)
Children: Tommy (9) and Betty Jean (7)

Samuel Cranston Family
Owns Cranston Hotel and Cranston Café (72), wife: Abigail (71)
Spinster twins, Milly and Molly (50) The Sweet Shoppe

Henry Driscol
Mayor of Oak Grove (50), wife: Trudy (45)
Adopted nieces: Caroline (15) and Elizabeth (10)

Gloria Hansen (25)
Librarian

Ann Madison (95) **"Miss Mattie"**
Oldest living resident of Oak Grove

Melba Maple (27)
Melba's Salon

Jack Reese
Reese's Market (38), wife: Mildred (36)

Elijah Seabaugh
Owns farm northwest of town (71), wife: Elizabeth (70) Cares for Nathan Black (14)

William Stanton (29)
Willy's Garage

John Walker Family
Sheriff (41), wife: Ann (39)
Children: Brenton (12), Preston (10), Josiah (8), Jordan (6), and Garrett (4)

Jim Walker Family
Fire chief and deputy (37), wife: Jennifer (36)
Children: Truman (12), Simon (10)

Gerald Williams
Oak Grove Drug Store (42), wife: Stella (41)

Matilda Watson (78) "Miss Tillie"

The Town of Oak Grove
—1946—

Chapter I

Wind blew through the trees with sudden, unexpected vengeance, as if in battle, bent on pushing the insufferable August heat to parts unknown. Swaying branches released dry, brittle leaves to swirl in wild abandon, and Leah stopped and looked up through the treetops. A small, dark cloud that seemingly came from nowhere was rapidly spreading across the sky.

Brushing a loose curl from her face, she sighed with relief and lifted long, dark hair from the back of her neck, relishing the unexpected cool breeze. Closing her eyes, she held her arms out and smiled with pleasure.

"Feels good doesn't it?" Mike asked, watching.

"Oh yes! It is wonderful," Leah exclaimed, smiling as he took her hand.

Gazing at her tenderly, he was overwhelmed once more that God had given her to him and wondered at her affect on him after all these years. Squeezing her fingers, he glanced up as thunder rumbled long and low. The storm cloud had darkened considerably and spread in all directions. Within minutes, the sun's filtering rays vanished completely, and the forest lay muted in shadow.

Breathing in the fresh scent of rain, Leah waited expectantly, hoping Johnny or Laura would think to close the windows.

"I wish the sky would open up and dump buckets of rain. I don't care if we get drenched." She would welcome anything that brought a respite from this unrelenting heat August held in its grip. Wiping perspiration from her forehead with the back of her hand, she looked around at the darkened forest.

"That would feel good, wouldn't it?" Mike asked, plucking a dead twig.

"Yes." Leah sighed, recalling the taunting, teasing thunderclouds that had appeared the last three days. Forming layer upon layer in the southwest, they had rumbled across the sky, promising a good drenching, and then blew off to the north, leaving nothing but a brief coolness in the air and a few raindrops. Within minutes, the sun's unrelenting heat bore down on the valley again, causing everyone to shake their heads in exasperation and seek a place to cool off.

Tying her hair back with a ribbon from her pocket, Leah looked at her husband, who had halted and was studying the sky thoroughly.

"We may just get wet," he murmured. A slow grin spread across his face as he looked at her, a memory of their honeymoon coming to mind. "You wouldn't want to get wet and look like a drowned rat, would you?"

Giggling, Leah recalled the day they were caught in a downpour while hiking. Married only three days, she had taken great pains with her clothing, hair, and makeup, ending up resembling a raccoon with mascara streaming down her face. Her hair hung limp, her clothes were soaked, and she had been mortified. Telling her she was still beautiful, Mike was surprised when his new bride sputtered words of anger, moaned with embarrassment, and resorted to tears.

"I did, didn't I?" Leah laughed, pleased that he remembered. A yearning to go back to that time tugged at her heart, and she tried to recall how long it had been since they had shared any length of time alone.

Chuckling, Mike agreed and pushed a low-hanging branch from their path. Accustomed to the woods, he walked surefooted, looking in all directions as he led her through trees and brush. Following closely, Leah admired his broad shoulders and thought him more handsome now than when they first married.

Glancing at her wristwatch, she realized they had walked approximately forty-five minutes. *The car can't be much farther,* she thought, wondering how Mike knew where he was going. Nothing, absolutely nothing, looked familiar.

It had been a long trek this morning, but one she enjoyed immensely. With its untamed beauty and varied sights, sounds, and smells, the dense forest was a world of its own. Coming upon a small stream, they paused to rest and watched two deer emerge from the trees, look around, and then slowly approach. Drinking the cool water, they looked up and then moved to another spot and drank again. Farther along the trail, a red fox appeared then just as quickly disappeared, a small chipmunk peered from the backside of a tree limb, and a bald eagle, visible through a break in the trees, soared high above with its wings spread against the sky.

The long-awaited visit with the Black family had proved more enjoyable than Leah anticipated. Isolated far atop one of the ridges, they were a mystery to those in Oak Grove. Wild tales, speculations, and no small amount of imagination surrounded the family, and if not for Mike's wanderings while hunting, he would never have stumbled upon Sally. Delivering the injured child safely home opened the door he needed, and through prayer, persistence, and repeated visits, Mike had eventually won Nathaniel Black's trust and friendship and was able to convince him of his oldest son's need for extended education and knowledge of the outside world. The only person to have visited their home, Mike respected their wish for privacy and had never revealed their location or taken anyone with him but Johnny, earlier in the summer, and today Leah.

Taking an immediate liking to Elizabeth Black, Leah had felt the woman to be a kindred spirit. *Spring Rain, what a beautiful name,* she thought, her attention now back at the cabin on the ridge and the petite, raven-haired Apache woman. Beautiful, almond-shaped eyes reflected loving kindness, and the copper tint of her skin only added to their warmth. *Ten children,* Leah thought, *how in the world—*

Stopping, she glanced up at Mike questioningly. He had halted abruptly, turned, and now enfolded her in his arms. "I believe we are lost and alone in the woods.

What, my dear, are we to do?" he asked, raising a dark brow, a rakish grin on his face, and his blue eyes teasing. Pulling her close, he kissed her tenderly for a long moment and then squeezed her tight and nibbled her neck.

Leah's laughter filled the forest, causing a squirrel in the tree above to look at them curiously and chatter from his lofty height. Placing both arms around Mike's neck, she pulled his head down and soundly returned his kiss.

Now her turn to raise a brow, she looked up at him. "Are you sure we are lost? *The preacher man* wouldn't be lying to his poor, innocent wife, would he?"

A deep laugh erupted, and he squeezed her. "Yes, that is what I am doing." He stood quietly for a moment, rubbing his chin against the softness of her hair. "Wouldn't it be nice—the two of us alone for a few days?"

Resting her head against his chest, Leah felt the solid, even beat of his heart, and she sighed in contentment, aware of the familiar scent of Old Spice and the feel of his arms around her.

"Why don't we? We haven't done that in such a long time."

"No we haven't, and I am sorry." He tenderly touched her cheek with his finger. "Will you forgive me for ignoring you?"

"You never ignore me. There is nothing to forgive."

"Yes there is, darlin', but thank you for being so gracious," he replied, kissing her cheek. Holding her close, he lifted his eyes to the threatening clouds, awed by God's display of majesty and power, and marveled once again that God loved him in spite of all his shortcomings.

"Let's make plans to go somewhere, just the two of us."

"Yes!" she exclaimed, hugging him tightly and smiling, dimples creasing both cheeks and her dark eyes sparkling.

A clap of thunder rumbled close, and Mike looked up at the swaying branches. Large raindrops fell against his face, and he knew it was coming.

"Come on. We better go before we get soaked. The car is just ahead."

Leah laughed merrily as they ran through the trees. Raindrops fell heavier, and Mike's laughter rang out as he pulled her along, and she relived that long ago day when they ran through the rain. Stopping, he turned and swung her up in his arms and over a huge fallen oak they crossed earlier that morning. Then, in one swift move, he jumped over the dead tree and pointed to the car as the heavens opened up with a downpour. Jerking the door open, Mike shoved her in, jumped in beside her, and slammed the door.

Leah's heart beat wildly as rain pelted the roof, and an unnerving, sudden darkness settled over the forest. Unconsciously holding her hand over her heart, she peered through the windshield at a green blur of driving rain and tree limbs.

"Trade me places, Leah," Mike yelled over the hammering rain. Pulling her across his lap and unceremoniously plopping her on the seat next to him, he slid beneath the steering wheel. Retrieving the key from the floorboard, he started the engine and paused at the expression on her face. "Don't worry, darlin'. We'll be okay, but I think we better get out of here."

A sudden urge to give it the gas entered his mind, but he knew that would be foolish. Rain was falling in torrents, and visibility was limited, to say the least. Wind and rain pummeled the car, another loud crash of thunder rolled, and lightning struck a tree, splitting a large branch, which fell to their left.

Squealing, Leah buried her face against his arm and clung to the side of his shirt with both hands.

"I'll pray. You drive."

Staring through pelting rain, Mike steered the car slowly along what was nothing more than an old wagon trail. Knowing in a matter of minutes it would quickly turn to a quagmire of mud, the possibility of getting bogged down was very real. So much for Leah's earlier opinion of it being "such a quaint, old wagon trail rich in history." They would travel this trail for another fifteen minutes, and he did not have a desire to add any more history to it than it already had.

The rain suddenly abated, and Mike looked up. Dark, ominous clouds were taking on an eerie, greenish tint. In the next instant, rain and hail were unleashed; a sudden gust blew a low-hanging branch against the driver's side, and several small limbs flew across the hood. Noting the trail filling with muddy water, he silently petitioned the Lord to prevent the car from getting stuck. Then, when another loud crack sounded close, he hastily added a request to prevent a tree from falling atop the car. Jagged streaks of lightning danced through trees in spectacular fashion, and he was amazed at the beauty in the midst of fury.

"Are you still praying?" Mike asked, knowing without a doubt she was.

"Yes," Leah replied, cautiously peeking up at him.

He gave her a reassuring glance. "Then you have nothing to worry about. God is our refuge and strength. You should watch this; it is spectacular."

Noting her husband's calmness, Leah closed her eyes and quoted the scripture to which he referred. "God is our refuge and strength, an ever present help in trouble."

"You believe that, don't you?"

"Why of course." Sitting up straighter, she stared through the window and watched in awe. The violent wind tossed tree branches, bent giant oaks and maples, and whipped brush around, rooting them out of the ground. Lightning jumped rapidly from cloud to cloud, striking trees at random and filling the air with loud, cracking noises. Thunder rolled, and driving rain hammered against the windows. *And here we sit,* Leah thought, *warm and dry.*

"I hope the children are at Sarah's," she commented, more to herself than Mike. Instructions to go to the Clark's in an emergency had been an understanding between the two families for years, and Leah found it a great comfort to know Sarah was close at hand.

"I imagine they hightailed it through the hedgerow in record time"—Mike chuckled—"with Laura leading the pack."

The hedgerow consisted of thick, wild sweet briar that grew along the back of both properties, its only break being a well-worn path that cut through the middle beneath an old arbor. With no children of their own, Reverend Clark and his wife bestowed much of their attention and love on the Daniels children, who wholeheartedly returned the affection. *Surely*, Leah thought, *they are at Sarah's*.

The car suddenly slid sideways, and her eyes flew to Mike as he turned the steering wheel first one way and then the other.

"Isn't this fun?"

"Fun?" Leah questioned incredulously. This definitely was not fun. "How much farther is the old mill?"

"Just a couple more minutes, and we will be out of the woods." He chuckled, noting her expression.

"I will be glad," she answered, one hand still maintaining a grip on his shirt as she stared straight ahead. Old Mill Road appeared through the trees, and she sighed in relief. *Thank heavens*, she thought then jumped as a thunderous crack rent the air and a towering oak shook. Leah's eyes widened as everything appeared to move in slow motion. The tree began to topple, tree branches and wild plants and weeds growing along the trail waved lazily, and Mike's movements appeared surreal. As if waking from a dream, she saw him stomp the accelerator and felt the car shoot forward, thrusting her back and against his shoulder. Twisting around, she looked through the rear window and watched the oak fall to the ground, barely missing the back of the car.

"Thank you, Lord," she whispered.

"Gusty winds, hail, and rain moving across the county; keep a watchful eye," Fred's voice warned on the radio. "I'll pass along an update when I get it; and now, here's another public service announcement from Brylcreem."

Melba crossed the salon floor and looked curiously out across the square, humming along to the familiar jingle "A Little Dab'll Do Ya." Wind blew tree branches, and the flag atop the flagpole flapped wildly. Milly and Molly stood in the door of the Sweet Shoppe looking at the sky, and Hank stepped out of the hardware store, pointed upward, and yelled something to Cooley, who was frantically finishing his mowing.

Trying to dismiss an uneasy feeling, Melba reminded herself that the clouds of the last three days had produced nothing. Yet Fred said there was a bad thunderstorm coming. Shrugging her shoulders, she returned to the shampoo bowl, where Trudy Driscol sat watching her.

"Say, did you hear what Fred just said?" Trudy asked, watching her unfold a shampoo cape. "He said rain and hail. *Humph*, everyone in the county will probably get it but us. You don't really think...I mean...We won't have a tornado, will we?" She glanced nervously over at Mildred, who was looking out the window.

"Oh, I don't think so, Trudy," Melba answered, turning the radio off. All she needed was Trudy and Mildred getting worked into a dither. "But we really do need rain."

"Land sakes, you are right about that. I believe I might have you do my nails, Melba. I like this new shade of polish."

"I can do that for you." Melba tested the water. "Are you going somewhere special this weekend?"

"Henry and I planned on going to—land sakes, it's getting blustery." Trudy stared at the window. "Maybe it will rain. Mary better take the sheets off the line. She changes our linens every Friday and insists on washing them up. I have told her time and again to wait until Monday when she does the rest of the laundry, but does she listen? No." Trudy shook her head and scooted back in the chair with a huff. "She always says, 'You never know when you might get comp'ny, and I don't want it on my conscience if someone has to sleep in a bed that's not fresh,' as if we didn't have a whole closet full of bed linens."

"Say, it sure looks like we might get something." Mildred turned from the window, glanced at Melba, and sat down in the chair. Picking up a *Modern Romance* magazine, she thumbed through it, feeling somewhat guilty and very confused.

Preaching on the subject of sex last week, Reverend Clark had made it very clear that God instituted that relationship exclusively for marriage. She could not have agreed more and hoped those to whom it applied were listening. With all the young people in the congregation, why, it was a subject they definitely needed to hear. Just a week before, Trudy had told her in confidence that Henry had said that Sam Cranston had told him that he and Abigail had noted a lot of sparking going on around the square, sometimes as late as nine at night. Mercy, hugging and kissing in public was downright disgraceful.

Yes indeed, it was a good sermon, and she glanced around to see if everyone was listening. Then her own cheeks grew warm with his next words: "Be very careful what you read and to what you listen. Some magazines contain stories and pictures that are not wholesome. It is tempting to look at them, and need I remind you that some of the radio programs are full of tempting situations? These types of habits can lead you astray if you are not careful."

He was speaking directly to her, she knew it. Shifting uncomfortably in the pew, her neck and face grew warm, and she wondered if she looked as red as she felt. Unable to look at anyone, she stared at the Sunday school attendance plaque, mortified that he chose such a subject to preach about. Nevertheless, she went home and promptly threw all of her romance magazines in the trash, vowing not to spend money on such nonsense anymore.

Now she wondered if perhaps she had not acted hastily. Was there really anything wrong with a love story? After all, Melba, being the good Christian woman she was, had the magazines right here in her salon, for goodness' sake. In a dither of confusion, she also wondered about watching *Faraway Hill* with Trudy yesterday. It all seemed so real when you actually watched it on television, much more so than listening to it on the radio. They were both caught up in the story, thinking what a sorry mess Karen had gotten herself into. Returning to her hometown after the death of her husband, she was pining away, in love with a man who was engaged to another woman. Mildred knew nothing good could come of that, but Trudy found it terribly exciting that Karen longed to kiss him.

"You mark my words. He is going to break off his engagement and marry Karen," Trudy had said. Then where would that leave the poor heartbroken fiancée? The young man would be in a pickle then, but, after all, it was just make-believe. Was it really wrong?

Sighing, Mildred stared at the floor. She would have to ask Reverend Clark about it. "Mercy me," she mumbled, a thought popping into her head. Perhaps he had watched *Faraway Hill* or looked at one of the romance magazines while preparing his sermon. No, she could not ask him. It would be too embarrassing. She could talk to Pastor Mike at the Baptist church but dismissed that thought immediately. He was much too young and handsome, and the thought of talking to him made her blush just thinking about it. Perhaps when September's Bible study on early church history rolled around, some of the other women would have answers or questions on the subject themselves. But then, how does one approach love stories and sex in the middle of the book of Acts?

"Mildred, are you listening?" Trudy looked at her strangely, wondering what in the world she was thinking.

"What did you say?"

"I said let's not get our hopes up. It looked like this yesterday and the two days before, but what did we get? Nothing, we didn't get a drop of rain. I declare, Melba, my flowerbeds are dried up to nothing, and Mary and I water them every day. It has not done a bit of good. I'll swan. You should see my poor day lilies. And the brown-eyed Susans and Queen Anne's lace along the road are withered to nothing." Trudy rambled on, examining the new shade of nail polish Melba had brought back from Chesterville.

"Say, Mildred, how are your flowers? Are they dried up also? Of course, you don't have nearly as many as we do. Henry keeps planting more every spring. Land sakes, you would think he has enough to do with all of his mayoral responsibilities, wouldn't you? But he says it relaxes him and he enjoys it, so I suppose—"

"Oh, hang your flowers, Trudy," Mildred commented irritably. Sometimes she just couldn't take all of Trudy's rambling, even if she was her best friend. Nervously rolling the *Modern Romance* magazine in her hands, she stared through the window.

"Well, I never," Trudy retorted, raising a brow and looking at Melba. "Just because they own the market doesn't mean she can … What are you looking at, Mildred?"

"You should take a look out here. I don't like the color of the sky at all. I believe we are in for a storm."

"Oh my heavens," Trudy exclaimed, putting a hand to her cheek. "I knew I should have kept my hair appointment this morning. But I thought I could get some shopping in and not have to make two trips to town if I waited until this afternoon, but Elizabeth had a mess in her room. I made her clean her closet, and you wouldn't believe all the junk she drug out into the middle of the floor. If I hadn't stayed there, well, it would lie there until Christmas and—"

The ringing telephone interrupted Trudy's rambling, and she set the fingernail polish on the counter with a frown. She didn't much care for the way Melba hurriedly grabbed the phone. After all, she was the mayor's wife and a patron and needed to get her hair shampooed and pin curled, go home, and get dressed. Henry was driving her to Chesterville for dinner. Impatiently drumming her fingers on the arm of the chair, she smoothed her dress and looked at Melba impatiently, observing the way her face lit up.

A look of concern replaced Melba's smile, and she turned away, murmuring quietly. Replacing the hand piece on the cradle, she glanced toward the window.

"That was Willy. He said Fred just announced that a bad storm hit Chesterville. It blew out the windows at C&G Hardware and damaged some roofs."

"Oh my word, we are going to Chesterville this evening for dinner!" Trudy exclaimed. "Is it coming this way? Do you think we should head for the café or drugstore?"

"I don't think so. Not yet ... I ... Willy just said to keep an eye on the sky." Melba glanced toward the window and casually draped a black cape around Trudy's shoulders. Sighing, she ran a hand along her forehead. Of all people to have in the shop! No two could get more hysterical than Trudy and Mildred.

A soft smile played around Melba's lips as she thought of Willy and how attentive he had become. She still found it hard to believe she had lived in Oak Grove five years and had never noticed him, not until the night of the circus. She had definitely noticed him that night. But he had stayed away, even after helping her home when she faked a sprained ankle. Melba knew he was attracted to her, but he avoided her. Therefore, it had been a total surprise when he stopped by one evening and invited her to accompany him to Miss Mattie's Fourth of July celebration. Whatever changed his attitude, she did not know, but she was very pleased.

Melba glanced toward the window again. The sky was becoming darker, and to stall a bit longer, she walked into the back room for fresh towels. Placing them on the shelf above Trudy's head, she noted Mildred nervously rolling a magazine around in her hands and her face taking on a look of panic as the fire whistle sounded. Its long, never-ending blast pierced the air, and Melba knew she needed to get herself and Trudy and Mildred to the café and down in the cellar.

Trudy sat straight up in the chair. "What is that? What is wrong?"

"I believe it is the emergency signal," Mildred remarked, standing to her feet with eyes as round as saucers.

Hurrying past the salon window with her head bent and one hand clutching her skirt, Gloria jerked the salon door open.

"We need to get to the café or the drugstore. Hurry, ladies."

"We are coming, Gloria," Melba replied, pulling Trudy up from the chair. Propelling her toward the door, she motioned Mildred to follow.

Still clutching the *Modern Romance* magazine, Mildred grabbed her hat and pocketbook and thrust an Edna's Dress Shop bag at Trudy, knocking her purse from the chair and spilling its contents.

"Oh, my word, Mildred, what are you thinking? Now look at what you've done," Trudy wailed, dropping to her knees. "Criminitly, if this isn't something."

"I didn't do it on purpose, for heaven's sake."

"No, of course you didn't, but you didn't need to throw my pocketbook at me."

"I did not throw your pocketbook. It was an accident, and if it wasn't as big as a suitcase…Here." Mildred retrieved a tube of lipstick from beneath the chair.

"Grab my Exlax, Mildred. It is right there under the chair…see?" Stuffing a significant amount of articles in her pocketbook, she watched Mildred grab the small, blue box. "It's a brand-new box. Just wait, you'll see," she said, looking up at Melba. "When you get a little older, you will have problems too…bloated, sluggish, and uncomfortable. I always keep it on hand."

"If you would eat more fruit, it would help. I have told you time and again—"

"I eat fruit!" Trudy retorted, jerking the laxative out of Mildred's hand and throwing it in her pocketbook. Standing to her feet, she glared at her. "You know I have never been regular; neither was my mother."

"Well, I have never in all my born days seen you so rude. You jerked that right out of my hand. You deserve constipation."

"Will you two hush?" Melba exclaimed exasperated.

"I think we really should hurry," Gloria commented, shaking her head at Trudy and Mildred, who had their backs to one another, clearly miffed.

Melba wanted to laugh. The fire whistle was blaring, Trudy and Mildred were mad at one another, and Gloria was standing in the door holding, for one reason or another, the world globe from the table in front of the library window.

"I am going to the café," Melba stated, grabbing the door. "Are you coming or not?"

"Oh, good gracious yes, Melba, don't you leave us," Trudy cried, bustling out the door.

Small twigs and blowing leaves struck their ankles as they hurried along the sidewalk, and Mildred let out a cry when the *Back to School Supplies* sign from the Dime Store sailed through the air in front of them. Plastered against the bank window, a brief moment of humor hit Melba as she thought of Michael Madison selling a large assortment of pencil boxes and Big Chief tablets in the bank. Halting in surprise, she stared as Clyde roared up and parked his taxi, its front wheels on the curb. Shouting something they could not hear, he waved, hesitated a moment, and then ran into the café. The glass in one of the street lamps shattered, Cooley ran toward his truck, and a man's gray hat rolled freely end over end down the sidewalk.

"Lord, have mercy," Mildred cried, colliding with Alan Miller as he stepped out of the Chronicle, the door slamming loudly behind him.

"I am sorry, Mildred. Ladies, hurry and get in the café. I am headed—" he yelled, halting in midsentence as they heard another clap of thunder and watched a jagged streak of lightning strike a large oak, one of its large branches cracking and falling onto the middle of the street.

"It's a twister. Oh my word, it's a twister," Trudy wailed, slapping at the shampoo cape. Flying around her like a witch's mantle, it caught a gust of wind and blew straight in the air then down over her head, stopping her dead in her tracks. "I can't see! Somebody help, oh, I am going to faint."

"You are not going to faint, Trudy!" Melba yelled, holding her skirt down with one hand and grabbing Trudy with the other. "I will not permit it. Do you hear me? Now let's get to the café." Melba pulled her along, fully exasperated. Of all people to be stuck with during an emergency!

At first warning, Ned had stepped out of his barbershop and into the café and was holding the door for them. "Come on, ladies, hurry. Get in here."

Ned jumped, and Melba gasped as a gust of wind blew the screen from his hand, banging it against the side of the building. The fire whistle continued, several folks ran in different directions, and thunder rumbled long and low. Gloria dashed through the opening, and Mildred and Trudy collided in the doorway.

"We are going to be blown away!" Trudy shouted. "Get out of the way, Mildred!"

"You get out of the way!"

"One of you step back," Melba yelled, wanting to slap both of them.

Grabbing Trudy by the arm, Ned pulled her back and shouted at Mildred, "Go on, hurry up, Mildred."

Wind slammed the loose screen against Melba's arm, and she stepped back, close to tears, a sudden panic seizing her. A firm grip encircled her wrist, and she felt a strong arm around her shoulders, pushing her forward. Glancing up, she sighed with relief at Willy's reassuring smile.

"Come on, Mel," he said calmly. Taking her by the hand, he steered her around the tables to the back of the café and down the cellar steps.

For a man of ninety, Benjamin Cook was amazingly agile. His mind was as sharp as a tack, and he found evidence of God's presence in everything he saw and touched. His skin was as dark as chocolate, hair white as snow, and he habitually smoothed a white mustache with his thumb and index finger. Dressed in his familiar faded overalls and a long-sleeved, plaid shirt, his presence was such a part of Oak Grove that one could not think of the town without thinking of old Ben and his blacksmith shop.

The usual group of men who gathered there had already gone home, and noting the rumble overhead, Ben stepped out on the small side porch, and peered up at the sky. Threatening black clouds churned, and wind blew against his face, evidencing a dramatic drop in temperature. Instinctively knowing what was coming, he headed indoors and made his way slowly through the house, closing windows. Stepping back into the shop, he secured the wooden shutters above the workbench and then headed to the double doors. Closing one, he glanced toward the firehouse and watched Jim Walker make a dash toward the door. *Ah expect he's goin' to sound the warnin',* Ben thought, pulling the other side closed and dropping the wooden plank in place.

Returning to the side door, he stepped out on the small porch where he had a clear view of the square, sat down in an old rocker, and watched folks scurry about. Ron, Oak Grove's mailman for the last ten years, was clutching his mailbag tightly as he disappeared into the post office, the loose White's Bakery sign swung precariously back and forth, and newspaper pages someone had left on one of the benches blew across the grass and into the street. Willy slammed the garage door and dashed across the square with his dog, Jack, at his heels, and Abigail Cranston and Lottie stood at the end of the hotel's veranda, waving for Milly and Molly to hurry. Hanging onto one another's arm, the two bustled across the street, and Clyde, making a quick left in his yellow taxi, slammed on his brakes to avoid hitting them.

Beginning low and rising in pitch, the fire whistle continued nonstop. To Ben's way of thinking, it only added to the confusion, scaring the daylights out of everyone, but he figured it got the job done. Looking up at the bell tower, he remembered his daddy ringing it during bad weather and disasters and thought how it frightened folks back then.

His brown eyes twinkled, and he chuckled as Trudy Driscol bustled along the sidewalk with a black cape flying behind her. A gust of wind blew it up over her head, and she came to a halt, waving both arms. Melba stopped, turned back, and said something, and they continued on to the café.

Edna closed the door of her dress shop and darted into the drugstore, and Jack Reese was out on the sidewalk in front of the market, uselessly trying to cover his produce with a tarpaulin. Cooley hurried to his old truck, threw pruning shears in the back, and jumped when a tree branch fell across the street in front of him.

Lifting his eyes to the roiling clouds, Ben watched wind whip through the trees. *This is goin' to be a good one.* Having seen plenty of storms in his ninety years, he always enjoyed watching the fury they unleashed. The calm, refreshing aftermath when the sun came out and presented the whole earth sparkling clean was something he relished. Inhaling the sweet fragrance, he watched the clouds open up with a downpour. Retreating, he pulled his rocker inside, placed it facing the door, and sat down to enjoy the show. Thunder rolled, lightning flashed, hail fell, and Ben calmly rocked back and forth.

"Ain't ya goin' to one of the cellars?" Cooley yelled above the rain and hail beating on the tin roof as he ran in. "It's a mighty big one comin', Ben. Don't ya hear that hail? We could get blown clean away!"

"Ah hear it, but ah reckon ah'll jest sit and watch," he answered, pulling his pipe from the pocket of his overalls. "The good Lord'll take me when he's ready and not before. Care ta join me?"

Hesitating a minute, Cooley took off his old, dirty ball cap and ran a hand through his unkempt hair. Slapping the cap on the side of his overalls, he peered through the open door and then turned back to Old Ben. "I shore hope Alice and the youngins took cover and got themselves in the cellar."

"Ah expect they did. Don't ya reckon Alice knows what to do?"

Watching old Ben puff his pipe, Cooley nodded. "She shore enough does." Mingled smells of rain, burnt wood, oil, and rich pipe tobacco were satisfying and comforting, and Cooley pulled an old stool next to Ben.

"I expect yer right about that, Ben. Ya know, what ya jest said about the good Lord takin' ya when he's ready. Well, ya cain't jump on the train 'til it pulls into the station now, can ya? I believe I'll just sit with ya a spell until she passes."

Retrieving a well-used pipe from his shirt pocket, Cooley tapped out the dregs from a couple of days ago and glanced at Ben. Considering it a luxury, he bought pipe tobacco when he accumulated enough change in an old Prince Albert can, long since empty.

"I'd be much obliged if I had a little of yer tobacco, Ben."

Passing him the pouch, he knew Cooley would be around in a couple of days with some piece of something to repay him, and he would add it to everything else he gave him through the years. The two friends sat quietly smoking their pipes. One man was old and wise, and the other young and simple, making his way through life the best way he knew how. They sat silently, enjoying the storm's fury through the open door of the blacksmith shop, white pipe smoke curling above their heads. The sky darkened until day looked like night, thunder rumbled, lightning flashed, and wind bent trees and tossed branches and leaves while rain and hail hammered the tin roof. All in all, Ben and Cooley agreed that *it was a right relaxin' afternoon.*

Chapter 2

Leah sighed in contentment, her head resting along the back of the tub. The warm water was relaxing, and she stared at the flickering candle, her mind drifting back over the day's events. The Black family was real to her now with faces and names and a home on the ridge. *Oak Grove may as well be a million miles away,* she thought, recalling Elizabeth's words of apprehension. *"This is all Nathan has ever known."*

Filled with compassion, she had placed both arms around the small Apache woman, promising to look out for her son.

Thunder rumbled in the distance, and she recalled this afternoon's storm and its unleashed fury that had transformed the forest into a place of both fear and wonder. The journey gave her a glimpse of God's creation undisturbed by man, and she now better understood Mike's love for the woods.

Yawning, she stepped from the tub, toweled off, and slipped into her gown. Climbing the stairs, she blew out the candle's flame, set it on the dresser, and picked up her hairbrush. Sitting in the middle of the bed, pulling the brush through her hair, she listened to the steady tick of the clock on the night table. The oil lamp atop the dresser glowed warmly, and the sound and scent of gentle rain drifted through the open window.

Relieved to discover no one was injured in the storm, Mike fell asleep almost immediately following their family devotion. He lay on his back with his face turned toward her. A dark curl fell across his forehead, and she reached over and tenderly pushed it back. The corners of his mouth turned slightly upward, and he appeared to smile even as he slept. His peaceful face fascinated her, and she knew if he awoke it would be instantly animated. Compelling blue eyes revealed his every emotion and were generally filled with amusement and accompanied by a warm smile that captivated her heart.

Not unaware of his handsome features, Leah was presently more fascinated with the peace on his face as he slept, and she breathed a silent prayer of thanks.

Mike's faith is extraordinary, she thought, studying him. *Everything is so simple. God says it, he believes it, and he applies God's Word and truth to every aspect of his life.* Nothing seemed to worry him, and she wondered if there was anything he even feared.

Rising from the bed, she cupped her hand and blew out the flame in the oil lamp and then walked to the window. Pulling the curtain aside, she looked out.

A cool breeze floated in, and she watched the moon peek through the clouds, shedding light on the old maple tree beyond the window. A few twinkling stars found their places in the sky, and sweet honeysuckle along the drive lent its fragrance. A faint rumble of thunder somewhere far away moved her, and she knew that God, who had controlled the storm today, had produced this evening's calm and was presently looking down on her with love. For several minutes, she stood unmoving. Overwhelmed, she sighed deeply, a prayer of gratitude and humility slipping from her as she dropped the curtain and crossed the room.

Slipping into bed, she rested her head on her husband's shoulder and smiled as he rolled and put his arms around her. Mumbling something she didn't understand, he pressed his face against her hair and was sound asleep again.

Before drifting off, the last thing Leah heard was distant thunder rumbling far away across the hills.

"What do you mean it's a mess? I like your hair." Willy sat on the sofa in Melba's living room watching her brush the long, red tresses the rain had turned into a riot of curls.

"Don't be silly. I look like Little Orphan Annie."

"Little Orphan Annie never looked so beautiful, and her hair is not nearly as pretty as yours." Impulsively reaching out, he touched the soft red curls.

Pleasantly surprised with the comment and the feel of his hand on her hair, Melba glanced sideways, observing the look on his face. Rubbing a curl through his fingers, he was studying it with unguarded fascination.

Noting her watching him, he grinned sheepishly and sat back on the sofa, embarrassed. Unconsciously rubbing his left thigh, he stretched his leg in front of him, laid his head on the back of the sofa, and stared at the ceiling.

"Do you know how long I have wanted to do that?"

"Do what?" Melba asked, studying his profile and thinking him quite handsome.

"Touch your hair."

"Touch my hair, whatever for?"

"That night at the circus…your hair looked so soft and pretty from the lights on the midway. I wanted to see what it felt like." Observing her hand on the sofa, he ran his finger across it. "I probably should not have told you."

"Why, Will, I don't bite," Melba commented softly. They studied one another for a moment, both aware of the gentle rain beyond the window and the soft glow of the oil lamp.

Staring into her eyes, Willy was aware of the familiar warning flag, and he deliberately removed his hand and looked away. "Are you sure about that?" Laughing slightly, he stood and walked slowly to the door. Staring out into the dark, he rubbed his left thigh again, and Melba knew it was bothering him.

It was a miracle Willy was alive. Severely wounded in the war, the doctors did not expect him to live and said if he did he would most probably lose his leg. Defying all odds, Willy had not only lived but kept his leg as well. Other than his occasional limp, like this evening, one would never know of his injury.

He never talked about the war, and Melba attributed much of his changing emotions to the horrors he had witnessed. Very aloof at times, he was also warm and caring, as he was tonight.

Seeing her home after the storm, he had checked to make sure there was no damage, retrieved a couple of oil lamps from the basement, and hung around until it appeared the storm had blown itself to parts unknown. They had laughed and joked while she prepared sandwiches, and he was more relaxed than she had ever seen.

Observing the rigid set to his jaw as he stood now with hands in his pockets looking out at the rain, she opened her mouth to speak and then stopped. There was a cutting edge to his words, and she wanted to walk over and shake him.

He was tall, trim with broad shoulders and strong muscles, and his dark hair had a bit of curl to it. But his eyes were what amazed her. Deep blue with a hint of gray around the edges, he had the longest lashes she had ever seen on a man. In sharp contrast, his facial features were strong and rugged, and he wore a serious expression much of the time. Emotionally, he held everyone at bay and watching him now, Melba sighed and wondered if he would ever let his guard down.

He turned and looked at her. "I guess I better head on over to the house. The rain has let up. Will you be okay?"

Smiling, Melba rose and crossed the room to stand next to him. "Yes, I'll be fine. I think the worst is over. Thank you, Will, for seeing me home."

Willy stared into her eyes, their color more intense from the emerald green of her dress. Its V-neckline lay softly on her shoulders, and he wondered if she knew how beautiful she was.

The same sweet fragrance she always wore reached him, and the memory of holding her close the night she sprained her ankle crossed his mind. Impulsively, he took her hand and opened the screen. "Walk out with me."

The rain had stopped but for a slight drizzle, the song of crickets and frogs filled the night air, and the moon appeared intermittently through drifting clouds. Stepping to the edge of the porch, Willy rested one arm on a pillar and casually draped his other arm across her shoulder. Jack raised his head, looked at them, and then laid it back down on his paws.

Neither spoke as they stood in the shadows, and Melba found it to be a companionable silence and enjoyed the feel of his arm on her shoulder. The unlit street lamps and windows up and down the street cloaked them in unusual darkness, and Melba unconsciously moved closer.

Willy took a deep breath, and she turned and looked up at him. The clouds had drifted, revealing his face in the moonlight. His eyes moved across her face from her eyes to her hair and then to her mouth. Her heart raced, and she was aware of nothing but Will as he bent his head toward her.

"Say, Melba! Is that you on the porch?" Mercy's voice called out of the darkness.

Groaning, Willy looked heavenward. "I could wring her neck."

Giggling, Melba stepped away. "Yes, Mercy, is everything all right at your house?"

"Yes, but ah'm bored stiff. Ah cannot see ta do anything, so ah'm comin' over for a while, okay?"

"Come on, Mercy. I was just leaving anyway," Willy called, shaking his head, suddenly frustrated. She might be Old Ben's great niece, and he was fond of her, but her timing tonight left much to be desired.

On sudden impulse, Willy turned with one swift move and wrapped an arm around Melba's waist and pulled her close.

"Willy, is that you?" Mercy called again.

Sighing, he squeezed Melba tight. "Would you like to see a movie Saturday night?"

Instinctively having wrapped both arms around his neck, she dropped them to rest on his chest. "I would like that very much."

"Ah'm sorry. Ah didn't know you were here, Willy," Mercy said, appearing on the sidewalk.

"I was just leaving," Willy replied, walking slowly down the steps. "Good night, Melba. I'll call you tomorrow. Come, Jack." Willy slapped the side of his leg, and Jack bounded off the porch and followed him down the walk, both disappearing into the darkness.

"Tomorrow?" Mercy whispered. "Melba, what is goin' on?"

Grinning, she turned to her friend. "Nothing. Whatever are you talking about?"

"Don't ya give me that, Melba. Good grief, ah'm your best friend. Now what is goin' on between you and Willy?"

Chapter 3

Dawn crept gently over the eastern ridge. Gray shadows of early morning revealed drawn shades and closed doors along Spruce Street, evidence that those closeted within still slumbered.

Mike strolled leisurely along the quiet street, enjoying the early morning hour with the one who was all things to him. Long ago, break of day had became his one ray of hope when all else was but confusion, heartache, and despair. Getting through each day was difficult, nights worse, and there seemed no balm for his heartache.

After one sleepless night, he stood at his bedroom window and watched the long, lonely night give way to a glorious sunrise. Quietly and gently, darkness slipped away, and a myriad of soft colors preceded the orange ball of fire that burst brilliantly above the treetops, stirring within him a glimmer of hope, and he knew he had witnessed a miracle. Tenderly and patiently, God tested his commitment, increased his faith, and he found a profound depth of God's love and comfort he had never known. Craving that early morning hour as a thirsty man craves water, he finally understood who he was, who he was not, and what the Lord wanted of him. The time of testing was lifted. He surrendered his life to God's ministry, and as peace filled his heart and soul, he found his relationship with Leah restored.

Pausing on the sidewalk, Mike watched pink streaks caress the sky then slowly spread above rooftops. Rabbits hopped here and there across wet grass, and a squirrel ran out on a limb above his head, flipped its tail, and stared curiously. Rays of sunlight fell on stained glass windows of the Methodist Church, and he studied their heightened colors a moment then continued on down the middle of the street. Approaching the square, he paused at the courthouse and looked around.

A large tree branch lay across the roof of the post office; cardboard was taped inside the cracked window of White's Bakery; and the Dime Store, the Flower Basket, and Ned's Barber Shop were missing shingles. Fruits and vegetables were strewn on the sidewalk in front of Reese's Market, and a shattered window of Baker's Clothier was boarded up. Street lamps in front of the Cranston Hotel and on the corner of Oak Street were broken, numerous small limbs lay about the square, and one large branch hung precariously from a tall maple next to the fountain. As though the storm had a sense of humor, the *back-to-school-in-Buster-Brown-shoes* sign was stuck in a corner of the bell tower.

Crossing to the bandstand, Mike sat down on the top step and lifted his eyes to the flagpole. No time for Cooley to lower it, the flag ruffled slightly in the breeze, and he was surprised it was not ripped to shreds. The morning air was fresh and pure, and wet grass glistened in the morning sun. Chirping birds flitted from one branch to the next, down to the ground in search of a worm, then back to the trees again. Mentally counting the chimes at city hall, he found the usual bustling square quiet and peaceful at six o'clock in the morning. Other than an open door at the Blacksmith Shop, there was no evidence of anyone stirring.

Mike Daniels was thirty-eight years old with dark hair and blues eyes. Standing an even six feet, his shoulders were broad, waist still trim, and he moved with an agility that stemmed from a life of hard work and love of the outdoors. A passionate man unafraid of showing emotion, he was a devoted husband and father; a warm, caring friend; and a pastor who shepherded his flock with love and sound guidance. Of strong conviction, especially concerning Scripture, he was not one to back down when confronted and was aware of how bullheaded he could be if he didn't allow the Lord to keep him in line. A keen sense of humor and a warm, friendly personality endeared him to all who knew him.

Noting the milk truck turning the corner at Oak and Main, he watched Melvin pull to the curb, slide the door aside, and step out. Wearing his familiar dark blue trousers and matching shirt, he stood for a moment looking at the truck's mud-splattered Dairy Fresh Milk logo. Shaking his head, he straightened his hard-billed cap that bore the same insignia and then turned and waved.

"Morning, Mike. You are out early."

"I am an early riser, Melvin. I walked down to check what damage we might have." Mike studied the man on the sidewalk in front of him. His cap was tilted back on his head, and his eyes roamed the square, taking everything in.

"Well, it's not as bad as I thought, but someone's going to be busy cleaning the place up. That was some storm, wasn't it?" he remarked, looking curiously at the sign in the bell tower.

"It sure was. Thankfully, we had no damage at our house and only lost electricity. How about your place...is everything okay?"

"Just dandy, Preacher, we didn't even lose our lights. It's this side of town that's down. I expect Union Electric will send trucks out as soon as they can."

"Thank the Lord for that," Mike replied, noting the uneasiness that crossed Melvin's face. "How are Mary and the kids?"

"They are fine, thanks. Well, I guess I better mosey on. Folks will be looking for their milk." He hesitated a moment and then stepped away. "Have a good day."

"You too, Melvin. My prayers are with you and your family."

"Well..." Melvin replied awkwardly, "I appreciate that."

Mike watched him step up into the truck, glance back, and wave. Circling the square, he parked in front of the café, alighted with a rack of milk bottles, and disappeared inside. He knew not to push Melvin but to wait on the Spirit's prompting.

Any mention of the Lord always made him uncomfortable. Choosing that to be a good sign, Mike continued to pray for the family and now lifted a prayer that their hearts might be softened.

Glancing across the square, he saw old Ben standing in the door of the Blacksmith Shop and rose to his feet. If there was anyone he would rather visit this morning than Old Ben, he didn't know who it would be. Raising his hand, Mike waved and headed toward the shop.

By eleven thirty a.m., Telephone Central was up and running, Hazel was back on the line, electricity was restored, and everyone was out and about. Nelson White and Tom Baker were at Hank's Hardware getting glass cut for their windows, and a new *back-to-school supplies* sign was in front of the Dime Store. A steady stream of folks paraded through the café and drugstore, making sure they hadn't missed anything and recalling previous tornadoes and earthquakes. The older folks decided last night's storm didn't amount to much and recollected when the bell signaled warnings, though they did concede that the new fire whistle had done a good job.

Melba's Salon was busier than usual and sounded like a chattering hen house. Amid the shampooing, curling, hair trimming, and dryers, Melba listened to where everyone had been and what they were doing when the storm hit.

Old Ben picked up shattered glass from the street lamps and helped Jack clean the mess in front of his market. Milly and Molly gave away *storm fudge* to any who happened by, and Sheriff Walker handed out candy sticks to children gathering trash and broken tree limbs from the square.

Alan Miller, taking pictures for *The Chronicle,* stood next to the bell tower with his camera aimed at Cooley, who was on the post office roof, assessing the damage of a large fallen branch.

"I'll need some help up here," he yelled to the men below. "This here tree branch is goin' to have to be chopped away from the tree a'fore we can shove her off the roof. 'Sides that," he continued, waving his arms as he called down the details, "there's a humdinger of a hole up here, 'bout two foot square that'll need patched up and covered over."

"Cooley, for heaven's sakes, stand still and quit throwin' yer arms around," Lottie called, shaking her feather duster at him. "Yer gonna fall off and break yer fool neck. And ya ain't gettin' any help from these old men down here," she declared firmly, deliberately eyeing up the four watching him. Staring at her husband's hand resting on a rung of the ladder, she narrowed her eyes.

"Yer all too old to be climbin' up there, and ya know it without me havin' to tell ya, 'specially you, Ben."

Surprised, old Ben wondered where she ever got the idea a ninety-year-old man would even think of climbin' up there. Land o' Goshen, the notion hadn't even struck.

Dusting the parlor of the Cranston Hotel and humming along with Frank Sinatra to "Oh, What It Seemed to Be", she had glanced through the window to see Paul carrying a ladder. Exasperated, she marched into the hall and out the front door in a huff. "I declare, that man's goin' ta be the death of me, and if he thinks he's goin' ta climb that ladder…we'll jest see 'bout that." she mumbled, following her husband across the street.

"I ain't gonna fall off," Cooley yelled back. "And I reckon yer right, Lottie. There's not a one of them old codgers that needs to be up here." Cooley looked down at the four old friends who regularly hung out at the Blacksmith Shop and grinned. Lottie and her feather duster appeared to have the upper hand.

Old Ben shook his head and glanced from Lottie to Paul. "Ah don't reckon ya should try it, Paul. Ya fell off that ladder last summer, and it might jest do ya in if ya fell agin."

"Ah didn't fall. It was an accident and—

"Well o' course it was an accident. I hope to high heaven ya didn't jump off the thing," Lottie retorted.

Joining Alan at the bell tower, Mike laughed at the exchange between the group. "Do you think perhaps we ought to step in and give Cooley a hand?" he asked, watching Lottie march back across the square muttering to herself.

"I guess we should. We might as well get ready for a lot of advice, though."

"I would say you are right about that," Mike chuckled. "Come on. I am ready if you are."

All was quiet in Oak Grove. The clock on the courthouse struck the midnight hour, soft breezes gently stirred tree branches, and a brilliant moon bathed the valley, painting a portrait not seen in any gallery. The quiet was interrupted only by those night sounds that accompany a peaceful, summer evening, and from all appearance, everyone had turned in for the night.

Oak Street cut through the center of town, wound its way east, and disappeared into the dark shadows of the eastern ridge. On the right and beyond the fairground, the Driscol home sat atop a small knoll surrounded by tall oaks and maples. Laden with fragrant jasmine blossoms, a white wooden fence wound its way up the lane to the large, two-story home. Blackberry bushes grew in abundance beyond a small pond that was home to several ducks, and the swing hanging from a large maple tree moved slightly.

A second-story bedroom at the southwest corner of the home overlooked the back lawn, and though the hour was midnight and the house dark, unlike those in the rest of the house, the young girl was not sleeping.

"Elizabeth, maybe we shouldn't do this," Laura whispered, watching her friend jiggle the screen back and forth.

"It's okay. I do it all of the time," Elizabeth replied over her shoulder as she gave a quick jerk on the left corner and the screen popped out, landing on her toe. "Ouch, *aaah*," she mumbled, hopping on one foot.

"*Shhh!*" Laura clamped a hand over her friend's mouth and glanced toward the door. "Elizabeth, you'll wake everyone."

"Okay, okay. I'm all right."

"I don't think we ought to do this," Noelle whispered.

Sitting on the floor, Elizabeth rubbed her toe. "Holy moly, that hurt."

Glancing at Noelle, Laura looked at Elizabeth. "Let's just sit here on the floor and eat."

"Oh, for crying out loud, that wouldn't be any fun." Elizabeth propped the screen against the wall, pulled the curtain back, and stuck one foot through the open window. Glancing back, she sighed loudly. "Come on."

"What if we fall off the roof?" Noelle asked with round eyes.

Half in and half out the window, Elizabeth looked at her in exasperation. "We are not going to fall off the roof. It's not that steep, see?" She leaned back and allowed them to poke their heads out into the night air.

"We are not as high as I thought," Laura said, looking at Noelle encouragingly.

"Oh good grief, don't be a fuddy-duddy. Come on, Noelle." Pulling her other leg through the window, Elizabeth stood up, looked back at her two friends, and grinned. "See?" she remarked, stretching her arms out to her sides.

Laura grinned. Standing barefoot on the roof in her yellow nightgown, Elizabeth reminded her of Wendy from Peter Pan, and she half expected her to fly off to Neverland. Giggling, she glanced at Noelle. "Come on. It will be fun."

"Hand me the quilt first and then the food," Elizabeth instructed, motioning Laura to grab the paper sack.

Eleven years old, best friends, and entering fifth grade within a matter of days, the three girls had just returned from seeing *Courage of Lassie* and were spending the night at Elizabeth's. One thing led to another, and Elizabeth had suddenly jumped from the bed and announced a midnight picnic on the roof. To be on the safe side, they waited until eleven thirty and then crept down the stairs, giggling and whispering, to raid the Frigidaire.

"Here." Noelle shoved the quilt through the window and stepped back, still unsure of what they were about to do.

Both girls watched Elizabeth spread the quilt on the roof. "If you don't lay something down, the shingles scratch your legs and hiney." Giggling, she looked back at them. "Okay, come on."

Glancing at Noelle, Laura grinned and stuck first one leg and then the other through the window and sat on the sill, her heart pounding. Inching her way, she crawled to the quilt, sat down, and gazed in wonder at the moonlit yard, pond, and trees along the distant ridge.

"Noelle, give me the food," Elizabeth whispered, sticking her head in the window.

Eyes as round as saucers, Noelle handed her the paper sack. The urge to jump in the middle of Elizabeth's canopied bed and pull the covers over her head seized her, and she stood with hands clasped, uncertain about this whole deal.

"Come on. I'll hold your hand," Elizabeth offered, passing the sack of food to Laura. Reaching through the window, she grabbed Noelle's hand and grinned. "You won't fall. I won't let you."

Sitting on the quilt, clutching the sack tightly, Laura smiled encouragingly and watched Noelle hesitantly climb through the window and out onto the roof, drop to her knees, and crawl toward her.

Digging into the paper sack, Elizabeth spread out what they confiscated from the kitchen, and for the next several minutes, they feasted, giggled, and whispered in hushed tones.

"This was a good idea," Laura whispered. She would never have thought to have a picnic at midnight and especially not on a roof. *Only Elizabeth could come up with an idea like this.*

"Golly, this is fun," Noelle said quietly, looking up at the stars. Dark braids hung to her waist, and she tucked her knees beneath her pink, cotton nightgown. Licking chocolate from her fork, she thought the sky had never looked so pretty and knew her mother would faint if she knew where she was right now.

"This is nifty, Elizabeth. It really is." Laura thought she had never seen anything more beautiful. A full moon illumined every bush, flower, and shrub in the yard, and she stared in awe at its reflection on the pond. The roof of the Seabaugh farm was visible in the distance, and her eyes followed the white fencing along the road. Other than the moon and stars, no other lights were visible, and she thought about her brothers and Shari asleep in their beds at home.

Swallowing a bite of chocolate cake, she grabbed the bottle of milk Elizabeth held and took a gulp, knowing her mother would disapprove if she saw her.

"I love to sit out here. Aunt Trudy would have a fit of apoplexy if she knew it," Elizabeth said, giggling. Lying on her back, she looked up into the night sky. "Caroline comes out here with me sometimes."

Tired, the girls lay on their backs looking at the stars in silence. The grandfather clock's faint melody sounded from within the house and then struck one o'clock.

"What's it like to have a mother and father?" Elizabeth asked softly.

Laura thought for a long moment. Elizabeth's mother had died when she was born, and she never spoke of her; therefore, Laura never thought about it. This was the first time Elizabeth ever asked such a question.

"Elizabeth, I don't think it is any different than your Aunt Trudy and Uncle Henry. They have always taken care of you and loved you."

"Yes, they have done that," she commented softly. "But it's not the same. They are my aunt and uncle, not my mother and father."

"I think they love you as much as your mom and dad would if they were here," Noelle remarked, sitting up and looking at her.

"No, you don't understand," Elizabeth replied, looking from one to the other. "I know they love me and Caroline, and we love them. It's just...they are Aunt Trudy and Uncle Henry. Neither of you know what it is like to have your mother die and your father run off and leave you."

Laura looked at Elizabeth's profile as she gazed up at the stars. Dark hair hung down her back, her nose tilted up a little on the end, and her blue eyes, usually full of mischief and humor, were filled with longing.

"I wish I had a mom and dad."

Laura and Noelle glanced at one another, not knowing what to say.

A shooting star streaked across the sky, and Laura sat up. "Did you see that? My Uncle Amos says when you see a shooting star, something good is going to happen."

"Really? I never heard that before. I wonder what is going to happen?" Noelle asked, yawning.

"Who knows, but I'm sleepy. Let's go to bed." Elizabeth rose to her feet and looked at Laura and Noelle. "Come on. One of you grab the quilt," she mumbled, tossing the sack of leftovers through the window.

Laura stood on the roof with the quilt in her hands and looked up at the night sky, thinking about what Elizabeth had asked. She couldn't imagine what it would be like not to have her parents. She didn't even want to think about it. Watching Noelle follow Elizabeth through the window, she passed her the quilt, and taking one last look out over the yard, she climbed back through the window and into Elizabeth's bedroom.

Chapter 4

Smiling, Willy reached for the bottle of Canoe Cologne from the top of his bureau. Thinking he needed a change for one reason or another, he purchased it on impulse one day at the drugstore. The description on the back of the box had read: *A masculine scent, possessing a blend of brisk citrus with accents of lemon and oak moss.* Wondering why anyone would want to smell like oak moss, he had placed it back on the shelf and walked away. Unable to shake the idea of his need for a change, he went back, took the bottle out of the box, sniffed it, and decided oak moss wasn't too bad. Two days later, he asked Melba for a date and sheepishly admitted to himself she was the reason for the much-needed change.

"You smell so good it is almost wicked," she commented the first night he wore it. Whistling, he put a few drops in his hand, rubbed it on his chest, and sat the bottle back on the bureau. Looking in the mirror, he buttoned his shirt, tucked its tail into his trousers, and straightened the collar. Though today's fashion for men was to wear casual shirts on the outside of their trousers, Willy didn't care for the idea.

Studying his reflection in the mirror, he aligned the buttons on his shirt with his belt buckle and straightened the collar a second time. He was oblivious to the shirt's fit across his broad shoulders or the rugged, handsome features of his face. Too many unpleasant memories and the will to survive through the years overshadowed all thoughts along those lines.

Whistling, he glanced at his wristwatch, suddenly impatient. He still had half an hour, and he combed his dark hair once more, feeling silly because it didn't need it. Halting abruptly, he stared in the mirror, a gut-wrenching sensation slamming him full force. His mother's eyes stared back, and for a moment, an unexpected, almost forgotten longing rushed over him. His eyes were just like hers; that was the only good thing he could remember.

A small boy sitting on her lap flew through his mind. Her eyes were soft and warm and sparkled when she laughed. Soft fingers stroked his hair while she read to him, and he had adored her. Then it all changed.

Fury began to build, and Willy stood unmoving, his jaw clenched and his blue eyes cold and hard as steel. "Get out of my life," he growled, staring into the mirror. Slamming the comb on the bureau, he turned, walked into the living room, and snatched up yesterday's paper from the coffee table.

A picture of Cooley on the post office roof was on the front page, and two smaller photos of the blown-out window at Baker's Clothier and the mess in front of Reese's Market were at the bottom. Attempting to read the article, he found he couldn't concentrate and, in frustration, threw the paper on the floor.

You would think after all this time I wouldn't allow her to get me so worked up, he thought, releasing a long breath. Laying his head on the back of the chair, he closed his eyes and welcomed features already so familiar: a few small freckles sprinkled across a pert nose, brows arched above brilliant green eyes, and soft lips curving into a sweet smile. A mass of red curls, soft to his touch came to mind, the smallness of her figure, and the sweet scent she always wore—

"Enough of this," Willy said, rising from his chair. Glancing impatiently at his watch, he walked to the door and stepped out onto the porch. Taking a deep breath and slowly releasing it, he felt the traces of anger subside, and he waved at Mercy across the street watering Old Ben's flowers.

"Stay, Jack!" Willy commanded and watched him lie back down on the porch with a pitiful expression. Crossing the yard, he headed toward the freshly washed and waxed Plymouth in the driveway.

It was the first and only car Willy had ever owned. With the bombing of Pearl Harbor, he had parked it in the garage, where it remained until he returned. The dark blue paint was unscratched and shiny, the interior still brand new, and the engine ran as smooth as any car he ever worked on. Closing the door, he glanced back at Jack, who sat on the porch watching. His anger forgotten, Willy backed out of the drive and headed toward Melba's.

Waving at young Ben carrying a piece of lumber across the yard toward his garage, he slowed for Simon, Jimmy, and Jake, who were riding their bikes down the middle of the street. Pedaling into the drive of the firehouse, they waved as he passed and watched him park along the sidewalk.

A smile spread across Melba's face as she heard Willy's step on the porch and his knock. Crossing the room, she opened the screen and looked up into his handsome face.

"Come in, Will," she greeted cheerfully, stepping aside.

Willy let the screen close slowly behind him, unable to take his eyes from her as she crossed the room, switched on a lamp, and then turned to face him. She looked beautiful, and for a fleeting moment, he thought he might be speechless and nervously collected his thoughts as she gathered her purse from the coffee table and laid a sweater across her arm.

The short-sleeved, turquoise, cotton dress she wore was soft and clingy, and the gathered top fell softly across her shoulders, forming a V-neckline. Willy's eyes traveled to the small gold locket lying against her neck. Then he noted her hair and smiled. She had done nothing but pull the top and sides back, leaving the rest to hang free. Had she remembered his comments about her hair the night of the storm and fixed it like this for him?

"You look beautiful, Mel."

"And you look quite handsome yourself," she replied, smiling. "Shall we go?"

"Yes. I am about to starve to death."

The evening was balmy, and the sun was beginning its slow descent behind the ridge as they walked out the door and down the sidewalk. Simon, Jimmy, and Jake gawked and grinned as they rode by and rode into Jake's yard across the street.

"I thought we would eat at Meadowbrook and then see *Road to Utopia*," Willy remarked, opening the door and watching her slide in. "How does that sound?" Leaning down, he rested an arm on the car door.

Turning with a pleased smile, Melba found his lips against hers; then he straightened, chuckled, and walked to the other side and got in.

Glancing sideways, Melba grinned. "I certainly hope you don't plan on manhandling me like that all evening."

Laughing, he pulled away from the curb. "I can't help myself, Mel. You are too beautiful for words, and I am putty in your hands."

"Putty?" she asked, laughing softly. "Then I suppose I can mold you anyway I want. Is that what you are saying?"

"You can try, but I don't know how far you'll get."

Mike lay stretched out on the couch with his eyes closed. Leah's voice drifted back and forth, and he was vaguely aware of her saying something about school clothes. Half listening, he knew he should be paying attention, but his other half was drifting off to sleep.

"Do you think that would be all right?" Leah asked, awaiting her husband's reaction. She just told him she was going to order twice as many school clothes for the children this year and several things for herself, even though she didn't need them.

"Sure, darlin'," he mumbled, faintly aware of the sound of turning pages and muffled giggling from the kitchen.

Leah shook her head, closed the Sears catalogue, and looked at her half-asleep husband. *I wonder what he would do if I ordered it all*, she thought and grinned. *Probably nothing. He knows I would never buy something we didn't need.*

Studying his relaxed form, a great love filled her heart. Mike was always there for anyone who needed him, and he ministered with genuine love, patience, and concern. Mrs. Tyler had taken a turn for the worse last night, and he had not gotten to bed until one thirty. Up at five, he then spent the greater part of the day helping young Ben paint Solomon and Grandma Hope's garage. She tried to convince him to do it another day, but he only smiled and said no. He gave his word and would rest later.

Praying the Lord would show her how to be of greater help, she also thanked him that Mike was able to rest almost anytime and anywhere he felt the need.

Flipping through the catalogue to winter coats, she found the boys' military-style jackets Johnny wanted—$9.50. It was a little expensive, but Jimmy would grow into it. "Let's see," she murmured, reading the description, "tan capeskin—*snappy as a salute and rugged as a marine.* Shoulder epaulets, zipper-front closing, and warm, cotton flannel lining."

It was a nice-looking jacket with two front pockets, and the rib knit cuffs and bottom would keep him warm. *He really does need a new jacket,* she thought. She almost dropped the catalogue when the front screen door flew open, banged against the wall, and Jimmy ran in with eyes as round as saucers.

Jolted awake, Mike jumped from the sofa, thinking he'd heard a gunshot, and stared at his youngest son.

"Jimmy, whatever is the matter?" Leah asked, coming to her feet.

"It's Willy!" Jimmy exclaimed, flopping down on the floor with a dejected look.

Leah and Mike glanced at one another and then back at their son.

"What's the matter with Willy, Son," Mike asked gently, wondering what in the world Willy had done to upset him in such a way.

He rose to his feet with a look of total dismay. "Willy kissed Melba! In the middle of the street and right on the mouth!" he exclaimed, stomping off into the kitchen.

A look of surprise on her face, Leah turned and looked at Mike, who sat back down on the couch, a grin spreading across his face.

The sound of kitchen chairs scraping the floor was followed by rapid footsteps, and Laura and Shari popped around the corner of the living room.

"Jimmy said Willy is kissing Melba in the street. Is he? What's going on?" Laura asked as Shari ran to the window and jerked the curtains back.

"I don't think he should kiss her in the street. People can see them," Shari stated, looking through the screen.

"Who's kissing who in the street?" Johnny asked, coming in the front door. "Who are you talking about?"

"I don't think he should do that," Shari said again, looking back at Mike. "Daddy, are we supposed to kiss in the street?"

"You, little lady, should not be kissing anyone," Mike replied. "But I don't think there is a law against kissing in the street. I was never arrested for it."

"And who, may I ask, have you kissed in the street?" Leah asked with a raised brow. "I know for certain it was not me."

"Did she kiss him back?" Laura asked, wide-eyed and smiling with her hands clasped together. "Oh, how exciting!"

Johnny stared at his little sister behind the curtains and then at Laura's dreamy expression. "Who kissed who? Never mind, I don't care." Flopping down on the end of the sofa, he noted the grin on his dad's face as he looked at his mom, who was standing with arms folded, staring back at him.

"Mike Daniels, you didn't answer me," Leah remarked. "I asked who you were kissing?"

"If you kiss in the street, you could get run over by a car or maybe Melvin in the milk truck," Shari said, her nose pressed against the screen.

"Good grief, Shari," Laura commented. "Who would be up kissing early enough for Melvin to run them down?"

"And I wasn't the only one who saw him," Jimmy exclaimed, coming back into the living room. "Jake and Simon did too and probably everybody in the world. I didn't think he would ever do that." Sitting on the floor with his chin in both hands, he decided he would never ever in his whole life kiss a girl.

"Would someone please tell me who you are talking about?" Johnny asked in frustration, watching his dad trying not to laugh.

"Do you think Sheriff Walker would arrest someone for kissing in the street?" Concerned, Shari stepped away from the window. She didn't think it was right, but Willy and Melba were both nice, and she didn't want to see either of them go to jail.

"Hmmm, I don't know." Standing to his feet, Mike crossed the room and grabbed Leah by the hand. "Let's find out. Come on, darlin'. We'll try it." Chuckling, he pulled her toward the door.

"Mike, are you crazy?" Leah laughed, grabbing the edge of the sofa with her free hand.

"No, you are jealous because I have never kissed you in the street, so I am going to make it up to you. Let's see if we can get arrested for it." Trying to maintain a serious look, he pried her hand loose and steered her toward the door.

"I am not jealous, and will you quit?" Leah laughed, looking up into her husband's eyes, which were full of merriment.

Laura laughed, trying to imagine what the neighbors would think if Dad dragged Mom into the street and kissed her.

"You aren't serious," Johnny exclaimed, wondering what was going on and what he had missed as he watched his mom uselessly try to free herself.

Leah found herself whirled around and Mike's arms wrapped firmly around her, pinning her arms to her sides.

"Mike, you are joking, aren't you?" she exclaimed, wondering just how far he was going to take this.

"Shari, when I get your mother out into the middle of the street and start kissing her, you run next door and tell Sheriff Walker, okay?" he said, lifting Leah enough that her feet were barely off the floor.

Shari stared wide-eyed and then giggled. There couldn't be anything wrong with kissing in the street. Daddy wouldn't do anything to get Mom arrested.

"Will you put me down." Leah laughed, suddenly none too sure he was not going to carry her outside.

Standing by the front door, he chuckled at Leah's useless attempts to free herself and looked in amusement at the expressions on his children's faces. Johnny was totally confused, and Laura sat in the armchair, her blue eyes bright with laughter. Shari's concern had changed to amusement, and she was jumping up and down giggling, and Jimmy still sat on the floor with a look of disbelief on his face.

"Is anyone going to tell me who kissed who?" Johnny asked loudly.

"It was Willy," Jimmy yelled above the uproar. "He kissed Melba on the mouth in the street, and just look what he started."

"Well, that will be all over town by tomorrow," Johnny commented. "Everyone will be talking."

"Oh, I can't wait to see them," Laura exclaimed, dreamy eyed. "He must really love her to kiss her in front of the whole world. I'm going to call Elizabeth and Noelle."

"He must be nuts," Jimmy mumbled, moving his finger in circles around his ear.

Mike laughed and released Leah. He couldn't wait to see Willy tomorrow.

Fluffing the pillow, Melba rolled to her side and stared through the window into the night. Usually guarded and emotions in check, Willy's relaxed, warm manner this evening pleased her immensely. Combined with his unpretentious personality that was so much a part of him, Melba found herself totally charmed. Dinner at Meadowbrook was excellent, and Bob Hope and Bing Crosby were hilarious, running all over Alaska in search of a gold mine in *Road to Utopia*.

Hugging her pillow, a slight smile curved her lips. Closing her eyes, she pictured Willy's handsome face when he leaned in the car window, kissed her quickly, and laughingly walked to the other side. Originating deep within, his laughter was deep and strong and moved her in a strange way she didn't understand.

Sighing contentedly, her mind wandered over the evening's events. They had talked and laughed on the drive home from Chesterville, going over the insanely funny parts of the movie. Will was curious about her life and listened intently while she told of her parents' accidental death, and she was touched when he reached over and held her hand when she told him of the automobile accident.

On arriving home, they walked hand in hand up the sidewalk and onto the porch. Not releasing her hand, he pulled her around to face him and stared at her for a long moment. She remembered nothing but the pounding of her heart and the expression in his eyes as he pulled her into his arms. His eyes searched hers as though looking for an answer to something, then pulling her close, he lowered his head and kissed her, and she found herself kissing him back. Raising his head, she felt his lips at her temple then he stepped back and smiled.

"Good night, Mel," he said softly. Then he turned and walked slowly down the steps.

Watching him walk to the car, she pulled her sweater close, a faint scent of his cologne clinging to it. Touching her lips, she wondered on the feelings he had stirred in her.

Chapter 5

"Dad-burn it! I'll be turned into a toad if you ain't cheated again," James complained, looking across the checkerboard at Phillip Driscol, who was grinning from ear to ear.

"I did not cheat. I don't have to cheat to beat you." Phillip glanced at Louis and old Ben with a grin. "Tell the old codger I didn't cheat. I have a reputation to uphold; my son's the mayor."

The two men, both in their seventies, sat on ladder-back chairs on either side of an old cracker barrel turned upside down and the checkerboard on top. The daily games would not be half as enjoyable without the arguing and cheating, even though they wouldn't admit it. For years there was an unwritten code that cheating was all right if you didn't get caught; not getting caught was more of a challenge than actually winning.

Old Ben rocked in his chair, puffing on his pipe and grinning. Phillip definitely had moved James's man when he leaned down to pick up his bottle of pop, but he was not about to say so.

The doors on the south end of the blacksmith shop were flung wide as usual, and a clear view of the square was visible through the screen that opened onto a small covered porch on the west. It was here Ben spent a good deal of his time when the shop was empty, rocking in an old wooden rocker and watching all the activity. A red Coca-Cola cooler, supplied with a variety of pop, sat to one side, a large thermometer hung on the wall to the right of the door, and an advertisement for AAA Root Beer hung on the other.

Inside, a black pot-bellied stove took up space in the middle of the shop, numerous pieces of equipment hung along the walls, and the forge and billows were where they had always been. A screen door at the north end led into Ben's kitchen, and windows over a workbench on the east welcomed early morning sun.

Unnoticed, Mike leaned against the doorjamb listening to the argument.

"Ya better watch what ya say. The preacher's here," old Ben warned, nodding toward the door.

"I guess I have already heard about everything, Ben. I just don't want to have to break up a fist fight." Chuckling, Mike walked over and sat on a stool next to the workbench. "Afternoon, fellas."

"Now let's see you cheat in front of the preacher." James rose and stepped out on the porch and rummaged around in the cooler. "Would you like a root beer, Pastor?"

"I believe I would, thanks."

"Dad-burn it!" he complained, returning and handing Mike his root beer. "Louis, I know you saw him move my man. Get on over here and take your turn. Hooking a thumb in his suspenders, he glared at Phillip. "Next time; I'll be hog tied if I don't beat you tomorrow."

Removing his feet from an old nail keg, Louis moved his stiff legs back and forth and then stood, marveling again that old Ben was able to get around as he did. Moving to the vacant seat opposite Phillip, he drew an exaggerated breath, cracked his knuckles and grinned. "Are ya ready ta face a real opponent?"

"Don't give me any of that malarkey. I can beat you any time," Phillip retorted without much conviction. Louis very seldom lost, cheating or not, and had finally resorted to playing the winner of three out of five games.

"Well now, Preacher, what do ya think of these here *bikinis?*" Louis asked, placing his checkers on the board.

Mike studied him a minute, not sure to what he was referring. The only Bikini that came to mind was that of the Marshall Islands, but by the look on Louis's face, he had serious doubts their thoughts were running along the same line. What on earth he was about to come up with was anyone's guess.

James, taking a seat on an old stool next to Mike, scratched his head. "You referring to Bikini Atoll over there in the Marshall Islands?" he asked, voicing Mike's thoughts. "I believe that's where Willy about met his maker.

"It sure was," Willy commented, standing in the door with a Coke in hand.

"Sit yerself down, Son," old Ben replied, indicating a small bench against the wall.

"What about the Marshall Islands?" Willy asked, throwing a nickel in a mason jar on the shelf, and popping the top off his Coke. Dragging the old wooden bench across the shop where he had a clear view of the garage and any customers who might drive in, he sat down and looked curiously at Louis.

James shrugged a shoulder and nodded toward Louis. "He was just getting ready to tell us something about bikinis."

"Now what were you saying?" Phillip asked, suspecting this was a ploy to distract him.

"A *bikini* is a new fangled swimmin' outfit women in Paris, France, have taken to wearin'," Louis stated importantly. "Yes suh, ah saw it with my own eyes. Sarah brung home one of them *Look Magazines* from the drugstore and showed it to me."

"What does it look like?" James asked, leaning forward. Glancing at Mike, he sat back and shrugged a shoulder.

Louis looked at Mike and shook his head. "Ya ain't goin' to like it, Preacher. It shore don't cover much. Land o' Goshen, it's jest two little strips of cloth that covers a woman's bosom and the other covers her...uh...well, her behind, if ya know what ah mean."

"I didn't know about it," Mike answered, noting the red hue creeping across Louis's face. "Perhaps it is nothing more than a passing fancy and will stay in Paris."

"Did you bring the magazine with you?" Phillip asked, glancing peevishly at Mike.

"No, ah'm not goin' ta carry somethin' like that out on the street. Ah declare, Sarah and ah was both shocked. Ah couldn't believe my eyes. She said ah'd looked at it long enough, and it wasn't fittin' to have somethin' like that layin' around, so she burnt it in the trash barrel."

"*Hmm hmm,* what's this world comin' to, Preacher?" Old Ben frowned. "Gosh a mighty, women runnin' around in nothin' more'n undergarments, no wonder youngins get so confused these days. There's too many temptations for 'em, ah reckon."

"The world is fine, Ben. It is how we choose to live in it and how we instruct our children that makes the difference. If we stick close to God's Word and teach it, our young people will know what is proper and what is not," Mike replied, wondering why he had not heard of this bikini. He would have to ask Leah if she knew anything about it.

"You are right about that, Pastor. Educating our children in every area of life is one of the most important things we can do." Phillip sat his bottle of pop on the floor and moved his man, thinking of Caroline and Elizabeth. Henry and Trudy had adopted his granddaughters when their mother passed away and their no-account father disappeared. He couldn't imagine those sweet girls giving in to the ways of the world. "You are right, Ben. Youngsters these days face a lot of temptation."

"That's for sure," James added. "Keep them busy so they stay out of trouble. I expect they don't have enough to do these days. They don't have half the chores I did when I was comin' up. Give them a little work to do and keep them in school and church. That'll keep them out of trouble."

"Ah declare, where's this summer gone?" Old Ben asked, shaking his head. "It seems like school jest let out, and now they're headin' back in how many days?"

"One week, Ben. Jimmy is counting the days and dreading it." Mike sat his bottle of pop on the work bench and grinned. "I remember how I hated to see summer end."

"Well," James replied, "I guess we were all that way, don't you think? I mean, what young boy likes school."

Ben chuckled and looked around at the men. "Well, sir, as best as ah can recollect, ole Tommy Seabaugh had the same problem. He was Elijah's uncle, yes suh, and he didn't want to go to school either." Old Ben stretched his legs in front of him, and leaned back in his chair, readying himself to launch into one of his tales.

Smoothing his mustache, he looked at Mike and shook his head. "His Momma brought him to school that fall kickin' and yellin'. Ah was just startin' first grade and didn't want to be there either, but watchin' him throw that fit made it all seem kind of worthwhile."

Old Ben looked at Willy as though an explanation was needed. "Back then, we all sat in one room. It didn't make no difference if ya was in the first or the twelfth grade. Miss Specklemeier was her name. She taught us all and was just as nice as all get out, but she never smiled much. Ah don't rightly know why she never smiled. Anyway, ah could see she was goin' ta have a time with Tommy right off."

Smiling at the twinkle in Old Ben's eye, Mike watched him fondly as he glanced down at the floor remembering. Shaking his head, he continued. "Well, Tommy came right regular for about a month or so. Then we had a touch of Indian summer, and that did it. Miss Specklemeier was tellin' us the story about George Washington crossin' the Delaware in the dead of night. Ah thought it was a pretty good one too, but old Tommy was jest starin' out the window, not hearin' a word."

Old Ben sipped his coffee and looked at Mike. "Ain't it strange what we remember about folks? Ah can still see the way she'd purse her lips up when she was mad and tryin' ta act like she wasn't."

Mike nodded. It was indeed strange the way a person remembered certain things, and he thought of the way Aunt Verona used to click her false teeth together when she ate.

"Well, suh," old Ben continued, "she stopped right in the middle of the story, pursed her lips, and lookin' over the top of her glasses like she always did, walked over and tapped his shoulder and asked, 'Thomas would ya rather come up here and sit on the stool in the corner with yer nose ta the wall or listen ta what ah am tellin' ya?'"

Old Ben threw his head back and laughed. Wiping his eyes, he looked at his listeners. "He said, 'No, ma'am, ah'd druther do neither. Ah'd jest as soon go fishin'.' And with that, he got up, walked over and jumped out the window, and lit out across the cornfield."

Laughter filled the shop, and Mike didn't know which he enjoyed more—listening to the tale or watching Ben tell it.

"Ya should of seen the look on her face. By the time Tommy got home, she'd already paid his folks a visit, and his daddy took him out behind the barn. As ah recollect, he couldn't sit very easy for a couple of days." Old Ben wiped his eyes again and stared through the window. "Ya know, he was a bright lad and never had any trouble catchin' up with his learnin' in spite of all the days he didn't show up. Miss Specklemeier never told on him again. I think she felt bad he got such a lickin'."

"Whatever happened to Tommy?" Mike asked, wondering why he had never heard of him.

Silence filled the shop, and Ben stared at the floor for a long moment and then spoke quietly, "He never came home. He ran away in '62 to join the 17th Missouri volunteers and was killed at Lookout Mountain." Ben stared through the window and spoke so quietly the men in the shop could barely hear. "He was only fourteen. No, suh, he never came home."

Chapter 6

The last few days of August flew by. Mayor Driscol called a town meeting to finalize Founders Day plans, Williams Shore Store advertised a new shipment of Buster Brown shoes, and mothers anxiously watched for school clothes ordered from Sears and Montgomery Ward. The Dime Store was a flurry of activity, with children selecting colored pencil boxes, book satchels, pencils, crayons, scissors, glue, Big Chief Tablets, erasers, and rulers. Ned's Barber Shop was livelier than usual from a flood of boys getting haircuts, and Melba missed her break two days in a row because of the rush for trimmed bangs, perms, haircuts, and quick finger wave instructions. Williams Drugstore found mothers stocking up on cod-liver oil, Smith Brothers cough drops, and Vicks Vaporub. Young girls glanced through magazines and picked out fingernail polish, while boys watched girls glance through magazines and pick out fingernail polish. Lunch at the Cranston Café was noisier than usual, started earlier, and lingered on until two. The St. Louis Cardinals and Los Angeles Dodgers were running neck and neck in the National League Pennant Race, and Trudy Driscol was aggravating Pastor Mike to plan a special welcome for Nathan Black.

Glad her school preparations were complete, Leah gave a sigh of relief and dropped clothespins into the green bag hanging on the line. Folding the sheet, she placed it in the basket and pulled the next one to her face, inhaling its fresh, line-dried fragrance. *Such simple pleasures,* she thought and then stood for a moment listening to birds chirp merrily. It was a beautiful, late August day, and the sky was a brilliant blue without a cloud in sight. A screen door slammed at the Walkers, and she recognized Jordan calling Josiah, Reverend Clark was hammering on something beyond the hedge, and the familiar clack of lawn mower blades sounded from the old Parker place.

It was unusually quiet. Mike drove Louise and Trudy to the Chesterville Hospital to visit Louise's mother, and Leah prayed for her health to be restored and that Mike be given an extra measure of patience with Trudy. Johnny was fishing with Brenton and Truman, Laura and Noelle had walked to the drugstore, Shari was over at Maggie's, and Jimmy and Zachary were headed to the Dime Store with a nickel each, hoping to find a rare and valuable baseball card in yet another pack of bubble gum.

Contented, she folded the last sheet and carried the laundry basket through the yard. Climbing the back steps, she stepped over their lazy cat, Midnight, who refused to move and walked into the kitchen. The pitcher of lemonade she prepared earlier looked inviting, and setting the basket on the floor, she grabbed a tall glass from the cabinet and then reached for another. Filling both with ice and lemonade, she pushed the back screen wide and stepped over Midnight again. Making her way down the steps and around the side of the house, she slipped through the honeysuckles to where Cooley was busily mowing.

His back was to her, and she watched him mow across the yard, turn, and come toward her. Lifting his eyes, he grinned and waved.

"Here, Cooley, have a glass of lemonade."

"Thank ya kindly, ma'am." Cooley smiled and pushed his ball cap back on his head and wiped his forehead with the back of his hand.

Thomas Jefferson Cooley was one of those individuals not easily forgotten. He stood about five feet nine inches and was slender in build and had a broad grin that traveled up into his eyes.

Not very educated, he was the school's janitor; caretaker of the square, fairground, and Baptist and Methodist churches; and he delivered coal in winter. Never at a loss for words, he said exactly what he thought, often getting himself in trouble.

A drinking problem behind him, he had gained weight in the last couple of years, giving the preacher all the credit. Joining Cooley in the jail cell after one of his episodes, Mike slammed the cell door and locked himself up to prove a point. Cooley had stared bleary-eyed and open mouthed, and the sheriff looked in bewilderment at his brother. Though both tried reasoning with their pastor, neither sheriff or deputy could convince him to come out. Requesting his one phone call to Leah, it had not taken twenty minutes for the information to get all over town. The deacons called a special meeting, Leah was bombarded with supportive friends, Trudy fainted, and Cooley became one of the most faithful members at Oak Grove Baptist church.

"I suppose Alice is busy getting Tommy and Betty Jean ready for school?"

"Yes, ma'am. Yer youngins ready?"

"They sure are," Leah replied, accepting his glass.

"I'm much obliged to ya for the lemonade. It hit square where I needed it." Cooley removed his cap, slapped it on the side of his leg, and looked at Leah. "I heard tell that one of the Black youngins is comin' down out of the hills and goin' to school."

Looking at her sideways, he plopped his cap back on his head; leaned toward her; and raised his brows. "Now would that be truth or not?"

Smiling at his direct manner, she knew if it were not so he would take it upon himself to go all over town to correct everyone. "Yes, Cooley, he is arriving tomorrow."

"Well, by jingees. Who would've ever thought they'd a come down out of the hills. Youins need any help with...what's his name?" he asked, cracking his knuckles.

"Nathan."

"Nathan. Youins need any help with Nathan, ya jest let me and Betty Jean know. We'll do what we can. Now go on back to the house," he said, grinning and motioning her off. "I got to finish mowin', and thank ya kindly for the lemonade."

Leah watched Cooley grab the mower handle and set off across the yard again, mower blades clacking. What a simple and uncomplicated man he was. Making her way around the honeysuckles, she looked up to see Mike leaning against the porch rail watching her, a grin on his face.

"What am I to do with you?" he asked as she climbed the steps and looked up at him. "I turn my back for an hour or so, and what do I come home to? I find you out here flirting with Cooley, having a party too," he commented, looking at both glasses. "What will the neighbors think?"

Leah laughed and returned his kiss as he bent down. "They will think you need to pay more attention to your wife."

Following Leah into the kitchen, Mike sat at the table and watched her fill two more glasses and replace the ice trays.

"How is Louise's mother?"

"Not well. She is very frail and is giving up all hope of getting better." Mike took a drink of the cold lemonade and set the glass on the table. "Louise became very upset when we were leaving. She doesn't say much, but she said three times that she didn't know what she was going to do without her mother."

"I feel so sorry for her," Leah replied. "Her whole life has consisted of working at the café and caring for Mrs. Tyler. She never had a social life or friends, so to speak, even though several have tried through the years."

"No, she is not exactly a social butterfly, is she?" Mike commented, gazing through the window.

Leah thought of the many times she invited Louise to church activities. She always declined with the excuse of looking after her mother, though Leah thought shyness had something to do with it. A great sadness washed over her. Louise would be all alone.

"She will be lost when Mrs. Tyler is gone. She has no one else."

Observing his wife's compassion, Mike took her hand. "Then we will have to carry her through when the time comes. The Lord will show us what to do, and it will be a blessing for Louise and for us also."

"Yes, of course, we will be there for her," Leah replied, watching Mike rub his thumb across the top of her hand. "And how was Trudy?" Mike didn't look too rattled, compared to some of the other times he drove her here and there. "I guess she is still wanting to surprise Nathan."

"Is she ever, but I told her not until Nathan gets used to all of us. Giving the poor kid a welcoming party would scare him to death," Mike answered, running a hand through his hair. "She's been about to drive me nuts, and I had to put my foot down."

Knowing how frustrating Trudy could be, Leah wondered just how firm he had been. "You know she is trying to be nice and make Nathan feel welcome. I hope you handled her delicately." Observing his look of exasperation , she propped her chin in her hand and studied his face as he stared through the window.

"Delicately?" Mike murmured, looking at her. "Don't worry, Leah. I was firm, but I did promise she could plan something when I thought it appropriate. I assured her that she was the perfect one to handle it and that pleased her."

Leah returned his smile. "You are right about that. No one can plan a special event like Trudy. I think you handled the situation beautifully."

The front screen slammed, and Jimmy stomped down the hall and into the kitchen. He wore a frown, his baseball cap sat at a crooked angle, and one pant leg was rolled up. Dragging a chair from the table, he sat down and dropped bubble gum, wrappers, and baseball cards on the table. "Never in my whole life will I ever buy another baseball card. I already have these, and Zachary wouldn't even trade me."

Mike looked at the frown on his youngest son's face and grinned. Jimmy was always *never again* going to do something or other.

"Oh, and Miss Gloria said to tell Laura her Nancy Drew book is overdue and she needs to return it."

"What were you doing in the library?" Leah asked, surprised he would think of going there on his own.

"Me and Zachary was looking for a book on maggots."

Chuckling at the expression on Leah's face, Mike looked at his son, not much surprised at his sudden interest, but he was curious as to what brought it on.

"Why in heaven's name would you want a book about…maggots, of all things," Leah asked, wrinkling her nose.

"We saw some on a dead cat on the side of the road. They were crawling—"

"That's enough. I don't want to hear anymore."

"But gee whiz, Mom, it was something about the way they wiggled and—"

"I said I don't want to hear about it," Leah repeated, standing and walking to the sink.

Exasperated, Jimmy turned to Mike. He didn't know why girls didn't like crawly things. "Dad, you need to go down there and talk to Miss Gloria. She said we surely couldn't be serious and the library didn't have a book on maggots. I bet if you went down there and talked to her, she would order one."

"I don't know," Mike replied, noting his earnest expression. "But do you know what?"

"What?"

"You will learn all you want to know about maggots in school."

Squinting, he stared at his dad. How could he always turn everything into a reason to go to school?

Stepping out on the porch, Willy glanced across the street at old Ben's. It was Wednesday; he would be over at his brother's. Bored, Willy sat on the porch swing, stretched his legs in front of him, and absentmindedly scratched Jack's ears. It was dusk, and familiar neighborhood sounds reached his ear. Aware of the restlessness that haunted him of late, he had spent the last three evenings cleaning out the garage and basement, but as soon as he settled down, it reared its head again. A deep sigh escaped, and he stared at the wisteria vines growing along the columns of Ben's porch. He was lonely. Recalling Uncle William and Aunt Lydia puttering around in the house, he realized he had been more attached to them than he ever knew. A frown creased his brow accompanied by a touch of melancholy. *Why didn't I realize that while they were still alive?*

A star appeared in the sky and a firefly caught his eye. The intermittent cicadas' song floated on the evening air and made him more aware of his loneliness. His eyes traveled to the lawn, and he wondered who mowed Melba's grass...or did she cut it herself? *I wonder what she's doing?* He knew his restlessness lay bound with her somehow, and it was becoming increasingly difficult to not think about her. How did that happen?

Frustrated, he stood abruptly to his feet. "Come on, Jack. Let's go for a walk."

Following him across the lawn, the border collie walked next to his master, turning his head to those whom Willy waved as if greeting them also. Passing the garage, Willy cut across the street and onto the square. No one was about, and the fountain's splash was peaceful and soothing. He paused in front of it, sat on the bench, and gave way to his betraying thoughts. A bright smile and green eyes drifted into his mind. *Why does she have to be so beautiful, and why does she occupy my thoughts so much?*

Confused, he rose to his feet and turned to call Jack. Though it was now dark, the street lamp's dim glow cast enough light for Willy to recognize the slight figure walking in his direction with Jack trotting alongside. A surge of pleasure rushed through him, and he walked toward her.

"Will you look at what Jack found?"

"Good evening, Will." Melba leaned down and scratched Jack's ears. "He found me over by the bandstand, didn't you, boy?"

Willy watched her pet Jack. Red curls fell across her shoulder, making it impossible to see her face, and he wondered if she was as glad to see him as he was her.

Straightening, she smiled and pushed a stray curl from her face. "It is such a beautiful evening. I've been in the shop all day, and after prayer meeting, I couldn't resist a walk in the night air."

"I couldn't either, so Jack took me for a walk, and here we are." Resisting the urge to reach out and touch her, Willy leaned down and picked up a stick. He tossed it, and they both watched Jack run after it.

"Well, what do you think? Should we walk along together or on opposite sides of the square?" Melba grinned, aware of her rapid pulse and the pleasure she felt.

Willy caught her hand and squeezed it. "I would like it better if we walked together."

Her hand felt small in his, and he glanced down at her again, wondering if she had seen the stupid grin plastered across his face when he saw her.

"What have you been doing all week?" he asked, realizing how much he had missed her.

"You wouldn't believe it. I think every young girl in Oak Grove needed her hair trimmed, and for some reason, many of the mothers are having something done also, and tomorrow and Friday will be the same."

"Well then, my hard-working, little girl," Willy teased, "I guess you ought to let me take you out to dinner and a movie Saturday night."

"That would be nice. What shall we see?"

Suddenly lighthearted, he squeezed her hand. "*Duel in the Sun* is playing at the Star, but I'll check *The Chronicle* to see what is playing in Chesterville."

Strolling hand in hand across the square, both were pleased with the turn of events. Crickets filled the August night, and a small breeze rustled oak leaves and stirred the scent of honeysuckle.

Stopping in front of the bandstand, Willy chuckled, remembering this was where Jasper hid while causing such havoc earlier in the summer.

"What are you laughing about?" Melba asked, looking up at him. The glow of the street lamp allowed her to see his face, and she once more wondered how they lived so long in Oak Grove and never noticed one another.

"I was thinking of this summer and all the commotion with Jasper."

Melba laughed. "Who would have thought a circus monkey was the culprit causing all the disturbance. It has been a summer of surprises, hasn't it?"

Willy agreed in more ways than one. Getting to know Melba was the greatest surprise of all. Turning his thoughts in another direction, he unknowingly asked a question that would carry an answer he would remember and reflect on the rest of his life.

"You said you were at prayer meeting tonight?" Not sure what it consisted of, other than the obvious, he was a bit curious. Pastor Mike often spoke of one thing or another happening at prayer meeting, but he never gave it much thought.

Melba looked at him, wondering if he was truly interested or only making conversation. Willy did not attend church anywhere, and she had pondered it quite frequently.

"I generally go every Wednesday. Pastor Mike brings a short Bible study, and we pray for one another…and others." Her voice was softer as she continued. "It is a special time, and I enjoy it very much. It helps me through the rest of the week."

"*Ummm.*"

Melba paused and tried to read his expression. "Willy, you are welcome at church anytime. You do know that, don't you?"

She held his gaze, and he instinctively knew his response would somehow make a difference. Her faith was strong, and not wanting to mislead her, he glanced up at the stars and thought about what she asked. Looking at her, he replied in a gentle tone, "Yes, Melba, I know I would be gladly received, and I cannot imagine you or Mike or Ben or anyone not making me feel welcome."

Dropping her hand, he looked steadily at her and realized, somewhat to his own surprise, that he wanted her to know his feelings. "I would make myself feel unwelcome."

Willy felt her hand on his arm and saw the questioning look in her eye. "But why? Tell me why you feel that way."

Silent for a moment, he tried to make sense of his thoughts and wondered why himself. He looked at the ground and then back into her eyes. "I don't know," he replied honestly. "I...don't feel like I belong." He studied her face, not knowing what to expect, and wondered if his answer disappointed her. He almost wished she would walk away, and yet, he didn't know what he would do if she did. Releasing a long breath and with a tone of regret, he spoke softly, "I am not good enough, Melba."

A small smile touched her lips, and Willy was taken aback when she reached up and kissed his cheek. "No, you aren't good enough, Will. None of us are, but God loves us no matter what we have done and in spite of what we think."

Surprised, Melba found his hands gripping her shoulders firmly and the look on his face intense. "But you haven't done anything, Melba. Not like I have. God would love you easily."

"Do you think I would lie to you, Will? Do you?"

"No, I don't think...no."

They stood facing one another in the dark, and, noting his confusion, Melba asked, "What did I tell you about God loving us?"

"You said he loved us no matter what we have done."

"That is correct. That is what the Bible says. It does not say God loves everyone in the world except William J. Stanton."

Suspecting she was on the verge of anger, Willy was amazed when she wrapped her arms around him and laid her head against his chest. "He does, Will. God loves you so much. He truly does."

Enfolding her in his arms, he tightened his embrace and held her close. She made it sound so simple.

Chapter 7

Circling the block, Mike noted Clyde's cab at Willy's garage. Chuckling, he wished he had witnessed yesterday's fiasco. Tinkering with the horn, Clyde had thought it fixed only to discover that not to be the case, and, of all people, Trudy was his passenger.

Relating the episode, Willy said Clyde was taking Trudy to Dr. Miller's because Henry forgot her appointment and had gone to Chesterville. Thinking it inappropriate in the first place for the mayor's wife to ride around town in a yellow cab with a dented fender, she became furious when he pulled out of their lane, honked at Elijah Seabaugh, and the horn stuck.

Clyde had waved at everyone staring, but Trudy was madder than a wet hen and voiced her indignation over the whole episode. Before he had the opportunity to assist her, she jerked the door open, stepped out, knocked her hat sideways, and dropped her pocketbook. Snatching it up with her face as red as a beet, she glared at him and yelled over the blare of the horn, "Get that fixed! I will walk home before riding in that infernal thing again."

Feeling the sharpness of her rebuke, Clyde circled the square and drove into Willy's garage with the horn still blaring. "Do whatever needs to be done," Clyde told him. "Just fix it, or Trudy will squawk about it every time I see her."

Mike chuckled and shook his head. He didn't know which he enjoyed more—the episode of Clyde and his cab or Willy's reaction to the hard time he and Ben gave him over kissing Melba in the street. Willy's face became red, he shifted in his chair, and then he attempted to refill an already full coffee cup. Mumbling something about nosy neighbors, he sat back down with a silly grin and looked at the both of them. "It is a free country, and I might just do it again the first chance I get."

Mike pulled up in front of the drugstore and stepped out. Closing the door, he studied a scratch on the old '39 Ford and then turned when he heard his name. Michael Madison, Oak Grove's banker, was walking toward him.

"Good morning, Pastor Mike."

"Good morning, Michael. How are you today?"

"Couldn't be better. Are you headed to the drugstore?"

"Yes, I am," Mike replied, "I need to get a tin of Anacin. Would you care to join me?"

"That's just where I was headed."

The bell attached to the door announced their entrance, and Gerald turned from the rack of magazines he was stocking and waved. "Good morning, Michael, Pastor Mike."

"Morning, Gerald," both answered, making their way to the soda fountain.

The black marble counter was bare but for napkin holders and round glass sugar containers. A covered cake plate, containing donuts from White's bakery, sat in the middle, and a basket of wrapped goodies from Milly and Molly's was on the end of the counter.

A large, ornate, framed mirror reflected stocked shelves of almost anything one needed: magazines, toiletry items, comic books, men's cologne, nail polish, first aid products, and beauty aids. A rack of greeting cards and post cards, as well as a jewelry case and another taller shelf containing Kodak cameras and film were located along the back wall.

The old floor bore numerous scuffs and dents, and an old black fan turned slowly overhead. Small, round wooden tables occupied the center, and toward the back, a closed door led to the pharmacy, its large, open window affording a view of shelves containing jars of chemicals, plasters, prepared pills, powders, medicated waters, herbs, and paregoric needed to fill prescriptions.

"What can I get you gentlemen?" Gerald asked. A thin man with an ever-present grin, he wore his usual white shirt and black bow tie, a freshly starched, white apron tied at the waist, and a soda jerk hat. Wiping his hands on a towel tucked in his apron, he reached beneath the counter for a couple of Coca-Cola glasses and glanced up, "The usual?" Adding cherry syrup from one of the fountain pumps, he filled the glasses with Coke and placed them on the counter.

"Thank you, Gerald," Mike replied, noting an envelope Michael had placed on the counter. "What is this?"

"It is a little something to use for Nathan Black," Michael commented, scratching his chin with a forefinger. "I don't know what his expenses might be, and I doubt that it will put Elijah and Elizabeth out any, but…this is something Ellen and I have prayed about. We want to make a monthly contribution for his needs and would like you to apply it however you find useful."

"Thank you, Michael, and thank Ellen too. This is very thoughtful and generous."

"This is something we feel led to do, and I would appreciate it if you kept it quiet."

"I certainly will, Michael. What is not used I will set aside for his brother, if that is acceptable," Mike said, slipping the envelope in his shirt pocket.

"Use your best judgment. It will be fine with us however you apply it. When is he to arrive?"

"I am to meet Mr. Black and Nathan at four o'clock this afternoon," Mike answered, glancing at the Coca-Cola clock. "I pray everything will go easy for him." Watching Gerald refill the candy rack by the door, he thought again of the adjustment Nathan would have to make.

The jingling bell ushered in Trudy and Mildred, talking a mile a minute. "Oh, Pastor Mike and Mr. Madison; you are just the two we are looking for," Trudy announced with a broad smile. "Mildred, isn't this nice? We have them both here together."

Placing her pocketbook on the table nearest the men, Trudy motioned to Mildred. "Now, dear, you sit right there, and, Pastor, you and Mr. Madison stay right where you are, and we'll take care of our business right now. Isn't this nice? Gerald, I'll have my usual, and bring Mildred the same."

Wondering how long this would take, Mike glanced at his wristwatch, 9:05. He was to pick Leah up at ten o'clock, and they were to check on Mrs. Tyler, have lunch with Miss Mattie, return home for the children, and be out at the Seabaugh Farm when Nathan arrived. And before that, he needed to run Anacin back to the church for Myrtle.

"Now then," Trudy said, rummaging through her pocketbook, "oh, here it is." Retrieving a slip of paper, she put her glasses on, glanced at her notes, and looked at Mike. "Henry gave me the schedule of events for Founders Day, and I need to know if you are going to have the sunrise service again this year…of course you will. Have you talked to Reverend Clark about it? He, of course, will participate also. It is such an inspirational way to start our Founders Day celebration, don't you think?"

Gerald sat two glasses of lemonade on the table and glanced at Mike with a grin before making his way to the other side of the soda fountain.

"Thank you, Gerald. Mr. Madison, we think you would be ideal for organizing the activities on the square this year. I know any ideas you have will be perfect, but Henry gave me a list of last year's events, and I have added a couple of my own thoughts. Mildred, did I give you that other slip of paper?" she asked, rummaging through her pocketbook again.

"No, you had all the papers together when we left Edna's. You were asking her about…that matter. It is in there somewhere," Mildred replied, watching Trudy empty its contents on the table.

Mike, watching Trudy's growing frustration and Mildred's annoyance as she sorted through the items, wondered how two women so different could be best friends. Trudy was forty-five years old, short, and on the plump side and always dressed in the latest fashion. She was obsessed with hats and today wore a green one with a wide brim and enormous bow.

Needing to always feel in control, Trudy bossed everyone, talked incessantly, and, as the mayor's wife, felt she should have a voice in all matters. But beneath it all, Mike knew how tenderhearted she was and how devoted she was to her two nieces.

Mildred Reese, on the other hand, was not quite as fashionable, and her clothing style was more tailored. Attempting to stay abreast of Trudy, she often put on airs, though deep down she was easily intimidated. Her greatest quality was doing what was necessary in a crisis and her worst was an uncanny ability to seek out the latest gossip.

Glancing at his wristwatch, Mike knew thirty minutes was about all he could spare, and with Trudy, that was near impossible.

"There it is," she remarked, producing a slip of paper. "Now, Mr. Madison, you look this over. I have a copy at home, and if you want to change anything, you go right ahead. Just let me know, though. And, Gerald, your idea last year of guessing the number of marbles in a jar was very popular. You are in charge of that again, if that's all right with you, Mr. Madison."

"Well, Trudy, I don't know if I am the right person to oversee the activities on the square because—"

"Nonsense, you are perfect. We all voted on it," she replied with a wave of her hand.

Figuring the *all* consisted of Mildred and Trudy, Mike glanced at Michael and grinned. He looked like a cornered rabbit.

"And I know your lovely wife Ellen will be most helpful. Everyone will assist in whatever way they can, and you don't know how much we appreciate your willingness to participate. Gerald, do you have my medication ready?" Trudy asked, sipping her lemonade.

Noting his friend's frustration, Mike wanted to laugh and decided he would grab the Anacin before he forgot.

"You're not leaving, are you?" Trudy asked anxiously, watching her pastor rise from his stool and head toward the *Health Products*.

Grabbing a tin of Anacin, Mike walked back to the counter and laid it down. "No, Trudy, I have a few more minutes before my next appointment. What did you need?"

"Well, Mildred and I are gravely concerned about something, and we need your advice as well as Reverend Clark's. Someone mentioned a new activity this year that I find questionable. Mildred and I both do, and I am sure others will also."

Trudy sat straight in her chair, placed folded hands on the table, and looked directly at him. "I think it would be a great tragedy to fall below the standards we have always maintained, a great tragedy."

The bell jingled again, and Abigail Cranston entered with Scooter, a small, black Scottish terrier trailing at her heels.

"Abigail, you are just in time. Mercy me, we could use your opinion on this subject too. Sit right down," Trudy ordered, shoving everything into her pocketbook. "Scooter, stop it. Abigail, why does he chew on my shoes? I never see him bothering anyone else's. Stop it now. Do you hear me?"

"Come here, Scooter," Abigail commanded, snapping her fingers at the little dog, who obediently sat down and looked up at her. "Good morning, Pastor Mike, Mr. Madison," Abigail greeted, smiling sweetly and sitting in the chair next to Mildred. "What are you discussing, and why do you need my opinion?"

"Can I get you something, Abigail?" Gerald asked, returning from the rear of the store with Trudy's medicine.

"Yes, Gerald, thank you. I will have a Coca-Cola, and I need some calamine lotion." Glancing at both women, she leaned forward and lowered her voice, "Sam's gotten into something, and he's itching everywhere...and I mean everywhere."

"Oh, dear, I suspect it is poison ivy. I had it once, and it was awful," Trudy said, shaking her head. "I don't *ever* go anywhere near the stuff."

"I have never had poison ivy. I guess I am fortunate." Mildred folded her hands and a thoughtful look crossed her face. "Although one time I did get in an awful mess of chiggers, and that is something to deal with, let me tell you. I have not sat on the grass since."

"My mother used to make a paste of cornstarch and buttermilk that helped. You might try that," Trudy offered. "She also used to—"

"Excuse me, ladies, but on what did you want our opinions?" Mike asked.

Sliding his glass across the counter, Michael rose to go, "If you will excuse me, ladies, I need to get over to—"

"Wait just a minute. We need your opinion," Trudy said."Sit down, please. This is too important. I will get right to it." Moving her foot, she bestowed an aggravated look on Scooter. "Now, this is the situation. Someone, and I am not going to say who, suggested this year for Founders Day we should...I hate to even suggest it," Trudy said, looking from Mildred to Abigail and then at Michael. Her eyes traveled to Gerald, who leaned against the counter listening, and then finally her gaze rested on Mike. Confident she had everyone's attention, she took a deep breath and continued, "Someone actually suggested we have a...a square dance." Dropping her bomb, she released a long, dramatic sigh; crossed her arms; and pursed her lips.

No one said a word, and expecting far worse, Mike chuckled. Michael looked at him strangely, Gerald busily wiped the counter with his tea towel, and Abigail clapped her hands enthusiastically.

Smiling broadly, she exclaimed, "Sakes alive, I think that is a marvelous idea. Why I haven't square danced in years."

"You think it is a good idea?" Trudy screeched. "Heavenly days, I would not have thought it of you. Why I am surprised, Abigail. You think we should turn Founders Day into a dance?" Flustered, Trudy looked from one to the other. "What do the rest of you think? Mr. Madison, surely you can't go along with this outlandish idea."

Looking as if wanting to bolt from his stool, Michael straightened his tie and cleared his throat. "Well, I don't know. I would imagine there are a lot of people like Mrs. Cranston that would enjoy it and—"

"A lot of people? Surely not! I declare, I have never square danced in my life." Trudy turned to Gerald, who was slowly inching his way to the back of the store. "Hold on there, Gerald. You're not getting out of this. What do you think?"

A sheepish grin on his face, he glanced at those staring at him and slowly strolled back behind the counter. "Well, I...kind of agree with Abigail," he said, glancing at Mike. "I mean...well...Trudy, I used to enjoy square dancing. I think it might be enjoyable."

"Well mercy me, Grandma would turn over in her grave. I can't believe you people. Do you realize what a rambunctious affair this could turn into and…what it could lead to? The next thing you know everyone will want to do the jitterbug, and we all know that is nothing more than the devil's work. Square dancing would just be the first step to something worse, wouldn't it, Mildred?"

"I am…certainly surprised…but maybe it wouldn't be…too bad if," Mildred answered hesitantly, glancing at the others, now none too positive square dancing was such an evil idea. After all, she and Jack used to enjoy it before they were married. "Perhaps we should ask Reverend Clark, and if he doesn't see anything wrong either, why I—"

"Well!" Trudy huffed, frowning at her betrayer. "We have never had square dancing on Founders Day. Pastor Mike, I know you will not condone such behavior," Trudy stated confidently and then narrowed her eyes. "Why are you grinning?"

"I am sorry, Trudy." Mike forced himself to rid the grin from his face and cleared his throat as he looked at Trudy's flushed face. "Founders Day has always been a great success, and the credit belongs to you. I appreciate that fact. I really do. But there is nothing wrong with adding something new or doing things a little different. If there are enough folks that want to have a square dance, I think you should consider it. After all, no one *has* to participate, and it is a group activity. I don't see anything wrong with it."

Watching Trudy's face, he knew she was not about to change her mind, not yet. She would come around in a few days after she gave it some thought and then be convinced it was all her idea. But for now, he believed it was a good time to make an exit. "And now, ladies, I have an appointment I must keep," Mike said, standing to his feet. "Give it some more thought, Trudy. I know you are very open-minded, and I am sure you will take everyone's wishes into consideration."

Patting her shoulder, he turned back to the men. "Michael, thank you again and give Ellen my regards." Dropping a quarter on the counter, Mike retrieved the tin of Anacin, turned to the ladies with a smile, and headed for the door. Stepping out onto the sidewalk, Trudy's voice followed him, "I declare, I just can't believe it has come to this. Have any of you seen the jitterbug?"

Appropriately named, Oak Hill sat on the eastern ridge and overlooked the valley. The forest along the ridge was most glorious when autumn's foliage burst into a riot of scarlet, yellow, and red as far as the eye could see. An occasional break in the trees allowed a brief glimpse of the home, only to be lost again amid oak, sweet gum, sugar maple, and cedar trees. The lane to Miss Mattie's wound uphill through the forest and leveled off at the summit. Rounding a bend of thick standing maple trees, the lane widened and continued beneath towering oaks and led to the front of Oak Hill, standing majestically at the end of the lane.

The three-story, white mansion graced the land of the original homestead and had an enormous front porch that extended along the front and around the east side of the house. Upstairs bedrooms opened onto a second-story balcony and afforded cool breezes on hot summer evenings and a magnificent view in the fall and winter. Large columns supported solid oak railings on both levels, and black shutters framed the windows, their lace curtains stirred by gentle breezes drifting across the ridge. Baskets of wandering Jew, Swedish ivy, and begonias added their beauty, and several pieces of white wicker furniture were scattered about on the porch.

A small dining table on the east veranda overlooked a meadow and pond, and it was here that Miss Mattie, Pastor Mike, Leah, Hannah, and Jeremiah were enjoying lunch.

"Elijah and Elizabeth are beside themselves," Mike commented, passing a platter of sliced roast beef. "They are like a couple of kids at Christmas."

Miss Mattie smiled and nodded. "It will be a wonderful blessing for them, as well as the young boy. My, but it will be grand to have a youngster around again."

"Lordy, when Deborah's here with the youngins, that's 'bout all we can manage anymore," Hannah replied, looking at Miss Mattie. "And ya ain't goin' ta fuss with me about it neither, 'cause we're all tuckered out by the time they leave."

Jeremiah looked at both ladies. "I kinda wish they'd stay a might longer when they come."

"That's cause ya don't do nothin' but let 'em follow ya 'round the barn and watch 'em crawl 'round in the hayloft," Hannah remarked to her husband of fifty years.

"It's me and Miss Mattie that's got ta see they're bathed, fed, and kept busy the rest of the time," Hannah continued, filling iced tea glasses.

"Now, Hannah, you know you enjoy the children," Mattie remarked, looking at her fondly. Hannah was like a child herself when Mark, Ruth, and Noah visited Oak Hill. Mattie's great-granddaughter, Deborah, always came along and stayed, but Hannah insisted on doing everything, in spite of Deborah's scolding.

"And yer the one that mopes around here a week after they've gone," Jeremiah commented, shaking his head. "She shore enough does, Pastor. Walks 'round here with a long face fer a good week and sniffles if she happens ta come across somethin' one of 'em left behind."

"Well, land sakes, of course ah miss 'em, ah shorely do, and ah won't deny it. It's lonesome when they're gone. That's for shore. But ah don't expect none of us could handle too long a bout of havin' 'em around."

"I expect you are right, Hannah. We have gotten too old to keep up with them. It is a pity too," Mattie replied, looking at Mike and Leah. "I guess that is why the Lord made parents young."

"Mattie, you will never be old. You enjoy life more than anyone I know," Mike chuckled, looking at her affectionately.

Anne Madison, ninety-five years old, was a slender lady with warm gray eyes who carried herself with regal bearing. In fairly good health, she now walked with the assistance of a cane, which she considered a nuisance. Mattie, a nickname given by her late husband Daniel, possessed great wisdom, was poised and gracious, demanded truth, and was a stickler for good manners and proper behavior. Though, as Mike had learned through the years, she had a tendency to give into the outrageous if the mood struck. She expressed love generously to all, and though blessed with great wealth, neither she nor her late husband ever considered one's social standing to have any bearing on their friendship, and both were often heard to remark that "the ground is level at the foot of the cross."

Comfortable and relaxed, Mike sat back in his chair and thought how much he enjoyed Thursday lunch with Miss Mattie. His eyes drifted up the hill to the original homestead still standing among a grove of oak trees. Presenting a picture of peace and serenity, it matched his mood as he listened to Leah describe Elizabeth and Nathaniel Black and their family and home on the ridge. Shifting his gaze, he watched her. After all these years, he still found his wife fascinating.

Dark hair curled on the ends and framed her heart-shaped face. Warm brown eyes sparkled beneath delicately arched brows, and her smile still took him back to that June evening he first laid eyes on her at an ice cream social. "Johnny is going to spend the first few days with Nathan, and I think that will help him somewhat. I certainly hope so," Leah continued.

"It will," Mike replied. "They hit it off pretty well, and I think it is an excellent idea. Thank you for praying about this with us."

"Why, of course. We prayed together, the three of us, every night for the Lord's will to be done in Nathan's life, and there is no need to thank us for it either."

"I just want you to know how much I appreciate your faithfulness," Mike commented. "Don't you love to watch the Lord answer prayer…how he moves in and lays out his plan?"

"Yes, indeed," Mattie replied. "It always amazes me how he considers our requests and grants them."

"What is even more amazing," Mike replied, "is how he prepares our hearts in advance in readiness to seek those requests. Then he molds and guides us so he can work his perfect will in and through us."

Leah spoke softly. "I watch for his answers throughout the day as Psalm 5 tells us, and I have especially pondered on it these last few days." Looking at Miss Mattie, Hannah, and Jeremiah, she continued. "Mike read it one morning during our quiet time together, and I never forgot it, 'In the morning, O Lord, you hear my voice; in the morning I lay my requests before you and wait in expectation.' It is one of my favorite scriptures."

"Yes, I know it well," Miss Mattie replied, smiling wistfully. "It is one among many that saw me through Daniel's passing. The Lord led me tenderly through that valley. I could not have made it without him." Mattie's eyes filled with love, and she looked at Hannah and Jeremiah. "Why, my soul, just think. Years ago, He saw my need and gave me the both of you to love."

"There ya go again, sayin' somethin' like that," Hannah replied, sniffling as she gathered the plates. "Good gracious, Miss Mattie, ya always say somethin' like that and…well, I'm gonna get the pie."

"Ye might jest as well sit back and wait a spell," Jeremiah said, shaking his head as his eyes followed Hannah. "She'll sniffle 'round in there a while afore she comes back actin' like nothin's wrong. She's been doin' that a powerful lot lately." Sitting forward, he looked at Mike. "Mebbe ya can help me know what's up there in her head. We been married so long, ah don't reckon ah remember when we wasn't, and ah still ain't figured her out."

Jeremiah scratched his white head and sighed. "Why jest the other day, ah tole her she didn't look near as old as she was, and ah even said she still got 'round as good as a cricket. Ah think it pleased her some too, cause she smiled and patted my cheek. Then the next thing ah know, she's cryin' and said yes, she did look old, and she pitied the poor cricket that couldn't get 'round any better than she did. Then she's tellin' me ah'm gettin' old too and walked off sayin' it's not been too bad married ta *this here ole man,* laughin' and cryin' at the same time. Now, ya tell me, Pastor Mike, what's a body to think?"

Chapter 8

The big bay plodded slowly down the road at a gait that appeared to be the only one he remembered. Days of running free across the field were long gone, and pulling the buckboard was about as much work as anyone expected of him.

Nathan Black sat on the wagon seat next to his pa and stared at the horse, its reddish-brown coat and black mane and tail as familiar to him as anything he knew. Riding bareback from the age of four, he remembered Thunder being old then, and although his pa had four other horses, he was still Nathan's favorite. Wondering if the old horse would miss him, he thought sadly, *He will miss the apples I give him.*

Glancing at his father, he took note of the familiar, old, gray hat sitting atop thick, sandy-colored hair. Violet eyes looked straight ahead, and the firm set to his jaw gave evidence that he was determined to do something neither wanted.

"I do not fancy this any more than you, Son," Pa had said as they walked together up the ridge one evening. "And I don't expect you to be happy about it, but that's tolerable. I can't fault you for that."

As they walked across the ridge and talked, he knew his pa was hurting, and they stood together, father and son, gazing down into the valley. The sun was sinking behind the hills, birds chirped as they nested in tree branches, and Nathan remembered his pa releasing a long sigh. Things were changing, and life would never be the same again. Nathan wanted to throw his arms around him and beg not to be sent away, but the desire for his father to be proud of him was stronger.

Nathaniel Black Sr., a towering man of great physical strength, felt as though his heart was being ripped from his chest. For the first time in his life, he felt emotionally weak, and he didn't like it. Laying an arm across his oldest son's shoulder, he looked across the hills, wondering where the years had gone.

He and Spring Rain came to these mountains shortly after their wedding. Critical tongues were sharp toward the young Apache girl he loved. When his own family showed signs of disapproval, Nathaniel could tolerate it no longer, and they set out on their own, making their way into the Ozark Mountains. God had blessed them in this time and place on earth, and things would have stayed the same if not for Mike Daniels...or would it?

Nathaniel turned and looked into trusting eyes so like his own.

"Sometimes a man is faced with a choice he'd druther not make, Nathan, but he knows if he falters, the one he loves will suffer farther on down the trail."

His words were uncharacteristically soft, and Nathan strained to hear what he was saying.

"A body sets his own feelin's on the shelf to do the right thing for the one he loves. You must remember that."

They stared at one another a long moment, and Nathaniel was aware of the signs that bore evidence of the man his son would become.

"I'd not allow such a thing, Nathan, if not for Mike Daniels. I'll tell you true, part of me is angry with him for findin' his way to our place." Shaking his head, he gazed off into the valley. "I suspect it's been three to four years now. He intruded, but I'll allow that it was God's way. If he wasn't huntin' this far up the ridge, he'd never found Sally when she busted her leg, and I'd have to swear he's been a good friend. You can trust him, Nathan. He's straight." Releasing a long sigh, Nathaniel put his hand on his son's shoulder. "And what he says is truth. I wasn't agreeable with him about you goin' over the mountain to school, and your mother surely wasn't, but...he is right. I know it now. It's needful and somethin' you deserve. I can't hold that from you. And you'll come home to visit a spell every full moon."

Lost in thought as he remembered that evening, Nathan's attention was drawn back to the present when his pa pulled on the reins and Thunder halted his slow gait.

"I expect we're here. " He nodded toward a white, two-story house sitting amid a grove of oak trees at the end of the lane. Another house, similar but smaller, sat a short distance to the left. "Yep, this is just the place Mike Daniels painted in my mind.

The two youngest Daniels children, sitting on the fence rail waiting, were curious as to the horse and wagon coming down the road and watched wide-eyed as the unusual sight turned up the lane.

"It's them," Shari exclaimed, looking at her brother and back at the wagon. "Golly gee, Jimmy, it's really them!"

"Boy howdy, they're coming in a hay wagon. Let's tell Dad."

Jumping from the rail, they ran through the yard and up the steps. "They're here," Shari yelled, jerking the screen wide. "They're coming up the lane right now!"

"And by horse and wagon," Jimmy exclaimed, looking at those gathered in the parlor. Mom and Dad were talking with Mr. and Mrs. Seabaugh, Laura and Johnny were playing Chinese checkers, and Liza stood in the dining room doorway with a handful of green and white checked napkins.

Mike rose to his feet and grinned at Elijah and Elizabeth. "This is what we have been waiting for. Shall we?"

"Land sakes alive," Liza commented, stuffing the napkins in her apron pocket. Following the others to the door, she stared at the strange sight coming up the lane.

She stared at the man on the wagon seat and could see from where she stood he was a large man. Wild rumors she'd heard ran through her mind, and for a brief second, she wondered what they would do if he was as wild a mountain man as everyone said, eatin' raw meat, drinkin' corn liquor, and throwin' hatchets at anyone settin' foot on his land.

"Lordy, Lordy, ah expect ya need ta forgive these sinful thoughts," she murmured quietly. "We asked ya ta do this very thing, so ah 'spect if ya sent 'em ta us, they ain't gonna kill us."

Liza's dark eyes traveled to the young boy sitting next to the man, and a broad grin crossed her face. "There he is. Thank ya, Jesus. We'll love him like ya expect us."

"Nathaniel, my friend," Mike greeted, walking down the steps and over to the buckboard. "It is good to see you."

The large man stepped down, nodded, gripped Mike's hand, and looked him steadily in the eye, seeking confirmation or an answer. He wasn't sure.

Mike placed a hand on his shoulder, aware of the emotion in the other man's eyes. "How have you been?"

"Fair to middlin' I expect." Nathaniel Black glanced at those gathered on the porch. He nodded to Leah, took note of the children, and rested his gaze on an older man and woman standing on the top step.

So, he thought, *them's the two who's goin' to look after my boy.* Anxious to get a good take on their character, he watched the tall, broad-shouldered man closely as he came down the steps and approached. He walked slowly and easily. There was a gentleness to his face, but the way he carried himself bespoke of strength, and Nathaniel instantly approved of the man.

Elijah Seabaugh looked Nathaniel Black directly in the eye, and the hand he extended was large, callused, and firm to the grip. Nathaniel studied the man. Clear, brown eyes were honest and warm; the tanned and weathered face bore evidence of days in the fields; and he stood erect and confident.

"Nathaniel, I am Elijah," he said, grinning broadly. "And this is Nathan. My soul, he sure looks like you."

Mike observed uncertainty in the young boy's face as he glanced from Elijah to his father, and he walked over to the wagon and smiled up at him. "Nathan, it is good to have you with us. Come on down, and let me introduce you to everyone."

Receiving a reassuring nod from his pa, Nathan slid from the wagon, his bare feet landing in the dust, and he removed his old, straw hat. His eyes on his father, he hesitantly came to stand before them and, extending his hand, found it enveloped in the larger hand of the man.

"Welcome, Nathan." The voice was deep and rich, and Nathan looked up into his eyes. There was something about him that reminded him of Pa.

"Nathaniel, I would like you and Nathan to meet Elizabeth Seabaugh," Mike said, turning to the sweet lady who had come to stand next to her husband.

"Mr. Black, I am proud to meet you," Elizabeth said, studying the man who was entrusting his son to them. Despite his ominous appearance, she instinctively knew there was a gentleness in him, and with a smile turned to the young boy standing awkwardly in front of her.

"Nathan, welcome to our home."

"Thank you, ma'am," he answered, remembering the manners Ma had instructed him. Nathan looked at the ground, unable to think of another word to say. *She's got the same Christian name as Ma*, he thought, with a melancholy feeling in the pit of his stomach.

"You may call me Elizabeth, but if Mrs. Seabaugh feels better until we get to know one another, that is fine."

Placing both hands in the pockets of his overalls, Nathan glanced at the woman's kind face and thought she was going to cry, but then she smiled. "Shall we call you Nathan? Or do you have a nickname?"

He nervously looked away, thoughts tumbling through his brain. He could never call her Elizabeth; Ma would frown at that. What did Johnny Daniels call her? And what was a nickname?

"Nathan?"

Pa's voice reached his ear, and he realized he hadn't answered. He didn't want to be called his nickname, whatever that was, so he guessed he'd better stick with Nathan. Opening his mouth to speak, a sense of pride and unexplained anger took hold.

"I would like to be called Nathaniel," he stated firmly, looking directly at her for the first time.

"Then Nathaniel it is."

Mike noted the surprised and pleased expression that crossed his father's face and the slight nod of head as he acknowledged his son's decision.

"Hey, *Nathaniel.*"

"Hey, Johnny Daniels."

"It's swell you're here. You'll have to meet some of the guys."

"I expect." He really didn't care if he did or not.

"I'm spending a few nights out here until school starts. I'll show you around the place."

Nathaniel Black looked at Mike with a slight nod of approval and then turned his attention to the other three children standing next to Mrs. Daniels.

"Welcome," Leah said. Standing before the young boy, she looked at him tenderly, wishing there was something she could do to set his mind at ease but knew nothing other than time and prayer would help him adjust. Looking into the remarkable violet eyes so like his father's, she smiled and placed a hand on his shoulder.

"I promised your mama that I would watch out for you, so the first thing I mean to do is give you a big hug." Pulling him into a warm embrace, Leah smiled and then stepped aside as Jimmy came to stand before him.

"She does that to everybody," he stated matter-of-factly. "You might as well get used to it. Say, do you like chicken and dumplings? Liza's fixed a big pot, and nobody cooks chicken and dumplings like Liza."

Mike placed an arm on each of his daughters' shoulder. "Now that you have met Jimmy, this is Laura and Shari."

Shari looked a lot like her ma, and he glanced at Laura. *She has a fine face*, he thought, noting her blond hair, blue eyes, and friendly smile. Feeling his face flush, he glanced away, wishing he was at home.

"I am glad you are here, Nathaniel," Laura said, smiling brightly. He wasn't anything as she had imagined.

He was tall for his age, and beneath the old straw hat was a shaggy mop of sandy-colored hair. His face was deeply tanned, and the color of his eyes was like none she had ever seen. Noting his shyness, she smiled reassuringly.

"Well, let's not stand out here," Elijah remarked, gesturing toward the steps. "Come on in the place, and we'll sit a spell. Liza has supper about ready, and we'll eat directly."

Making his way reluctantly up the steps, Nathaniel felt a tug on his shirt sleeve. "You'll like it here. It's nifty," Jimmy said, grinning. "There are horses and cows, chickens, and pigs and rabbits; and you should see the lambs. Do you like lambs, Nathaniel? I'll show them to you if you want."

The small boy followed him through the door, over to the sofa, and, managing to squeeze between him and Pa, continued. "And there's the old bull. I don't like him. He's mean."

Nathaniel looked down at Jimmy. He reminded him of his five-year-old brother Andrew. He was always jabbering about something too.

"But you have to watch out for that old nanny goat, or she'll get you right in the butt. She butts *almost* everybody, even Johnny."

"She gets you just as often as she does everyone else, so don't sit there and act like she doesn't," Johnny answered. "But he's right, Nathaniel. You better stay away from her."

"Buttin' Beulah, that's her name," Shari piped up. "Do you want to go see her, Nathaniel?"

"No one's goin' anywhere," a voice called from the dining room. "It's time ta eat, so don't get it in yer heads ta go runnin' off outside. Ya jest as well wash up and get in here."

Nathan stared at the slim black lady standing in the doorway. He had never seen anyone like her. A yellow bibbed apron covered the faded, blue dress she wore, and a red and white bandana was wrapped around her kinky black hair. She held a tea towel in one hand, a large wooden spoon in the other, and her dark eyes circled the room, resting on Shari and Jimmy.

"And don't ya two be haulin' this young man out all over the barnyard jest yet. Ah've seen ya out there teasin' my Beulah," she said, shaking the spoon at them. "She never butts me, but ah declare, ah'd butt ye too if ah was her."

Nathan sat unmoving, not knowing what to expect from this bold, dark-skinned woman. Her black eyes moved to his father. White teeth gleamed as she smiled, and she placed both hands on her hips.

"Ah'm Liza. Welcome ta the farm, Mr. Black, and ya too, Nathaniel. We're mighty proud ya be sharin' supper with us. We been prayin' fer youins ta get here. Why, Jacob's got a new fishin' pole ready for ya," she exclaimed, her eyes resting on Nathaniel. "Land sakes alive, what a handsome young man ya are. And ah reckon yer brothers and sisters are just as purty. How many of youins are they?"

Nathan hesitated a moment and then answered quietly, "I've got five brothers and four sisters."

"Well now, that's a mighty nice family ya have there, Mr. Black, mighty nice. Ya jest bring them all around one of these times. All ah have ta do is grab a bigger cook pot. Miss Elizabeth, supper's ready anytime ya have a mind ta gather 'round the table." Looking back at Nathan, she grinned again. "My my, but we sure are proud ta have ya here." Flashing another smile, she turned and disappeared.

Mike looked at Leah and grinned. As long as Liza was around, he figured things would run pretty smooth. She would get to the root of any problem that might arise.

"Dad," Preston yelled from the back porch, "Miss Tillie wants you to come over and check the alley. She says the Yanks are out behind the garage."

Shaking his head, Sheriff Walker glanced at his wristwatch, six thirty, right on time. Miss Tillie's calls began earlier in the summer, about the time folks started missing things. After much confusion and several sleepless nights, it was discovered the robberies were linked to the mystery of Jasper and the unexplained ringing of the town square bell. Tillie Watson had Hazel ring him every couple of weeks now to report someone snooping around her house trying to steal her grandmother's silverware, a gift from General Robert E. Lee.

Seventy-eight, Miss Tillie lived alone in a large Victorian house at the corner of Church and Pine streets. A tall, slender woman with a mind of her own, she was always a bit eccentric but became increasingly more so after the unexpected death of her husband of fifty years. Most days, Miss Tillie was fairly normal, and then other times, her behavior was quite peculiar. On those occasions, she donned one of many old gowns and bonnets from a trunk in the attic and was once again a young southern belle living on a plantation in Virginia. Sitting on her front porch, she shared lemonade and teacakes and told outlandish stories to any and all who happened by. Most in Oak Grove were used to Miss Tillie and took it all in stride. John's only real concern was when Hazel rang to inform him, "Miss Tillie is out in her Tin Lizzie again."

The 1926 Model T Ford Runabout was a forty-year wedding anniversary gift from her late husband. The shiny, two-door, black automobile was a top-of-the-line vehicle equipped with electric starter and horn, wire wheels, imitation leather seats, shiny black fenders, and splash aprons. But Miss Tillie's greatest delight was the front windshield, which she proudly demonstrated for her lady friends, opening and closing it at every opportunity. All in all, she was quite proud of the whole *contraption*, as was her wont to call it.

Miss Tillie in her shiny, black Model T was a sight to behold in 1926, zipping down the street at thirty-five miles per hour, and it had taken Harold all summer to explain the various functions of its three floor pedals, two steering column levers, and floor lever. After several weeks, he was fairly certain she understood and held his breath when she climbed behind the steering wheel and leaped and lurched down the road.

Tillie finally mastered it, filling Harold with a sense of accomplishment that quickly turned to dread. Insisting on driving maximum speed, she felt *more comfortable* using both lanes and preferred stopping by stamping on both floor pedals.

Following Harold's death, the Tin Lizzie was parked in the garage and only seen when Miss Tillie was not quite herself and took it out for a spin, scaring everyone half to death. The general consensus was the old car brought back memories of Harold and the summer she learned to drive, so no one complained much.

After driving four times around the square one day, John finally got her attention and motioned her to pull over. In haste, she mistakenly accelerated, drove across the sidewalk into the honeysuckles, slammed on the brakes, and then accused him of running her off the road. Instructing her to park it in the garage and not drive again, he was flabbergasted when she produced a current driver's license and said she had as much right to the road as anyone. When he followed her home at ten miles per hour, she drove across her lawn, around the side of the house, to the alley, and into the garage. He was totally amazed she hadn't ripped the whole side of the garage off.

Willy used every excuse not to sell her gasoline, and Clyde offered free cab fare. Dr. Miller made a house call once a month, David Reese delivered her groceries, and John lectured her every time he caught her driving. Pastor Mike and Reverend Clark were no help. She made it abundantly clear they were to preach the Word of God and not her driving. Refusing them admittance, she cheerily visited through the door or on the front porch, and as for the rest of the folks in Oak Grove, they figured the simplest and safest thing to do was to stay out of her way.

"Can I go?" Brenton asked.

"You might as well. Come on, we should get back in time for the ball game."

"I'm going too," Preston called, jumping from the back steps. Crawling into the back seat, he grinned at Brenton. "I wonder what battle took place this time."

Backing out of the drive, John looked in the rearview mirror. "You boys mind your manners and don't encourage her to get started on one of her tales."

"But her stories are nifty, Dad," Preston piped, "even if they are all a pack of lies."

"She doesn't know they are lies. She gets confused."

"She's all gussied up," Brenton whispered as they pulled up in front of the large home.

Sitting on the porch swing wearing a medium blue taffeta tea dress and a matching dark blue felt bonnet, Miss Tillie looked every bit the grand Southern lady. A pink lace shawl was draped across her shoulders, and her spectacles were perched on her nose.

Pointing a gloved finger, she exclaimed, "You go on out back and get that Yankee out of my garage, General. He's been there all afternoon, as sure as you're born. I know what he's up to. He is waiting until dark to sneak in here and take my silverware."

"Good evening, Miss Tillie. You look absolutely charming this evening. Don't you fret about a thing. I'll check it out right now."

"Thank you kindly, General. I didn't want to have to use my pistol. Did I tell you General Robert E. Lee gave that silverware to my grandmother? He sure did. He brought it from Arlington house, just as sure as you're born." Petting Charlotte, her fat, white lap cat, she eyed up Brenton and Preston. "I see you brought two of your men."

"Yes, ma'am, I sure did. If there are any Yankees in your garage, we'll rout them out," John replied, grinning at both boys before disappearing around the corner of the house.

"Well, bless my soul, that's a comfort. Well, then go on. Get about your business," she commanded, retrieving a glass of iced tea from the small table next to the swing. "The general needs your help."

Finding his dad coming around the side of the garage, Brenton wondered what he would do if someone suddenly jumped out. The idea gave him the willies. Maybe Civil War ghosts really did live around here, as Miss Tillie claimed.

"Say, Brenton, do you remember that day she said the Yankees were right over the ridge and she went to Hank's for bullets?" Preston asked uneasily, glancing over his shoulder.

"Yeah, but Hank didn't sell her any." Brenton looked at his brother's face and glanced back at the house. "But what if she bought some in Chesterville?"

"Holy moley! She might get in her Tin Lizzie and go on a shooting spree," Preston exclaimed, wishing Dad would hurry.

"She's not going to do that. Gee willikers, Preston, Miss Tillie's not crazy."

"I don't know. She's batty one day, and then when Mom and Mrs. Daniels visit her the next day they say she's normal," Preston replied, watching his dad step out of the garage and slide the door closed.

"That is pretty weird, isn't it? I hope I don't ever get like that."

"You won't. She's a lady, and you are a boy."

"What does that have to do with anything?"

"Because something happens to ladies when they get old."

"What are you talking about!"

"I heard Mrs. Driscol talking to Mrs. Reese one day in the drugstore about having a *change in her life*. She said she wasn't looking forward to it either, but it happened to all women sooner or later. Mrs. Reese said she heard that some women go crazy. I betcha that's what happened to Miss Tillie."

"Well, boys, let's go home and listen to the ball game," John said, walking toward them. "Everything's taken care of."

"Did you rout him out, General?" Miss Tillie asked.

"Yes, ma'am. They are retreating…hightailing it across the ridge."

"I thank you kindly, General. Would you or your men like a glass of tea?"

"No thank you, ma'am, not this evening. I will next time."

"I guess you better go then, or you will never get back to camp before dark. And don't dawdle around. Those Yanks will be back looking for you just as sure as you're born."

"Yes, ma'am. We are on our way right now," John replied. "You have a good evening, Miss Tillie, and don't worry about a thing."

"Mercy sakes, General, I almost forgot. You tell General Lee that Miss Tillie sends her warmest regards."

"I sure will. Good evening, Miss Tillie."

"Good evening, General."

Chapter 9

September ushered in that sense of normalcy that accompanies the beginning of another school year. Sitting in his rocker on the small side porch of the shop, old Ben leisurely puffed his pipe and thought about Carrie. How he wished she were there last night when Ben and Lizzie came to tell him they were getting married. He could just hear her. *Now, didn't ah tell ya. All that frettin' fer nothin'. The good Lord always works things in his own time.*

Mercy was ecstatic, and Ben wondered how long he would have to wait to see her happily married. She and Saul had courted all summer, but they seemed to be nothing more than good friends. He removed his hat and scratched his white head. *Maybe ah'm just so old, ah don't know what's goin' on,* he thought, placing the hat on his knee.

"I expect yer right, Carrie," he spoke aloud. "Ah'll let the good Lord handle it and not fret on it."

Across the shop, the checkerboard sat atop the cracker barrel in readiness for the day's game, and he grinned as he made his way to the kitchen. Yesterday, James and Phillip vowed to never play each other again, and he wondered how many times he'd heard that through the years. "Pert near once a month ah suspect." He chuckled, refilling his cup.

Replacing the percolator on the stove, he sat down at the kitchen table and rubbed his chest. There it was again, that same pain he noticed lately. He ought to call Doc Miller, but he would only tell him what he already knew; besides, it would just worry Mercy. *How long, Lord? How long 'til ah get to see yer face?*

A new 1946 Mercury sedan slowly passed on the street, and Ben admired its green color, figuring it must have cost the driver a pretty penny. *Wonder who that might be,* he thought as the vehicle slowed and pulled up in front of the Cranston Hotel. *Someone jest passin' through ah expect.*

Opening the car door, a well-dressed man stepped out, absentmindedly smoothed his mustache, and looked at the small shops lining the sidewalks. Across the street sat a large, white, impressive building with a clock on the front, currently chiming ten o'clock.

"Madison County Courthouse," he murmured, reading the words across the front. "This is it."

Looking behind him, he was pleased with what he saw. A black, wrought-iron fence surrounded a large, white, two-story home amid two enormous maple trees. Black shutters framed its windows and wide steps led up to a large porch. Round, white columns at both ends and on either side of the steps rose to support a second-story veranda that overlooked the square. Displayed on the lawn, a white, wooden sign identified it as the Cranston Hotel in black bold lettering. He smiled with satisfaction. *Perfect, just perfect.*

Closing the car door, he acknowledged a greeting from an elderly gentleman who was headed toward an old building with Blacksmith painted on its side. A tall, young man pumped gas at Willy's Garage, and across the street, a young couple entered the Cranston Café.

"You are all daft," a short, robust man called to the sound of laughter as he exited a small shop, its function clearly identified by a barber pole and Ned's painted on the window. The man paused a moment to speak with another gentleman entering Oak Grove Community Bank, then continued on his way.

The stranger stood quietly, smiling with pleasure. This was like stepping into a Norman Rockwell painting. Allowing himself a leisurely perusal of the other side of the street, his gaze traveled past White's Bakery, Edna's, the Dime Store, and an enticing little place called the Sweet Shoppe. A sign in a window at Hank's Hardware advertised a sale on Benjamin Moore Paint. There was the Oak Grove Post Office, and around the corner sat Baker's Clothier and Williams Shoe Shop. Just beyond the courthouse and across the street from the Oak Grove Library, the Star Theater's marquee advertised *Boom Town* with Clark Gable and Spencer Tracy. A shop with Melba's painted on the window, the Chronicle News, and Reese's Market comprised the rest of the shops.

There was peace and satisfaction here. He could sense it. An urge to get back in the car and drive away gripped him. *What gives me the right to disrupt these people's lives,* he thought for probably the hundredth time. Realizing he was clenching both fists, he flexed his fingers, took a deep breath, and stared up into the blue September sky. It was now or never. It was time to find out.

Preferring to drive and take time to collect his thoughts, he walked around the front of the vehicle purchased specifically for this trip. Stepping through the gate, he strolled up the sidewalk and climbed the steps, praying he would not regret what he was about to do.

"Why, good morning," a plump, rosy-cheeked little woman said, smiling sweetly as she greeted him at the door. White hair was pulled back in a bun, a pair of spectacles was perched on her nose, and over a blue and white flowered dress, she wore a white apron tied at the neck and around her waist. "Is there something I can do for you?" she asked, pleasantly. "If you are looking for a room, this is the perfect place. I am Abigail Cranston, and we would love to have you stay with us."

Andrew returned the smile and glanced around the large foyer, aware of the smell of beeswax and fresh-cut flowers. Something about the place bespoke of home, and he immediately felt at ease.

"As a matter of fact, yes." He chuckled, liking her direct, warm manner. "I do need a room, and you are correct. This looks like it just may be the perfect place."

"My stars, I am so glad. This is Scooter," she offered, stepping aside to reveal a small, black, Scottish terrier at her feet. Scooter looked up, barked, and then ran around his feet and flopped down on the floor.

"Now would you look at that. Scooter likes you." Leaning toward him, she softened her voice and added, "If he doesn't, he will go after your shoes."

Inquisitive, she now studied him a moment, wondering on his accent, then walked to a tall, walnut secretary against the opposite wall and pulled out a beautiful side chair and sat down.

Abigail glanced up at the well-dressed young man, hoping he would stay a while. It had been some time since anyone took a room for more than a couple of days. "We love to have folks stay with us when they are passing through. It brightens our day," she commented, opening a black, leather-bound guest register. "Why, my stars, we used to have folks stay her for a month or more at a time, but not too often anymore. Nevertheless, I am happy you have chosen to visit Oak Grove, and if you need help locating anyone or anything, you just let me know. If you will, just sign your name, Mr.—"

"Baxter, ma'am. Andrew Baxter."

"Well, Mr. Baxter, if you will sign here, we will get you taken care of," she commented, turning the register and handing him a fountain pen.

"Will your business keep you through the weekend or just this evening?" Flushing, she touched her cheek. "Oh, my stars, I don't mean to be nosy. Please don't think so. It is just that Lottie will want to bake something special. She tends to spoil our guests, which is not a bad thing, of course. We do like our guests to feel comfortable, but it is just that…oh for goodness' sake, she would be terribly disappointed if she didn't have the opportunity to bake you something. My stars, but she would be in a dither if she didn't. That is why I was wondering how long you planned to stay."

Andrew smiled at her flustered face, signed his name with a flourish across the page, and returned her fountain pen. "I will definitely be spending the weekend, Mrs. Cranston. In fact, I may be here several days."

"Oh my, but that is wonderful. I have just the room." Opening a side drawer, she removed a key and rose to her feet, smoothing the front of her dress.

"Pardon me, if you tell me the cost, I will pay in advance."

"Mercy sakes no, it is four dollars a night, but you can pay when you leave."

"For all I know, I may be run out of town on a rail and not able to pay," Andrew laughed, pulling a bill from his wallet. "Seriously, Mrs. Cranston, I prefer to pay in advance. This should take care of the first week. Would you perhaps have a room overlooking the square?"

"Why, of course," she replied, accepting the twenty-dollar bill. Looking at it for a moment, she put it in her apron pocket and smiled. "Thank you. Now let me show you around the place."

Andrew followed, watching Scooter traipse along at her heels, the sound of his paws clicking along the floor. Appreciating the rich workmanship of dark mahogany banisters and gleaming waxed floors, Andrew was well pleased and followed Mrs. Cranston up the carpeted stairs, where they turned right and stopped at the first door.

"This is my favorite room. I hope you find it comfortable," Abigail commented, pushing the door wide.

Stepping inside, Andrew glanced around with pleasure. They stood in a small, comfortable sitting room. An overstuffed, brown chair and a table with a reading lamp sat to the right of French doors that opened onto the balcony. Against the wall on the right was a bookcase containing several volumes, and an open door on the opposite wall revealed a large four-poster bed. Walking into the bedroom, he noticed a writing desk, an armoire, and another door leading into a bathing chamber.

"This is very nice. I shall be most comfortable here. Thank you," Andrew remarked, returning to the sitting room. Crossing to the French doors, he opened one and stepped out onto the veranda, admiring the view below. "This is perfect."

"Good. Now, breakfast is at seven, lunch is at noon, and supper is on the table at five. If you are not here on time, don't worry yourself none. Lottie will keep it warm on the stove. And you are welcome to help yourself anytime, day or night." Abigail handed him the key and made her way to the door. "There will be fresh washcloths and towels on the credenza in the hall every morning, and if you need anything, you let us know," she said, pausing in the doorway.

"Yes, ma'am, I will," he replied. Though asking no questions, he knew she was curious as to his presence in Oak Grove, and he deliberately turned away. Walking across the room, he made a pretense of looking at the books on the shelf. "Oh, Mrs. Cranston, if I may ask, I usually attend church. Could you tell me where I might find one tomorrow morning?"

Abigail smiled with pleasure. "Why, we go to the Baptist church out on Spruce Street. You are welcome to come along if you like. The Methodist church is three blocks west, or if you prefer, Chesterville has a Catholic church."

"Thank you, I will settle in, have some lunch, and then perhaps drive around a bit and get my bearings."

"Very well, then," Abigail replied, stepping out into the hall. "We shall see you at lunch. Come along, Scooter." Closing the door, she stood a moment and stared down the hall.

"I wonder who he is and where he is from. He sounds like a foreigner," she mumbled as she made her way down the hall and staircase in search of Lottie.

Chapter 10

"It is good to meet you, Andrew," Pastor Mike commented, shaking the hand of the man he just met. "I am pleased you chose to worship with us."

"Likewise, Pastor. You have a beautiful church, and your congregation is one of the warmest and friendliest I have had the opportunity of meeting, although I can't say I enjoyed your sermon," Andrew replied, his eyes displaying a bit of humor as he unconsciously ran a thumb down the side of his mustache and smoothed the dark, well-trimmed beard with a thumb and index finger. "Do you always step all over people's toes?"

"I am afraid I don't have anything to do with that. I preach what the Lord tells me, so you will have to talk to him about that," Mike replied, chuckling. "If I stepped on your toes, I don't apologize in the least."

He had taken an instant liking to the slender, dark-complexioned man standing in front of him. Andrew Baxter was well polished, friendly, and possessed an inner strength and depth Mike recognized instantly.

Laughing at Mike's comment, Andrew tilted his head sideways, a look of merriment in the dark blue eyes, and Mike studied him a moment. There was something vaguely familiar about that gesture, but it lasted only an instant and was gone.

"I would like you to meet my wife, Leah," Mike commented, putting an arm around Leah's back and drawing her forward.

"Mr. Baxter, we are very pleased you visited with us this morning. Will you be in Oak Grove long?"

Looking down at the attractive woman, Andrew admired the delicate lines of her face and warm, dark eyes. "Thank you, I enjoyed the service. I suppose I might stay a few days. I was passing through and found your small town to my liking. It is a quaint little place, and a few days' rest might do me some good. Perhaps, I can learn what small town life is really like."

"I am sure you will find it most pleasant," an articulate voice spoke from behind.

Turning, Andrew looked into the gray eyes of an elderly lady, and for a brief moment, he had the uncanny feeling his soul was laid bare. She was thin with white hair, and he guessed her to be at least ninety. There was a dignity about her that he had seen in few people, and, although she held a cane in her right hand, she stood erect. Andrew knew instinctively this was a woman of great wisdom and foresight.

She would no doubt demand answers and get to the root of any problem, despite her age.

"Mr. Baxter," Leah said, taking the woman by the arm, "this is Miss Mattie, one of our most beloved church members."

"I am the oldest church member," she stated with a smile as she looked at Leah and then back at Andrew. "Ninety-five, and I do not mind telling you either. How old are you, Mr. Baxter?"

Andrew chuckled at her directness and took her soft hand in his. "Miss Mattie, is it? I am very pleased to meet you. I am thirty-nine years old."

"Thirty-nine; you have much to learn and a long road to travel, but you will make it." Looking directly at him, she nodded and patted his arm. "The Lord has given this preacher much wisdom. He can help you. Think on it." Glancing at Pastor Mike, she looked back at Andrew. "I detect an Eastern accent. Boston?"

"Connecticut, ma'am."

"Connecticut," she replied, studying him. "I was there on business with my husband a few times. It is a beautiful place. Now if you will excuse me, there are children anxiously awaiting a piece of candy. You will remember what I told you?" she asked, holding his gaze a long moment. Turning, she patted Pastor Mike on the arm and made her way down the steps.

Perplexed by her comments, Andrew nodded at Pastor Mike and Leah and then made his way down the step. He knew the Lord blessed certain people with special insight and wisdom; his grandmother was a prime example. Without a doubt, this elegant lady was one of those, and she was probably correct. *Before this is all over, I will need help ... if nothing more than someone to confide in.*

Stepping from the sidewalk, he placed a brown fedora on his dark head and continued to watch as she slowly made her way to a wrought-iron bench beneath an oak tree. A slim black lady followed closely, took a seat next to her, and handed her a red and white box. Andrew smiled as several small children eagerly gathered around.

"Well, son, most folks 'round these parts call me old Ben, and ya jest as well too."

A very elderly black man's hand rested firmly on Andrew's shoulder. "Ah've got the Blacksmith Shop, and if ya got a mind ta get inta a heated game of checkers, drop in and watch some of these old codgers make blamed fools of themselves."

Andrew chuckled, observing the twinkle in the dark eyes. "I might just do that, thank you."

"That'd be dandy. It'd be powerful good ta have somebody stir up a little competition fer a change." Reaching inside his suit coat, he produced a gold watch fob and timepiece. Raising the hinged cover, he checked the time, snapped it shut, and returned it to the inside pocket. "Ah understand yer stayin' at the hotel. The shop's directly behind."

Patting Andrew on the shoulder again, he started to move away and then paused. "Do stop in fer a spell. Somebody's always about." Switching an old Bible to his left hand, he gripped Andrew's hand firmly. "Proud ta have ya with us this mornin', son."

Andrew smoothed his beard thoughtfully as he watched him walk slowly away. There was a depth to the old gentleman that was unmistakable, and he was curious as to his presence. Supposing he normally attended another place of worship, he rapidly dismissed the idea as he glanced around. He was evidently a member of this congregation as well as the man standing by the car and the woman sitting next to Miss Mattie. And there was the young couple he assumed recently became engaged, since several ladies made a fuss over the slim girl and several men shook hands with a tall, robust man who appeared somewhat embarrassed with their enthusiasm.

Accepting Abigail's invitation to accompany them, he now looked around for their whereabouts. Spying them visiting with a rather portly gentleman he had not met, he grinned when a young girl about ten or eleven ran up and asked him something, tugging irritably on the collar of her dress. Staring intently at the young girl, Andrew took in the dark hair and delicate bone structure. A red ribbon in her hair matched the dress she wore, and, even before she whirled and dashed away with a wide grin, Andrew pegged her for a tomboy. She moved as one who spent a lot of time outdoors, and he watched in fascination as she fairly skipped across the lawn to join two other girls about the same age.

Inhaling the early September air, his attention was drawn to a young woman exiting the church. She stopped and spoke with Pastor Mike and his wife and then turned and continued down the steps.

The artist within Andrew surfaced, and he noted every detail of the petite, attractive, woman. She wore a two-pieced, brown dress and a small matching hat that sat jauntily to one side of a beautiful head of red hair. What he wouldn't give to have his paintbrush. She would be wonderful to capture on canvas.

A multitude of portraits and landscapes flew through his mind, flashes of people and places. He had not been in Oak Grove twenty-four hours and knew this was a gold mine that could keep him busy for months.

"Mr. Baxter, we are ready to head home directly, if you are," Sam Cranston spoke, breaking Andrew's train of thought.

"Yes, of course, Mr. Cranston."

"I told you to call me Sam. Everyone else does," he said, rubbing his midsection as they walked slowly toward the parking lot. "I declare, I'm hungry. I expect you are too. Lottie has a roast in the oven, and I guarantee you it's the best you will ever taste."

"That sounds delicious, Sam. I cannot remember when I last had a good, home-cooked meal."

"I'm coming," Abigail called, scurrying toward them. "Mercy me, I promised Lottie I would frost the cake, so we best hurry. She always rushes home to get dinner on the table when we have guests, and she will be beside herself if I don't get there pretty quick."

"Milly and Molly went with her, so quit your fretting," Sam reassured.

"I do not want anyone going to any extra trouble because of me, Mrs. Cranston," Andrew said, opening the door for her.

"Why thank you, Mr. Baxter, but frosting a cake is no trouble. My stars, we have to have cake. It is Sunday."

Smiling, Andrew closed the door and turned back for another glimpse of the red-haired young woman, but she was nowhere to be seen.

"Willy, this is so nice. I have not been for a ride on a Sunday afternoon in such a long while."

Grinning, Willy tugged on her hand. "Can't you sit a little closer? I'm lonesome with you way over there."

Flushing with pleasure, Melba scooted across the seat. She was home from church no more than thirty minutes when he arrived at the door asking her to go for a drive. She grabbed a sweater and they were out the door.

"Where are we going?"

"Somewhere special," Willy replied.

Melba smiled in sheer happiness. She couldn't believe the change in Will. Earlier in the summer, he all but ignored her. He was hesitant at first, and she knew it had something to do with his past, but the more they were together, the more he opened up. The wall around him was slowly beginning to crumble, and beneath his cool aloofness, she was discovering an attentive, thoughtful, and passionate man. Willy would not talk about his mother, who was the root of his heartache and bitterness, and Melba prayed for the situation daily. Confiding her concerns with Pastor Mike, she was relieved to know he had been praying for Willy a long time.

Wind blew through the windows, tossing Melba's hair in all directions, but she didn't care in the least. Will liked her hair loose and free, and lately, that was what mattered.

"I'm about to starve to death. How about you?" he asked, glancing at her and then back to the road.

"Yes. Let's eat soon, or I am going to climb over the seat and eat while you drive," she laughed, glancing at his profile. He looked quite handsome. Dressed in brown, cotton twill trousers and a brown and green plaid flannel shirt, she wondered if he ever thought of how handsome he was.

"I've got the perfect spot. We are almost there." Slowing the car, he looked searchingly through the trees. "It is right along here somewhere—"

"What is right along here?"

"You'll see. It's a surprise." Turning onto a narrow road overgrown with weeds, he drove a few feet, cut the motor, and looked at her with a broad grin. "Here we are."

Melba looked at him curiously. "Are you crazy?"

"Come on." Grinning, he opened the door, stepped out and waited as she slid across the seat.

Grabbing a quilt, he tossed it across his shoulder and retrieved the picnic basket they had hurriedly filled. "I have been called worse. Let's go."

The old road they followed was overgrown with tall grass and goldenrod and meandered through the trees. It curved sharply to the right, and Melba smiled in delight at the sight of a small meadow blanketed with a profusion of violets and an old barn in the middle of the field.

Observing her expression, Willy grinned. "We are not having a picnic in the barn."

"I should hope not. It looks like a good wind would blow the thing over, but where in heaven's name are we going?" Melba asked, following him through a tall patch of Queen Anne's lace.

"You will see. It's a climb, but it is worth it." Turning, he smiled as he took her hand and they began an uphill trek.

"Are you sure you know where you are going?"

"I've been here several times. Don't worry, hon."

For the next ten minutes, she followed Willy as they steadily climbed uphill, following no visible path. *At least he seems to know where he is going,* she thought, stumbling over a rock and grabbing the back of his shirt.

Halting, Willy gripped her arm and pulled her up next to him. "You sure have a problem with falling," he chuckled. "I think you do if for attention, like the night at the circus."

Melba's mouth dropped, and she stared at him. "You knew?" she asked in astonishment. "You knew all this time and did not say anything?"

"Of course I knew you were faking. If you were that desperate for my attention, I figured I might as well go along with you."

"I was not desperate for your attention. Do you know how guilty I have felt about that night?" Placing both hands on her hips, she faced him. "You just let me stew about it, didn't you? Why didn't you say something?"

Willy laughed and then became serious. Slipping an arm about her waist, he pulled her close, kissed her, and then smiled. "Because it is one of the nicest things anyone has ever done to me, and it gave me the excuse to get to know you. Are you sorry about that?"

"Well...of course not."

"All right then," he said, pointing up the ridge to a clearing of blue sky. "Right there, that's where we are headed."

Adjusting the blanket over his shoulder, Willy squeezed her hand and they continued on. Halting a few feet from the top, Willy sat the picnic basket on the ground and removed the quilt from his shoulder. "Okay, close your eyes."

"What?"

"Close your eyes, and don't open them until I tell you."

Curious, Melba raised a brow, grinned, and then complied.

"Are they closed good and tight?"

"Yes, and I am not peeking."

Sliding an arm around her waist, he gripped her arm firmly, and they haltingly continued uphill.

"I've got you. It's just a couple more steps," he murmured, "and don't peek."

With eyes closed, Melba felt much like a child at play and grinned, thinking how silly they would look to anyone who saw them. Birdsong permeated the forest, a crow called in the distance, and she felt and heard twigs crunch beneath their feet. The woodsy smell of the forest was pleasant, and she was aware of the scent of Will's cologne. Conscious of his arm about her waist and the other gripping her arm, she was unusually content and was disappointed when he suddenly halted and stepped away.

"Just a minute," he said, taking her by the shoulders and turning her to the right. "Okay, Mel, now you can look."

Opening her eyes, she stared in delight at a small valley between two mountain ridges. Water cascaded over a cliff, and tumbled into a pool, meandering through the valley and glistening in the sunlight. Orange butterfly weed grew profusely, and an old log cabin sat in the shade of a couple of large oak trees. What was once a sheep pen sat to the right, a barn stood behind the cabin, and on the south side a wire fence hosted a crop of black-eyed Susans.

Melba looked up at Willy, her eyes glistening with tears. "Oh, Will, it is beautiful."

Grinning, he pulled her close. "It is, isn't it? I found this place several years ago. I don't even know if anyone remembers it is still here. It doesn't appear that anyone ever comes around. This place is special to me. It is my place."

Standing silently, they gazed down into the valley, and Melba realized he was revealing something private. His arm tightened around her shoulders, and he said softly, "I have never brought anyone here, but I wanted to share it with you."

He stared intently at her, and there was something new in his eyes. Touching his cheek with her hand, she smiled tenderly. "I am glad, Will. I am so glad you brought me here."

Grinning, he wrapped both arms around her and squeezed. "And I am glad you like it. Let's have our picnic right here. I'll get the blanket and picnic basket."

Watching him walk down the hill, she turned and looked out across the valley. *I wonder who lived down there and how long ago? How could anyone forget a place like this?*

"Will?" she called as he strode back up the hill. "How did you know of this valley?"

Placing the basket on the ground, he spread the blanket out and then straightened and looked at her for a long moment. Glancing up into the sky, he was silent and then came to stand beside her and gazed off into the distance. Reaching down, he took her hand in his and studied her face a long moment, and she knew whatever he was about to say was not going to be easy.

"I found this place when I was fourteen. It was my first summer in Oak Grove, and I ran away from my aunt and uncle." He looked at her hesitantly for a minute and then down across the meadow, silent and lost in thought.

Please, don't let him withdraw from me, Melba prayed silently, watching the changing emotions cross his face. *Not now, not when he is just beginning to open up.*

"My mother sent me here to live," he said quietly, a frown on his face. "She died a couple of weeks later...I...hated her." Tossing the small stick he held in his hand, he stared at the ground. "I hated everyone, especially her. When Uncle William told me she died"—Willy hesitated, looked at her, and then stared off into the valley again—"I was glad. She couldn't hurt me anymore."

Melba's heart ached, and she realized she was scarcely breathing as she stared at him, tears blurring her eyes. The pain in his face was sharp, and, checking the impulse to reach out and touch him for fear he would stop speaking, she stood quietly.

"The day he told me she died, I left the house and started walking. I didn't know where I was going. I just headed for the woods." Willy's voice was softer now, and Melba stepped closer. "I walked along thinking I was finally free of her, and then I realized that in death she had trapped me completely. Nothing would ever change now. It was too late. Everything was still the same and always would be.

"I probably wandered in circles. But it became dark, and I was hungry and tired, so I sat down to rest. The next thing I knew, it was morning."

Looking at her, Willy saw tears running down her cheeks, and a look of tenderness crossed his face. "Oh, hon, I am sorry." Pulling her into his arms, he released a long breath. "I didn't mean to make you cry. I shouldn't have said anything."

Melba laid her head against his chest, feeling a close, intimate sensation that was new. "No, please, Will, tell me," Melba whispered.

"This is where I woke up." Lifting her chin, he gazed into her eyes. "Nothing was ever pretty in my life, not after the age of five...nothing. The world was ugly and frightening and cruel. But when I woke up that morning and saw this place, it reminded me of a picture I saw in a book once. I used to imagine I lived there...and my mother loved me. I would run and play, and we were happy. But it was just a picture, and after a while, I forgot about it until that morning when I awoke."

Looking out across the valley, Willy's eyes traveled up into the blue sky and then back to her face. "I don't understand it, but somehow I felt this special place was just for me. It didn't make sense to me then, and it doesn't today. But that's the way I feel, and I have returned here many times."

"Oh, Will," Melba said softly, wrapping both arms around his neck. "This is your special place, and you did not stumble upon it. God brought you here. He loves you now, and he did then. Can you understand that?"

"I don't know, Mel. I just don't know."

"You will one day," she replied, smiling happily. "I am so glad you brought me here and told me how you found it."

"Are you?" he asked, amazed that he had actually told her about that day so long ago and more amazed that she understood. Willy stared at her closely. Different than anyone he had ever known, there was something about her that allowed his feelings and thoughts to surface with a will of their own. He had feared if his past were known she would walk away and never speak to him again, and he didn't know what he would do if she did.

"Of course I am. I want you to share your thoughts and feelings with me."

Relief washed over him, and he laughed. "Do you know what I would like to do?'

"What?"

"One of these days I would like to buy that farm down there. Do you think I would make a good shepherd?"

Melba looked at him, trying not to laugh.

"You don't think I could take care of a herd of sheep, do you?"

"In the first place, it is a flock of sheep, not a herd of sheep. But I guess if you—"

Willy laughed. "I don't think so either. I wouldn't know the first thing about taking care of sheep or any other animal, as far as that goes. Jack is as much as I can manage."

Melba grinned at his laughing face and had to agree. She could not imagine Willy tending a flock of sheep either, but she could imagine him living right there in the valley. "Why don't you?"

"Why don't I what?"

"Why don't you buy that farm? It is what you really would like to do, isn't it?"

He studied her face a minute and then looked across the valley, and Melba could see his mind working. "I don't even know who owns the place, and if I did, they would probably want a fortune for it."

"Well, you will never know unless you inquire about it, will you?" She let her gaze roam slowly over the hills, the waterfall, and the cabin. Yes, she could definitely see Willy living there. Turning her attention back to him, she realized he was watching her and grinning.

"I just might do that."

"You should."

"I am serious, I might. It is a beautiful place."

"Yes it is. You should do it."

"You don't think I will, do you?"

"If you really want to, you will."

"Well, I just might."

Giggling, Melba walked over to the blanket, sat down, and opened the picnic basket. "You should," she said, staring him straight in the eye.

Staring back, he strolled over to the blanket and sat down. "Hand me a chicken leg. I need something to help me think."

"I have to have another piece of pie, darlin'," Mike said, walking into the kitchen. Reaching around her, he kissed her on the neck, picked up the apple pie, and looked at her with a grin. "I don't know which is sweeter, you or the pie."

He chuckled at the expression on his wife's face. "No question about it, you are sweeter. But like Momma always said, 'It is sinful to let good food go to waste.' Would you like a piece?"

"Goodness no. I am too full," Leah replied, watching him retrieve a dessert plate from the cabinet.

Cutting a generous slice, Mike turned as Shari and Jimmy scuffled through the back door.

"Daddy, can you die from the cramps?" Shari asked.

Pausing with a bite halfway to his mouth, he looked at her in surprise. "What?"

Jimmy sighed loudly. "She wants to know if you can die from the cramps. You can't, can you?"

Leaning on the kitchen table with his chin in his hands, he looked at Mike and rolled his eyes. "I told her people died from the cramps in olden times, but now Dr. Miller can give you a shot for it, and just your neck and jaw swell up."

Smiling, Leah looked at him and shook her head."You are thinking of mumps, Jimmy. Mumps cause your neck and jaw to swell." Watching him spoon a bite of pie into his mouth, she frowned, "Don't eat out of the pie pan. You know better than that."

"Dad does."

"I do not eat out of the pie pan."

"Yes you do. Mom brought some of that rhubarb pie home from the church dinner, and you ate it right out of the pan."

"Oh. Well, you see," Mike replied, glancing at Leah, "it was the one and only piece left. That's different."

Shaking her head, Leah looked at him and then at her youngest son. "It is not proper to ever eat out of the pie pan. Now hurry and get your bath. Then you may have a piece."

"Okay, but Shari's not talking about mumps, Mom. She's talking about the cramps. I think it's going around, and I sure don't want to get it," he called, scurrying down the hall.

"Can you, Daddy? Can you die from the cramps?"

Leah looked at Shari's worried face. "Where did you hear about cramps?" she asked, wanting to laugh at the bewildered look on Mike's face as he stared at her.

"This morning at church. I heard Elizabeth tell Laura that was why Caroline wasn't there. She was sick with the cramps, and Mrs. Driscol had to stay home with her. Elizabeth said 'You'd think she was going to die.' Is she going to die?"

Mike glanced at Leah, down at Shari, and then back to Leah again. Looking heavenward, he grabbed a glass of milk in one hand, his pie in the other, and answered, "No, Shari, Caroline is not going to die from cramps. Your mother will explain." Heading to the living room. he figured Leah could handle this much better than he could. After all, he would have his turn with Johnny and Jimmy.

Leah sat down at the kitchen table. "You mustn't worry about cramps, Shari. Teenage girls and women have cramps all of the time, and it is kind of like a tummy ache."

Sitting on the kitchen chair swinging her legs, she furrowed her brows thoughtfully. "Do boys have cramps?"

"No, boys do not."

"Gee whiz, that's not fair. Why do we have to have stomach aches and they don't?"

"Shari, God did not make boys' bodies to experience anything like that."

"But why? If a girl gets cramps, boys should too."

"Because," Leah answered patiently, "God made men and women's bodies different for a very special reason, and that reason is very wonderful. He created us so when a man and woman love each other and get married, they can have babies."

"Babies! Oh good grief," Johnny exclaimed, standing in the doorway. "I wanted a piece of pie, but forget it." Rolling his eyes, he retreated into the hall.

"You'll never believe what's going on in there, Dad," he said, sitting on the couch.

"Yes, I would. That's why I am eating my pie in here."

"What's going on in the kitchen?" Laura asked, overhearing their remarks as she came downstairs. "Dad, Jimmy is filling the tub with too much water again."

"All right, I'll talk to him," Mike replied, setting his fork and plate on the coffee table. Rising from the sofa, he started for the stairs and then paused as the telephone rang.

"What's going on in the kitchen?" Laura asked again.

"Mom is telling Shari about the birds and bees. I don't know if . . ." Johnny's voice trailed off, and he and Laura both turned to their dad. He was talking about Uncle Amos.

"I understand, Paul. Certainly, I will put her on the train first thing in the morning. Let me get her. I know she will want to speak with you."

Laying the telephone's hand piece on the table, Mike walked into the kitchen. "Hon, Paul is on the telephone. You need to speak with him."

Leah looked at her husband, and a sinking feeling hit the pit of her stomach.

"Uncle Amos is in the hospital," he said gently.

Alarmed, she rose from the table and walked toward him.

Stopping her, Mike lifted her chin. "They think he may have had a stroke, Leah. He is comfortable right now, but you need to speak with your brother."

Following her to the small table in the hall, Mike laid an arm across her shoulder as she spoke into the telephone, "Paul, what has happened?"

Wandering down the stairs in his pajamas, Jimmy perched on the arm of the sofa and looked around. Why did everyone look so weird?

Placing the hand piece in the cradle, Leah looked up at Mike with watery eyes. "Paul said Uncle Amos got sick this afternoon, and—"

"I know, darlin'," Mike said, gathering her in his arms.

"What happened to Uncle Amos, Dad?" Johnny asked.

"I'll explain in a minute, Son. Come on, Leah, let's sit down," Mike suggested, steering her to the sofa.

"Uncle Paul called to tell us Uncle Amos is sick," Mike began, "and the doctor thinks it is best if he stays in the hospital a couple of days."

"What is the matter with him, Daddy?" Laura asked, tears filling her eyes.

"They do not know for certain, but they think he may have suffered a slight stroke, and that means he had an episode where he was a little confused."

"The doctors have given him medication," Leah said, hoping to reassure them. "Uncle Paul said he is very comfortable and is now asleep."

"And that is a good thing, because he needs rest right now," Mike added. "Let's pray and ask God's healing and blessing on Uncle Amos."

Their family prayed together all of the time, but tonight was different. They were praying for Uncle Amos, and a sudden fear gripped Johnny. He couldn't imagine Uncle Amos sick...or worse. He didn't want to think about that.

His dad's strong, confident voice, speaking to God like he was sitting there in the living room with them, was comforting and soothing, and he felt the strength in his dad's hand. He had no doubt God was listening.

"We love you, Father. Thank you for what you are about to do for Uncle Amos, and this we ask in Jesus's name. Amen."

"I feel much better." Leah sat back and ran her fingers through Laura's hair.

"How long will Uncle Amos be in the hospital?" Laura asked.

"I don't know, sugar. Mom will call and let us know."

"Call?" Leah asked, looking at him strangely.

"Yes, darlin'. I told Paul I would put you on a train tomorrow morning. You need to be with Uncle Amos and your parents," Mike replied, looking at her questioning face.

"But I can't go off and leave all of you alone. It is just too much. There is school and laundry and—"

"No, it is not too much," Mike replied firmly. "The children are not babies anymore. I am a grown man capable of handling things around here, and besides, the children are in school all day."

"Yeah, Mom, we can handle things," Jimmy said with a grin.

"Dad's right," Laura added. "We will be okay for a few days. Don't worry about us. I will help Dad."

"But, Mike, you don't realize what all is involved with—"

"I don't want to hear another word," Mike said sternly. "I told Paul I would have you on your way in the morning. He is going to drive from Sheridan and will pick you up at the depot. Besides, you would be wondering what was going on and how he was doing every waking minute. It is settled; you are going. Now I suggest you start packing. I will have Hazel ring Oliver for your ticket," Mike remarked, glancing at his watch, eight thirty. It was past Hazel's working hours, but she wouldn't mind. Out of courtesy, Oak Grove abided by Telephone Central's unwritten law of telephone time between the hours of 8:00 a.m. and 8:00 p.m., with the exception of emergencies.

Telephone Central, nothing more than a small room in Hazel's home, contained all the telephone equipment necessary to connect the citizens of Oak Grove, and it had taken no more than three weeks for Hazel to have her fill of everyone's enthusiasm. Happening to be in Mayor Driscol's office, Mike witnessed her tirade the morning she marched in without a knock, hello, or how do you do.

"They can come right back and remove all of that equipment unless some guidelines are established. Good Lord, I hardly have time to eat. Neighbors are ringing neighbors right next door. Now don't that just beat all? I guess they can't step out back and yell across the fence anymore? Lordy, you would think Oak Grove is some high falootin' place."

Looking from one to the other, she shook her head and pointed her finger at Mayor Driscol. "Something has to be done, I have a life too, you know."

Whirling around, she marched out of the office and slammed the door behind her, leaving Mike to wonder if she realized she was wearing two different shoes.

Picking up the hand piece, Mike pressed the button a couple of times and waited for Hazel's voice. "What's the problem, Pastor Mike?"

"Hazel, I hate to bother you this late in the evening, but—"

Chapter 11

Andrew laid his paintbrush on the palette, stepped back, and studied the canvas, satisfied with what he had captured. Early morning sun rays streamed through oak branches, dappling the square's lush, green grass. The bell tower and flag pole stood like a couple of sentinels in the middle of the square, high above the bandstand and bubbling fountain. Quaint shops surrounded the place, and all he had left was to apply detailing that would add an extra amount of charm. As far as he was concerned, the square was the very essence of Oak Grove. *I'll finish the detailing later,* he thought, raising the coffee cup to his lips and grimacing at the cold taste.

Leaning one shoulder against a pillar, Andrew enjoyed a sense of peace that was rare lately. Of slender build, he stood about five feet eleven inches and moved with an agility and purpose to his steps that portrayed a man of confidence and direction. Absentmindedly stroking a well-trimmed beard, he pondered once again his purpose here. A handsome man, Andrew was not unaware of his appeal to women, and what little attention he paid them only added a mystique that attracted them all the more.

A woman used to having her way, Claudia Kendall exhausted every female wile she knew and in frustration spat words of contempt at him, "Andrew, you are insufferable, unfeeling, and married to your work."

Dining in a small café in Paris, he had looked steadily across the table and calmly agreed. Infuriated, she grabbed her handbag and with a look of disdain assured him he would grow to be a lonely, old man and stomped off, leaving him alone and very relieved.

One woman had captured his heart, and he had loved her completely. He also knew he could never settle for a marriage of convenience or companionship and had long ago made up his mind that if God created another that came even close, he would wait for her.

A clacking noise reached his ear, and he watched Paul appear around the corner of the hotel pushing his mower. Andrew grinned, recalling the argument at breakfast.

"Now, Lottie, ya know ah enjoy mowin' the grass, and it'll be the last time 'til next spring. Ah'll start on the garage tomorro'."

"But the grass don't need cuttin," she complained.

"Yes, it does. It needs *tidied* up one last time. Do ah tell ya how ta run the hotel, or cook, or clean?"

"Tidied up, ya jest said that cause ya know ah like things *tidy*. Go on; cut the grass. Everbody'll think yer daft, mowin' grass that don't need cuttin'."

Andrew gazed around, realizing he could not have found more perfect lodging in Oak Grove. From the balcony's vantage point, he could see everything as folks went about their business.

A frown crossed his face and his brows furrowed as he wondered again if he was doing the right thing. Circumstances had not changed, and the reason for his presence was as strong as ever, but there was something about this small town. This place was…what? It was what he longed for. The people here were settled, roots were strong, and he could not have picked a better place if the decision would have been his.

Miss Mattie's words echoed in his mind. "He can help." Ninety-five years of wisdom and keen insight had pegged him in a matter of minutes. Andrew saw it in her eyes and heard it in the tone of her voice. *Maybe I ought to talk to Pastor Mike*, he thought and then shook his head. *No, not yet.*

He watched a couple of older men heading toward the Blacksmith Shop and remembered old Ben's remarks about the checker games and his invitation to drop by.

The old gentleman would be marvelous to capture on canvas, and his thoughts traveled to the woman with beautiful features and red hair. Both were extraordinary, but it would take time to study them. And time was uncertain, but more so, did he want to commit himself to such a project? Neither was typical of the subjects he usually painted, and he was reminded again as to his preference for landscapes and inanimate objects. They didn't drain him emotionally.

Dipping the paintbrush in a jar of turpentine, his thoughts traveled to those individuals he painted in the past. For the most part, they were strangers: people in parks, the lonely, poor, young, and the old. They were easy to portray, but characters he found unique were those with heart and spirit. Once found, he waited patiently for that unguarded moment when the soul was exposed and he caught a glimpse of that which made the person who they were. For some it took longer, but sooner or later it came and with varied emotions. He caught it in a split second in the midst of laughter, tears, fear, joy, or anger, and then labored unceasingly until he captured that which he saw in a way that was astonishing. Did he want to commit himself to that again? He didn't know.

Born with a gift of painting, he never expected to fulfill his dream. But with the unexpected death of his beloved grandmother, he found himself alone and the sole heir of her inheritance, a beautiful estate in Connecticut.

Standing next to her grave with a heart full of memories, he bade farewell to the last person in his life that loved him. Her faithful, old butler stood a few feet away and slowly approached when Andrew turned to leave. Reaching in his suit coat, he produced an envelope.

"I promised Miss Rebekah I would see you got this."

Andrew looked into the sad eyes and nodded his head. "Thank you, Cletus."

Sitting on a bench beneath a blossoming dogwood, Andrew read his grandmother's last words written in her familiar elegant script.

June 6, 1943

Andrew, my beloved grandson,

Think only of how I have loved you when you read these words. Though my journey has taken me from you, it has ushered me into the presence of those we both love. Be happy for me. I lived a long and full life with no regrets, and you will too. Always remember, Andy, use the opportunities the Lord gives. Along with the responsibility and accountability of those gifts, He adds joy and fulfillment to life with an abundance of peace at the end of the journey.

You have overcome much in thirty-six years, my dear, much to which others would have succumbed. But it has made you a strong man, and I know love and joy await you. No regrets, I don't want you to have any regrets, and I encourage you in the endeavor we so often discussed. Use what I have given in that effort. Nothing could make me happier than to see it come to fruition, as I know it will. I know you have heard it before, but I must say it once more. "Paint, Andrew. It is God's gift to you." You are smiling as you read these words. I know you are. But, my dear, he has made it your dream. Make your dream a reality and be happy once more.

Until then,

I love you, Grandmother

He remembered that day clearly, sitting on a bench, staring at the sheet of paper in his hands. The same numbness he felt once before held him in its grip, and he stood to his feet when Cletus touched his arm. A slight fragrance that his grandmother always wore reached him as he slipped the letter in his pocket, and a tender smile touched his lips.

"Thank you, Grandmother," he whispered and walked away, his mind made up.

Andrew invested his grandmother's endowment, and leaving his law practice behind used his savings to take a bold step of faith into the art world. After but a few showings, his talent rapidly drew attention, and his paintings sold at astonishing prices. Ironically, the portrait that gained the most recognition and highest bids was one done from memory and now hung in his grandmother's sitting room.

Retaining Cletus and the rest of the household staff, he had worked and traveled, periodically returning to the home he loved. On his last visit, he knew he was ready to carry out what must be done, and one month later he found himself in Oak Grove.

Drying his hands on a towel, he ran a comb through his hair. He would walk over to the Blacksmith Shop. Glancing at the painting once more, he nodded in satisfaction and walked to the door. Locking it behind him, he strode down the hall to the staircase. The grandfather clock struck ten a.m., and he paused. Lottie stood at the bottom step.

"Mr. Baxter, ah'm goin' quiltin' this mornin' and prob'ly won't be back 'fore lunch, but there's sliced chicken in the fridge and a pot o' soup on the stove." Turning to leave, she stopped, turned around, and shook her finger. "Ya better eat too; it's good. And ah expect ya ta eat some more of that coconut cake. We need ta finish it off."

Andrew watched her plop a straw hat atop her head and make her way down the hall toward the back of the hotel. He felt like a child again with Grandmother telling him to eat his lunch.

"Thank you, Lottie," he called, descending the stairs. Though not having a clue what he might expect to find at the Blacksmith Shop, he was looking forward to it. Reaching for the doorknob, Andrew swung the door wide and, much to his surprise, found a beautiful woman in his arms.

"Whoa! Are you all right?" Amazement, concern, and delight crossed his face as he stared down into a pair of green eyes.

"I am so sorry," Melba apologized, embarrassed. "I should have knocked. I was looking for Mrs. Cranston." Aware of his hands on her arms, she stepped back, realizing this was the Andrew Baxter everyone was speaking of.

Pleased with his good fortune, he grinned and held the door wide. Bowing in a flamboyant manner, he swung his arm to the side and bade her enter.

"I am Andrew Baxter, at your service, my lovely lady," he said with an exaggerated Southern drawl. "And who might you be, jumping into my arms without so much as a proper introduction?"

Melba shook her head and laughed. "I am Melba Maple, sir, and I did not jump into your arms. I fell into them when you jerked the door open and frightened me."

"Then you must forgive me. I most assuredly did not mean to startle you," he replied with a feigned look of remorse. "But frankly, my dear," he drawled, "I cannot think of a better way to have made your acquaintance."

Rolling her eyes, Melba smiled and stepped into the foyer. Glancing into the parlor, she turned back to the man standing in the open doorway grinning at her. He was not as tall as Will or nearly as attractive, but Melba found him very nice looking with an overabundance of charm that he expertly knew how to apply. Though his teasing was flirtatious, it was good natured and did not come across as inappropriate.

"Mr. Baxter," Melba began, placing a small package on the secretary, "you should be warned that it does not take folks in Oak Grove long to discover everything they can about a stranger in town. Let's see," Melba said, tapping her chin with an index finger. "I believe you are from somewhere East, Connecticut is most everyone's opinion because of your license plates, but several insist it to be New York."

Watching in amusement, Andrew studied the contours of her face, the marvelous mass of red hair, her engaging smile, and a delicately arched brow as she turned and looked at him thoughtfully.

"You are well educated and polished, the new Mercury Sedan you drive indicates wealth and prosperity, and the general consensus is that you are a successful lawyer or doctor…oh, and several of the ladies attest to the fact that you are a *perfect gentleman, suave and handsome enough to bring on a case of the vapors*," Melba said, imitating his drawl and placing a hand to her forehead.

Bursting into laughter, Andrew took her hand and bowed low, glanced up with a wicked grin, and drawled once more, "I am flattered and appreciate the kind ladies' opinions, but, Melba, my dear, I fear yours is the only opinion this Southern gentleman desires."

Frowning, but with eyes alight with humor, Melba shook her head slowly. "I would guess this is as far south as you have ever ventured, so, *Rhett Butler,* you can drop the Southern drawl and own up to who you really are. And…if you have any deep, dark secrets, you better keep them under lock and key, or they will be bandied about all over town before you blink twice."

Andrew laughed. "I am duly warned, Melba. Thank you." She was more beautiful than he remembered.

"And of what is Melba warning you?" Mike asked, standing on the porch watching the exchange.

"Good morning, Pastor Mike," Melba answered, red faced. "I was just telling Mr. Baxter of the curiosity he has stirred."

Mike laughed and looked at Andrew. "You sure have, but I doubt that bothers you much, does it?"

"No, if that is all I have to worry about, I would say I am very fortunate. It is good to see you."

"If you two gentlemen will excuse me, I need to get back to work. Mr. Baxter, I left a package for Mrs. Cranston. I am sure she will see it, but if she does not, would you—"

"Of course. I will make sure she gets it," Andrew replied, smiling. "I am so very glad we *bumped* into one another this morning, Melba."

"It was very nice to meet you as well. Pastor, I trust you will keep our new friend in line. I think he is going to need it." Laughing, she turned and walked out the door.

Andrew turned to Mike. "It is good to see you."

"I was wondering if I might introduce you to some of Oak Grove's finest."

"I think I just met one of them." Andrew grinned, stepping out onto the porch, "but I would enjoy meeting more, so let's be about it. I was hoping for some companionship this morning. Should I be on my best behavior?"

Mike laughed. "Quite an elite bunch hangs out in the Blacksmith Shop, but I don't think you need to worry."

Walking down the hotel's wide steps, Mike opened the black, wrought-iron gate at the end of the sidewalk and waved at Paul. "Why is he mowing? It doesn't—"

"Don't even go there." Andrew laughed. "That was this morning's argument."

"I see." Mike chuckled, thinking of Lottie and how she fretted much of the time. "Are you enjoying your stay with the Cranstons?"

"Yes, I am very comfortable. Sam and Abigail are wonderful people, and Lottie...well I guess you know Lottie."

Mike laughed and nodded his head. "I sure do."

Strolling toward the shop, Andrew asked, "How long have you lived here?"

"The Lord brought us here ten years ago, and we love it. There is nothing on earth so satisfying as being in the Lord's will, and if he chooses my ministry to remain here for the rest of my life, I will be happy. This is...a special place."

Mike pondered the man walking at his side and knew he was not familiar with life as it existed in Oak Grove. What would bring a city man here?

"You indicated Sunday you were not familiar with small-town life. You will probably find it quite different than to what you are accustomed."

Andrew strolled slowly along with both hands in his pockets, looking at the sidewalk as though studying his answer, and Mike knew whatever reason the Lord led him here, he would know in due time.

"The people here are good, decent folks. Of course, everyone knows everyone else's business, as Melba indicated, but they stand by one another through thick and thin. Theirs is a way of life passed from one generation to the next, and they know nothing else. Most families have roots dating back over one hundred years."

Nodding his head, Andrew glanced at Mike, a peculiar expression on his face.

"Living in a large city, one does not find something like...this," he said, lifting a hand and glancing around. "Nice, very nice. You would probably find it hard to believe that I know nothing more about my neighbor than his name. I never thought of it, but maybe my neighbor prefers it that way," Andrew said, chuckling.

Mike studied his face. There it was again. Something was familiar, but for the life of him, he didn't know what it was. "You have never been here before, have you?"

"No, why do you ask?"

"Just curious, you remind me of someone, but I cannot think who it might be. I will think of it sooner or later I suppose."

"I guess everyone reminds someone of another person in one way or another. Mrs. Cranston reminds me so much of my late grandmother I find I want to hug her every time I see her."

"Abigail is typical of many of our folks. If you visit long enough, you will see what I mean. Most are very genuine and caring. They are more than neighbors, Andrew. They have shared heartache and the agony of war, struggled through the Great Depression, helped one another through sickness and tragedies...and good times too."

Andrew nodded, and the two men walked along quietly.

"Will you be here long?"

"I don't know," Andrew replied honestly.

"Well, I am sure you will find it enjoyable no matter how long or short your stay may be. My family and I would like to get to know you."

"Your family…you are fortunate," he said, a faraway look in his eyes. "Any man would wish for such as you have."

Mike glanced up at the sky. "Yes, God has blessed me. I have four wonderful children and a sweet wife that I don't know what I would do without. Though I fear I am about to find out."

"Is something wrong?"

"Oh no," Mike replied, noting his concern, "Leah's uncle is sick, and she's gone to see about him. I put her on the train a few minutes ago. The children and I are going to be on our own a few days."

"Do you think you can handle it?"

"I guess I will find out, won't I?" Mike replied, chuckling. "We will be fine. I can't imagine why we wouldn't. Do you have family?"

For a moment he did not reply, and when he glanced at Mike, he spoke quietly. "No. My grandmother was the only one, and she passed on three years ago." Nodding his head toward the large wooden building with *Blacksmith* painted across the side, he looked at Mike and grinned. "So this is where the elite hang out?"

"This is it. Come on."

"I am so happy for them," Melba said, filling Mercy's tea glass. "It has been a long time since we've had a wedding, hasn't it?"

"Yes, ah can hardly believe it. My brother, Ben, gettin' married," Mercy said softly, her eyes watery. "And Lizzie is so sweet. Just think, she'll be my sister."

Melba hugged her friend and smiled. "Have they set a date?"

"November 16, and Ben asked our cousin, Noah, ta be his best man. They have been close since they were little boys and were always in some sort of mischief of one kind or another."

"Have I met him?"

"Ah don't think so. He hasn't been home in a long time. Ah guess since before the war. Ben said he is plannin' on stayin' through Thanksgivin'. Oh, Melba, it will be so wonderful ta have him home for the weddin' and the holidays."

Sitting across the table, Melba smiled at her friend. "That Ben, he always said he and Lizzie were just friends, but I knew better."

Mercy laughed. "Ah was hoping for quite some time, but Ben has always been so private when it comes ta personal matters. Momma and Daddy are thrilled, and Uncle Ben is so pleased. He keeps telling me if ah would get married he could die in peace," she said, laughing.

Melba squeezed her friend's hand. "Oh, Mercy, I am so happy for your family. Weddings are wonderful, and they bring such joy and happiness."

"Maybe there will be another weddin' soon?" Mercy asked, grinning mischievously.

"You and Saul?"

"Goodness gracious no, ah was thinkin' of you and Willy."

Melba's eyes widened, and she sat back in her chair. "Me and Willy? Why would you think that, Mercy?"

"Willy is in love with ya. Surely ya know that."

"He has never said as much. I know he cares for me, but *love,* I don't know."

"Just because a man does not say it does not mean he doesn't feel it," Mercy replied. "Now be honest; don't' ya think Willy loves ya?"

Melba's mind had wandered along those lines, but she was confused. If she was honest with herself, she guessed she hoped he did love her, but it was easier not to dwell on the subject.

"Melba, do ya not care for him?" Mercy asked. Perhaps she was wrong. "Ah am sorry, ah should not have said anything."

"No, it is all right, Mercy. I care a great deal for Willy, but I try not to think about it. It frightens me, and I am not sure…oh, I don't know. When my parents were killed, I was so lonely for so long, and I always supposed that one day I would get married. But now that the *one day* may be here, it scares the daylights out of me." Melba looked at Mercy and grinned shyly. "Sometimes I long to hear Will say he loves me, but I don't know what I would say or do if he did."

Mercy reached over and touched Melba's hand. "Maybe the question should be how would ya feel if he did not love ya?"

"Oh, Mercy, I am afraid it would break my heart."

"Then ah think ya have your answer."

"But Willy is not a Christian, Mercy. What do I do about that? I can't marry someone who is not a man of faith."

"Then ya must make that clear to him."

"But I can't. He hasn't approached the subject or even declared his feelings." Melba wiped a tear from her eye and released a trembling breath. "I pray for him daily, and that is of the utmost importance right now."

"Yes, of course, ya are right about that. Have ya spoken ta Pastor Mike?"

"I talked to him about my concern for Willy's salvation. He prays for him too, but I have not told him of my feelings."

"Maybe ya should, Melba. Pastor Mike is a wise man, and he would give ya good advice. Besides, ah wouldn't be surprised if he doesn't already suspect how ya feel."

Mercy glanced at the clock. "Oh! Melba, ah was supposed to be at Uncle Ben's ten minutes ago."

"Then you better go." Rising from the table, she looked at her friend and smiled. "We must continue this conversation at a later time, and I want to hear about you and Saul."

Walking to the front door, Mercy turned and looked at her. "There is not much ta tell about Saul, ah'm afraid. He is a busy man, and ah don't think romance is on his mind, but that's okay."

"Just because a man does not say it does not mean he doesn't feel it," Melba quoted, grinning.

Laughing, Mercy hugged her. "Everything will turn out fine for ya, Melba. Continue praying for Willy, and let love take its course. God will work things out. He has his own plan for you and Willy."

"Thank you, Mercy." Watching her walk down the steps and through the yard, she thought on what she had said. *God will work things out.*

"Pastor Mike, this is Pete Callahan. Could you come over to my office? We have a bit of a problem with Nathaniel and Johnny."

"Yes, Pete, I will be right there." Replacing the hand piece, he rose and walked to the small room that served as Myrtle's office on Monday, Wednesday, and Friday. A mimeograph machine occupied one wall, a window another, and a small desk with a telephone and typewriter sat against the back wall, where Myrtle was presently cleaning its keys with a small brush.

Myrtle Tucker was a forty-eight-year-old spinster who never wore makeup and dressed in the plainest of fashion. She was the elementary school music teacher, church pianist, and Mike's self-appointed secretary for the last eight years.

Unashamedly honest and blunt, she hated change of any kind and constantly argued with him, saying, "Leave things as they are. It's worked for the last fifty years." Her idea of pastor was one of dignity, and she was forever telling him to wear a necktie, to which he balked and she complained. Purchasing two, in case of an emergency, she kept them in a bottom file drawer and proudly retrieved one on the rare occasion he deferred to her opinion.

Respecting his leadership and knowledge of Scripture, she accepted his decisions, admitted when he was right, and fretted over him like an older sister or aunt, their relationship one of friendship, affection, and honesty.

"Myrtle, I have to go out for a few minutes."

"When will Mrs. Daniels be back?" she asked with compassion, wondering why men didn't ask for help when they needed it.

"Friday," Mike answered. "And it will be none too soon."

"Praise the Lord," Myrtle exclaimed, much too enthusiastically for Mike's way of thinking.

Standing in the doorway, he watched her slide a piece of paper into the typewriter.

"What?" she asked, looking at him curiously.

"Do I really look that pathetic, Myrtle?"

"Well now, Pastor, not pathetic exactly. I think *frazzled* would be more accurate. You are gaining firsthand knowledge of how much responsibility a wife and mother carries on her shoulders day in and day out." She leaned forward and looked earnestly over her glasses. "Men just can't handle the everyday—"

"I know, Myrtle. I have to go over to the school, and I don't know how long I will be gone," he replied, stepping into the hall. He didn't need a speech. Lord only knows he could write one himself after the last three days.

"Trudy rang," Myrtle called after him as he strode down the hall. "She said to tell you Mildred was bringing supper tonight and it will be something you don't have to worry about burning. And you really should put on a tie, since you are going over to the schoolhouse!"

Running a hand through his dark hair, Mike muttered, "Put on a tie to go over to the school." Reaching in his pocket for his keys, he realized they were on his desk and in exasperation retraced his steps and met Myrtle coming out the door displaying them in the palm of her hand.

"I think you will need these.

"Thank you, Myrtle."

"Take the rest of the day off and tomorrow too." she called as he got in the car.

"What now?" Mike spoke aloud.

He had never seen tide turn so swiftly and completely. Monday started out fine. He saw Leah off at the depot with all the confidence in the world and then dropped by the hotel and invited Andrew along to the Blacksmith Shop.

After a round of checkers and accompanying arguments, old Ben entertained them with one of his tales about a barn dance turned pie fight after someone spiked the apple cider. Laughing, they left the shop with Andrew committing himself to a game on his next visit, and they headed down the sidewalk toward the square. Agreeing what an unforgettable character old Ben was, Mike chuckled when Andrew told him of his desire to paint him. He couldn't imagine Ben posing to have his portrait done.

Deciding to drop by the drugstore, they ran into Trudy purchasing SSS Tonic.

"You better stock up on some of this. It's an old Indian remedy, you know," she explained, setting the bottle on the counter between them. "It is good for your blood, and you mark my words, it will keep you from coming down with something this winter. I make sure we have a bottle in our medicine chest all winter long."

"Mr. Baxter is it? I am Trudy Driscol," she said, perching on the stool next to him. "My husband, Henry, is the mayor. He said you were in church Sunday and was disappointed not to have had the opportunity to speak with you. I wasn't able to make it. Caroline wasn't feeling well, so I stayed home with her. Land sakes, I hate to miss church, but sometimes a body just can't help it now, can they?"

"No, ma'am, I guess not."

"I will tell Henry we met, and I know he wants to make your acquaintance. He is such a busy man, but I know he will make time to see you. If there is anything I can do while you are in town, you let me know. I want you to enjoy your stay."

Continuing, she gave him Oak Grove's schedule of events for the next six months and then unleashed such a barrage of questions that Mike, out of sheer compassion for Andrew and exasperation with Trudy, stepped in and rescued him with the idea of driving out to the old mill.

What was he going to do with her? She tried his patience more than anyone he had ever known and even confessed to Leah one evening that she was his *thorn in the flesh.*

Almost out the door, Mike found his arm in a death grip and Trudy in his face. "For goodness' sake, Pastor, I almost forgot. You are always so good to help everyone. I want to do the same. Mildred said that Jack said that when he was getting a haircut that Ned said that Ellie said she stopped by the church this morning and Myrtle said Leah would be gone for a few days. You poor thing."

"Trudy, we will be fine," Mike answered, noting the mirth in Andrew's eyes. "I don't foresee any—"

"Yes indeed, you are going to be fine," she exclaimed, interrupting. "You are not to worry about a thing. We will take care of you and those children. My word, but it will be a joy to look after you. It will give our Sunday school class an opportunity to serve the Lord by serving you. It is the very least we can do, and it will give us such pleasure. Now, supper will be delivered at four every afternoon, and that's that. All you will have to do is warm it up."

Thanking her warmly, Mike breathed a sigh of relief and gratitude. Good grief, he hadn't even thought of supper and realized Trudy had come to his rescue, not just today but for the rest of the week. *What a blessing she is,* he thought guiltily.

How things managed to go downhill after that he did not know, but downhill they went at full throttle. He visited Louise's mother, ran by Reese's for MoonPies, stopped back by the church to give Myrtle his sermon notes, and was home by 3:20 with ten minutes to spare. Glancing down at Midnight, raising a fuss and rubbing against his legs, he realized he forgot to feed her and headed for the Frigidaire. *Leftover meatloaf ... might as well get rid of that,* he thought. *Supper will be here at four.* Scraping it into her bowl, he grabbed *The Chronicle*, sat down, and glanced through it.

Five minutes and thirty seconds later, as to his best estimate, everything went downhill. Jimmy burst through the door stating it was his last day of school because he wasn't going anymore since Mrs. Thompson informed them that next week they would be getting booster shots and Miss Myrtle showed up with a dumb song they had to learn for Founders Day.

Johnny was in a bad mood because some of the guys were mouthing off about Nathaniel, and he couldn't understand why they just didn't leave him alone. It had something to do with the new girl, Lacey, who evidently liked Nathaniel, and the other guys were mad cause she was quite a *dish.*

Trudy bustled through the door with a pot of green beans, an apple pie, a loaf of homemade bread, and a casserole that "will just need to be heated for thirty minutes." She fluffed the sofa pillows, straightened the newspaper, and raised a brow at a couple of MoonPie wrappers on the coffee table and an empty coffee cup on the floor next to his chair.

"*Tsk, tsk,* what would Leah think?" she clucked. Picking up three Marvel comic books, she placed them in the magazine rack then stood with hands on her hips and looked around. "You mustn't let Leah come home to a mess. She has a lot on her mind with Uncle Amos sick, and I know how she keeps house."

Ignoring her perusal of the living room, Mike walked her to the front door and was genuinely thanking her for supper when the back door slammed and Shari called, "Dad, Midnight just threw up in the kitchen, and it looks like meatloaf."

With a look of disbelief, Trudy whirled and screeched, "Surely you didn't feed that cat meatloaf? Leah only gives her dry Ken-L-Ration!"

Mike stared at her, wondering how she knew Leah fed Midnight Ken-L-Ration when he didn't even know it. He scratched his head and stared out into the yard. What was wrong with meatloaf? He ate it.

"Oh my word! Land sakes, you just better hope it doesn't give her the trots."

With a feeling close to panic, Mike stared at Trudy and mumbled something about Midnight having a strong stomach, thanked her again, and almost had her out the door a second time when Laura walked into the living room and asked, "Dad, didn't you do laundry?"

It took another fifteen minutes to convince Trudy he was capable and would take care of the wash tomorrow. There was no way he would allow her to hang his underwear on the line, and she left only after he promised she could come back and clean before Leah got home. And that was only the first day.

Parked at the curb, Mike made his way along the rock wall bordering the playground, recalling one other trip to school. Johnny was in third grade and thought it a good idea to put marshmallows on Mrs. Charles's desk chair. What would he find today? Crossing the schoolyard, he climbed the steps and opened the door, the familiar smell of oiled floors, crayons, chalk, and glue greeting him. The corridor was quiet, and out of curiosity, he paused at the first-grade room and glanced through the door. Jimmy and Zachary were at the pencil sharpener giggling. Mrs. Thompson snapped her fingers, said something, and both boys returned to their desks. Mike shook his head. Their desks were behind one another, with Jordan Walker's across the aisle. How long would that last?

Walking the length of the hall, he paused outside the principal's office and observed Johnny and Nathaniel seated in chairs along one wall and one of the Stevens's boys and Charlie Hawking across the room. Opening the door, he walked in as Pete Callahan came from his office.

"Pastor Mike, come in. I appreciate you coming." Shaking his hand, Mr. Callahan glanced at the boys and then turned to Mike. "I knew you would want this brought to your attention. We had a little episode at lunch."

Mike nodded, looked at Johnny and Nathaniel and then glanced at the boys across the room. "You are most definitely correct about that."

"If you will come with me, boys, we will discuss this in my office."

After all was said and done, it appeared the *dish,* Lacey Bingham, had taken a liking to Nathaniel which made Billy angry enough to throw a punch and get knocked to the floor. Charlie jumped in to help Billy, and Johnny, feeling it his duty to even things up, joined the fray. Billy had a black eye, Charlie's face was scratched, Nathaniel had a busted lip, and Johnny had two buttons torn off his shirt. And after all that, they agreed girls weren't worth it and they were now friends.

Chapter 12

To Mike's way of thinking, after the first three days of Leah's absence, he was sure things could not get any worse. But then again, what did he really know? If not for the fact that he knew the Lord was allowing this humbling experience, he would have been totally frustrated. As it were, the kids were supportive and nightly devotions precious, as each offered suggestions and informed him how Mom did it.

"Dad, Mom says that three hundred twenty-five degrees is a good temperature for heating and baking most anything," Laura offered the third evening. Monday's pork chop dinner was burned beyond recognition, but he refused to take the blame for that. Directions taped to the top of the casserole lid were smudged, and the three looked like a five, so he heated it at five hundred degrees for forty-five minutes. Polishing off the pot of green beans, homemade bread, and apple pie, no one really complained, and they even formed a pact to not say anything, to avoid hurting Trudy's feelings.

The second night he read the directions three times. *Bake covered thirty minutes in preheated oven at three hundred twenty-five degrees.* How was he supposed to know Abigail Cranston's Chicken Fantasy was frozen? It was in the Frigidaire when he came home, and the directions said *bake covered*, so he didn't even look at it. Why he ever listened to Shari's suggestion to "bake it twice as long and turn the heat up, Dad," he didn't know.

Evidently, word got out. During music class, Myrtle asked Jimmy how things were going, and *old honest Abe* told the truth. So the third evening they fared better. Mildred Reese arrived at four o'clock on the dot with fried chicken, mashed potatoes, corn, salad, and chocolate cake. Placing it all on the kitchen table, she looked him directly in the eye and stated there was not a thing he needed to do but call the children in, sit down, and eat.

We survived, Mike thought as he stood at the depot and glanced at his wristwatch once more, two forty-five. Fifteen more minutes and Leah would be home, and was she going to be surprised. Trudy and Mildred had arrived early that morning, and within two hours, the house was spic and span. Lynn Miller and Ellen Madison pulled up right as he was leaving for the train station with a pot roast, potatoes and carrots, a tossed salad, rolls, and banana cake.

Cooley rattled up the street in his old pickup and delivered the ironing that Alice had volunteered to do. Helping Mike carry clothes baskets in the house,

Cooley told him he "heard tell how he didn't know nuthin' about housework, and he'd a give him a hand if he would've knowed it." To think Cooley thought him inept left him a little irritated.

Releasing a sigh, Mike let the happiness and anticipation that had been building all morning have free rein, and he knew the turmoil of the past week didn't amount to anything. Leah was coming home, Uncle Amos was out of the hospital, and he and the children survived it all.

Walking to the end of the depot, a grin crossed his face as he remembered Jimmy and Johnny's indignation over their newly acquired pink undershorts.

"My robe is brand new, Dad, and it is *red*. Didn't you know it would fade, and why didn't you sort the clothes before you washed them?" Laura asked, trying not to laugh when Jimmy stated he would not wear underwear at all before he wore pink splotchy ones.

A silly grin on his face, Mike gazed toward the west, imagining how all of this would be related to Leah. Things had not been really that bad. So what if he messed suppers up, Johnny had a fight at school, laundry wasn't done perfectly, Midnight threw up in the kitchen, and one morning he got the lunches all mixed up. Things could have been a lot worse.

"Ya goin' ta tell me what's ailin' ya? Or ya just goin' ta sit there and grunt ever' time ah say somethin'?" old Ben asked, studying Willy. The two sat in Ben's kitchen, a set of dominoes, as yet, untouched in the middle of the table.

"What?"

"Ah said, what's ailin' ya? There's somethin' on yer mind."

"Oh, nothing, nothing at all. Come on, let's play," Willy replied, reaching for the box.

"Well, son, ah don't expect it'd be much of a game. Ya came over here tonight 'cause ya don't know what ta do with yerself, and ah expect a game of dominoes won't take care of yer problem. So what's the use of pretendin'?"

Willy glanced at his old friend, frustrated that he could read him so clearly and, at the same time, relieved he could. Surely, if anyone could help, Ben could.

"I've been wondering about something, Ben," Willy commented, studying him. The thought of him not being there one day flashed through his mind, and for a moment, a sickening feeling welled up inside.

"What are ya wonderin' 'bout?"

"Well, Ben, I wondered how—" Willy began. Losing his former train of thought, he suddenly wanted Ben to know how much he meant to him. Much to his regret, he failed to tell Aunt Lydia and Uncle William, and he didn't want that to happen again. "I have not had many people who...what I mean is, I—"

Ben watched him struggle for words, perplexed by his attitude, and sat back in his chair with his thumbs hooked in his suspenders. "Sometimes when yer tryin' ta say somethin' it's easiest if ya jest take a deep breath and throw it out."

Sliding the domino box back and forth, Willy looked at the old, brown, wrinkled face as though seeing it for the first time. Ben's thick, white hair and bushy mustache were in stark contrast to the dark skin. A pair of wire spectacles sat on his nose, and wise, gentle brown eyes watched him patiently.

"You mean a lot to me, Ben. I want you to know that."

"Ah'm proud ta hear yer words, and ah love ya like one of my own, Willy. Watchin' ya grow and struggle through the years has made me tender toward ya. Ya've had a mighty hard time." Ben studied the young man he was so fond of and wondered on the bitterness buried deep inside.

"Yer Uncle William used ta come over every evenin' jest like ya do," Ben commented, pulling his pipe from the pocket of his overalls. He studied it a minute, remembering. "We'd sit a spell and talk, mostly about ya. He loved ya much, Willy, him and Lydia both. Ah know ya had a hard time believin' that. He tole me as much."

Ben chuckled and shook his head. "Stubborn, willful, rebellious, that's what ya was. But yer not the only youngster who got started out on the wrong track comin' up, and ya won't be the last. That's all behind ya now. Yer a right respectable young man."

Observing his sincerity and gentleness, Willy was touched by his words, aware of a soft feeling inside that was familiar of late, mostly where Melba was concerned. Somehow, she managed to bring out a lot of feelings he never felt before.

"Yes sir, ya've been through a lot. Not only did ya survive almost losin' yer leg and the horrors of war, ya've seen the death of Lydia, William, and yer mother," Ben said, noting the unconcealed anger on his face at the mention of the latter.

"Now," Ben said, "ah've rambled on long enough. Are ya goin' ta tell me what's ailin' ya or not?"

A small grin crossed Willy's face, and he sat back in the chair and stretched his long legs in front of him. "I wanted to ask you a question."

"Ask away. If ah know the answer, ah'll tell ya."

Willy scratched the side of his nose and drummed his fingers on the table. "How important is church to you?"

Looking steadily at him for a minute, Ben sat forward with both arms on the table. "Are ya wantin' ta know how important church is ta me, or do ya want ta know how important it might be ta one particular little red-haired gal?"

Willy grinned. "Maybe both."

"Well, sir, it's one of the most important things in my life. Ya see, goin' ta church is a result of lovin' the Lord and wantin' ta worship him."

Observing his curiosity, Ben nodded and walked to a small desk in the corner of the kitchen, removed something, and then walked back to where Willy sat. He stood quietly for a moment and then laid a Bible on the table in front of him.

"Church might be an important part of my life, son, but not the most important. Walkin' daily with the Lord, that's what counts. When yer born again, ya learn ta love him cause of all he's done for ya and 'cause he loved ya first. And ya'll learn all that in this here old Bible."

Old Ben's voice softened, and he continued. "Ah didn't deserve it. No sir, he loves me, and my salvation was a free gift…jest like this here old Bible ah'm givin' ta ya. It's there if ya want it. But ya got ta pick it up and take it."

Ben watched the emotion on Willy's face, and for a brief second, a glimmer of hope appeared and then just as quickly vanished. Leaning toward him, Ben spoke quietly, "Willy, ah suspect the Lord's dealin' with ya or ya wouldn't be askin' 'bout it. Here," he said, tapping the Bible. "Take this home and read it. God's Word has all the answers ya'll ever need."

Staring at the worn Bible, he glanced at old Ben, "Thank you, Ben. You and Pastor Mike…when we sit here Thursday mornings, I see…something." Willy was quiet for a moment, a serious look on his face. "I see it in Melba too."

Old Ben nodded and puffed his pipe, not saying anything for a bit. "That pretty little thing is a young woman of strong faith, Willy. Ya need ta heed that."

The two sat quietly, and Ben watched Willy stare at the wall.

Glancing over at Ben, Willy rose from the table. "I guess I'll go on over to the house." Picking up the Bible, Willy looked at him with a strange expression. "Thank you, Ben. I'll take care of this."

"Ah know ya will, son," he replied, rising and following him to the front door.

Pausing, Willy stood still a minute, enjoying the feel of Ben's strong hand on his shoulder. Turning, he looked at the old man, his heart full of emotion. "Good night, Ben."

"G'night, son," Ben replied, watching him walk down the sidewalk and cross the street with Jack at his heels. Closing the door, Ben smiled and made his way back to the kitchen table. Sitting down, he laid a hand on his old, brown, leather Bible and closed his eyes. "Thank ya, Lord. Ya'll jest have ta bring him along as ya see fit, and ah'm here, so jest tell me what ya want me ta do for him."

Willy raised a foot on his front step then, on impulse, turned and headed across the yard. His footsteps fell rapidly on the sidewalk, and Jack trotted alongside, eager to be going somewhere. He was thinking of nothing but an urgent desire to see Melba. They had a date tomorrow evening, but he did not want to wait, and a compelling force seemed to propel him along.

His footsteps quickened until he stood in front of her house. Walking up the sidewalk, he took the steps two at a time and knocked. Jack flopped down in his usual spot, and Willy looked around. The light was on, but he didn't hear anything and knocked again.

Melba stood in the bedroom listening. *Who could that be? Probably Mercy.* Making her way into the living room, she ran her fingers through wet hair.

Donning an old shirt and a faded pair of slacks, Melba walked barefoot across the floor. She opened the door and was surprised and pleased to see Willy standing there.

A wide grin spread across his face, and he grabbed her around the waist and pulled her close. Turning in circles, he joined her laughter and then stopped and looked down at her. The laughter was gone, and something akin to awe crossed his face. Closing his eyes briefly, he opened them and stared intently at her. Mesmerized, Melba was unable to look away and unconsciously moved closer, aware of nothing but the look on his face.

Willy lifted a wet curl and ran it through his fingers. Releasing it, he raised her chin and ran his thumb across her bottom lip.

"I love you, Mel," he whispered, brushing his lips across hers. He held her close, relishing every emotion, and knew he was in a place he had never been.

Looking up into his face with wondrous joy in her heart, Melba touched his cheek. How long had she loved him? A tender smile touched her lips, and she wrapped both arms around his neck. "I love you too, Will."

Andrew sat on a bench on the balcony outside his room. The detailing finished on his painting, he was enjoying that sense of accomplishment he always experienced when completing a project.

The stores were busy with Friday night shoppers, and he stared across the square at city hall and absentmindedly stroked his beard as he counted the chimes, seven o'clock.

"I have been here one week. I suppose it is time to be about it," he spoke aloud, standing to his feet.

Stepping into the sitting room, he closed the French doors, walked into the bedroom and over to the dresser. Running a comb through his hair, he stared intently at his reflection in the mirror. There was nothing familiar that he could see. Nodding in satisfaction, he spoke aloud, "Andrew, you are just a stranger passing through."

Returning to the sitting room, he took one last look at his painting and then walked out the door, locking it behind him. Pausing on the porch, he noted several in the drugstore, and making his way down the steps and sidewalk, he closed the gate behind him and crossed the street.

A buzz of voices greeted him, and he recognized a few faces he had met earlier in the week. Hank from the Hardware Store sat at the counter between Ned and another man he did not know. Two women chatted animatedly by the magazine rack, and an older woman was waiting at the back counter for Gerald to fill her prescription. The small tables were occupied, and Trudy Driscol and two other women sat at one.

"Yoo-hoo, Mister Baxter," Trudy called in a shrill voice, waving a hanky.

Nodding, Andrew smiled and made his way to their table, all the while watching her beaming face. This was his second encounter with the woman. He guessed her to be about forty-five, and, although short and on the plump side, she bore evidence of once being a lovely, young woman.

"Good evening, Mrs. Driscol...ladies."

"Please, would you join us, Mr. Baxter?" Trudy invited pleasantly. She was just telling Mildred and Gloria how handsome and mysterious he was, quite the man of the world.

Returning her smile, Andrew glanced at the others, pulled a chair out, and sat down. "It would be a pleasure, thank you," he replied, noting a pink blush staining the cheeks of the younger woman.

"Mr. Baxter, I would like you to meet my dearest friend, Mildred Reese. Her husband owns Reese's Market, and if you haven't already met, this is Gloria Hansen. She is Oak Grove's very own librarian and also relieves Hazel at Telephone Central."

"I am very pleased to meet you," Andrew remarked, smiling at the thin woman next to Trudy and then the younger woman, who showed obvious signs of discomfort. Guessing her to be about twenty-five, she was slender and would not be considered beautiful, but apple cheeks and a heart-shaped mouth gave her a fresh, natural beauty. Shifting slightly she smiled, lowered her eyes, and then looked back at him, her clear, hazel eyes reflecting a wholesomeness Andrew had not seen in a long time. Though his first impression was shyness, he sensed a boldness about her also.

"Lottie made the most delicious meal this evening," he said, ending his perusal of the younger woman, "and I am afraid I stuffed myself to the point of passing up dessert. Now I am ready for an ice cream sundae. How about you ladies?" he asked, looking from one to the other. "It is my treat, and will I take no for an answer? I don't think so. This is my first Friday night in Oak Grove, and I am going to celebrate."

"Well," Mildred replied, smiling broadly, "I do have a few minutes."

"Mr. Baxter, I declare, it will ruin my diet. I have to watch my weight," Trudy replied, shaking her head and smoothing the front of her dress. "If I didn't, why mercy sakes, I would be as fat as a toad. Mildred and Gloria are fortunate, but me...land sakes no. I can just look at something and feel it settling on my...well, you know."

"Now, Mrs. Driscol, continue your diet tomorrow. One ice cream sundae is not going to push you over the top, is it?" Andrew questioned, knowing it would not take much convincing.

"Well no, of course not." She laughed. "You talked me into it."

"Good, and what about you, Mrs. Hansen?" he asked, smiling as Gerald approached.

"How are you this evening, Andrew?"

"The only way I would be any better is for you to bring me a large chocolate ice cream sundae with nuts and whatever these three new lady friends of mine wish, please."

Gerald grinned and placed a pencil behind his ear. "I suppose you will all want your usual, or will you try something different tonight? The same then," he said as they indicated their usual preference.

Touching her hat and smiling, Trudy leaned forward. "Are you comfortable at the hotel? I know Lottie is a wonderful cook. It is quite a popular place this time of year, and with Founders Day just a few weeks away, you are fortunate you already have a room. It is usually booked full that weekend. I do hope you are here for the celebration. The hotel meets your satisfaction?"

"Oh, quite so."

"Good. May I ask where you live and what brought you to our town?"

"Trudy, forevermore! You are downright nosy, I declare," Mildred said. "Why on earth would you ask such a thing?"

The younger girl shook her head and rolled her eyes, blushing when she caught Andrew smiling at her reaction.

"Oh for goodness' sake, Mildred, I am not nosy. I am only curious and interested. Mr. Baxter, if you would rather not say, that is perfectly all right. But as the mayor's wife, I want to make sure one and all feel welcome and comfortable. You do understand, don't you?"

"Of course, Mrs. Driscol. It is rare indeed to come across people as friendly and kind as those I have met in Oak Grove. My home is in Connecticut, but I spend a good deal of my time in New York City, and people there are not so friendly and caring.

"New York City!" Mildred exclaimed. "How terribly exciting. My word, but I have always wanted to travel there, but I fear I never will."

"Henry and I traveled as far as Baltimore. My family is there, and we try to get back every couple of years, but we have never made it to New York," Trudy replied. "One of these times we will."

"Here you are," Gerald said, placing the sundaes on the table. "I hear you were over at the Blacksmith Shop."

Sitting back in the chair, Andrew chuckled. "It is quite an interesting place," Andrew said, sitting back in his chair. "They even talked me into a game of checkers on my next visit."

"I'll warn you, they cheat like all get out."

Andrew laughed. "I am already aware of that."

"Sure am glad you're visiting with us. Excuse me, folks. I have a customer at the counter. Enjoy your sundaes."

Spooning a bite of ice cream in his mouth, he looked at Trudy. "Did I understand you to say you have family in Baltimore?"

"Yes, my parents and most of my relatives. Henry, of course, is from right here. We met in Ocean City. My father took our family there on vacation, and Henry happened to be there for his uncle's funeral. We met on the boardwalk one afternoon and began talking. Mercy me," Trudy sighed, "that was so long ago. We met every day after that and fell in love right then. After writing back and forth for a while, we were married, and I came here to live."

"How nice. Marrying, raising a family, and living your life in one place sounds perfect."

Shifting in his chair, his eye caught Mildred's gesture as she reached across the table and patted Trudy's arm. The two women looked at one another, and he wondered if he had said something wrong.

"My life would indeed be perfect if I had not lost my sister. We were so close."

"Mrs. Driscol, I am very sorry," Andrew responded genuinely. "I certainly did not want to bring up painful memories. Please forgive me. I am truly sorry if I upset you."

"No, no, you did not upset me. It is quite all right. It was a long time ago," Trudy answered, patting his hand. "I have much to be thankful for, and my memories are fond ones. Mary was a remarkable young woman."

"I am sure she was. I know what it is to lose a loved one myself. Memories are precious aren't they?"

"Yes they are, and I have many. Oh, dear me," Trudy exclaimed, glancing at her watch. "Henry and the girls must surely be waiting. The girls went to the movie, and it was over ten minutes ago. I really must be going." Rising, she gathered her pocketbook and an Edna's Dress Shop bag. "Now if you are going to be here for a few more days, we would love to have you to dinner. I will send Henry around to check with you. He told me just this afternoon how bad he feels that you have been in town one week and he has not met you. Gracious, but he is so busy preparing for Founders Day, but he did say he stopped by the hotel one day. Did Abigail tell you?"

"As a matter of fact, she did. I am sorry I missed him," Andrew answered, rising.

Smiling, she straightened her hat and patted his shoulder. "If he doesn't see you tomorrow, then perhaps we will see you Sunday at church. Well, I must go. Thank you, Mr. Baxter, for the ice cream."

"It was my pleasure."

"Mildred, come along. We will drop you off on the way."

"It was so nice to meet you, Mr. Baxter, and thank you for the sundae," Mildred commented, gathering her things. "I hope you enjoy your stay in Oak Grove."

"I am sure I will, Mrs. Reese. It was a pleasure to meet you also."

Andrew watched the two ladies walk away and turned his attention to Gloria.

"I must be going also," Gloria murmured, "but I am happy to have met you."

Somewhat surprised when she spoke, Andrew looked at her curiously. Her voice was soft and silky and not what he would have imagined at all. He knew many women to feign that tone of voice, but for this young woman, it was genuine.

Andrew stood to his feet, noting she was only a couple inches shorter. "I suppose your husband is waiting also?"

Gloria's eyes widened, and she smiled as she picked up her pocketbook. "I am not married, Mr. Baxter."

"I see. Well, then if you will allow me," Andrew said, steering her toward the door, "I will see you out, and then I believe I will return to my room. I have an early morning tomorrow."

Stepping onto the sidewalk, Gloria turned and faced him. "Then I shall say good night."

"Good night, Miss Hansen."

Watching her walk away, Andrew wondered how she was getting home. "Miss Hansen?"

Surprised, Gloria turned to see him walking toward her. "Yes?"

"You are walking home?"

"Why, yes. I only live six blocks away, and it is—"

"I cannot let you walk home alone. Permit me." The notion of a young woman walking alone in the dark was foreign to his way of thinking, and he…he couldn't allow it.

Gloria laughed softly, "I walk all of the time, Mr. Baxter. It is quite safe, I assure you."

"That may be, but where I come from, young women are not safe to walk alone in the dark, and I would feel much better if you humored me. Do you mind?"

"Very well then, thank you, Mr. Baxter."

"Would you mind calling me Andrew?" he asked, stepping around to the curb side of the walk. "Mr. Baxter makes me feel old."

"Only if you call me Gloria."

"Then it is a deal," Andrew answered, grinning.

Returning his smile, Gloria felt her cheeks flush and hoped he would not notice.

Chapter 13

"Thank you for dinner, Leah," Andrew said, relaxing in a white Adirondack chair in the Danielses' backyard. "I can't remember when I enjoyed a meal more. I have not had much family time since the death of my grandmother."

"You are quite welcome, Andrew. I am glad you are comfortable with us."

Mike settled back in the red metal glider, his arm around Leah's shoulder. "I don't know how comfortable you would have been last week when Leah was gone," he chuckled, squeezing her shoulder. "It was a little on the hectic side."

"From what I hear, the general consensus around town was much worse." Andrew laughed and then became serious. "Forgive me for not asking, Leah. How is your uncle?"

She sat comfortably in the crook of her husband's arm, his hand casually resting on her shoulder, and Andrew turned his eyes away. The intimate contact stirred an ache within him he doubted would ever go away.

"He is much better, thank you. Momma sprained her ankle, so he is staying with my brother, Paul. Hopefully he will soon feel up to visiting."

"Did his wife pass away?"

"No. Uncle Amos is a bachelor. He lives across the orchard from Momma and Daddy, so, needless to say, he has always been a very great part of our family, and we love him dearly."

Andrew smiled wistfully. "That sounds nice…family being so close. My parents died when I was small, and my grandmother raised me and my brothers. Then I lost both of them in the war."

Mike studied the loneliness etched in the face of this man he was becoming fond of, and he gently tightened his grip on Leah's shoulder. Giggling and the sound of rattling dishes drifted through the kitchen window, Johnny's voice rose in complaint of too much trash in the waste can, and Jimmy's voice called from the front yard, "Laura, Elizabeth is here."

The sounds stirred him, and he prayed never to take them for granted. Leah and the children were everything to him, and he could not begin to imagine life without them. Leaning forward, he looked at Andrew compassionately.

"I am so sorry, Andrew. It has to be a very traumatic experience to lose your parents as a small child and then both brothers. I cannot begin to know what that must have been like."

"Thank God for my grandmother. We...my brothers and I were staying with her while our parents were vacationing. They were...killed in a boating accident. I don't believe the authorities ever determined what actually happened."

Resting a hand on the arm of the chair, he gazed up into the maple tree and spoke softly. "I was only four and my brothers seven and nine. Grandmother took care of us and did an excellent job too, I might add," Andrew said, smiling. "I will always be grateful for her love and support. She maintained a family atmosphere for us, but I long to have a normal family life, a wife and family of my own."

"Of course you do," Mike replied, knowing he'd make a good husband and father. The depth and quality to his character was unmistakable. "Sometimes, Andrew, the Lord has us wait for that which we long, and his timing is always right, always."

Andrew looked at Mike for a long moment and then glanced away. "I was married once...but it was brief. I loved her too much, maybe." He sighed, thinking the conversation was getting too serious and grinned at Leah.

"I used to tell Grandmother I was patiently waiting to find someone like her, and she would say, 'God didn't intend for a man to marry his grandmother, so wait for the one he has chosen for you.'" Andrew chuckled, and then grew serious again.

"I want what you have. And I will wait for it, but sometimes I get so lonely."

"You are exactly—"

"Mr. Baxter! Aren't you an artist?" Shari called, running down the back steps, followed by Laura and another young girl.

Skipping through the yard, she came to stand before him, and he smiled at the little girl, so like her mother. Her brown hair was cut at the shoulder, facial features were perfect, and she displayed an engaging smile that created dimples in both cheeks.

"I told Laura and Elizabeth you are a famous artist, and they don't believe me," she stated, frowning at the other two.

Andrew chuckled at the expression on her face and then turned his attention to Laura and the young girl, Elizabeth.

She was the little tomboy in the red dress he had seen at church. A pretty little thing, she had an olive skin tone, and big, blue eyes that presently studied him with a look of skepticism.

"Well, are you a famous artist or not?"

Andrew threw his head back and laughed. "Well, little Miss Elizabeth, yes, I am an artist, but I would not say I was famous."

"Then you are not so great after all. I thought—"

"Andrew," Leah interrupted, "this is Elizabeth Driscol, who I think has forgotten her manners."

"I am sorry, Mr. Baxter. I am pleased to meet you." A sheepish grin crossed her face, and she glanced at Leah, hoping she wouldn't say anything to Aunt Trudy cause she would surely drag out that book by some lady named Emily Post and make her read about proper etiquette. She and Caroline had thrown it in the trash one day, only to have Aunt Trudy find it and tearfully confront them, saying she only wanted them to be proper young ladies. Uncle Henry felt so sorry for them he said that he hadn't thought anyone read it and he had thrown it away, which only left Caroline and Elizabeth feeling all the more guilty.

Frowning at Elizabeth, Laura looked at Mr. Baxter. She thought he was very nice. He told them all about New York, his home in Connecticut, and several other interesting places. He had even been to Paris.

"I bet you are famous," Laura remarked. What do you draw?"

"Actually, I paint, and I enjoy it more than anything."

"Can we see your pictures?" Elizabeth asked, dropping on the ground next to Laura. "I have never met a real artist. My sister Caroline can draw pretty good, but all I draw are stick figures, and they don't look right. But I am very good at everything else," she stated matter-of-factly and then glanced at Laura when she poked her in the side.

"I want to see your pictures."

Studying the stubborn set to her chin and her impish smile, Andrew mentally added her to his growing list of possible portraits. There was fire and spirit in this little girl, and she would grow into a fascinating young woman who knew exactly what she wanted.

"I have a better idea. You can watch me paint," Andrew suggested. "Choose something or some place and let me know tomorrow at church. I will see what I can do."

Observing their pleased expressions, Andrew smiled and rose to his feet. "But for now, I must be going."

"You may not know what you are getting yourself into, Andrew," Mike chuckled, also rising.

"I will enjoy it, and I am sure it will not be boring. Leah, thank you again for dinner. I enjoyed it much more than you know."

"So we can choose anything we want, and you will paint it. Is that correct?" Elizabeth questioned.

"Anything," he promised.

Giggling, the girls looked at one another and then ran off across the yard.

"You're nifty...for an artist," Elizabeth called back as she chased Laura around the side of the house.

Leah shook her head and laughed, slipping an arm through Mike's as they strolled through the yard. "Elizabeth is quite rambunctious, but she is precious. She is the total opposite of her sister."

"I guess that is a blessing," Mike laughed. "I don't know if Trudy and Henry could handle two Elizabeths."

"Henry Driscol is the mayor, isn't he? I have not had the pleasure of meeting him, but I have met Mrs. Driscol," Andrew remarked, grinning. "I would venture to say Elizabeth is more like her mother."

"I suppose she may have a couple of Trudy's characteristics," Mike replied, shaking his head, "but Trudy is not her mother. Caroline and Elizabeth are the daughters of Trudy's sister. She died when Elizabeth was born, and they were left without a father, so Trudy and Henry adopted the girls and raised them as their own."

Andrew shook his head and sighed, "There is a lot of sadness in this world, isn't there? Thank the Lord there was someone to care for them."

"You must come back and visit again, Andrew," Leah remarked, touched by his compassion.

"I will look forward to it. I appreciate you sharing your home and family with me, Mike," Andrew said as they walked around the side of the house. He paused and looked into the eyes of this pastor. "I mean it. Thank you."

"I am happy you spent time with our rowdy bunch," Mike answered, placing a hand on his shoulder. "And I echo Leah's words, Andrew. As long as you are in Oak Grove, drop by anytime."

Mike watched him walk to the car, open the door and then turn and look back. A strange feeling came over him. Who was it? Who did Andrew remind him of?

Spoons was a favorite game in the Daniels household, and tonight was especially enjoyable, because Nathaniel had never played. After the first few rounds of holding too many cards, passing in the wrong direction, and being the last to grab a spoon, he finally caught on.

Sitting in a circle in the middle of the floor with the smell of popcorn and sound of laughter, Mike glanced at Leah and smiled, each reading the other's thoughts.

It was good Leah was home, Uncle Amos was doing well, and everyone was healthy and happy. Nathaniel, adjusting well, was spending the night and enjoying himself, in spite of all of the ribbing Elizabeth was giving him about being such a lousy player.

Mike thought of Andrew and knew he would have enjoyed this evening and wished he would have suggested he stay.

"It is your deal, Dad," Laura said, handing him the cards.

Shuffling, Mike passed four to each, glanced at the cards in his hand, and drew one from the pile. Passing a queen of hearts to Elizabeth, he heard her groan and then pass it to Jimmy. Mike watched in amusement as cards were passed around the circle. Shari bit her lower lip and passed a card to Leah, who picked it up, dropped it, and grabbed it again. A dimple threatened with the faintest hint of a smile and then became more pronounced when she laughed and passed her card to Johnny and quickly grabbed a spoon.

Not paying attention, Mike was without a spoon and the object of everyone's laughter.

"That's not fair," he complained, tossing his cards down.

"Poor Pastor Mike, you're getting too old and slow for Spoons," Elizabeth taunted, tilting her head sideways and glancing up at him with a mischievous grin and merriment in her eyes.

Surprise, truth, and denial came together, hitting Mike full force like a bucket of cold water, and he stared dumbfounded. *It couldn't be,* he thought, staring at her.

"Mike?" Leah asked, looking at him curiously.

"Nathaniel, it is your deal," Mike heard Jimmy say as he stood to his feet in bewilderment and ran a hand across his forehead.

"I think I have lost for the last time tonight. You go on and play," he said with a grin, attempting to mask the feelings rushing through him.

"Sore loser, that's what you are," Elizabeth teased.

"I guess I am." He laughed, a hundred thoughts swirling through his head. Nodding reassuringly at Leah's questioning gaze, he glanced at those on the floor. "Go ahead and play, I am getting a Coke."

Walking down the hall into the kitchen, he stepped out onto the porch and closed the door quietly. "Oh, Lord, is it so?" he murmured, looking up at the moonless sky and trying to absorb his swirling thoughts. Gazing at the stars, he silently awaited an answer. *One thing at a time... Lord, help me to... just one thing at a time.* Closing his eyes, he released a slow breath and welcomed the gentle calmness that surrounded him.

"All right then," he whispered, "it is in your hands." Looking out into the night, he wondered how he could have missed that which was so evident. Turning and entering the kitchen, he retrieved a bottle of Coke from the Frigidaire, popped the cap off, and returned to the living room and sat in his chair.

Elizabeth was dealing, and Mike watched her. She tilted her head and flashed Laura an unmistakable grin. Why had he not put the two together? With the strange sensation he was seeing Elizabeth for the first time, he looked in amazement at the dark hair and olive skin tone so like another. The blue eyes full of mirth and that look on her face when she tilted her head and glanced up at him. It was the same familiar look he had tried to place the last several days. Resting his head on the back of the chair, Mike closed his eyes and released a slow breath. *Andrew Baxter... I know who you are and why you are here.*

Chapter 14

Glancing at his wristwatch, Mike picked up his Bible and sermon notes and headed for the door. Most Sundays, he walked across the street to collect his family and then milled around in the vestibule visiting with his congregation, but today he sought the quiet of his office.

There was nothing he could do or say at the present time. He had no proof, and there was nothing on which to base his assumption, other than observation and instinct. But he knew, he knew without a doubt, that Andrew Baxter was Caroline and Elizabeth's father. What effect was this going to have on them and the whole Driscol family? What were Andrew's plans? His face, etched in loneliness and longing, surfaced in Mike's mind, and he now knew to whom and why this morning's message was given him.

Pausing at the door, he looked down at the worn Bible in his hand, amazed once more how God drew his attention to a specific passage of scripture and laid a message on his heart.

Strains of "Down at the Cross" reached him, and Mike closed his eyes and prayed, "Oh, Lord, I look to you in the coming days for wisdom, strength, and understanding. So many lives are going to be touched. Give me patience and wisdom for what lies ahead. Thank you for bringing about this miracle, and I know you will do it in your time and in the power of your love and understanding. You said your words would not return to you void, and I am claiming that promise this morning."

Standing with his hand on the doorknob, he allowed God's peace to permeate his heart; then he opened the door, stepped out, and strode down the hall. Voices rose, and Mike joined in the familiar hymn as he walked to the second pew and stood next to Leah.

Ned was singing lustily and waving his arms in time with the music. Continuing to the last note of the last verse, he then took his seat on the front row, and those in the choir found their seats.

Robert Miller rose and made his way to the pulpit. He was a short man, and what hair he had left was sprinkled with gray. As Oak Grove's doctor for over thirty years, he knew everyone's aches, illnesses, and heartaches and had delivered a good portion of the congregation; therefore, everyone figured he should make the announcements every week, since he knew all that was going on anyway.

"Good morning." Removing his spectacles, he wiped them with his hanky. "I hope you are as proud to be in the Lord's house this morning as I am. Willy, it is good to see you today." Replacing them, he nodded and glanced over at Andrew. "Mr. Baxter, glad to have you join us again, and if there is anyone who has not had the good fortune to meet this fine young man, you do it before you leave today."

Andrew smiled and nodded at those looking in his direction and noted Gloria Hansen looking attractive in a dark green suit and matching hat. Flashing a friendly smile, she turned her attention back to Dr. Miller.

"This Tuesday at six o'clock the Founders Day committee will meet at the Methodist church to discuss the sunrise service. Oh, and Trudy has a sign-up sheet in the foyer for meals and times allotted each day to look in on Mrs. Tyler."

Nodding his approval, he looked at Trudy. "I am sure this will be a great help to Louise. Thank you, Trudy, for taking care of that. I dropped by yesterday, and Mrs. Tyler is feeling much better. Grandma Hope's back pain is much improved, and she is up and about. I expect she will be here next Sunday. We can thank the Lord for the both of them, and I believe that is all I had—" His last words were drowned out as Myrtle launched into the introduction of "Footprints of Jesus."

"Mike," Leah whispered, leaning toward him, "did you know Willy was coming this morning?"

"No, but I suspect Melba had something to do with it," he replied, grinning and gently squeezing her hand.

Turning her attention back to Ned, Leah joined her voice with the rich baritone of her husband as they sang the old hymn.

Walking to the pulpit, Mike looked out across the congregation and this church he loved. Old, oak pews were filled with familiar faces on either side of a center aisle, and the wood floor was waxed and shiny, thanks to Alice Cooley. A large, open Bible and bouquet of autumn flowers graced the Lord's supper table in front of the pulpit, and the sunlit vestibule was visible through open double doors in the back.

Allowing the congregation a few minutes to pray silently, he asked the Lord's blessing on his message and those for whom it was prepared. Then opening his Bible, he turned to the passage of scripture.

"This morning I will be reading from Jeremiah chapter twenty-nine, beginning with verse eleven," he said and waited a moment. He then read in a strong, confident voice, "For I know the plans I have for you, declares the Lord, plans to prosper you and not to harm you, plans to give you hope and a future."

For the next thirty minutes, Andrew listened to Pastor Mike speak of the promise of which Jeremiah wrote, expounding thoroughly and straightforwardly on the passage. The familiar words took on new meaning for Andrew. He had read the well-known passage several times, but this morning, the meaning was clear and fresh. Although the man at no time singled him out, Andrew knew the words were for him, and it also was very clear that his presence in Oak Grove, if for no other reason, was to hear what Pastor Mike was saying.

"Move ahead in your life despite the past. The past is behind you. It is over. Did you hear what I said? The past is over. There is nothing you can do to change it. God has plans for your life today and for your future, and he will enable you to fulfill those plans, or he would *never* have set your feet on the path he has chosen for you."

Andrew sat unmoving, allowing the words to sink in. Unconsciously smoothing his beard, he realized that the Lord was using this man to assure his coming to Oak Grove had been right.

"Follow God's agenda, not yours. Our agenda leads off the path, it always does. It is his plan that works and brings fulfillment. So stay close to him, my friend. Stay so close that there is no doubt with each step you take. God does not expect or want us to live in doubt and fear. So get rid of your doubt, follow the Lord's leading."

Mike closed his Bible and looked out across the congregation. "I think one of the hardest things for us is patience...but it is necessary. Much of the time one's walk consists of small, slow steps, but...those slow steps pave the road God has chosen for you...and for me. And that road, you will find, is the road that will fulfill his plan for you, and you will find it is paved with boundless hope."

Pausing a moment, Mike stared down at his Bible. Looking up, he spoke in a softer tone, "You may not be spared pain. You may not be spared suffering or hardship. The road we travel occasionally encounters suffering. But...if you are following God's lead, you can be assured he will see you through to the glorious end. And you will find it will be worth it, more than you can ever begin to imagine."

Chapter 15

The last of September flew by, ushering in brisk, cool days of October. Ridges surrounding Oak Grove were a riot of red, gold, scarlet, amber, and purple. Wood tables at Reese's Market were filled with pumpkins, gourds, Indian corn, and an abundance of fruits and vegetables; Gerald's caramel apple sundae was a hit; and the fourth graders' annual Founders Day painting contest entries were displayed in the bank. Gloria's library window was an autumn masterpiece and displayed Andrew's painting of the town square, his name scrawled across the bottom left corner with a small card that simply read *Heart of Oak Grove.*

Trudy was aflutter with Founders Day one week away, scurrying here and there and checking everyone's assigned duties. The barber shop, café, drugstore, and blacksmith shop buzzed with preparations and tales of previous years. Men and boys, glued to radios, voiced their opinions while they slept, ate, and argued baseball as the St. Louis Cardinals and Brooklyn Dodgers ended the season in the first-ever tie for the National League Pennant Race. Jubilation, pride, and boasting abounded when the Cardinals won the first two out of three and went to the World Series to face the Boston Red Sox and Ted Williams.

Andrew Baxter was now a familiar face in Oak Grove, and Nathaniel Black, after an awkward start at school, had adjusted and was found to be a promising running back for the Oak Grove Tigers.

"I don't see why I was picked to recite the dumb poem," Jimmy complained, a frown on his face as he sat at the breakfast table Friday morning. "Everyone will laugh."

"No they will not," Leah replied, pouring milk into his Wheaties. "And you should consider it a privilege. Your brother recited it when he was in first grade."

"I did, didn't I?" Johnny remarked, looking up from Buck Rogers's picture on the back of the cereal box. "I forgot about that."

"And you did a good job," Leah said. "You didn't miss a word."

"Thanks, Mom."

Shari wiped the milk from her mouth with the back of her hand. "Seems to me they could pick out something a girl did. I *know* girls came along on the trip, didn't they, Mom?"

"Yes of course. And I am positive they contributed a lot along the way," Leah said, having noted Shari's small bit of jealousy over the attention her brother was receiving.

"Then why didn't they write it down?"

"I imagine some mothers or young girls kept journals. It would be very interesting to read them wouldn't it?"

"Well I wish they would find one of them," Jimmy grumbled, "and then you could stand up there and read it, and I wouldn't have to."

"It is eight forty-five. Are any of you going to school this morning?" Mike asked, standing in the doorway, "Or is this a day off?"

Leah glanced at the clock. "Oh my goodness. It is time to go or you will be late."

A flurry of activity erupted. Cereal bowls were dropped in the sink, lunches grabbed from the cabinet, and after a quick hug and kiss, they were headed out the back door.

"Nathaniel's coming home with me after school," Johnny said, holding the screen open. "He gets to sit on the bench tonight and might even get to play a little. I hear the guys think he is pretty nifty since he started practicing…you coming, Jimmy?"

"Yeah," he replied, shifting his books. "You know, Dad, how you always say that sometimes a man has to do things he doesn't want to but has to anyway? Well, this is one of those times for me, and I do it under protest." Plopping his baseball cap on his head, he marched out the door, down the steps, and ran through the yard.

"What is he protesting?" Mike asked, looking at Leah.

"Reciting the Founders Day poem. It would be just like him to clam up and refuse."

"He will do fine, darlin'. He knows it by heart. I heard him practicing in the bathroom. And he is proud that he was asked. He's just a little embarrassed and pretending it's not a big deal."

"I hope so. But sometime he can be so stubborn," Leah said, pouring Mike's coffee.

Adding a bit of brown to the reddish mixture on the palette, Andrew blended it with his brush and glanced at the old mill, a perfect match. He studied the canvas a moment and then laid the brush aside, his desire to paint vanishing as the beauty and peace of the wooded area beckoned.

He glanced around. Surrounded by tall grass and wildflowers, the mill sat at water's edge, its color faded to a pale, rusty red. *Seabaugh Mill,* painted in bold, white letters long ago, was barely readable, and trickling water drew his attention. He watched the stream in fascination as it flowed from somewhere high on the ridge and down around the now motionless wheel. Cascading over several large rocks, it pooled into a fairly large swimming hole where a wooden dock jutted away from the bank and a small fishing boat, floating in the lazily flowing water, bumped rhythmically against its side.

Spring fed, he thought, watching as the stream narrowed and disappeared through the trees. Releasing a sigh, he stared at a patch of yellow wildflowers, brilliant in color where the sun broke through trees. He had missed much in his life. Some circumstances he had no control over, and others had been his own fault. A cool breeze stirred, and he smoothed his beard and watched gold, amber, and red leaves drift leisurely to his feet. A woodpecker's busy hammering reached his ear, and he closed his eyes, allowing the sounds and smells of the forest to soothe his soul.

"There, that is what I want you to paint," Elizabeth's voice echoed in his memory as she pointed to a weeping willow tree in the empty lot next to Pastor Mike's house. "You said you would paint anything for us, and we play under there all the time," she had said, looking up at him with the same grin he remembered from pictures he had seen of himself as a boy.

Looking down into her face, he had wondered how he had managed to fool anyone. Her eyes were his, their skin tone identical, and the dark shade of their hair the same. Reaching out and grabbing his hand, she had laughingly pulled him toward the tree. Mesmerized, he had been overwhelmed that she was a part of him and had nearly pulled her close. Often wondering on his reaction if he ever saw his daughters, he now realized nothing had prepared him for the powerful, emotional turmoil and fierce longing to tell them who he was.

What sweet agony, Andrew thought, gazing up through tree branches. *My daughters, so near and yet so far. Will they ever know the truth? Will they love me or hate me?* He closed his eyes, and Caroline's face swam before him. Jolted to his very core the first time he saw her, there was no need to ask. The minute she stepped through the church door and walked toward him, he could do nothing but stare as she passed and entered the sanctuary. Her resemblance to Mary was striking.

What was he to do? The sun was warm on his back as he strolled along the edge of the stream. *Oh, Lord, show me what to do. The last thing I want is to hurt them.* Perhaps it would have been best if he had not come to Oak Grove. Releasing a long sigh, he tossed a twig in the water and knew that was not so. Even if nothing came to fruition, it was worth seeing them and knowing they were happy and cared for.

Follow God's agenda, not yours. Mike's words came slowly and clearly as Andrew recalled his message. *Stay close to him, my friend. Stay so close that there is no doubt with each step you take, and you will find that the road you are walking is the one he has selected. You will find it paved with boundless hope.*

Relief welled up inside, and Andrew smiled. "Thank you, Lord. Thank you for speaking to my heart. Keep me close to you, one step at a time, just one step at a time."

Walking back to his paint and easel, he gathered them up and looked around. There would be a lot of activity here the next few days with Elijah preparing for

Founders Day, but he would return when things were settled. For now, he wanted to remember this minute, and he gazed around, imprinting the scene in his mind. He would paint it from memory, just the way it looked this minute, and it would be his reminder of God's presence and comfort.

"If yesterday's game was any indication of the rest of the series, I declare it'll be a good one," Ned commented, holding scissors in midair and glancing around the shop. James, forgoing the checker game, was in the barber chair, and Pastor Mike, along with several others sat in wood chairs along the walls.

"You can say that again," James replied. "My soul, I was on the edge of the sofa. The dad-burned game had me so tense Miriam said I was going to have a spell if I didn't relax."

Closing the *Field and Stream,* Sheriff Walker shook his head. "It was a pretty tense last couple of innings, wasn't it? I really thought Pollet was going to hang in there, but…ah, when the chips are down, he doesn't have what it takes."

Mike watched him lean back in his chair, grin at James, and then turn his attention back to Ned. Casting him an irritated look, Ned shook his head and glanced at Mike through the mirror.

Framed in dark mahogany, its corner shelves held vacation souvenirs comprised mostly of a variety of shaving mugs and coffee cups, a miniature of the Washington Monument from Henry Driscol, a framed picture of Betty Grable someone clipped from a magazine, and a hula dancer with a clock in her belly.

Pausing, Ned leaned a hand on the counter and looked at him. "Are you kidding? Pollet doesn't have what it takes? Of course he does, he always does. He was tired. That was the problem. A pitcher can only do so much, you know."

Red faced, Ned turned back to James and ran a comb through his hair. "If you haven't got the worst mess of hair I've ever seen on a man."

"Yeah, well the way yours is disappearing, you'll wish you had some of this mess one of these days, and thin it out like you did last time," James retorted. Glancing through the mirror, he winked and said, "You might have hit the nail on the head, Sheriff. I heard several say Pollet lost the game, but do you know what I think? I think they lost their momentum. That's what happened."

"The Cardinals did not lose momentum," Ned exclaimed, thumping James on the head with his comb. "That's the dad-burndest fool thing I ever heard tell…lost their momentum."

"Oh, don't get yourself in a dander," James remarked, chuckling. "Calm down before you botch my haircut. I'm not paying fifty cents for a haircut that doesn't look right."

"Did I ever give you a bad hair cut?" Ned asked, stepping back and frowning. "Did I?"

"No, but there's always a first time, and I can see you're getting mad 'cause your face is red."

"I don't think it would matter much if I did," Ned remarked, running a comb through the red, unruly hair. "It's always a mess anyway. And I am *not* mad."

Mike watched in amusement as the subject was dropped, and they sat in companionable silence, the wall clock's tick and snip of scissors the only sound.

Unable to resist, Mike leaned back with a serious expression. "Well now, I think I'll just put my two cents in. I don't think they lost momentum. When Rudy York got a piece of the ball and sent it into the left-field bleachers, that turned the tide."

"Don't start it up again, Pastor," Jack Reese said. "I have to get back to the market, so hurry up, Ned."

"All right, all right, hold your horses. I'm finished. I just have to put a little Vitalis on his hair. Why didn't you say you was in a rush." Putting a dab in his hand, he rubbed it through James' hair, combed it, and then removed the barber cape and picked up his Coke.

"Say," James said, examining his hair in the mirror. "What do you think of the big square dance Saturday evening?"

Jack moved to the barber chair and sat down. "Mildred told me to agree with whoever I was talking with. She can't make up her mind about it. At first she and Trudy were against it, well Trudy still is. But now that everyone in town thinks it's a good idea, Mildred's not so sure it's a bad idea."

"Miriam plans to get me out there, but I told her at our age our get up and go already got up and went. But I wouldn't mind watching some of the young folks," James replied. "What about you and the wife, Sheriff?"

"I think we might try it. Spade Jackson is supposed to be one of the best callers around."

"I promised Ellie we'd give it a whirl," Ned said, grabbing a clean comb. "What about you and the missus, Preacher?"

"You just never know. We might show everyone up," Mike answered, grinning and wondering what Leah would do if he grabbed her and swung her around on the dance floor. *She would do all right,* he thought, *but I would look like an idiot.*

"Trudy would faint right on the spot," Jack laughed. "She's still trying to convince everyone it is not a good idea, and she was counting on you, Preacher, to nix the whole idea."

Mike laughed. "There is nothing wrong with square dancing, but I wouldn't want to be the cause of Trudy fainting on Founders Day, so I guess we will just watch. Besides, I don't know how."

"You don't know how?" Ned asked. "Boy howdy, I thought everyone knew how to square-dance."

"I'm afraid not, Ned." Mike answered. "I spent most of my time hunting, fishing, or out doing something on the farm and never gave much thought to it. I can move around to a slow tune, but that's about it."

"Well, I'll be...I sure figured everyone could square-dance. Back in my day, we square-danced at all the special doin's. What do you think of Andrew Baxter? Do you think he'll still be in town?"

James sat down in the chair Jack had just vacated and crossed a leg. "I can't see why he would leave with Founders Day four days away. He was over at Old Ben's a couple of times and was asking about it. Seems like a pretty nice fellow, if you ask me."

"Seems to be. He came in one day last week, and I gave him a trim. For a city slicker, he didn't act much different than anybody else. He said he was from either New York or Connecticut. I was a little confused," Ned said, placing the barber cape around Jack's neck.

"He works and stays in New York a good deal of the time," Mike replied, "but his home is in Connecticut. He has stopped by the house a few times, and we have become quite fond of him. He is a good man."

"What's he doing in Oak Grove?" Jack asked curiously. "He's got no folks here, and Sam Cranston doesn't know much about him other than he was passing through and decided to stay a while. Sam said he seems to have made himself at home."

"I guess when you have a lot of money you can pretty much do what you want," Jack said. "I can't say I blame him. If I had a job that gave me freedom to move around at will, I would too."

"What kind of job does he have that he earns so much money?" Ned asked, looking at Mike. "Doesn't he have any family or obligations? You know, we really don't know much about him, do we?"

"Well, fellows, I guess when he feels comfortable enough to share his life with us, he will. I do know he had a successful law practice before he took up painting. That seems to be what he loves most."

"Well he sure can paint," James said. "That picture Gloria has in the library window looks like you're standing right in the middle of the square. He is talented all right."

"He sure is," Jack said, "but I am still curious. Why Oak Grove? Why is he here?"

Chapter 16

Standing in front of the library window admiring Gloria's autumn display, Andrew stared at his painting. Everything about it beckoned, and he knew it would always be more than an image of a sleepy little town. His gaze moved across the flower-bordered bandstand and fountain, the bell tower, flag pole, and walkway that cut through the middle of the square with its honeysuckle, oak trees, and surrounding shops. No, to him it represented much more: people and roots and families and purpose and love. His brush had expressed all that he longed for and missed.

Most everyone commented on it, and Mayor Driscol expressed a desire to purchase it. The thought of his painting hanging in the Driscol home irked him. *He has both my daughters. Isn't that enough?* A frown crossed his handsome face, and he absentmindedly smoothed his beard and sighed in frustration. Placing both hands in his pockets, he continued to study the painting, aware of his irritability. Knowing he would never part with it afforded him a sense of satisfaction, and the smallest hint of a smile touched his lips.

Sitting at her desk, Gloria watched him through the window. Her heart beat rapidly, and she was suddenly angry with herself. *He doesn't even know I am alive. He is a nice man, and I am acting like a schoolgirl.*

Startled when he stepped toward the door, she hurriedly grabbed a book.

"Good afternoon, Gloria." Closing the door, he flashed a smile that would make any woman giddy, and she wondered how many women had fallen for it.

"Good afternoon, Andrew."

"I was admiring your window display. It is nice, *very* nice."

"Thank you." Flushing, she watched him approach her desk. "Your painting is the element that makes it."

"You are too modest. You have a talent for arranging things. Do you mind?" he asked, pointing to a chair.

"No, please sit down."

Noting Louise across the room with two books and a puzzled expression, Gloria rose and glanced at Andrew, who picked up a book from the return table. "Excuse me a moment, Andrew. Louise, can I help you find something?" she asked, thankful for the distraction.

"No. I want both of these for Mother." Depositing the books on Gloria's desk, she looked curiously at Andrew.

"How is Mrs. Tyler?" Gloria asked, removing the cards from their pockets.

"She's about the same." Signing the cards, she stood ramrod straight and watched Gloria stamp return dates.

Noting the woman's stern face, Andrew wondered at her brittle manner and then reminded himself he did not know her circumstances. Staring unseeing at the book in his hand, he listened to her curt replies to Gloria's questions and then looked up when she loudly cleared her throat.

Staring at him with a raised brow, she lowered her gaze to the book he held, *Little Women* by Louisa May Alcott.

"They tell me this is a good book," Andrew grinned, holding it up. Instead of the expected smile, he received a stone-faced expression; then she turned away.

Suppressing a grin, Gloria commented softly, "It is very good, Andrew, though I doubt you would enjoy it. But then again, maybe you would, if that is your preference. Here you are, Louise, tell your mother hello for me. I hope she is feeling better."

Pushing the hair net behind her ear, Louise retrieved her books, glanced suspiciously at Andrew again, and headed for the door, pulling it firmly closed.

Looking at Andrew, Gloria grinned, "Did you really want *Little Women?* I have some Nancy Drew mysteries that might interest you more."

Sitting back in the chair, Andrew chuckled. "No thank you," he replied, again admiring the silky voice and friendly smile. *She has no idea,* he thought, placing *Little Women* on her desk. "I guess I did not make a very good first impression, did I?"

"Don't worry about Louise. She never says much," Gloria explained. "She doesn't mean to be rude."

Resting an arm on her desk, Andrew shook his head. "She seems an unusually sad individual. I understand her mother is ill?"

"Yes, very," Gloria replied. "From what I understand, her heart does not pump the way it should, and she is very weak." Conscious of his arm's close proximity, she moved hers and, placing both hands in her lap, sat back. "Louise takes care of her mother, and they have no other family around here. They are very close."

"That's too bad. Family nearby can be very comforting," he murmured quietly, glancing up as Leah walked through the door carrying several books.

"Good afternoon, Andrew…Gloria," she remarked cheerfully. "And how are both of you today?"

"I am fine, thank you," Andrew replied, admiring her delicate features as she deposited the books on the return table and spoke with Gloria. The artist within wholeheartedly appreciated beauty wherever or in whomever he saw it, his perusal often creating misunderstandings in many of the female gender.

She is a classic beauty, Andrew thought, studying the heart-shaped face. Long lashes framed dark eyes, her nose was straight, and her mouth beautifully formed. Dimples creased both cheeks as she smiled at Gloria, and he figured Mike had not stood a chance when she bestowed that smile on him.

"I believe I have them all," she commented, double-checking. "Nancy Drew, The Bobbsey Twins, Hardy Boys, and The Boxcar Children. Laura is still reading a Nancy Drew book, but it is not due yet."

"That's fine," Gloria said, pulling them toward her.

"Your painting is beautiful, Andrew," she said, glancing toward the window. "You have captured the life of Oak Grove."

"Thank you, Leah."

"Gloria, your window display is attractive as always," she remarked, pondering the fact that Gloria seemed a little flustered. She hoped she was feeling all right. "Gloria always does such a wonderful job decorating. You should see how nice the church looks at Christmas, Andrew. She makes it looks so beautiful."

"Thank you, Leah, but it is nothing. Anyone could—"

"No, not just anyone," Andrew said, noting her flush-stained cheeks. "It requires imagination and thought to arrange things nicely."

Her face suddenly very warm, Gloria gathered several books that needed filing. "Excuse me," she said, aware of Leah's question as she headed toward the fiction section.

"You are going to the football game Friday evening, aren't you?"

"I have not been to a football game in years," Andrew answered, trying to recall the last game he had attended. In fact, as of late, he was trying to recall several things he had not done in a long time.

"Oh you mustn't miss it. A lot of folks who return for Founders Day make it a point to arrive Friday for the game and the bonfire and chili supper beforehand. You would enjoy it, Andrew."

"I think I might just do that."

"Good, Mike and I will look for you. I must hurry along. The children will be home shortly. Thank you, Gloria," Leah called, moving toward the door.

"You are welcome, Leah," Gloria answered, sliding the last book into its proper place and feeling somewhat guilty. She had not eavesdropped. *I really wasn't*, she reasoned, staring at the book on the shelf. *It was not a personal conversation, and they were right here in the library.* But she had deliberately listened for Andrew's response.

"Do you have Thomas B. Costain's *The Black Rose?*"

Caught off guard and with a feeling close to panic, she turned and looked up into his face. His eyes, a darker hue from the navy blue V-neck sweater he wore were questioning, and she suddenly found it difficult to breathe.

"Actually, yes," she replied, moving away. "I just placed it on the shelf about a month ago. Let's see...yes. Here it is." Retrieving it, she turned to find he had followed and was standing behind her.

"Great, I was afraid you would not have it," he said, his eastern accent terribly romantic. "I have not taken the time to read in a long while, and I miss it. You have a nice library, Gloria. Do I need to fill out a card?" he asked, turning the book over to read the back matter.

Caught between Andrew and the bookshelf, Gloria felt trapped. Her heart beat rapidly, and for a brief, ridiculous moment, she wondered if he could hear its pounding. Staring at his bent head, she gave a start when he glanced up and looked at her.

"I do, don't I?"

"Do what?"

"Fill out a library card."

"Oh," Gloria answered, embarrassed. "Yes, it will take just a moment."

He stepped aside, and Gloria moved to her desk and removed a card from the top drawer. "I need your name and address, and…well, you can read for yourself." Feeling foolish, she watched him rapidly fill in the information and sign his name with a flourish, noting his left-handedness.

"Thank you, Gloria. I am looking forward to reading this," he remarked, glancing up. Her hazel eyes were soft, and the unmasked virtue and purity of blush on her cheeks was precious. *So refreshing, if she only knew how becoming that is.*

"I hope you enjoy it," Gloria murmured, wondering at his expression. "Is something wrong?"

"No, Gloria. You are very rare, do you know that?" Observing her puzzled expression, he smiled and then walked to the door.

Both relieved and disappointed at his departure, Gloria stood speechless, wondering what he had meant.

Chapter 17

By nine o'clock, Oak Grove was a flurry of activity, everyone adding finishing touches to Founders Day preparations. Cooley had repaired and painted the bandstand's loosened latticework from Jasper's escapade earlier in the summer and painted the trash barrels red "so's they catch everbody's eye."

Old Ben, with the help of the shop's regulars, had the forge ready and hammer and anvil in place, as well as bellows, tongs, files, and grinders. He would fill the vat with water tomorrow.

Listening to chatter of when so-and-so did this or that on previous celebrations, Melba laughed aloud when Hazel swooped into the shop early for her perm and announced, "I'll swan. I hear Trudy's voice in my sleep: 'Hazel, ring me Mildred; Hazel, ring me Pastor Mike; Hazel, ring me Sheriff Walker; Hazel, ring me, ring me—' Land sakes! She's about to drive me batty. Gloria is relieving me, and she can deal with her now. I duly warned her."

A banner displaying "Oak Grove's 66th Annual Founders Day Celebration" was strung across the front of city hall, red, white, and blue bunting was draped along the Cranston Hotel balcony, and every shop on the square proudly displayed an American flag. The Sweet Shoppe advertised Founders Day Fudge, and several were already guessing how many marbles the gallon jar in the drugstore contained.

Cranston Café's Founders Day menu, contributed by Andrew, was painted in a patriotic theme and displayed on an easel outside the door, makeshift picnic tables afforded extra seating on the square, and every store window posted a schedule of activities and entertainment by the Jordan River Gospel Singers, the Ozark Mountaineers, and a special appearance of Spade Jackson and his Square Dancing Strings.

Cooley, after spending the last two weeks working on the "hoedown dance floor," as Trudy called it, was quite proud of his results and had nothing more to do but throw down some saw dust. Receiving several compliments, his pride was bruised when Trudy mentioned using it for the cakewalk.

"Yer goin' to mess up my brand new floor by paintin' a circle of squares all over it, ain't ya?" he complained, pointing his finger. "I ain't paintin' it. I'll tell ya that right now."

"Good heavens, Cooley, don't get your dander up," Trudy remarked, straightening her hat.

Get my dander up, Cooley thought, watching her fiddle with the concoction and wanting to tell her it looked like someone ran over it with a truck and dragged it through a pile of leaves.

"I didn't expect you to paint it," she said, rummaging through her handbag. "Mildred and I will."

"You and Mildred?" Cooley had screeched. "Now, that there would be a fine mess, two ladies tryin' to paint. I'll have you know, I built that dance floor, and I'll be dogged if I let anyone mess it up. I'll jest paint her myself, and I don't want to hear nothin' more about it."

"Good heavens, Cooley, if you feel that strongly, then paint it," Trudy replied, exasperated. "Bright yellow would show up nicely." Patting his arm, she smiled sweetly and headed toward the door.

"By jingees, she got me to do jest what she wanted, didn't she?" Cooley asked, removing his ball cap and scratching his head as he turned to the grinning faces of those seated at the soda fountain.

With everything ready and set to go, all breathed a sigh of relief, and Founders Day gave way to the fourth game of the World Series, with men gathering in Ned's, the Blacksmith Shop, and drugstore, listening in frustration as the Boston Red Sox beat the St. Louis Cardinals 6–3.

Standing on the porch of the large, Victorian home, Mike stared at two pumpkins by the door and wondered what warranted such an urgent visit. Myrtle left two notes on his desk, and, upon arriving home, Leah said Miss Tillie was most adamant about seeing him as soon as possible.

Normally, she would instruct him to sit in the wicker chair and then disappear to return with a tray of cookies and lemonade and announce he was not to talk about her coming to church. Often their conversations were meaningful, and just as often she rambled on about nothing in particular. When confused, he would listen to her reminisce about life on the plantation, tell which family members supposedly served with General Lee, and usually thought him to be one of any number of individuals she had known in the past. Hearing footsteps, he stepped back and smiled when she opened the door.

"Good morning, Miss Tillie."

"Good morning, Pastor Mike. Won't you come in?"

Surprised, he looked at her closely as he stepped inside and closed the door. For all outward appearance, she appeared to be in a normal frame of mind, and his curiosity was heightened as to the reason for his visit and the privilege of entering her home. Glancing around, he admired rich furnishings that far exceeded what he had been told.

"Please, come in and have a seat," Miss Tillie offered politely, crossing to the chairs by the fireplace.

"Would you care for a cup of tea?" she asked, reaching for a porcelain teapot.

"Yes, I would, Miss Tillie, thank you." Sitting back, Mike's gaze traveled to a portrait above the fireplace. A slender, dark-haired, young woman wearing a long, green velvet gown stood on a staircase. Her only jewelry was a strand of pearls and a sapphire ring on the hand resting on the banister. A soft smile touched her lips as she admired the single rose she held. Staring at the portrait in wonderment, Mike recognized the young girl and focused his attention on Miss Tillie as she poured their tea.

She wore a modest cut, rose-colored dress with a froth of white material at the neck and a white shawl draped across her shoulders. Her once dark hair, now mostly gray, was pulled back and fastened at the nape of her neck, and though the bloom of youth was long gone, Mike saw faint traces of the lovely young woman in the portrait.

"Yes," she smiled, "the young girl in the portrait is me. It was quite a long time ago, and there has been quite a lot of changes…cream and sugar?"

"Sugar please."

"I hope it is to your liking; I add a hint of mint," she commented, delicately adding cream and sugar to her own.

Watching her, Mike had the distinct feeling he was looking at someone he had never seen. Not much of a tea drinker, he was surprised with the pleasant flavor and knew when he had stepped through Miss Tillie's front door, he had stepped over a threshold into a world of surprises. "This is very good," he said, setting the cup and saucer on the table and glancing at the portrait again. "We all change through the years, but I will be honest, Miss Tillie. I recognized that beautiful young girl in the portrait."

Laughing, Miss Tillie placed her cup and saucer on the table. "A preacher with charm…I would say Mrs. Daniels was defenseless when you were courting her."

Chuckling, Mike crossed a leg. "I don't know about the charm, but you are correct about my pursuing her. I was determined to marry Leah the first time I saw her."

"My gracious, but isn't love grand. I am not too old to remember," she said softly, sipping her tea. "Tell me, how is Mrs. Tyler?"

"Not well at all," Mike replied, thinking how bad she looked that morning. "I believe the end is very close."

"Oh dear, poor Louise. She will be lost without her mother." Shaking her head sadly, she sighed and looked at him questioningly. "And Grandma Hope, I understand she fell."

"It will take more than a fall to get Grandma Hope down. They feared she may have broken a hip, but as it turned out, she was only bruised and sore."

"I am very glad to hear that. One never knows when something…unexpected might occur." Placing both hands in her lap, she looked at him intently. "I suppose you are wondering why I so urgently wanted to speak with you."

"Yes, ma'am, I am curious. How can I be of help?" he asked, finding it hard to believe this was the same woman who often ran him off her porch, occasionally dressed as one stepped from a page in history, and drove her Tin Lizzie recklessly through town, scattering folks in all directions.

"You were busy yesterday, and I now realize today is much better to speak with you anyway. Everything I need to show you is here, and we have plenty of privacy."

Absentmindedly fingering the brooch at her neck, her next words were soft. "Pastor Mike, what I tell you must be held in strictest confidence. Do I have your word?"

"Of course, Miss Tillie, I would never betray your trust."

"Very well, then." Smoothing the front of her dress, she stared at her hands a moment and then looked up, tears brimming in her eyes. "I know you are aware that I get...confused at times."

He nodded his head in acknowledgement, and she stared at him a long moment. He had such a compassionate, honest face, and she knew him to be the one who would help.

"I do not know what happens to me, Pastor Mike," she said quietly, gazing at the falling leaves beyond the window. "Most of the time I am fine. Then occasionally I...I find myself a young girl again at home in Virginia. It is hard to explain."

Fear crossed her face, and Mike thought she looked like a little, lost girl. Leaning forward, he took her hands. "Miss Tillie, I will not begin to tell you I understand what happens or how you feel, because I do not. But I know it has to be frightening."

Patting his hand, she smiled and sat back. "Not so much anymore. But what does concern me...I have occasional longings to retreat there and stay. And that is why I need to speak with you."

"All right, tell me how I can help?"

Walking across the room to a tall secretary, she unlocked it and retrieved a wooden box. Returning to her chair, she held it in her lap and studied it a moment.

"A day may indeed come when I retreat into my past and not return. Because of that probability, I need to explain a few things. And it is necessary that I do so while I have all my faculties and you are confident I know exactly what I am saying and very clearheaded with what I am doing, but . . ." she said, gripping the box firmly, "you must promise to guard this and reveal its contents to no one unless I give my consent...and then, only if I am in a normal frame of mind."

The box she held was of rich walnut with the initials MJC carved in gold on its lid. Admiring its intricate workmanship, Mike wondered what secrets lay within and then looked up as she continued.

"Pastor Mike, you must promise not to return this box if I ask for it when I am confused...even if I insist. Never under those circumstances allow me to have it. The contents of this box must be shared with the right people at the proper time. If in the future I become...incapacitated, I will leave it to your discretion to reveal its contents when and in what manner you think best. Do you understand?"

"Miss Tillie, are you sure you want to entrust this box and its contents to me? Perhaps there is someone else that—"

"No! There is no one else. I have asked the Lord to show me who to share this with, and he chose you."

Mike studied her, absorbing her declaration. He was accustomed to the Lord's leading and direction in his life, but Miss Tillie's change of attitude took him off guard. Deep inside he felt she was a believer, but her belligerent attitude toward him had always confused him.

"Just because I would not allow you in the house and told you not to preach to me about coming to church does not mean I don't love the Lord. Oh, I was angry with him a long time for taking my Harold home so soon, but he has loved and taken care of me through the years. I came to terms with Harold's passing long ago, but...for one reason or another, stubbornness mostly, I never returned to church. And now I am not sure I know how...with the spectacle I occasionally make of myself."

Leaning toward her, Mike took her hands again and looked directly into her eyes. "Miss Tillie," he said quietly, "you are *not* a spectacle. You are *Mrs. Matilda Watson,* and the folks in Oak Grove love you just as Leah and I do. You must believe that and allow us to show you by trusting us. Do not shut us out of your life any longer. You said the Lord chose me...Then let me help you in more ways than one. Leah and I both will help in any way we can."

Dabbing tears with a lace hankie, she smiled and patted his hand. "Thank you, Pastor Mike. I will try. I really will. But for now, I must tell you who I am."

Unlocking the box, she handed the small key to him. "It is the only one I have, so do not lose it. Papa gave me this box on my thirteenth birthday, and I would hate for you to have to break its lock." She sat back in her chair and looked fixedly at him. "Most folks know me as Tillie Watson or Matilda Watson. My maiden name was Matilda Jane Compton. Papa owned a tobacco plantation in Virginia—Edgewood. When my parents passed away, everything was divided among my three brothers."

Sighing, she folded her hands and looked at him sadly. "World War I took all three, and within a short time, Edgewood was gone, along with all traces of our family legacy."

Removing a document from the box, she handed it to him. "This is my birth certificate. I want to show you these papers so there is no margin of error."

Mike looked at the yellowed document, its writing penned in antique script stating Matilda Jane Compton was born August 16, 1868, to Amelia Rose Compton and William J. Compton. Returning it to Miss Tillie, he watched her replace it and remove another.

"I had two sisters. Isabelle was two years younger and died of an illness no one understood. This box contains her birth and death certificate as well. My other sister was three years older than me."

Pausing a moment, Miss Tillie sighed and laid her head against the back of the chair. "We were so close, Elizabeth and I, and I wanted so to be like her. We laughed and shared secrets and...all those things sisters share. One summer a gentleman, Jonathan Wilkins, came to do business with Papa, and Elizabeth fell madly in love with him. As it happened, Papa adamantly refused to allow her to marry him, saying she was much too young...so they ran off and got married."

Mike looked at the birth certificate much the same as the first and read that Elizabeth Ann Compton was born June 4, 1865, to Amelia Rose Compton and William J. Compton.

"Of course we did not hear from Lizzie for a long time," Miss Tillie continued, replacing the documents. "I was crushed. We had shared so much, and I missed her terribly. Then about two years later, I received a letter...the only one I ever got," she said softly, removing an envelope from the box. "She told me of the birth of her son and how happy she was, and she wrote of how she missed and loved us all. Whatever happened after that, I do not know. I replied but never heard from her again. Then Harold and I married, and we stayed in Virginia for quite some time, but...when Edgewood was sold, we moved here. This is where Lizzie lived when she wrote to me," she said, handing him the envelope.

Turning it over, Mike stared at the return address, Elizabeth Wilkins, 246 Lancaster Avenue, New Haven, Connecticut. Thoughts swirled through his head. Where had he seen that address? *Andrew's business card,* Mike thought, glancing up at Miss Tillie in confusion.

"Pastor Mike," Miss Tillie said softly, "Andrew Baxter is my great-nephew."

Mike sat unmoving, trying to grab onto this unexpected turn of events. "Miss Tillie," he replied, releasing a long breath, "did you ever think...I mean, just because Andrew is from New Haven, Connecticut, and—"

"Do you think the name Wilkins and New Haven have no relevance with Andrew Baxter?" she asked, removing a small envelope from the box. "I think it does, Pastor. Whether his name is Baxter or Wilkins, perhaps this may convince you. As sure as you're born, I knew who Andrew was the first time I saw him. He came into the post office one day while I was there, and I knew immediately."

Knowing the envelope she handed him contained a photograph, he sat for a moment then slid it out and stared in amazement. It was of another place and another time, but the man in the photograph could have been Andrew. Releasing a slow breath, Mike sat back in his chair and studied the man in the photo. His arm was around a lovely, young woman holding a small boy, and they were smiling at the camera.

"This is Elizabeth?"

"Yes, she included it in her letter." Taking the photo, Miss Tillie looked at it a long while and then spoke. "She was so in love with him, and he loved her too. By the way, Pastor, Elizabeth's husband's name was Jonathan...Jonathan *Andrew,* and the child was named after him, Jonathan Andrew II. I believe that would make our Andrew...Jonathan Andrew Wilkins III, wouldn't you say? "

Melba looked at the short love note Willy had tucked in the shop door that morning. Smiling, she glanced at her watch, hardly able to contain her happiness. They would share supper together again this evening. What had she done to deserve such joy? Continuing rapidly along the sidewalk, she was unaware of the man stepping into her path until they collided and she felt herself falling. Strong hands gripped her arms firmly, and she stared up into laughing blue eyes.

"Would you look at this? She jumps into my arms a second time. I surely must be the luckiest man in the world…or irresistible." Still maintaining his hold, Andrew grinned down into Melba's flushed face.

"Andrew, I am so sorry. I was not watching where I was going."

"My, my, but what I would not give if those stars in your eyes were for me," he said with an exaggerated sigh. "To be loved by such a beautiful woman…ah, my heart's greatest desire."

"Oh, for heaven sakes, will you quit flirting," Melba said, laughing at the lovesick expression he bestowed.

"Me? Every time I turn around you are throwing yourself at me."

"I am not, and you know it," Melba replied, smiling at the ridiculous grin on his face.

"Then does this mean you are still in love with Will?" he asked much too loudly.

Her cheeks growing warm, Melba glanced through the window of Ned's Barber Shop. Every man in the shop was staring at her with grins that matched Andrew's.

"Will you be quiet? You don't have to shout."

"Why not? If I was in love, I would shout it from the rooftops," he exclaimed, raising his hand in the air. "Come on; let me yell it to everyone. Melba is in love with Willy!"

"Andrew, stop it," Melba giggled. "Everyone will think we are crazy."

"I will if you allow me to walk you home. I presume that is where you are headed in such a rush at four o'clock. Preparing a romantic dinner?"

Melba shook her head. "Don't you have anything else to do?"

"Nope, not a thing." Chuckling, he fell into step. "I have one hour before dinner, and if I arrive too soon, Lottie will put an apron on me. Do you know she made me set the table the other day? Now I am more punctual about my arrival for dinner."

Melba laughed. "You have been at the hotel too long. You need to find a place of your own."

Suddenly serious, Andrew looked at her, opened his mouth to speak, and then closed it again and unconsciously smoothed his beard.

Sensing she had said something wrong, Melba glanced at him as they strolled slowly along the street. A cool breeze ruffled tree branches overhead, releasing autumn leaves to fall lazily across the sidewalk at their feet.

"If only life was that simple." Walking along with hands in his pockets, Andrew stared straight ahead and spoke softly, "but it is not, and that is unfortunate."

"I am sorry, Andrew. I don't know your personal life or why you came to Oak Grove, but I hope you find what you are searching for."

"I do too, Melba," he replied, pausing and looking through the window of Reese's Market.

Jack Reese was bagging groceries and chatting with two women while a couple of small boys were counting pieces of candy and dropping them into a paper sack. Glancing over at the Cranston Hotel, his gaze traveled to the second floor and the French doors that led to his room.

"I like it here," Andrew said. "You are fortunate to call this place home."

"I love it here too," Melba replied, plucking a leaf from an overhanging branch. "I have lived here five years and do not regret my move at all, especially now."

"No, I guess you do not," he said, studying her thoughtfully. "I suppose there is a definite future for you and Willy?"

Melba's face warmed, and she looked away. "Yes, although Will and I…I do not want to rush into anything."

Andrew stopped abruptly, turned, and stared intently at her, his voice low and firm. "Do not waste a minute, Melba. Time is too fleeting. The love God grants two people is one of his greatest gifts…Don't…don't lose it," he remarked quietly.

There was a sadness in his manner, and his dark blue eyes were seemingly trying to tell her something. She watched him smooth his well-trimmed mustache and run a hand across his beard. Andrew was handsome, rather striking, with his dark hair and olive skin, and she studied his face, realizing that in spite of his charm and light-hearted behavior, he was a person of great depth and principle. Perhaps that was why he never offended her with his inane, flirtatious manner. But he was a mystery. Who was Andrew, what had happened in his life, and was there a woman who shared it?

Crossing in front of the fire house, a gust of wind whipped around the corner, and Melba pulled the front of her cardigan close, thinking on his words.

"You are absolutely right, Andrew. Love is a gift from God, and we should never treat it lightly. And it comes when we least expect it. Do you know I lived here five years and didn't even know Will until this summer? Then one night I looked at him, and…well," Melba said with a small smile.

Glancing sideways, he chuckled. "Willy is a lucky man, Melba. And you can tell him I said so."

The sun was sinking behind the ridge as they made their way down Pine Street. Someone was cooking supper, and Andrew breathed in the delicious aroma.

"Pork chops, I believe. That is what Lottie is fixing for dinner. Last Friday she inquired about my favorite meals, and Monday morning there was a menu hanging on the Frigidaire." Andrew chuckled, remembering her remark at breakfast. "She also told me I could help with dinner anytime I took a notion."

"That sounds like Lottie. Mrs. Cranston would have scolded her if she'd heard her."

"Oh she did. I thought they were going to get into a scrap right there at the breakfast table. Mrs. Cranston said I was a guest and was not expected to do anything. Of course Lottie's reply was, 'Guest? Andrew's been here a long enough spell he's practically family, and he'll feel even more at home if we treat him as such,'" he said, mocking her perfectly.

Chuckling, Andrew remembered the exchange and realized Lottie was right. The hotel was starting to feel like home. "That remark touched me. I…I really like Oak Grove and the people here."

"I am so glad, Andrew. Maybe you will make it your home one day?"

He was silent for a long moment and then turned to her with a strange expression. "It would almost be too good to be true."

"Andrew, you must do what you feel is right, and I think you probably could do whatever you wished," Melba replied, wondering on the mystery surrounding him. She had heard many speculations, and though no one really knew anything for certain, he was well liked. "But whatever you decide, make sure you have prayed about it and know that it is what God wants."

"Now you sound like Pastor Mike," he replied, grinning.

"Well, here I am," Melba stated, stopping in front of her house. "Thank you for walking me home, Andrew. I enjoyed it."

The house was small and neat with black shutters. A sidewalk and steps led up to a wide porch with a swing at one end and a white wicker chair and small table at the other. A well-tended flower garden was planted along the porch, and he found the home suited Melba perfectly.

"It was my pleasure, Melba." He looked at her for a moment and then smiled wistfully and touched her shoulder. "Thank you for being a friend, and remember what I said. Time is fleeting, Melba. You and Willy must grab love and happiness and hang onto it. I wish the best for the both of you."

Patting her shoulder gently, he smiled again and then turned and strolled leisurely down the sidewalk. A burden for the slender, attractive man settled on her, and Melba felt there was something wrong. She prayed he would find what he was searching for.

Chapter 18

"Peter, the Methodists outdid themselves this Founders Day," Mike said as they stood on the steps of the Methodist church. "I ate way too many pancakes."

"I admit it too, Mike. Everything was delicious, wasn't it?" Patting his round belly, Reverend Clark studied the trim form of his Baptist preacher friend and shook his head. "One of these days you will round out like me. You just wait." His gaze traveled up to the cloudless sky, and he sighed with pleasure. "My, what a marvelous day the Lord has given us."

The two men stood in companionable silence, the sound of chatter, laughter, and clink of plates, cups, and utensils reaching their ears from an open basement window of the fellowship hall.

Breathing in the invigorating October air laced with fresh brewed coffee, sausage, and bacon, Mike watched orange and red maple leaves drift lazily to the ground, creating a multicolored carpet. "It truly is a beautiful day, Peter."

"There you two are." Smiling broadly, Trudy stepped out the door. "I have been looking everywhere for you."

"Good morning, Trudy," both men chorused.

"The pancake breakfast was wonderful, Reverend Clark. I declare, it really was."

Watching her absentmindedly straighten her hat, Mike wondered for the hundredth time where she managed to find such creations. This one fit like a bucket. An abundance of multicolored leaves and acorns graced the front, and a huge, orange bow and brown feathers adorned the whole right side.

"The breakfast committee should be congratulated. I will make certain Alan mentions it in *The Chronicle*. And I was so pleased with this morning's sunrise service. My soul, it was such a blessing. Thank you both for making it so inspirational. The choir sounded like heavenly angels," Trudy exclaimed, placing a hand over her heart. "My, my, gathering on the square for worship will always be one of my fondest memories. There is just something special about it, don't you think? And the weather, I declare, it could not be a more perfect day, although there is a bit of a chill, but nice and refreshing, don't you think? Our back thermometer read fifty-eight degrees. Mercy me, but I am glad I wore my suit jacket."

"Mornin', Preacher, Reverend Clark," Cooley said, stepping out the door with baseball cap in hand. "Mornin', Trudy," he commented stiffly, still somewhat miffed that she messed up his dance floor with cakewalk squares.

"Good morning, Cooley. I didn't see Alice and the children. They are here, aren't they?"

"Yes, ma'am, they's still downstairs eatin' pancakes." Motioning his thumb toward the door, he hesitated and looked at her hat. "Where'd ya unearth that bonnet?"

Placing a hand over his mouth and coughing, Mike's eyes traveled from Cooley to Peter and then back to Trudy, who stared at Cooley, a brow raised and lips pursed.

"And what is that supposed to mean?"

"It means where'd ya get your bonnet? What'd ya think I meant? I jest asked."

"Well, I declare," Trudy exclaimed in amazement, a pleased grin spreading across her face. "You want to purchase one for Alice, don't you?"

Astonishment crossed Cooley's face, and Mike braced himself for what might spew out of his mouth.

Scratching his head, Cooley glanced at Mike uncertainly and then back at Trudy's hat. "Well, I don't rightly know about that, but...uh...your bonnet shore is somethin' all right."

"Excuse me please," Reverend Clark said, running a finger around the inside of his clerical collar, "I need to speak with Henry regarding an event." Hurrying down the steps, he headed toward a group of men and then stopped, turned back, and grinned at Mike.

Peter, you chicken, you bolted and ran, Mike thought. Shaking his head, he stuck both hands in his pockets and looked back at Trudy, whose voice rose in volume. "Mercy sakes, Cooley, you really do admire my hat."

His face a bright red, Cooley shifted from one foot to the other, and his eyes darted to those within earshot. "Well, by jingees, now that ya ask," he said loudly, "I'd say it's right seasonal with all them there leaves and nuts. Ya best hope a squirrel don't take note, or he'll be chasin' ya all over the countryside." Guffawing, he slapped the side of his leg. "That there was a joke, ya know."

"I certainly hope so!" Trudy retorted, noting several glancing their way.

"Awww, Trudy, ya know I was jestin'. It's a right fine bonnet."

Fingering one of its leaves, she looked at Mike. "What about you, Pastor Mike?"

"What?" Caught off guard, Mike watched her raise and tilt her head, deliberately affording him an unwanted perusal of the awful looking thing.

"What do you think of my hat? Do you like this one or the one I wore last Sunday?"

"Yeah, Preacher, which one of them bonnets do ya reckon ya like best?" Cooley asked, leaning toward him with an outrageous grin plastered on his face. "I expect ya got a real good look, standin' up there in the pulpit and all."

Mike glared at Cooley, knowing what he was up to, and then scanned the church lawn for a glimpse of Leah. *Where was your wife when you needed her?*

"Now tell me what you really think, Pastor," Trudy continued, turning her head one way and then the other. "I can't make up my mind. I thought this one suited Founders Day, but the one I wore last week would have also. I asked Henry which was more appropriate, but he only said a hat is a hat, so he was no help. I really would like your opinion."

"By jingees, I would too," Cooley interjected, the silly grin still in place. "Come on, Preacher, tell us what ya think?"

"Well, I think both hats are...remarkable, Trudy. In fact, all your hats are *indescribable,* and they...well, no one else could wear them," Mike replied, trying to remember what monstrosity she wore last Sunday. And what difference did it make which one he liked? The one on her head was the one she had decided to wear.

"I expect I'd have to agree with ya on that, Preacher. Them bonnets jest *epitomize* yer personality, Trudy."

Raising a brow, Mike stared at him, wondering how *epitomize* made its way into his vocabulary of slang and bad grammar.

"That there's my word of the week," he stated proudly. "Me and Alice learn a new word every Monday. Heard 'em talkin' about it on the radio the other week right after *Fibber McGee and Molly* was over. We thought it'd be a good idea," he said, waving a hand in the air. Tapping the side of his head with an index finger, he said importantly, "It never hurts a body to exercise his brain, and this ole noggin needs some exercizin'. But now, then, let's get back to Trudy's bonnet. She wants to know which one ya like best, this here bonnet or the one she wore last Sunday." Pointing a finger at Trudy's hat, he then hooked both thumbs in his suspenders and grinned, awaiting Mike's answer.

Observing the silly grin, an urge to choke Cooley floated around in the back of Mike's mind, and he entertained the idea he should have left him in jail when Sheriff Walker had him there. Rubbing his fingers across his chin, Mike turned slowly with a thoughtful expression and studied her hat.

"Hmm...I can't choose, Trudy; I really cannot. I guess we will have to let Cooley decide. What do you think? Which one do *you* like best...this one or the one she wore last week?" Mike asked, watching his grin turn to a scowl.

"Now, Preacher, I reckon she don't really want my notion about this. No, sir, it's yer thoughts Trudy wants, so I'll let ya take another crack at it."

"Oh, you two," Trudy gushed, looking from one to the other. "Cooley, sakes alive, I was not aware you admired my hats. You know, now that I think about it, I have too many, but don't tell Henry I said so. And there are several I do not wear any longer. I will box them up and give them to Alice. I know she would enjoy wearing them, and you will have the pleasure of seeing them on her. Mercy sakes, why didn't I think of that before? What do you think of that idea?"

Startled, Cooley glanced at Mike with a direct appeal for help. Grinning slightly, Mike glanced up into the branches of a large oak. He was not about to get involved in this discussion. The urge to hightail it like Peter gripped him, but watching Cooley shift uncomfortably from one foot to the other was enough to keep him planted.

"Trudy, that is a very generous offer. Wouldn't you agree, Cooley?"

Scratching his head in exasperation, Cooley looked at him with narrowed eyes and then turned back to Trudy. "Well now I don't know much about ladies' bonnets and such, and since I'm not the one that'll be wearin' 'em, I expect ya should jest ask Alice herself. O' course, I reckon there's plenty other ladies who'd love yer bonnets, and they'd need 'em more than Alice—"

"No, no, I want Alice to have them. I can see them on her now; I surely can. I will just do that," Trudy replied, delighted. "You tell her I'll see she gets them one day this week, and don't you forget either." Filled with pleasure, Trudy headed for the steps and then turned back. "Oh, Cooley, I must say you did a fine job painting the cakewalk squares, a much better job than Mildred and I could have done, thank you. Gracious me. It's nine forty-five. I must see if everything's ready for this morning's ceremony. I trust Jimmy is ready to recite the Founders Day poem? I am sure he is. My soul, but committee chairman is a lot of work. I shall see you at the bandstand." Smiling, she touched her hat again and bustled down the steps.

Although Trudy's act was one of generosity, Mike couldn't help but feel sorry for Alice and the unexpected gift coming her way. Glancing sideways, he observed the frown on Cooley's face.

"Her and Mildred," Cooley remarked irritably, plopping his cap atop his head. "I caint see why they couldn't of jest marked squares in the street with chalk like they always do. I worked hard on that dance floor, Preacher, real hard. And they had to ruin it jest so they'd have a *permanent* cakewalk site. Ya know she did it 'cause she was against the square dancing."

"Now, Cooley," Mike replied, placing a hand on his shoulder, "did you ever stop and think that not only will the square dancers appreciate your hard work but those participating in the cakewalk will too? They will always remember what a fine job you did constructing the dance floor and providing a perfect place for the cakewalk. I think it is a contribution everyone will be grateful for."

Staring up into the trees, Cooley straightened his ball cap and then grinned. "By jingees, I never thought of that. Maybe it wasn't such a bad idea after all. Everbody'll know where to head when it's time for the cakewalk from now on, won't they?"

"They sure will. It will be an established fact that the cakewalk has its own official area, and it is all because of you."

"Ah, now, it's not that big of a deal, but thank ya for yer words," he replied, both proud and embarrassed. Smiling, he folded his arms and stood erect for a minute and then suddenly turned to Mike with a frown. "Blame it all, if messin' up my dance floor wasn't enough, now I'm goin' to have to look at them dad-burned bonnets all the time, and Alice is gonna skin me alive. She ain't goin' to like them things."

"You have to admit it was generous of Trudy. Women like hats, Cooley. Alice might enjoy them."

"Them things? I don't expect so…and if she does end up with 'em, it's all your fault."

"My fault?"

"Yes, sir. It's yer fault for gettin' me involved in this whole bonnet discussion in the first place."

"I did not get you involved in anything. You came out and asked where she got her bonnet."

"Well, it's jest what ya was wonderin' too, now wasn't it? Ya was just plumb too scared to ask."

"I was not afraid to ask. I was *smart* enough to *not* ask. Sometimes it is best to just look and not comment. What one person finds pleasing may not be to someone else, so it is wise on certain occasions to not say anything. That way you won't hurt anyone's feelings. That is the smart thing to do."

"There ya go…ya gonna preach me a sermon? I expect next ya'll be tellin' me there's somewheres in God's Holy Bible where it says somethin' about not askin' about bonnets?"

Bursting into laughter, Mike put his arm across Cooley's shoulder. "No, it doesn't, Cooley, but it does say that laughter is good for the soul, and I appreciate you making me feel good. You are a real blessing to me, do you know that?"

"No, by jingees, I didn't know that, and I appreciate yer words, Preacher. I sure enough do."

"Sit with us, Andrew." Leah indicated an unoccupied chair and smiled at the man her family was growing so fond of. Like many others, she was curious about his presence in Oak Grove. He did not attempt to hide his past and spoke freely of his childhood and years as an attorney. Sharing much of his life and home in Connecticut, he also unreservedly spoke of his travels abroad, his art gallery in New York, and his grandmother.

"You were not saving it for someone, were you?"

Shaking her head, Leah watched him take the seat and look around. What was this warm, caring man, who seemingly had everything, doing in Oak Grove? She asked Mike a few times, but he always replied, "The Lord brought him here, so let's enjoy his friendship." That Mike knew something she did not was evident, and she respected his silence on matters he was not at liberty to discuss.

"I am glad you are here to enjoy Founders Day with us, Andrew. "

"I am too, Leah. It is quite different than anything I have ever experienced," he said, his gaze roaming the crowd for two faces he longed to see.

Wood, folding chairs from the sunrise service were quickly filling for the eleven o'clock program, Mayor Driscol was speaking with Mayor Carter from Chesterville, the high school band had assembled, and Myrtle was coaxing an intimidated elementary choral group to line up.

Several children dressed in period clothing fidgeted on the front row, and Leah watched Jimmy and prayed he would feel confident while reciting the poem. A tender smile on her face, she thought of early this morning when he came into their bedroom for a *dress rehearsal* and stood at the foot of the bed, stared at the ceiling, and silently recited the words.

Glancing around, she caught sight of the tall form of her husband making his way in her direction. He stopped and spoke with Melvin and Mary, and she recalled Mike's words to "be patient and love and pray for them." *Perhaps one day,* she thought, watching Mike slowly move through the crowd. She smiled at the display of affection he received as he paused to say a word here and there. Greeting everyone with his ever-present smile, he casually laid his hand on a shoulder, touched another on the back, and shook hands with most everyone. At present, he stood with his head bent, listening to Lynn Miller. With a broad grin, he looked at Alan, shook his hand, and laughed at something said and then patted Lynn on the arm. Turning, his gaze found Leah's, and with a smile she knew to be for her, he nodded and continued making his way toward her.

"Is Founders Day always this well attended?" Andrew asked, amazed at the number of people gathered.

"Oh yes, and by two o'clock this afternoon it will be so crowded you will think everyone in the county is here."

"Well I know for certain there is not a room left at the hotel," Andrew remarked, thinking of those he met at dinner last night.

All arriving within an hour of one another, Andrew found the sound of extra footsteps in the hall, doors opening and closing, and conversation and laughter drifting through the hotel created a festive atmosphere. By the time dinner was served, he had met everyone and knew where they lived and how they had come to know the Cranstons. Lingering over coffee and enjoying their jovial camaraderie, he lost track of time and almost missed the kickoff at the football game.

"The hotel is always full this weekend, from now through the holidays," Leah said. "Our little town seems to draw tourists this time of year."

"I can see why; the valley is beautiful, and the town is charming."

"Hi, darlin'," Mike said, taking a seat and sliding his arm along the back of her chair. Reaching across, he shook Andrew's hand. "What do you think of Founders Day, Andrew?"

"Very enjoyable, good football game last night, this morning's sunrise service blessed me, and what can I say about the pancake breakfast."

"I know what you mean."

Mike's eyes roamed the crowd. "Are the kids all in place?"

"Yes, but Jimmy is very nervous. What will we do if he clams up and refuses to say anything?"

"He will do fine, darlin'. We prayed about it this morning."

"Oh, I am so glad," Leah said softly, studying her husband's profile. So that was what Jimmy wanted when he ran up asking for Mike's whereabouts. Upon questioning, he said it was something he needed to "talk about with Dad, man to man."

Chatter and laughter subsided, and all eyes turned toward the front as Oak Grove's school band and the choir began the first strains of "My Country 'Tis of Thee."

Taking note of their children, Mike and Leah glanced at one another and grinned. Shari and her best friend Maggie were holding hands and singing lustily, and Johnny was clearly uncomfortable standing next to Kim Reese, who had developed a crush on him. Jimmy was not singing at all, and Laura, standing next to Elizabeth, turned and looked at her in astonishment as her off-key voice rose several decibels. Elizabeth was not making any attempt to hide the fact she preferred to be anywhere but where she was, and with a look of satisfaction, she folded both arms and promptly sat down, ignoring the chuckles and the look Myrtle bestowed upon her.

Though a little confused as to the why, Mike was not surprised. Elizabeth was Elizabeth and generally said and did what she thought. Noting the stubborn set to her jaw, he grinned and then turned his attention to the podium. Mayor Driscol looked at his notes and cleared his throat while Trudy smiled proudly, her hat's orange bow and feathers blowing in the breeze. Scheduled for this year's invocation, Peter Clark sat next to her, and Miss Mattie, oldest living relative of the original founding fathers, occupied the fourth chair. Old Ben and Elijah Seabaugh were in the second row next to William Hunter, Jeremiah Smith, and Dr. Miller, all ancestors of the early settlers.

The program proceeded much the same as previous years. Following Mayor Driscol's welcome, the Pledge of Allegiance was led by one of the senior boys, and then Reverend Clark gave the invocation. Myrtle, face red as a beet, glanced at Mike and nodded her approval of his tie as she moved to the podium.

Speaking loudly into the microphone, she announced that Oak Grove's elementary and high school choral group would present "God Our Help in Ages Past." Closing his eyes, Mike listened to the old refrain, reflecting on the early settlers' faith and all they endured. The brisk, October air was clean and pure, the sun warm on his back, and Leah's arm linked within his filled him with love. Relishing the peace flooding his soul, he sighed deeply and then found the brief reverie suddenly interrupted. Opening his eyes, he stared at Elizabeth, who once again was all but shouting the last chorus.

Suppressing his laughter, Mike glanced at a shocked Trudy and then at Henry, who merely shrugged his shoulders. Leah masked a grin behind her hand, and several laughed aloud. Shaking his head, Mike glanced to his right, his gaze resting on Andrew, whose eyes were riveted on Elizabeth. The tender expression on his face laid bare his feelings and the turmoil he was experiencing. From where he stood, Mike saw the whites of Andrew's knuckles as he gripped the back of the chair in front of him. Lost in a world of his own, he watched his daughter as though mesmerized. Andrew's head turned slowly, and he looked at Mike, the depth of his love clearly exposed. Nodding slightly, Mike looked away and watched Trudy rise and step behind the podium, his heart aching for his friend

Touching her hat, Trudy looked curiously at Elizabeth and then cleared her throat, smiled, and looked across the crowd. "Now, dear friends, it is with great pride and pleasure that I introduce Oak Grove's first-grade class. They will present details of our founding fathers' journey and settlement of the valley. The presentation will conclude with the annual recitation of our Founders Day First Grade Poem. Written in 1860 by seven-year-old Jedediah Seaubaugh, it describes his father's thoughts of that journey. This year, Jedediah Seabaugh's poem will be recited by Jimmy Daniels."

Smiling proudly, Trudy took her seat, and the first-grade students filed past the crowd, and after a bit of confusion and switching places, they finally assembled on the steps. In turn, they announced the names of the settlers and shared facts of their journey, hardships encountered along the way, and a host of other particulars until each student had given some tidbit of information.

Mike felt Leah's hand slip into his when Jimmy stepped out of line and took his place at the podium. Dressed in a pair of black, button-fly trousers with suspenders, a white, cotton, collarless shirt, and a black, wool felt hat on his dark head, he looked every bit a young boy of 1860. Standing quietly, he hooked one thumb in his suspenders and put his other hand behind his back. Frowning, his eyes roamed the crowd, and then he turned and looked behind him. Mike saw old Ben nod his head and say something and then Jimmy turned back and stared at his feet.

Now, Son, come on. You can do it. We prayed about this, Mike thought, feeling Leah's hand tighten in his.

Trudy cleared her throat, those gathered became very quiet, and then Jimmy raised his head and looked across the crowd until his eyes met Mike's. Hooking both thumbs in his suspenders, he took a deep breath and then spoke in a loud, confident voice.

"A poem by Jedediah Seabaugh—"

Unfaltering, he recited the poem word for word and, much to Mike and Leah's surprise, even threw in a little flair on the last verse, holding a hand up to the hills.

Tall oak trees, deer, land, and clear streams,
Our fathers found the home of their dreams.

Looking intently into the crowd, he pointed his finger and with great emphasis proclaimed,

Father would often turn to me and say
Always remember to thank God when you pray
For He gave us this valley: Oak Grove, our home.

Smiling proudly, he bowed gallantly and waved as he took his place among the first graders. Removing the black, wool cap, he scratched his head and turned around in his chair and flashed a broad grin at his dad and mom.

Leah was correct. By two o'clock, Oak Grove was overflowing with people, the parking area full, and automobiles parked along streets for several blocks in all directions.

A steady flow of customers mingled in the Sweet Shoppe watching the candy-making process and good-naturedly attempting to distinguish Milly from Molly. Red wrapped Founders Day assorted chocolates were purchased as fast as they were boxed and free samples readily consumed.

Across the street at White's Bakery, the tantalizing aroma of brewed coffee and fresh-baked pastries filled the air. Fluffy, light, and delicate tarts, éclairs, petite fours, crème puffs, and napoleons filled glass cases, and donuts, coffeecakes, raspberry Danish, and sweet Brioche were boxed in anticipation for tomorrow's breakfast.

Many curious folks milled around the courthouse looking at artifacts, pictures, old documents, clothing, and records from the early days. Several of the townsfolk, wearing period clothing, moved among the visitors answering any and all questions relating to what a typical day might have been in 1830.

At the blacksmith shop, old Ben and young Ben demonstrated the once necessary trade of fashioning iron rims for carriage and wagon wheels, horse shoes, fireplace racks, and pothooks. Wearing leather apron and gloves, old Ben heated iron, hammered it into shape, and then cooled it, all the while spinning tales of a long-ago day when he was a boy, much to the delight of his listeners. Meandering about outside the large double doors, folks waited patiently for the next hay wagon that would transport them to the fairgrounds or the old mill.

Across the street at Williams Drugstore, the soda fountain was two deep with customers awaiting one of Gerald's famous creations and his *ultimate chocolate soda*. Reminiscing and visiting, they caught up on the latest news and learned what had transpired in the lives of those they had not seen since last year. Young and old good-naturedly argued over the marbles in the gallon jar and eyed up the seventeen-dollar Philco some lucky winner would take home.

Stepping out onto the sidewalk, Andrew glanced around, still chuckling at Ned's remark that the marbles in the jar came from Gerald's head. The Harmony Quartet filled the air with "Shine on Harvest Moon," Bingo was in full swing, and Cooley's dance floor swarmed with cake walkers moving to music from a Victrola on the porch of the hotel. The mixture of aromas in the air reminded him he was hungry, and he weaved his way in and out of the crowd toward the café, his eyes peeled for a glimpse of Caroline or Elizabeth. A long line of folks with the same idea was ahead of him, and he stepped to the back of the line, catching sight of a dark-haired young girl that reminded him of Elizabeth, and he grinned.

What on earth possessed her to sing so loudly this morning? She was undoubtedly demonstrating a point to someone. He also had done many foolish things as a boy to prove something he thought important at the time. *She is like me in more ways than one,* he thought with a mixture of pride and dread. *She is the one I will have to contend with.* Having nothing to base his assumption on but instinct and Mary's memory, he knew Caroline possessed her same sweet, forgiving nature, whereas Elizabeth...well, she was too much like him, and the hurdle would be great when the truth was known.

Elizabeth's face swam before him. She was so like him. How had he fooled so many people with only a beard and mustache? Recalling her hand movement as predominately left, he looked at his own, another small fact that she was a part of him.

Pastor Mike knows, he thought. *I saw it in his eyes, but how?*

Caroline came to mind, and he scanned the crowd for a glimpse of her, again amazed how much she looked like Mary.

"Are you looking for someone?"

Green eyes met his, and he grinned with pleasure, "Hello, Melba. Yes, I was...looking at the number of people that has flooded our little town."

"It is amazing, isn't it? They come from miles around every year. Most are the same folks, but there are always some here for the first time, like...Mr. Andrew Baxter, a famous New York artist."

"I don't think one could call me famous, but thank you," he replied, studying the beautiful face. The October sun streaked the mass of red curls with highlights, and her eyes sparkled with humor. A few freckles were sprinkled across the bridge of her nose, red lips curved into a bright smile, and he again found himself wishing for a paintbrush.

"Have you taken a wagon ride up to the old mill?" Melba asked, uncomfortably aware of his perusal.

"No, but I plan on it," Andrew commented, trying to decide if a formal portrait would suit her or a natural setting as today. Studying the green of her eyes, he knew it would be the most difficult shade to match.

"Not until I moved to Oak Grove had I...Andrew, for heaven's sake, will you stop staring at me. Do I have something on my face?"

"No," he laughed, smoothing his beard. "Your face, my dear, is perfect and one I would like to paint. I was studying your features."

"I did not know your talent included portraits, and why on earth would you want to paint me?" Melba asked, astonished.

"You reflect spirit and character," Andrew said matter-of-factly, continuing his scrutiny. "Painting an individual is much more than transferring an image to canvas. It is portraying that which sets him or her apart from everyone else. That is what I strive to capture."

Amazed at the character of this man she was coming to know, Melba studied him. He was a mystery. One minute he was an outrageous flirt with not a care in the world, and the next he revealed a depth one would never expect.

Pleased with her interest, Andrew hesitated and then asked, "Would you consider it?"

Awaiting her answer, he watched uncertainty cross her face and realized he was more than willing to commit himself to the time and effort it would take. A few weeks ago he was uncertain, but now…he needed and wanted time to know his daughters.

A shy smile touched her lips. "My goodness, it would be an honor, Andrew, but I think I would feel…strange somehow. I don't know. I am sure there are others that you find interesting."

"Sure, I have selected several, but you were the first to catch my attention. A portrait takes a lot of time, patience, and hard work. I may not be here long enough to paint all those I would like."

"Who else do you wish to paint?"

"Oh, I would love to paint old Ben," he replied, nodding his head. "He is full of wisdom and depth, and also Miss Mattie. She exemplifies grace and possesses a rare insight and knowledge that few people gain in this life. Then there is Cooley." He chuckled, noting her surprise. "He is one of a kind, unpretentious, and completely genuine."

Melba watched him run a thumb and forefinger across his mustache, astonished that within such a short time he saw attributes in people she had known for years and not noticed. "Also, there is Mayor Driscol's niece, the little dark-haired girl, Elizabeth."

The tone of his voice softened subtly, and Melba gazed at him curiously. Had she imagined it?

"She is full of life and quite spirited. One day she will be a remarkable young woman." Clearing his throat, he looked at her strangely and then smiled. "Well enough of that. Where is Willy?"

"Actually, here he comes now." Melba smiled as Willy walked toward them. Andrew quietly observed the way her face lit up, and Willy saw no one but her.

The hay wagon bumped along, leaving a small trail of straw. The hills were a riot of color in the glorious October sun, and Mike marveled at the beauty. He was as content as he had ever been. Chatter and laughter and the frequent toss of straw added to an already festive atmosphere, and Cooley, sitting on the wagon seat with reins held loosely in his hands, sang above the noise his own off-key rendition of "You Are My Sunshine."

Glancing up into the blue sky, Mike knew today would be tucked away in many a mind and reflected on through the years. Leah leaned comfortably against him, and he wondered what more a man could want out of life. He was conscious of a slight fragrance of her hair, and reflected on lifting her into the wagon a few minutes ago. Her trim form was not much changed from when they first married.

Laughing at something Ellen Madison said, she laid her head against his shoulder, and he impulsively rubbed his chin against her hair. Leah was the love of his life, and in a moment such as now, the sharp, clear memory of that long ago time, when he thought her lost to him forever, surfaced. Turning, she smiled at him, volumes of unspoken words passing between them.

"I did not know that," Ellen remarked excitedly. "Leah, did you know Lynn and Alan are expecting?"

"Yes," Leah replied, her attention drawn back to the women's conversation. "Isn't it wonderful? I am so happy for them."

Turning his ear from the women's conversation, Mike's gaze traveled to Andrew, sitting on the back of the wagon listening to Phillip Driscol earnestly tell him something. Watching the two, Mike pondered Phillips's reaction when he discovered the man he was speaking with was the father of his granddaughters. As loving and proud as any grandfather, he had doted on Caroline and Elizabeth from the first day Henry and Trudy had brought them home to Oak Grove. Would he feel threatened or pleased when he learned that their father, long since dead to them, was very much alive…And what about Henry and Trudy?

"Daddy," Shari said, tapping his shoulder as she knelt behind him.

"What, sugar?" Mike asked, noting the frown on his youngest daughter's face.

"Jimmy said all of the MoonPies are his. Are they?"

"What makes Jimmy think they belong to him? Did he give you a reason?"

"He said since he recited the poem today he should get all the MoonPies and when he gets home, he's going to put them in his room."

Frowning at her brother, she shook her head and looked at Mike. "I don't think that's fair. I sang, and so did Laura and Johnny."

"Come here." Pulling her around, Mike sat her on his lap and held her tight, allowing her legs to dangle from the side of the wagon.

Overhearing the complaint, Leah looked around at her beaming face as she tossed straw on the road. "Well, look at you, Shari."

Smiling, she tossed another handful. "This is fun. It is more fun than sitting in the middle of the wagon with Jimmy."

Noting Mike's arm firmly around their daughter, she smiled and fastened her sliding hair barrette. "You aren't afraid sitting on the edge of the wagon are you?"

"Nope, Daddy's holding me tight."

"Then you are safe, aren't you?" Leah asked, kissing her forehead and glancing up at Mike with a tender smile.

"You know what, Daddy?"

"What?" Mike asked, looking at the upturned face so like Leah's.

"It is pretty special that Jimmy was picked to recite the poem. I guess he should get the MoonPies if he wants them, 'cause he didn't make one single mistake, did he?"

"No, he did not. I was very proud of him."

"Me too, I've never been proud of him before. It's kind of nice for a change. I guess he deserves them."

Mike chuckled and hugged her. "Well, we'll see about that."

"All right folks, jest keep sittin' 'til I get pulled off the road," Cooley yelled over his shoulder. "I don't want none of ya hurt."

If one thought the square was crowded, the fairgrounds were more so, with meandering folks talking, laughing, and observing a time in history come alive. A covered wagon was laden with items used by the early settlers, and several folks were dressed in period clothing: long dresses, bonnets, buckskins, and boots. Women cooked over open fires, young boys split logs, and men cleaned shot guns and told of shooting, skinning, and preserving animal hides.

A large kettle of apple butter lent its aroma to the brisk, cool air, and across the field, Lottie and Hannah busily made soap from a concoction of lard, wood ashes, and a bit of lavender for fragrance. The cooled bars, once cut and wrapped in colorful paper, were tied with ribbon to quickly become souvenirs for many.

Tables were laden with a variety of fruit pies, an assortment of cakes, every cookie imaginable, homemade breads and rolls, canned pickles, beets, jellies, and jams. Doilies that Grandma Hope made while recuperating from a back injury were displayed and sold along with quilts, pot holders, intricate tatting, and embroidered pillow cases and linens. Colorful knitted sock caps, scarves and sweaters were purchased for upcoming winter months, as well as afghans and shawls for the ladies.

Grandma Hope sat at a spinning wheel, several men from the lumber company displayed their skill at making chairs, benches, and small tables, and the homestead area featured a small cabin raising.

Several watched the horseshoe tournament underway, and an even larger crowd surrounded a large pen where several children chased a greased pig with a two-dollar bill tied to its tail. One last wild dive and Simon Walker jerked the bill from its tail, becoming the winner of the ten-to twelve-year-old division.

"Well, that is the last contest of the day," Alan Miller stated, looking at Ron Hanson and Eli Smith. "You two catch that pig and get him back in the truck."

"What makes you think you aren't going to help?" Ron replied, resting an arm on the fence post and waving to several passersby.

Glancing up at her older brother, Gloria laughed. "I have to see this. You have not chased a pig in forever, Ron."

"Well, sis, you aren't going to see me now either. Eli will do it."

"I don't think so. I promised Mary I would square-dance, and she won't like it if I smell like a hog."

Grinning at the arguing, Gloria walked away and fell into step with her sister-law-law, Betty and Lynn Miller.

"Congratulations, Lynn," Gloria commented, observing her glowing face. "I am very happy for you and Alan."

"Thank you, Gloria. What are they arguing about?" she asked, glancing back at the trio.

Gloria's gaze fell on Andrew talking to a gentleman she had never seen. He looked incredibly handsome wearing brown slacks and a tan shirt beneath a dark green and brown, plaid, crew neck sweater. His dark hair was tousled from the breeze, and she watched him unconsciously smooth his beard, and a broad grin crossed his face when the gentleman said something.

"Gloria?" Lynn asked, looking at her strangely.

"What? Oh, Lynn, I am so sorry. I did not hear what you said."

"It doesn't matter. I wondered what the men were talking about, but here they come. I think it is time we headed back to town for the square dance, don't you?"

"Yes, I think so," Gloria murmured, feeling the warmth of her cheeks. She had been caught admiring Andrew. Had Lynn noticed?

"Now remember, Gloria, I am depending on you to keep Ron busy most of the evening," Betty commented, pulling her along. "He tried to show me how to square dance all week, and I did promise to give it a try, but I don't know."

With the sun sinking behind the ridge, the late afternoon air had turned cooler, and Gloria threw her cardigan across her shoulders, wondering if Andrew would square dance. Somehow she doubted it.

"Don't be bashful, and don't be afraid. Swing on the corner in a waltz promenade," Spade Jackson called loud and clear.

White lights swayed and twinkled around Cooley's dance floor as square dancers swirled and swung their partners to a lively fiddle and banjo. Laughing at bumbling mistakes and the frequent loss of partners, those participating for the first time provided great entertainment for onlookers preferring to rest on picnic tables, benches, and wooden folding chairs. Children raced back and forth, and many folks strolled beneath the oaks in the cool, night air, the half moon's glow and corner street lamps lighting the square.

"Oh, how Daniel and I loved to square-dance," Miss Mattie sighed. Sitting on one of the benches and tapping her cane, she watched the fiddler and banjo player with delight as they increased the tempo and those on the dance floor laughed uproariously at one another.

"If I was just a couple of years younger, I would be out there kicking up my heels."

"I don't doubt that in the least, Miss Mattie." Mike chuckled, glancing fondly at the stately lady sitting on the bench beside Leah and Hannah.

"I suppose I could try, but—"

"Lord have mercy, Miss Mattie," Hannah exclaimed, turning wide, black eyes on her. "Ya'll do no such thing. Fall down and break yer neck, and then wouldn't ya know Jeremiah and ah'd have ta haul ya home or over ta Doc Miller's. Ya can come up with some of the foolest notions ah ever heard tell." Shaking her head in exasperation, she glanced up at Mike. "Pastor, ya tell her ta stay sittin' and get that harebrained idea out of her head right now."

"Oh, Hannah, you know I have more sense than do something so foolish. I fear I might trip someone with my cane."

"Well, ah should hope so, land sakes."

"No, those days are gone," she said softly, turning a deliberate gaze on Mike. "Now what is the matter with you, Pastor Mike? Why do you not have this pretty wife of yours out there? And do not give me some pitiful excuse like Reverend Clark, saying it is not proper and he is too old. You are young yet."

"I might be young enough, and I could not have a more beautiful partner, Miss Mattie," he replied, grinning at Leah, "but my wife knows my dancing ability. Out of mercy, I will not embarrass her."

Raising a skeptical brow, she turned to Leah.

"Thank the Lord for small favors, Miss Mattie," Leah whispered. "He does know his limits. Although very agile otherwise, he does lack something on a dance floor if the music is something other than a slow song. He does all right then, but...we better just sit and watch."

"Very well then," Mattie replied, patting Leah's hand. Turning, she stared at Andrew standing next to Mike with his hands in his pockets and watching the hilarity on the dance floor. "And what might be your excuse Mr. Baxter?"

"Me?"

"Yes, you. What is your excuse?"

Glancing apprehensively at Mike, Andrew turned back to Miss Mattie, the thought crossing his mind that it would not be unlike her to call someone over to drag him out there.

"I am sure I have never learned to...dance like that," he replied, nodding his head toward those who appeared to be running in confused circles.

"Oh, goodness gracious, there is nothing to it. You just follow along and do what everyone else does."

"I think I will just watch," he replied, noting Mike's grin.

"I do not know what is wrong with this younger generation. Before you know it, you will be like me...unable. Then you will wish you had. Regrets are unnecessary burdens," she said, thumping her cane on the ground.

Andrew studied her a moment, pondering on her tone of voice and knew she was aware he was watching her. Turning her head slowly, she looked up at him and commented softly, echoing his grandmother's words, "Do not store up regrets, Andrew."

Staring into the warm, gray eyes, he knew she was not referring to dancing. He had experienced the same uncanny feeling the first time they met, and he couldn't help but wonder what she knew.

"I will try not to, Miss Mattie."

"Well, Pastor Mike, I have to admit," Trudy Driscol stated, coming to stand beside him, "I was wrong, and you were right. I believe everyone is enjoying the square dance. My word, but so many have thanked me for coming up with the idea. I had to think about it long and hard, but now I…why, even the youngsters are trying it. Did you see them? Land sakes, I would much rather see them square-dancing than kicking their legs around doing that infernal jitterbug. This is more like a game, isn't it? Yes, I think it was a splendid idea."

"I must say, Trudy, you did another marvelous job organizing the events, and I believe this year is the best," Mike replied, noting her pleased expression. "I think you made a wise choice to include the square dance."

"I agree with Pastor Mike, Trudy," Miss Mattie commented. "We could not have Founders Day without your planning expertise. Thank you, my dear, for all your hard work."

"Thank you, Miss Mattie, for your speech. It was wonderful. Land sakes, but I was worried when they told me you were not feeling well earlier in the week."

"It was nothing, my dear, just a little spell of old age that bites occasionally. And speaking of old age, I think I shall take this old body home, put on my gown and robe, and drink a nice cup of hot tea. I have had enough excitement for one day."

Taking the arm Andrew offered, she rose slowly to her feet and glanced once more at the couples on the dance floor waiting for the music to begin again. Looking up at Andrew, she smiled and patted his arm. "You need a nice, pretty girl to court, Andrew. It would be good for you. Everyone needs someone. Now," she said, glancing at the others, "I must say good night."

"Let me walk you to the car," Mike offered, stepping over and taking her arm. "I see Jeremiah is waiting."

"I told him we would be ready to leave at seven thirty, and I do not have to look at my watch. Jeremiah is very punctual. Good night, Leah, Andrew. Come along, Hannah."

Running a hand across his beard, Andrew watched Pastor Mike lead her across the square, his hand beneath her elbow. Hannah carried the afghan she had thrown across her knees and was talking animatedly as they approached Jeremiah waiting by the '41 Packard. Miss Mattie reminded him of Grandmother. *Perhaps it is her wisdom,* he thought with a touch of melancholy. Another burst of laughter caught his ear, and he turned back to the dance floor.

Gerald Reese looked strange, minus his soda jerk hat and white apron, and as though free to be someone else for a short time, he swung his wife around with all the carefree abandon of a much younger man. In fact, Andrew mused, they all did. Hank and Sally appeared to know exactly what they were doing, and Sam and Abigail Cranston and their guests were totally enjoying themselves and appeared more practiced than the others. Willy was having difficulty, and in a moment of confusion, he and Melba, Michael and Ellen Madison, and Jim and Jennifer Walker all collided. The look of surprise on their faces quickly turned to a fit of laugher. Then they seemed to get back into the swing of things.

Chuckling, Andrew figured square dancing could not be that difficult, and what difference did it make anyway? No one seemed to care if they were doing it correctly or not. How different this was from New York. Grinning, he thought of some of the women he had dated in the past and how mortified they would be if exposed to a night such as this. As far as he was concerned, they did not know what they were missing. How refreshing, he thought, his eyes falling on Cooley.

He stood directly across the dance floor tapping his toes and gesturing wildly as he talked to everyone within earshot. Old Ben and several of his old cronies were gathered close to the water fountain observing everything, and a group of teenagers talked animatedly among themselves

His gaze rested on Caroline smiling prettily at a young man he knew to be Peter Williams. He was clearly smitten, and a gut-wrenching sensation filled Andrew when she tossed her head to one side, lowered her eyes, and glanced coyly up at him. How could she have grown up so fast? She should still be five years old, and who and what kind of young boy was this Peter Williams anyway? His father owned the shoe store, but he knew nothing else about him. Smoothing his beard, he watched and realized he had been just as smitten with Mary, and a deep, buried longing crept to the surface.

The music stopped, and his attention was drawn back to the dance floor. Directly in front of him, Ron Hansen continued to swing his sister in a circle and then abruptly released her. Staggering to the right, Gloria held out a hand to catch herself, and Ron grabbed her by both arms to prevent her from falling. Looking up into her brother's laughing face, she fell into a fit of giggles and pounded his shoulder with a small, closed fist.

Her thick, dark hair, unusually loose and free, swung around her shoulders, and lifting a hand, she brushed it away from her face. Large hazel eyes were bright and full of merriment, her cheeks glowed, and her smile was one he had not seen. Andrew stared at the young girl as she walked from the dance floor. Gloria was a very pretty, young woman.

"Mr. Baxter, are you enjoying yourself?" Trudy asked. "I am so happy you chose to stay in Oak Grove for Founders Day. Aren't you, Pastor Mike?"

"Yes, I am," Mike replied. "Was it worth it, Andrew?"

"Indeed, it has been a most enjoyable day. I would not have missed this for anything in the world. In fact, I hope to make it again next year."

"I'll swan, but that would be wonderful," Trudy exclaimed, placing both hands together. "You must really come out to the house and have dinner with us soon. My gracious, we would love that, and I apologize again. My goodness, where are my manners? I have just been so busy with preparations for Founders Day that—"

"Don't give it a second thought, Mrs. Driscol. You have had a lot of responsibility on your hands," he replied, wondering if visiting the house Caroline and Elizabeth called home was a good idea.

"Elizabeth hung the willow tree painting in her bedroom. That was so nice of you. It is beautiful, and she is quite proud of it. You must really come and see it. I will check Henry's schedule and—"

"Aunt Trudy," Elizabeth exclaimed, rushing up with a look of exasperation, "if Preston Walker doesn't leave me alone, I'm going to knock his block off."

"Elizabeth, you will do no such thing!" Trudy exclaimed, shocked. "Oh, dear, where is Henry. Laura, what did she do?"

"She hasn't done anything, Mrs. Driscol," Laura answered, looking at Elizabeth and then up at her dad, "not yet anyway."

"I am. I am going to punch him in the nose."

"Elizabeth! Whatever is the matter with you?"

Andrew watched his daughter in amusement. She stood with arms akimbo and a frown on her face. Her head was tilted sideways, her jaw set at a stubborn angle, and her blue eyes dark with anger. Laura appeared ready to laugh as she looked from Trudy to her father, and Noelle, fiddling nervously with one of her long braids, was watching Elizabeth with wide eyes.

"What is the problem, Elizabeth?" Mike asked with a slight smile. Placing a hand on her shoulder, he glanced briefly at Andrew and then back at Elizabeth.

"Pastor Mike, Preston won't leave me alone. He is a brat!"

"Elizabeth!" Trudy exclaimed, placing a hand to her cheek. "My gracious, don't be saying such things, especially not in front of Pastor… You shouldn't talk like that at all."

"Elizabeth doesn't think Preston is really a brat," Laura remarked, looking at Trudy and then back at her father, rolling her eyes. "She just—"

"Yes I do. He is a brat."

"Preston may be a little rambunctious, but I don't think he is a brat," Mike said, his hand still on her shoulder as he looked down into eyes that clearly betrayed Andrew's secret. Glancing at Leah with a grin, he winked and then turned back to Elizabeth.

"When others do things that annoy us, it is usually best to overlook it. As I recall, one Sunday someone glued several Annie Armstrong Easter offering envelopes together while I was preaching," he said, wanting to laugh at the culprit's guilty face. "But I just paid it no mind and figured it would not happen again."

"Oh dear," Trudy mumbled, frowning at Elizabeth. The Annie Armstrong envelopes; she had complained to the WMU ladies herself that some young person needed a good lesson in respect, and here it was Elizabeth all the time. She just knew it.

Tapping a toe impatiently, Elizabeth looked up at Mike and then glanced down at the ground and played with a button on her sweater. Sighing, she looked at Laura then back at Mike.

"Well… but… Preston thinks he is so smart! I can run faster than him. I outran him today, and now he keeps saying he *let* me win. He picks on me at school and brings me junk like we are best friends or something. What do I want with an old, dirty rabbit's foot and a cricket?"

Making a muscle, she shook her head and retorted, "He tells me how strong he is. Gee whiz, I don't care if he is Superman."

"Well," Mike replied, scratching his chin and glancing at Andrew, who was watching her with affection and trying not to laugh, "I think Preston is probably trying to show you how much he wants to be your friend."

"My friend? He already is my friend. I think he's doing things backwards, or he's lost all his marbles," she said, running a finger in circles by her ear as she looked at Laura and Noelle and giggled.

"Well that is my opinion. What do you think, Andrew?"

"I would have to agree with Pastor Mike, Elizabeth. Boys do things sort of backwards some of the time."

"Some of the time?" she asked, looking up at him curiously. "Did you ever do anything backwards, Mr. Baxter?"

Andrew stared down into his daughter's eyes, a strong urge to hug her holding him in its grip. "I am afraid so, sweetheart," he said softly, unaware of his term of endearment. "I have done things backwards and upside down many times for the sake of a pretty young lady."

Laying his Bible on the night table, Mike switched the lamp off, rolled to his side, and pulled Leah into his arms. A tender smile touched his lips as she snuggled close. Her slow, even breathing bore evidence of slumber, and he inhaled the familiar fragrance of soft hair against his cheek. His gaze rested on the bureau mirror, and he watched the shadowed reflection of tree branches beyond the window sway and dance in hypnotic rhythm. The clock's slow, regular tick added to the sweet peace and quiet of an end to a perfect day.

Worn out when they returned home, baths were taken, and Jimmy, with a change of heart, shared MoonPies with everyone as they gathered for their devotion.

Leah stirred slightly, and Mike cuddled her close. Andrew's lonely face came to mind, and he could still see the love and anguish in his eyes as he watched Elizabeth. It was heartbreaking. If only he could help him, give support and encouragement, anything. But he would have to wait for Andrew to confide in him. *Lord, this is another situation of which you are in control. I will wait for you to show me what to do for all of them, Andrew, Caroline and Elizabeth, and Henry and Trudy. And, oh Lord, Miss Tillie. I don't know how all of this is going to play out. I really need your guidance in that state of affairs.*

A dog barked somewhere, and the image of Jack following Willy came to mind. He had no doubt that Willy and Melba were in love. It was obvious. He was happy for them but also troubled. Willy was happier than he had ever seen him, had come out of his shell, and attended church regularly, but Mike suspected the latter was to please Melba. If that were the case, their relationship would never stand. Her faith was strong, and she would want a husband who shared it. *Lord, you promised your word would not return to you void, and I am trusting that the messages you give me will touch Willy's heart. He has been running from you so long, I would think he would soon tire of it.*

Yawning, Mike closed his eyes and thought of Mrs. Tyler and Louise and how close the end was. *Take her gently and peacefully home, Lord. She is ready. And help me to minister to both when the time comes.*

Eyes heavy and his body relaxed, the last thought in Mike's mind as he drifted off to sleep was standing behind the church by the Sumac bushes and Jimmy's dark eyes looking up at him, "Dad, I need you to pray with me about this dumb poem."

Chapter 19

Cold and rainy, the weather on October 31, 1946, reflected the feelings of many in Oak Grove. Staring at the withered flowers on the mound of dirt, Mike was oblivious to the wind and misting rain. The Lord had sustained all of them the last couple of days, and he knew Louise would know God's strength and comfort in the months to come. He was sure of it.

Mrs. Tyler's passing was peaceful. The telephone woke him from a dead sleep, and he knew before he lifted the receiver and heard Hazel's voice the time had come. The clock on the bedside table read 3:35, and within twenty minutes, he was pulling up in front of the Tyler home. Louise met him at the door teary eyed and said she believed Mother was waiting for him. Sitting next to the bed, he took her hand and looked down into the ashen face. Opening her eyes, she smiled faintly and then closed them again, feebly trying to squeeze his hand. Clasping her frail hand in his, Mike prayed and spoke quietly to her while Louise sat on the edge of the bed and cried softly. Dr. Miller arrived and confirmed what Mike knew. Shaking his head, he patted Louise's shoulder and then sat in a rocker across the room. Mildred Reese arrived forty-five minutes later, and, taking matters in hand, brewed Louise a cup of tea, put the percolator on the stove, and began tidying up. Early morning hours passed slowly as they watched and waited, and at 7:35, Ruth Ann Tyler slipped peacefully away and journeyed home.

Thunder rumbled in the distance, and Mike looked up at the sky and then the forest beyond the cemetery. Brilliant leaves, their colors muted from the gray mist, would soon be gone and branches would be stark and cold through the long winter months. A soft smile crossed his lips. Spring would follow, bursting forth overnight and bringing new life, hopes and dreams, babies, and the inevitable loss of other loved ones.

"Thank you, Lord," he spoke aloud. "Thank you for loving us the way only you do and for holding us in the palm of your hand from one season to the next."

Mist turned to drizzle, and he turned and headed toward the church. Quickening his pace, he reached the church steps and took them two at a time, the rain turning to a downpour as he opened the door and stepped in.

"Out in the rain and without a hat!" Myrtle exclaimed in exasperation as he passed her door.

"Good morning to you too, Myrtle," he called, stepping into his office.

"I don't know why you don't listen," she said, standing in the doorway with one hand on her hip. "I'll swan, but you are a stubborn man, Pastor Mike. Why in heaven's name don't you take care of yourself. I pity poor Leah, I sure do."

"I take care of myself," Mike replied, draping his jacket across the back of the chair by the bookcase. Snatching it up, she hung it on the hook behind the door, a routine he had grown accustomed to over the years.

"Your jacket belongs on the coat hook; the chair is for sitting," she used to say but now only snatched it up and hung it on the hook. Clucking around like a mother hen, she would retreat back across the hall and then return with his coffee.

It hadn't taken Mike long to recognize Myrtle's need to look after someone, and he was her target, so he allowed her to scold, reprimand, and advise him on any and all matters. He occasionally humored her on something she felt strongly and also praised her when she actually came up with a good idea. All in all, their relationship was warm and congenial.

"Myrtle, when was the last time I was sick?"

"You had the grippe two years ago, and don't tell me you didn't. I talked to Leah, and she told me how sick you were. A preacher is not above illness, you know."

"I hardly think that counts. Everyone in Oak Grove had it, so—" Mike replied, looking at her curiously. Something was different about her this morning. She wore one of her typical, tailored dresses, dark hair streaked with gray pulled back and held in place with bobby pins, and she was presently looking at him over the black rims of her reading glasses. *Myrtle is wearing lipstick,* Mike realized surprised. "You are wearing lipstick, Myrtle."

"The weather makes my lips dry," she retorted, turning red, "and don't try changing the subject," she threw over her shoulder, stepping across the hall to her office and missing the grin that crossed his face.

"You just ask to get sick," she continued, reappearing with his coffee. "Anyone with any brains knows you don't run around bareheaded in cold weather."

"Thank you, Myrtle. There is nothing like a warm cup of coffee on a cold, rainy day."

"Cold, rainy day he says," she mumbled, watching raindrops hit the window. "At least I have sense enough to wear my headscarf. If I didn't, I would be sick as sure as anything."

"Well, I don't have a headscarf."

"That's it, just poke fun. Maybe I'll get you one for Christmas," she retorted, crossing the room.

"If it matters any, I think your lipstick looks nice," he remarked, watching her stare through the window. "It gives you color and a nice healthy look."

"In another month this will be ice and snow," she answered, ignoring the compliment. "Then you will be ill for sure."

"No I won't. You know I very seldom get sick," Mike replied, sipping his coffee and thanking the Lord for his good health. "Besides, it isn't that cold. Old Ben's shop doors are still open. When he closes them, then you know it is cold."

"That might be so, but he at least keeps a good warm fire going and wears a hat like every other man in town."

"Will you quit worrying? I am used to going bareheaded. That makes a difference, you know."

"What makes a difference?" Dr. Miller asked, appearing in the doorway.

"Dr. Miller," Louise exclaimed, looking at Mike in triumph. "Maybe you can tell this hardheaded preacher he should wear a hat in weather like this. He is going to catch his death if he doesn't." Shaking her head, she frowned at Mike and then looked at the kind man in the doorway.

"Would you care for a cup of coffee?"

"No, Myrtle, thank you. I only have a few minutes." Stepping aside, he allowed her to pass.

"In trouble again, are you?" Robert Miller chuckled.

"I guess you might say so," Mike replied, grinning. "What brings you out in this rain?"

"I have to make my calls whether it rains or not," Dr. Miller said, shaking raindrops from his hat. "I don't have to tell you what that is like, do I?"

"No, you don't. What's on your mind?"

"We need to talk about Miss Tillie," he said, taking a seat in the chair. "I don't know what to do with her."

A feeling of trepidation crept over Mike at the concern on his face. "What is wrong with Miss Tillie?"

"Her spells are lasting longer, Pastor, and it worries me. I went by Monday, and we had a good visit talking about Founders Day and this and that. She was even raking leaves."

"Why on earth was she doing that?" Mike asked. "I told her Johnny would rake her leaves."

"I asked her the same thing, and she said it was such a pretty day she wanted to spend some time outdoors. She was fine, but when Margaret dropped by yesterday, she was out on the porch dressed in all her finery and waiting for Jake, whoever that might be, to bring the carriage around. She said they were going into Richmond. This morning I figured she would be back to normal, but when she opened the door, she was all gussied up again, complaining Sadie didn't polish the silver as she should."

Chuckling, Dr. Miller looked at Mike and shook his head. "She said if the Yanks were going to steal her silverware, it should at least be nice and shiny."

"She is always concerned with her silverware," Mike replied, smiling slightly and wondering why, out of everything she owned, her silverware was so important. "What should we expect, Robert?" he asked, tapping a pencil on his desk.

"Her symptoms should gradually occur more frequently and last longer." Running a hand through his thinning, gray hair, he shook his head, "but it is puzzling. The intervals are actually getting longer. I believe this is the first spell she's had in almost a month. Nevertheless, if the pattern persists and she stays confused for any length of time, I fear what she might do or where she might go."

Doctor Miller shook his head in frustration, sat back in the chair, and, removing his spectacles, rubbed his eyes, sighed, replaced them, and looked back at Mike. "I don't think she should be living alone."

Leaning back in his chair, Mike watched rivulets of rain stream down the window pane. Phillip Driscol had explained his responsibility in full detail when he had agreed to become Miss Tillie's power of attorney. Decisions made in her best interest were his at this point, and though they had talked at length about many things, Mike realized there were delicate matters he and Miss Tillie still needed to discuss.

The two men sat silent for a few minutes, the only noise that of the clock on the shelf and Myrtle striking typewriter keys across the hall.

"I really believe she should not live alone anymore, Pastor Mike, and I hate to burden you with this, but I am very concerned."

"Miss Tillie is not a burden, Robert," Mike replied softly. Turning away from the window, he looked across the desk at the kind doctor who had given so much of his life to the folks in this town. "We just need to find out what the Lord wants us to do. Is there the possibility that someone could live with her? Or do you not recommend such an arrangement?"

"That would be the ideal situation." Running his finger around the brim of his hat, he sat forward in his chair and looked at Mike. "She is as healthy as a horse physically and would not require much care. She just needs someone in the house to keep an eye on her during her bad days, but who? She has no family that I know of."

No one but Andrew, Mike thought, but that was out of the question, since Andrew did not even know.

"I suppose we could ask around, but I can't think of anyone right off the top of my head."

"Robert, we can look around all we want, but the Lord has already chosen someone to meet her need. Let's just allow him to show us who that might be."

Doctor Miller nodded in agreement and smiled at the man across the desk. He possessed a great deal of wisdom for a man of his years. Never in his life had he ever met a man who could take a problem or concern and turn it over to the Lord so quickly with such trust and confidence as Pastor Mike.

"Then that is just what we will do." Standing to his feet, he leaned toward Mike and lowered his voice. "Is Myrtle wearing lipstick?"

Chuckling, Mike rose and glanced toward the door. "Yes, she is. I guess we are seeing a wild side of her we didn't know existed."

"I wonder if it has anything to do with Clyde?"

"Clyde?" Mike asked, surprised. What on earth would Clyde have to do with Myrtle's lipstick?

"His cab was parked at her house one evening last week, and I don't think he takes piano lessons." Grinning, he slipped into his coat. "I know Clyde is lonely since Gertrude died. It has been about four years I expect, hasn't it?"

"I think closer to five," Mike said, recalling Clyde dropping off a box of bulletins for Ron a couple of weeks ago. He had hung around and talked to Myrtle for several minutes.

"I believe you are right, Mike. Well, I guess I need to make some house calls instead of standing around starting rumors, don't you think?"

"I suppose so. I will drop by and see Miss Tillie today, Robert," Mike said, following him to the door. "Thanks for coming by. Be praying with me on this matter."

"I will, and I wanted to thank you for your message at Ruth's funeral yesterday. It was very comforting and full of assurance. Several have commented on it."

"That was the Lord's doing, Robert. He gave me the words."

"That was very evident. I must go, and *yes*, you probably should wear a hat in this weather," he remarked loudly. Glancing at the top of Mike's head, he grinned and glanced across the hall. "Good day, Myrtle."

"Good day, Dr. Miller," she answered, smiling at Mike.

Standing in his doorway he watched Dr. Miller walk down the hall and then turned and observed Myrtle rummaging through the side drawer of her desk. *Myrtle and Clyde?*

"What? Did you need something?" she asked, glancing up. What was he staring at?

"Oh...no, nothing. I am going over to Miss Tillie's and then checking on Louise."

"You heard Dr. Miller, wear your hat."

Replacing the last five book returns, Gloria walked to her desk, placed the ink pad and date stamp in the side drawer, and retrieved her handbag. Out of sorts, she didn't know if she wanted to punch someone or just sit down and have a good cry. *Good grief,* she thought. *What is the matter with me?* Retrieving the key from her handbag, she snapped it shut. *Why am I so angry?*

Lifting her coat from the rack, she slipped it on, grabbed her umbrella, and realized Andrew was the cause of her anger. He had been in the library...what, three times? Dropping by to deliver his painting, he returned twice for books. What did she expect? She had asked to display his painting. He was pleasant and chatted on each occasion, but was that supposed to mean something? No, it did not mean a thing, and she realized she was angry with herself for acting like a love-struck teenager. Andrew was a gentleman who treated her with respect and kindness. Of course if she were Melba, he would be falling all over her.

The top desk drawer ajar, she walked over, slammed it shut, and sighed. Why couldn't he notice her a little anyway? It was not Melba's fault that she was pretty. Besides, she was in love with Willy.

Key in hand, she walked to the door and glanced at the window display. A couple of flowers were askew, and she straightened them, her gaze moving to Andrew's painting. She studied it a moment. It was very good, and she wondered if he knew how talented he was or how handsome.

He is probably the most attractive man I have ever met, she thought. Sighing, she tucked the flowers in place and glanced up, her face turning ten shades of red. There he stood, grinning at her through the window.

Feeling exposed, her heart pounded as she watched him walk toward the door. Surely he could not know what she was thinking.

"Are you locking up?" Dressed in a pair of gray trousers, a gray and black striped shirt, and a black, leather jacket, Gloria thought he never looked so handsome.

"I was just leaving. Did you need something?" An urge to slap his handsome face entered her mind, and she stared at him. Where on earth had that thought come from? What was wrong with her?

"I was returning my book," he replied, holding it up. "Lottie threw me out of the kitchen because I agreed with Mrs. Cranston that her beef stew could use a little more *something,* and she asked us both to go about our business," he said, chuckling. "I happened to remember my book was due, so I thought I would return it. I am sorry; I did not realize it was four o'clock."

Looking at her curiously, he titled his head and studied her. "Your face is flushed. Are you feeling all right?"

"I feel fine, thank you." The words came too fast and sharp, and she immediately regretted it. It was not his fault he did not find her attractive or that she felt like a starry-eyed, young girl when he was near. "I am sorry. Let me have it, and I will take care of it."

"I can bring it back tomorrow."

"No, that is not necessary, Andrew," Gloria replied, reaching for the book.

Maintaining a firm grip on it, he turned his head a little to the side and looked at her closely. "Are you sure you are okay?"

Acutely aware of his hand maintaining its hold, and with a surprising boldness Gloria jerked the book from his hand. "Thank you, Andrew. I will take care of this tomorrow. Now if you will excuse me, I was just leaving."

Raising a brow, Andrew was taken aback by her unusual rude behavior, and he watched her place it on her desk with a thud and then turn and walk toward him with a look something akin to defiance. Anger had turned her large gray eyes almost blue, a flush of pink stained her cheeks, and Andrew once more was aware of how lovely she was. Perplexed, he stepped toward the door and placed a hand on the doorknob, watching her fiddle with her handbag, glance at him, and then look away.

Why she is about to cry, Andrew thought, noting the watery eyes. "Gloria," he said, placing both hands on her arms. "What is the matter?"

"Nothing, I am fine."

"No, you are not. Something has upset you. What is it?" he asked, genuinely troubled. She always seemed so in control. "Perhaps it is none of my business."

Observing his concern, Gloria felt guilty and stared beyond him through the window, the touch of his hands on her arms unnerving, to say the least. She was acting absurd and should not treat him this way.

"Andrew, I am very sorry." Stepping away, she spoke softly. "I have had a very trying day and…am out of sorts. Please forgive me for taking it out on you."

"Well now, my favorite little librarian, there is nothing to forgive. We all have days like that. You just need to yell at someone," he replied. "Isn't that what you would like to do?"

She had to agree with that and glanced at him sheepishly. If he only knew he was the one she wanted to yell at.

"I knew it. Come on."

"What?" Gloria asked as he took her by the arm and steered her out the door.

"We are going somewhere to let you yell your head off." Taking the key from her hand and locking the door he then glanced around the square. "How about the bell tower? You could shout at the whole town from up there. Or perhaps the acoustics would be better on top of the courthouse."

Gloria stared openmouthed then observed the humor on his face and laughed. "Wouldn't everyone in Oak Grove think I had gone mad?"

"That is better. You have a beautiful smile, Gloria, and I like it much better than that old frowny face you were wearing."

"I am really sorry, Andrew. Thank you."

"It is my pleasure, my sweet friend. Allow me to walk you home."

"That is not necessary. You probably—"

"Please allow me. I cannot go back to the hotel just yet, or I may find myself in trouble again. And besides, I would not want a goblin to get you."

"All right then, since you are so frightened of Lottie, you may walk with me," she answered with a bright smile, dropping the key in her handbag.

All traces of anger gone, she breathed in the brisk, late afternoon air and welcomed its coolness against her warm cheeks. She was aware of the scent of his cologne, his presence, and the sound of their footsteps on the sidewalk. Her heart hammered, and she didn't care. She would enjoy their walk together.

Relaxing, she turned and smiled. "What have you done with yourself all day, besides make Lottie angry?"

Glancing sideways at her, he grinned and stepped around her to walk next to the street. "I caught up on my correspondence, made rounds at the café and drugstore, drove to Chesterville for paint supplies, and ended up in the blacksmith shop. Oh, and I visited Willy at the station for a while."

"Then you have had a good day, haven't you, except for making Lottie angry."

"Yes I have."

They walked in silence for a couple of minutes, and Andrew wondered on her quietness. "Are you sure there is nothing bothering you? You are unusually quiet."

"I am fine, thank you. I was just thinking. You are comfortable in Oak Grove, aren't you?"

Strolling along, looking at the damp leaves beneath their feet, Andrew thought on her question a moment, thinking she stated it perfectly. "Yes, Gloria. I never imagined a small place like this had so much to offer. I am used to large cities and the traffic, noise, and hustle and bustle. But you are right. I am comfortable here."

"Hey, Miss Hansen—"

"Hi, Truman," Gloria answered, smiling at the brown-haired young boy who braked his bicycle and adjusted *The Chronicle* bag on his shoulder.

"Hi, Mr. Baxter."

"Hello, Truman."

Removing a newspaper, he handed it to Gloria with a small grin. "Here, I am not sure, but I think your paper is on your roof, because I didn't see it hit the ground after I threw it...sorry."

"That's okay, Truman. Thank you."

"You're welcome."

Watching him pedal away, Andrew turned to Gloria. "You see, that is what I like about this place. Where I come from, you buy your newspaper on the corner, and if it is delivered, he doesn't care if you get it or not."

"Truman is a nice boy."

"He is Jim and Jennifer Walker's son, isn't he?"

"Yes," Gloria answered, waving at Sally Wilson, who was retrieving her paper from the yard. "He has a younger brother, Simon."

Andrew took Gloria by the elbow, and they paused as a car drove slowly across the sidewalk and into the drive in front of them. Smoothing his beard, he watched wistfully as a young girl in a witch's cape and hat jumped from the porch and ran to greet her father.

Crossing the street, they made their way down the block. Sounds and smells of an October evening floated on the air. A door banged shut, and a dog barked as it chased some children in the yard across the street. A voice called for supper, and its aroma, mingling with the autumn leaves at their feet, was pleasing. Andrew felt the chill in the air and wondered if the drizzly rain would stop for the evening's trick-or-treaters. Realizing Gloria had stopped walking, he turned and looked at her. She was staring at him, her clear eyes wide and questioning.

"Which do you prefer?"

"Which do I prefer? I am not sure I know what—"

"Which do you prefer, Andrew," Gloria asked softly as she touched the sleeve of his jacket and looked up at him, "your city life or this?"

Andrew stared intently into the gray eyes. Melba had touched on the same subject a few days ago but was not as direct as Gloria. It was comfortable and somewhat pleasant to have someone delve into his thoughts and feelings on a more intimate level.

"I don't know. I enjoy my life in New York and all the advantages it affords, and I love my home in Connecticut. But there are things here that I do not have there."

"What things?" Maintaining her direct gaze, she touched her dark hair with a hand. "I have never been to a large city, but I cannot imagine what you find here that cannot be found in Connecticut or New York. They sound like wonderful places."

"They are, and you would probably love it, but here…there is a solidness," he said, gesturing with a closed hand, "and goodness, and this is where—"

Stopping abruptly, he turned and slowly began walking, realizing he had almost said this was where Caroline and Elizabeth were.

"This is where what?" Gloria asked, falling into step.

"This is where I prefer to be right now."

"I am glad you prefer to be here, Andrew. One day, when you are back in New York or Connecticut, I hope you will remember us fondly."

"Oh I shall. Oak Grove is one place I do not think I will ever forget. Now what about you? Tell me about your day."

Rolling her eyes, Gloria laughed. "My day was pretty much the same as always. I hoped the new shipment of books would come today, but it didn't. So I spent some time working on a project, which was a futile attempt."

"And what is that?" Andrew inquired, trying to imagine what project she would be involved with.

Glancing up, she smiled shyly, a pink blush staining her cheeks. "You would not be interested."

"Yes I am," Andrew replied sternly. "You do not know me well enough to know what might interest me."

The humor in his eyes betrayed his seemingly harsh comment, and she smiled. "All right, you asked, so I will tell you. I am drawing plans for an antique shop."

"Antique shop? I did not know you held an interest in antiques." They crossed the street and stepped onto the sidewalk. "I think that is a wonderful interest, Gloria. My grandmother's home is filled with treasures and antiques. She loved them too. I would like to see your plans sometime."

"You would laugh. I use nothing but a ruler and am trying to draw it to scale, though I am sure it is all wrong. My dream is to have a large, two-story home filled with antiques. It has to have a tea room for the ladies to sit and visit and rooms where they might spend a weekend if they so choose, and…I know what you are thinking."

"And what am I thinking?"

"You are thinking I should be practical. There are only certain seasons of the year that I would have any business, and it would never pay for itself."

"Those are very practical points, but that is not what I was thinking."

"No?"

"I was wondering what your husband would think of living in a house full of ladies all of the time."

"But I don't have a husband—"

"Not at present, Gloria, but speaking of being practical, you are much too young and beautiful to not consider the fact that you will marry. Surely you have thought of that."

"Of course, but I have not met the right man."

"You have never considered anyone?" Andrew asked in amazement. Though it was none of his business, he was genuinely interested. "Have you never been in love, Gloria? I am sorry. That is none of my concern."

Her heart pounding, she glanced sideways at him. "Marriage is a lifelong commitment that should not be entered lightly. I would love to have a family, Andrew, and hope to one day, but until I meet the man who...loves me the way I love him, I will concentrate on dreaming of owning an antique shop."

"Good for you. Everyone deserves true love, and everyone should have a dream. My grandmother made my dream of painting come true. I could not have done it without her. Have you always held an interest in antiques?"

"Yes, I have wanted my own home and antique shop for a number of years, but unless a long-lost relative dies and leaves me a bundle of money, my dream will never come true, but I can dream anyway." She laughed softly.

Suddenly serious, she spoke quietly. "It is just a dream, but it is something to plan and long for. What would we have if we did not have dreams?"

"You are right, Gloria. Sometimes it is the dream that helps us through rough times."

"Here we are. Thank you, Andrew," she said softly, her silky voice reaching his ear.

"For what?" he asked, looking down into her upturned face. She was so young yet mature in many ways. She knew exactly what she wanted.

"Thank you for lifting my spirits and walking me home. Now Lottie is already angry with you, so I don't think you should be late for supper."

Opening the gate, she turned back and looked at him, her gray eyes soft and warm. "You are a nice man, Andrew. I will always remember you."

He watched her walk up the sidewalk and onto the porch. Opening the door, she turned and smiled, then disappeared inside. Standing outside the gate, he stared at the little house and thought of the young woman inside. *Why in heaven's name hasn't some man snatched her up?*

Chapter 20

Angrily throwing a shoe in the closet, Melba stomped into the kitchen, tears brimming in her eyes. She had given Willy every benefit of the doubt, but she had had it. She had done nothing wrong, and if he was trying to prove something, he had most definitely succeeded.

Filling the tea kettle, she set it on the burner, stood with arms folded, and waited for the water to heat. What had happened? To see one another daily and then suddenly everything comes to an abrupt halt? After Lizzie's wedding shower Sunday afternoon, she was tired and hadn't thought much about it when he did not call. Monday was rainy, and, feeling a cold coming on, she was thankful it was her day off. It had proved to be the perfect time to stay in and clean her kitchen cabinets. When Willy didn't call that evening, she considered perhaps he was not feeling well either. By Tuesday, she began to fret and thought to call him, but from the salon window, she saw he was working and appeared fine. Assuming to see him that evening, she was clearly irritated by eight when there was no word, no phone call…nothing. Wednesday morning she awoke mad, her anger growing with each passing hour. Lunch rolled around, and, heading toward the café, she looked across the square to see him leaning against a car talking and laughing with Sheriff Walker. Evidently he did not miss her at all. Gritting her teeth, she stepped into the café, waved at Mercy, took her plate, and headed back to the salon, wondering why she had ordered it. She was not even hungry. At prayer meeting, she had not heard a word Pastor Mike said about the first chapter of John and hurriedly left, mumbling something she didn't remember when Leah stopped to ask if everything was okay.

Mercy was no help. Catching up to her, she patiently listened as Melba angrily voiced her frustration the entire seven blocks home.

"Don't be angry until ya find what the problem is. Melba, ya know Willy loves you. Perhaps he needs time ta—"

"Needs time to what?" she snapped irately, then felt guilty. Mercy was trying to help, and it would do no good to take it out on her.

"Give Willy a chance ta explain. Wouldn't ya want the same consideration?"

"I would never—"

"Never say never," Mercy said, shaking her head. "Just remember, Willy loves ya."

Glancing at the stove, Melba groaned in frustration. She had not even turned the burner on.

"Forget it," Melba spoke aloud to an empty kitchen. "I am not interested in tea or Willy. I am going to bed."

Flipping the kitchen light off, she marched into the living room, was halfway to her bedroom, and heard a knock at the door. Knowing it was Mercy making herself available for a good heart-to-heart, Melba swung the door wide and stared speechless.

There Willy stood with a wide grin on his handsome face. "Hi, hon'," he greeted, stepping inside and pulling her into his arms. "I missed you."

Gazing at him in bewilderment, a surge of joy rushed through her, and Melba was acutely aware of his familiar aftershave as he bent his head toward her. A sudden flood of anger engulfed her, and she jerked away.

Taken aback, Willy straightened, wondering what in heaven's name was wrong and then suddenly found her back presented to him. She stood stiff and straight and tapped her right toe impatiently. Confused, and with a small inkling somewhere in the back of his brain that he was about to tread into deep water, he plunged in. "What's wrong, hon'?"

"What's wrong?" she asked incredulously, whirling around. The fool did not even realize something could be wrong, and she had stewed and fretted four days.

"Oh, absolutely nothing, *William*," she remarked, crossing the room to stand in front of the window with arms folded and glaring at him.

William? She's never called me that before, Willy thought, a warning signal penetrating his brain. Rubbing a hand across his chin, he stared at her and then glanced away, his eyes falling on the telephone. *Perhaps it would have been a good idea to—*

"Now let me see," Melba commented musingly, tapping her chin with a forefinger as she paced back and forth studying the ceiling thoughtfully. "Should there be something wrong?"

Halting a few feet away, she bestowed an icy glare, and Willy knew beyond a shadow of a doubt he should do or say something, and it better be good, and it better be quick.

"What do you think?" she asked quietly, her footsteps carefully measured as she came to stand before him, her face close to his and her eyes flashing sparks of anger. "What could possibly be wrong?"

"Hon', I have been thinking ... well, I thought maybe if ... I needed some time—" Willy stammered, feeling like an idiot and all the while thinking she had the most beautiful green eyes he had ever seen.

"Oh, of course, Will, that sounds *so* reasonable," Melba retorted angrily, moving away when he reached for her.

I need to do something, Willy thought nervously, noting the rapid pulse at her throat. She was madder than he supposed, and by the clench of her hands, he knew she was trying to maintain a grip on her anger.

"Hon', I know I should have called," he said apologetically, moving slowly toward her, aware of her rigid stance as she stared at the wall.

"And why call? To inform me that you were okay?" she queried with a deadly calm, stepping toward him. "Or perhaps you should have called to inform me you broke both legs and were *not* okay, or just maybe there were things you needed to do. Hmmm?" she questioned, raising a brow.

"Well," Willy replied, stepping back.

"Or maybe," she continued, lowering her voice and stepping toward him again, "you just needed time alone for one reason or another. In that case, it would have been *nice* if you would have let me know. But I suppose there were other more important things on your mind."

"There was nothing more important…I just wanted to—" Willy began, his mind racing for something to say as she took another step forward and he retreated again.

"Of course, it doesn't really matter anyway," she remarked, lifting her chin and looking at him through narrowed eyes. Melba knew she was being unreasonable, but she didn't care. He had made her miserable for the last four days, and if she wanted to play the martyr, she would. He would not hurt her and get away with it.

"It has actually been a very enlightening experience. At least I know where I stand. I am not that important, so please leave."

"Now just a minute," Willy retorted, his own anger building. He was tiring of this whole business. She was going too far. "You can be as angry as you want with me for not calling. I should have. I know that, and I am sorry."

His irritation clearly evident, he leaned down and stared into her face. "But don't you ever, ever say you do not mean anything to me. I love you," he stated flatly in undoubtedly the most unromantic manner a man could utter those three little words.

"And you have such a novel way of showing it, don't you, Will?" Melba commented sarcastically, tossing her head and turning away.

An urge to shake her seized him, and he reached out, grabbed her by the wrist, and turned her around. Placing both hands on her shoulders, he took a deep breath, and then spoke firmly and evenly. "You are going to listen to me. I love you, Mel, and you will hear what I have to say—"

"What *you* have to say? What about what *I* have to say? Is this what you call loving someone?" she asked, her eyes glistening with tears. "Letting me worry and wonder what is going on, not hearing from you, making me think all kinds of things. Is that what you call love? I call it being rude."

Jerking angrily away, she stalked across the room and stood with her back to him once more.

"Oh, I see. So if I understand all this correctly, you are the *expert* on love," Willy commented, his turn to be sarcastic. "I guess your idea of love is *not* trying to understand what the other person is going through."

"Exactly! You are not trying to understand what I have gone through the last four days when I was wondering what was wrong. You do not even know how to understand when I do not understand what is happening. And you have the nerve to say I am not understanding?" she flung back at him.

"You are not making any sense," Willy retorted through gritted teeth, shaking his head. "You are not even allowing me the opportunity to explain. You are being downright unreasonable."

"I believe I asked you to leave," Melba stated angrily. "I do not think this is a good time to discuss this, so please go."

"No!" Willy replied, striding across the room. Gripping both arms, he turned her around and looked down into her face, his eyes blazing with anger. "I will not leave until I am allowed to have my say."

"After four days, I hope you can at least come up with some excuse that might carry some importance," Melba answered angrily, tears spilling over her lashes. "But I seriously doubt it."

Frustrated, Willy lifted his eyes to the ceiling and then looked back down at the top of her head and commented softly, "Maybe you will not think it is important after all."

"I don't care about anything right now," Melba replied, tears streaming down her cheeks. "I told you to leave, and we will talk later."

"And I told you no!" He would stand there all night if need be until she listened.

"There is nothing more to be said."

"Yes there is."

"No there isn't."

"Yes, Mel, there is," Willy replied adamantly.

"What?" Melba asked impatiently, rolling her eyes. Why was he being so stubborn and unreasonable? Why didn't he just go and leave her alone. She was in no mood to listen to anything he had to say.

"Marry me."

Silence filled the room, and blue eyes stared into green. Willy watched changing emotions cross her face, and he thought she had never looked more beautiful. He stared at her, taking in the tear-sparkled eyes, flushed cheeks, and tousled red curls, soft against his hands. Realizing he was holding his breath, a gut-wrenching feeling hit him, and he knew her answer was no. None of this had gone the way he planned.

"Wh...what?" Melba asked softly in amazement.

Out of everything he planned to say, Willy could not think of a word and stood frozen to the spot, unable to do anything but look at her. If she said no, he did not know what he would do.

"That is what you have been...you...I didn't...oh my," Melba mumbled quietly, fascinated by the intense emotion in his eyes.

"Will you, Mel?" he asked softly, touching her cheek. "Will you marry me?"

Tears flowed down both cheeks, and Melba laid her forehead against his chest. She welcomed his embrace as he pulled her into his arms.

"Is that the reason you stayed away?" she asked, gripping the front of his shirt.

"I was trying to think of a special way to ask you, and I wanted it to be something we would always remember," Willy replied, thinking this had to beat any marriage proposal ever offered.

"I don't think we will have any trouble remembering tonight," Melba said, grinning.

"Probably not, but I really wish you would give me an answer."

Smiling happily, she threw both arms around his neck. "Yes, Will, yes. I will marry you."

Chapter 21

Monday proved rainy and chilly, a moderate breeze making it feel much cooler than forty-eight degrees. Fastening the top button of her jacket, Leah stared at the enormous locomotive idling on the track. Loud, squeaky, clanking noises filled the air, and a small boy pressed against the Pullman window. The nine fifteen Sunshine Special was right on time.

"Now, Louise, don't you worry about a thing," Leah said, holding both her hands. "You spend time with your aunt and try to enjoy yourself. Mike and I will keep an eye on the house."

"I don't know…It has just been so long since . . ."

"Louise," Mike said, placing a hand on her shoulder, "you and your mother's sister will have so much to talk about. I know it will be bittersweet, but I think it will be good for the both of you, and we will be waiting for you when you return."

"All aboard! Please step up, all aboard!" Standing at the boarding steps with pocket watch in the palm of his hand, the conductor snapped it closed, slid it into an inside pocket ,and glanced in their direction.

"Oh, dear, I guess it is time. Thank you, Pastor Mike, for everything. And you too, Leah. I don't know what I would have done without you at Mother's passing."

Hugging her close, Leah stepped back and smiled. "We will be praying for you, Louise."

"I know you will. I will see you in a couple of weeks," she said, retrieving the small suitcase from Mike. Smiling nervously and eyes wide, she turned and walked across the platform.

"I hope she enjoys herself," Leah commented, waving as she turned then boarded the train.

"Mrs. Tyler's sister was very sincere about this, and it will be good for the both of them," Mike said, watching the conductor perform his last minute duties.

Two long whistle blasts signaled its departure, and they watched the powerful locomotive come alive. Iron wheels turned slowly, thick, black smoke billowed from the engine's chimneys, and blasts of steam filled the air with a chugging sound. Picking up speed, the Sunshine Special hissed and chugged and disappeared around the bend.

"Louise will have a lot to do when she returns, and I think this trip will prepare her for that," Mike said as they walked to the car.

"I am so glad her aunt is returning with her. That will be a great help."

Opening the door, Mike watched Leah slide in. "Yes, her aunt is a very sweet lady. I am glad she suggested this trip." Closing the door, Mike walked to the other side and then halted. A young, black man was walking toward him in the drizzling rain, carrying a suitcase. There was something familiar, and Mike looked closely as he neared the car, trying to recall where he had seen him.

"Good morning. I am Mike Daniels. Can I give you a lift somewhere?"

A broad smile crossed the young man's face, and he sat his suitcase on the ground and grabbed Mike's hand. "Noah, Pastor, and ah'd be obliged, thank ya."

Mike laughed in recognition and slapped him on the shoulder. "Noah, Noah Cook. Why how long has it been?"

"Ah didn't think ya'd remember me. Ah believe it's been six and a half years, mebbe seven."

"It is good to see you. Get in, and we will give you a lift." Opening the back door, Mike slid the suitcase across the seat and looked at Leah's questioning face. "Leah, you remember Noah."

"Why of course. How are you, Noah?" Watching him settle into the backseat, Leah grinned. "You would not be here for the wedding, would you?"

"Yes'm, ah shore am. Nothin' could keep me away from that. Ah cain't believe Ben's finally gettin' married. That poor girl shore don't know what she's gettin' herself into," he replied, laughing as he removed his cap and laid it on the seat.

"I imagine Lizzie can handle him," Mike commented, starting the car. "I cannot tell you how nice it is to see you again, Noah." Glancing in the rearview mirror, he grinned. "I believe the last time you were home, old Ben threatened to run both you and Ben out of town."

Noah chuckled and shook his head. "Uncle Ben, he was always goin' ta do somethin' or th'other ta us. We was like a couple of jack rabbits runnin' around jest lookin' for mischief. Ah shore do miss those days. And how about ya'selves and them youngins? They's three of 'em, ain't they?"

"Actually, we have four. I guess you have not been back since Jimmy was born." Leah looked over her shoulder and smiled. "But we are all fine and healthy."

"Ah don't spect ah'd know any of 'em anymore. Been gone too long, and ah been thinkin' about that. Mercy and Ben both wrote and said Uncle Ben's slowin' down a might."

"I guess he is somewhat," Mike replied, glancing through the mirror again, "but he is going strong for ninety and still keeping things lively at the shop. That is where you are going, I presume?"

"Yes, suh, ah'd like ta spend as much time as ah can with him while ah'm home. Ah wasn't supposed ta arrive for another five days, but they was a change in my plans, so here ah am. It'll be a surprise too, 'cause he don't know ah's comin' in early."

"I am sure he will be pleased," Leah said, knowing how thrilled he would be to see his great-nephew.

Passing the garage, Noah leaned forward and looked curiously out the window. "Is that Willy?"

"Yes, it is," Mike answered. "He runs the place now."

"And how's Mr. and Mrs. Stanton? How might they be doin'?"

"They have both gone on to be with the Lord since you were here, Noah."

"Ya don't say. Well, ah shore hate to hear that…not that they're with the Lord, ah shore don't mean that. It's jest that ah'll miss seein' 'em across the street from Uncle Ben's. Is Willy livin' there in the house?"

"He sure is," Mike answered, halting at the stop sign. "Willy is doing very well for himself."

"Well now that's good ta hear. I've thought about him now and agi'n. He had a lot of misery when he was a youngin."

"He is also getting married," Leah commented, turning to face him, "although they have not set a date yet."

"Ya don't say. Ain't that somethin'. Who's he marryin'?"

"I don't think you know Melba. She has only lived in Oak Grove for about five years."

"No, ma'am, ah don't expect ah do."

"Here you are, Noah," Mike said, pulling up next to the old, weathered building. Turning to the young man in the backseat, Mike shook the hand he offered. "We sure are glad you're home."

"And It's shore good ta be back and good ta see the both of ya," he said, opening the door and stepping out. "Thank ya kindly for the ride."

"No problem, Noah. We hope to see a lot of you while you are here."

"Ah expect so. Thank ya agi'n." Grabbing the suitcase, he tipped his hat to Leah and with a grin from ear to ear, remarked, "Uncle Ben's gonna be as surprised as an old hound with no fleas when ah walk in."

After many an afternoon spent on Miss Tillie's porch and colder days talking through the door, sitting in her living room was an experience Mike was as yet unaccustomed to.

Presently he and Leah were enjoying a cup of tea, checking on her frame of mind, and hoping to approach the subject of living arrangements.

"This tea is very good, Miss Tillie," Leah commented, setting her cup in the saucer. "Mike told me how he liked it, and he is not much of a tea drinker."

"I am glad you enjoy it, Leah. Why as sure as you're born, this is the only way we drink tea in Virginia. I add…mint."

"Hmmm, I do taste mint," Leah commented thoughtfully, "but there is something else that—"

"Oh that. It is Berta's recipe. She created it especially for Mama. I always add a smidgen."

Lifting the cup to his lips, Mike inhaled the fragrance and took a sip. Mint flavoring was evident, but now that Leah mentioned it, there was something else. He held the warm liquid in his mouth for a minute and then swallowed. "Blackberry, do I taste a trace of blackberry?"

"Well my soul, Pastor Mike. Yes, there is blackberry in the recipe, but that is all I am going to tell you. Berta would turn over in her grave if she thought I was giving away her secrets."

"Well, I think it is delicious," Leah replied, wondering just exactly what ingredients Berta's recipe contained.

"Miss Tillie, I am looking forward to seeing you in church Sunday. Mike told me you planned to worship with us again." Leah patted her hand and smiled with pleasure. "I cannot tell you how happy I am."

"My dear, it is time to put my stubbornness aside. I have to admit, though, I am somewhat nervous. It has been so very long."

"Not a thing to be nervous about, Miss Tillie," Mike said. "Your spot next to Miss Mattie is still there. It has not gone anywhere."

"Now you sound like her. She tells me much the same thing. What a good friend she has been through the years."

"She is that, indeed," Mike replied, feeling much relaxed after his hectic morning.

"Did you know she visits me every Tuesday without fail and always makes it a point to remind me how wrong I have been through the years." Smiling, she smoothed the front of her dress. "She prays for me daily. I do not have a chance with a force like that prodding me along, do I?"

Leah laughed lightly and squeezed her hand. "I have had many people pray for me through the years too, Miss Tillie. Aren't we glad they do?"

"Oh yes," Tillie replied, "but even knowing so, I still worry that…but—" Her voice trailed off, and she became very quiet. Sitting back in her chair with hands folded in her lap, tears sprang to her eyes. "I fear that I may—"

Noting her apprehension, Mike leaned forward and commented softly, "Miss Tillie, I have no doubt you will conduct yourself with proper etiquette, whether you feel as normal as you do today or as the elegant lady who appears from time to time."

Visible relief washed over her, and she spoke quietly, "This is a big step for me."

"Yes it is, but there is nothing for which you are to be concerned, and I will come early for you—"

"No, no," she stated, raising a hand in objection, "that will not be necessary. I can drive myself."

Leah's eyes flew to Mike, and he wanted to laugh at her expression. An image of Miss Tillie driving her Tin Lizzie through the fence, across the cemetery, or worse flashed through his mind, and he knew this needed to be nipped in the bud.

"Miss Tillie, you know what Sheriff Walker says about you driving," he began.

"Oh, pish-posh. Sheriff Walker worries too much. I can drive just fine, and I will."

"That may be so, but—"

"Mike," Leah interrupted, "Miss Tillie enjoys driving, and she should if she wants. But I am certain, Miss Tillie," she said, smiling sweetly as she looked her straight in the eye, "you would agree that with winter upon us and the ice and snow, well, one never knows what the weather might be on a Sunday morning. It would be a terrible thing if you slid off into a snow bank…Of course, Mike or any number of men would willingly come to your aid. That would be no problem, but I know how you would fret about disrupting the worship service, or perchance, someone becoming injured."

Miss Tillie stared at the warm dark eyes and pondered her train of thought and motive. Snow banks and injuries? This young woman was not fooling her in the least, but she was graciously allowing her to make her own decision, and for that, she was grateful. Inclining her head and smiling slightly, Miss Tillie deferred to the younger woman and spoke quietly, "Leah, you are quite right. I certainly would not wish to disrupt worship service if I, *perchance,* did slide off into a *snow bank.* Now, what did you have in mind?"

Leah smiled happily, knowing she had not fooled Miss Tillie at all. "I think Jeremiah should come for you. After all, he drives Miss Mattie and Hannah right by your house every Sunday morning."

Miss Tillie laughed and shook her head. "You have no idea how many times Mattie's uttered those very words."

Having watched Leah's handling of the situation, Mike reclined comfortably in the chair, "Now with that taken care of, there is something else I would like to discuss."

Uncrossing a leg and sitting forward in his chair, Mike looked pointedly at Miss Tillie with a gaze she recognized as stubbornness.

Glancing from one to the other, Miss Tillie slowly sat her teacup in the saucer and then, just as stubbornly, stared back.

"I am very honored, Miss Tillie," Mike said sincerely, "that you entrusted me with your personal matters. I take that responsibility very serious, otherwise, I would not have agreed."

The sound of her husband's voice was strong and confident, and Leah prayed silently for Miss Tillie to accept his words in the spirit they were intended.

"And that includes your physical well-being. I would be amiss if I did not consider that, and it is something I know the Lord expects of me."

Petting Charlotte who curled in her lap, Tillie wondered on his manner and was suddenly fearful of what he had in mind. "Are you going to tell me something I do not want to hear, Pastor?"

"I hope I never have to do that," Mike replied gently, "but if circumstances arise and I need to, I certainly will."

She studied him a long moment, and Leah watched her gaze shift to the window. Raindrops hit the pane, a log cracked in the fireplace, and Charlotte purred contentedly.

With a slight nod of her head, Tillie Watson looked at Mike and spoke quietly. "That was a good answer. I know you will always do the right thing. Now, what is it?"

Mike spoke softly but firmly. "I want you to think about something, Miss Tillie, and I want you to give it a lot of consideration."

"And what might that be?"

"I would like you to consider a house guest."

"A house guest!"

"Yes, someone you would welcome into your home as a companion of sorts."

Staring at him, she shook her head and then looked at Leah, down at the floor, and then back at Mike again. "Why in heaven's name would I want someone living in my home? I am quite used to living alone. I do things my own way, and I am perfectly content. Besides," she remarked, raising a brow as though she had him over a barrel, "who would put up with my foolishness when I get...confused?"

"And there you have it," Mike replied. "Your spells are lasting longer. They are not as frequent, but they are lasting longer, and Dr. Miller and I are both concerned. I think it would be a good idea, and I would like you to give the matter a lot of thought."

"Just like that?"

"Just like that," he replied, observing her look of defiance.

"Well, now I just do not know about that," she said, turning her eyes to a falling log in the fire. What was she going to do? Was everyone now going to tell her how to live her life? *Oh, Harold, if you were only here...but you are not.* She sighed miserably. Lifting her eyes, she looked at Mike and knew what he said was true. But she would not give in, not yet.

"It is something I need to ponder. You did say I should *think* about it."

"Miss Tillie, I want you to give it a lot of thought," Mike commented. "It is an important matter we need to consider together. We will pray about it and wait to see who the Lord sends our way."

Allowing her to quietly absorb the idea, Mike looked at Leah and then stood and stoked the logs on the fire. Glancing at the portrait above the mantel, he thought how Miss Tillie's life had changed and turned to look at the proud head bent in thought. He touched her shoulder gently and then walked to his chair and sat down, watching as she raised her eyes to his and sighed.

"As sure as you're born, I should have run you off the porch one more time instead of inviting you in."

Mike chuckled and sat back in the chair, relieved at her manner. "You did many a time, didn't you?"

"I know, and I am sorry, shame on me. I declare, Pastor Mike, I do not know what I was thinking, behaving so badly. Mama would be mortified with my lack of manners."

"Don't feel too badly, Miss Tillie." Leah giggled. "I have felt like running him off a time or two myself."

"I tried it with Harold once, but he only laughed and said he would think about it. My, but that was a long time ago, and now...please have another," she said, passing a plate of sugar cookies, her thoughts tumbling. Perhaps it might be nice to have someone in the house for a change, then again, maybe not. What if it turned out to be someone on the peculiar side. Well as sure as you're born, she would not put up with that. *I will have to think on this,* she thought, turning her attention back to her guests.

"Tell me, Pastor Mike, how is Andrew Baxter enjoying our small town? Does he plan on staying?"

"I believe Andrew finds Oak Grove very pleasant, and I don't know anything for certain, but I expect him to stay around awhile."

"Then I believe I would be much disappointed if I did not get to know him. Perhaps you will bring him around for a visit, Friday perhaps?"

Watching him over the rim of her teacup, she smiled sweetly, and Mike realized he was seeing a very crafty side of Matilda Jane Watson.

She had nonchalantly approached the subject of her great-nephew in front of Leah with all the ease and innocence of any hospitable neighbor. If there was any small amount of hope in Mike's mind that she might drop the issue of their relationship, he now knew it was gone.

Looking at her a brief moment, Mike chuckled and nodded his head. "I will see what I can do, Miss Tillie. I am sure he would enjoy it."

Leah lowered her teacup and glanced between Miss Tillie and her husband. She had missed something. What was it?

Chapter 22

"You have a meeting tomorrow at one o'clock with the Thanksgiving committee, per Miss High-and-mighty. I'll swan. Trudy's called twice to remind me. She knows I have a calendar on my desk to keep track of everything. Lordy, sometimes I could strangle her."

Mike glanced up from the mail he was reading. "Why do you let her get you so riled up, Myrtle? She is never going to change. She just wants to make sure things are—"

"She is plumb bossy, and you know it," Myrtle retorted. "She thinks I am incapable of handling your phone calls. Well, I have done it for years with no complaints. Here," she said, waving a handful of notes in the air before slapping them one by one on the desk in front of him. "Phillip Driscol says to drop by his office any time you get a chance. Ben and Lizzie cannot make their meeting with you tonight and would like to make it Thursday, if that is convenient. Andrew Baxter returned your call, and Miss Mattie wants you to bring Miss Tillie along Thursday for lunch. Now does that look to you like I am incapable of handling things around here? One of these days, just one of these days, I'm going to slam one of them bonnets down around her ears."

"Ummm, thank you, Myrtle," Mike replied, grinning. Gathering the small slips of paper scattered about, he thought of driving to Chesterville to pick up Johnny's gun from the sport shop. His birthday was less than two weeks away, and he couldn't wait to see his face when he gave it to him. *Maybe Andrew would like to ride along.*

Aware of the silence, Mike glanced up and noted Myrtle standing at the window staring at nothing in particular. He studied her a moment. He had gotten used to the lipstick, but this morning there was something different.

Turning, she looked at him, smoothed the front of her brown, tailored dress, and commented, "I might leave a little early today, if that is all right."

"Sure, is there something you need to do?"

"Do I question your personal affairs?" Myrtle asked, raising a somewhat darker than usual brow, a stain flushing her cheeks. *She's wearing rouge,* Mike thought, studying her closely. And her hair; it was held back with a barrette instead of the usual bobby pin.

Leaning back in his chair, he tapped a pencil on the desk and grinned. "As a matter of fact, you do, Myrtle. You love to keep track of me. But that's okay, I know you have my best interest at heart, although, *I* respect *your* privacy."

Rolling her eyes, she turned back to the window, and Mike was struck with the thought that perhaps something was actually troubling her.

"I am sorry, Myrtle. If you are ill or have a problem, you know you can confide in me."

"I am not *ill*, and I don't have a *problem*," she answered, exasperated. Crossing the room, with chin in the air, she grabbed his coffee cup and marched across the hall.

"Got some shopping to do?" he called, now curious as to why she needed to leave early. Occasionally she did so around Christmas, but it was way too soon for Christmas shopping.

"No."

"Oh," Mike replied, retrieving a slip of paper from his shirt pocket. "Myrtle, would you add the Stevens family to those receiving Thanksgiving baskets?"

"Yes," she replied, returning with his cup. Placing it in front of him, she reached for the small slip of paper with Stevens scribbled across it and looked at the top of her pastor's dark head.

"I suppose it is too farfetched to think I might have something fun planned."

Mike laid his pen down and glanced up, wondering what on earth Myrtle considered fun.

"Well I should hope so," he replied, watching her sit in the chair across from him. "Do you?"

"Do I what?" she questioned, fingers drumming the arm of the chair

"Do you have something fun planned tonight?" Mike asked. For someone planning a fun evening, she sure was fidgety and out of sorts.

"Actually, an old friend and I are going to dinner."

"That is nice. Is she visiting or just passing through?" Lifting a sheet of paper from the side drawer, he jotted down the beginning of his sermon outline then realized Myrtle had not answered. He glanced up to find her staring at him.

"Actually, my friend is a...he."

Mike stared across the desk, an incredulous look on his face. Myrtle had a date?

"Well, heavenly days, you don't have to look so shocked. My word, can't I have a male friend if I want?"

"Well...of course. Yes...yes, you most certainly can, Myrtle," Mike replied, hoping he didn't sound as shocked as he felt. "I am glad there is someone that...Who is this male friend?"

"He is just a friend, good heavens." Rising to her feet, she headed toward the door. "I will call Lizzie before I forget and tell her Thursday evening is okay. It is convenient for you, isn't it?"

Nodding, Mike stared after her and then gazed through the window, mulling the idea over in his head. Myrtle had a date. How did this all come about without his knowledge? Of course, it was her business, and it would be nice if she had a companion to keep her company, but Myrtle knew nothing about men.

Rising, Mike strode across the hall and stood in the doorway watching her open a box of bulletins. "This...friend of yours; do I know him, and does he live in Oak Grove?"

"Why do you want to know?" she asked, peering at him over the rim of her glasses.

"Because...I want to make sure he is someone that—"

"That what?"

"Just how well do you know this friend?" he asked, leaning against the door jam, wondering who and what sort of man this *friend* was.

"Oh for evermore, I told you he is an old friend."

"Do you mean old as a friend from a long time ago, or is he old like an old man?"

"What difference does that make?"

"A lot; there are some old men who look for someone to take care of them. I mean...*not* that I think that is the situation here, but—"

Standing ramrod straight behind the desk, she retorted, "I will tell you right now, I am not about to become some old codger's babysitter. And what makes you think he is an old man? Never mind," she said, waving a hand in the air and plopping another stack of bulletins on the desk. Placing both hands on her hips, she stared straight at him. "Since you think I am an old lady, quite naturally an old man would be taking me to dinner, wouldn't he?"

"I don't think of you as an old lady," Mike replied, thinking he should retreat to his office.

Myrtle set the empty cardboard box on the floor and looked at him. "You know he could be much younger than you suppose."

Now it was Mike's turn to stare. There was no way he would allow some younger man to trifle with Myrtle's emotions. As far as he knew, she had never dated and could be easily hurt.

Watching her stack bulletins on the shelf behind her, Mike rested an arm against the wall and asked curiously, "Well, is he?"

"Is he what?"

"Is he young?"

"I didn't say he was young. I said he *could* be, and why are you concerned?"

"I just think you ought to...be careful."

"Careful?" Myrtle laughed. "I am forty-eight years old and going to dinner with a friend. Land sakes, what do I need to be careful about, that he will stab me with his fork?" Her eyes widened, and she sat down in her chair. "Well, my word, you are worried about me, aren't you?"

"No, of course not. I am not worried, exactly...well maybe a little," he answered, noting her smug look. Now this was a turnabout. After fussing and worrying about him all these years, the shoe was about to go on the other foot.

"My, my, but it sure is nice to have someone concerned about me. That's your phone ringing. You'd better answer it."

She is not going to tell me who he is, Mike thought, exasperated as he stepped across the hall and answered the telephone, "Hello."

"Daddy?" Shari's voice sounded in his ear.

"What, sugar." Sitting in his chair, he glanced across the hall. Myrtle had her compact out and was freshening her lipstick.

"Laura won't let me cross the line in our room, and I need to get something out of the closet. Will you tell her to give me a pass?"

Scratching his head, he decided two daughters too sick to go to school were evidently on a rapid road to recovery. "Where is your mother?"

"She went to borrow a lemon from Mrs. Clark to make us cough syrup. We have honey but not a lemon. What if she doesn't have one either? I don't want to take that other yucky stuff."

"I don't blame you, but why do you need a pass for your closet?" he asked, looking heavenward as Myrtle blotted her lips, dropped the lipstick and compact in her handbag, and smoothed the back of her hair.

"Cause we divided our room in half, and the closet is on her side."

"That hardly seems fair."

"But the bureau is on my side, and I have the mirror."

"I suppose everything is fair and square then. What do you need from the closet that can't wait until your mother gets back?" Why in heaven's name did they divide their room in half?

"My shoes."

"Aren't you in your pajamas?"

"Yes, but I need my shoes."

"Why do you need your shoes when you are supposed to be in bed?" Mike asked, grinning. The little squirt was doing nothing but aggravating her sister.

"Cause."

"Cause is not a good enough reason as far as I am concerned. Maybe you can explain it better to Mom." Hearing a long sigh, he chuckled. "Go back upstairs and wait until she gets back. I am sure she will figure something out."

"Okay."

Eight or forty-eight, the female gender was making his life confusing today.

"Are you busy?"

Looking up at Andrew standing in the doorway, a grin crossed Mike's face. "Not with anything that can't wait. Come in and sit down," he said, thankful for male companionship.

Andrew hesitated briefly and then removed his jacket and draped it on the back of the chair. "Lottie said you called, and I had a couple of errands to run, so I thought I would drop by to see what was on your mind." Taking a seat, he smoothed his beard and allowed his gaze to roam the office.

Mike's desk sat in the middle of the room, shelves against the wall behind him contained a variety of books, Bibles, and commentaries, and a large window on the right gave one a view of the forest.

"I am glad you came by," Mike said watching him take a seat. "I wanted to ask a small favor, one I think you will find enjoyable and interesting, to say the least."

"Sure," Andrew replied, "anything. What can I do for you?"

"Actually, it is not for me. It is for a sweet lady that you could make very happy." Mike laughed at the expression on Andrew's face. "No, not that."

"Okay then. If you were going to play matchmaker, I would have to decline," Andrew chuckled.

"No, no. Would you like a cup of coffee?" Mike asked, starting to rise.

"Thank you, no. I don't believe so."

Sitting back in his chair, Mike looked at Andrew, recalling his likeness to the man in the picture Miss Tillie had shown him. "I called to invite you to lunch Friday, if you have no other plans."

"None that I know of. I would like that," Andrew replied, somewhat relieved. He didn't know what to expect when Lottie told him Pastor Mike called. The one thing he knew for certain was this man somehow knew his secret.

"Good, we will have lunch with one of the sweetest ladies in Oak Grove, Miss Tillie Watson. I don't think you have met."

"No, I do not believe we have."

"I was telling her of your painting, and she wants to meet you. I think you will find her very enjoyable, although, I must tell you she suffers with intermittent spells of confusion, but that only adds to her charm."

"Ah, the infamous lady and her Tin Lizzie."

"Yes, although it has been a while. She is a very warm, wonderful lady, Andrew," he said in a softer tone, "and I know you will grow quite fond of her."

"I am sure I will," he answered, wondering on the last comment. Why would he grow fond of her? Studying the man across from him, Andrew looked into the deep blue eyes and took in the honest face and sincere manner. Why did he think this conversation was something other than an invitation to lunch? He was becoming paranoid.

Andrew looked down at the floor a long moment and then lifted his gaze to the window and the barren trees of the forest beyond. This was as good a time as any. Rising from his chair, he pushed the door closed, hesitated, and then turned around. Clearing his throat, he stood in front of Mike's desk with both hands in his pockets and looked intently at him.

"I am curious. Would you mind telling me...how did you know?"

A slight smile crossed Mike's face. Rubbing his fingers along the pages of his Bible, he said quietly, "Elizabeth."

"Elizabeth?" Curious, Andrew sat back down in the chair. "I don't understand."

"Do you remember my saying you reminded me of someone? Need I say more? You could never deny her, Andrew. Your daughter looks just like you."

Mike observed the deep breath and strong emotion that crossed his face, clear evidence of the truth. "It was not something I pondered on and figured out. Quite the contrary, it caught me by surprise. Elizabeth spent the night with us and was making fun of me during a game of spoons." Mike shook his head and laughed softly. "I believe she said I was a sore loser, if I remember correctly. Anyway, she laughed and looked up at me with her head tilted sideways like you do, and in that instant, I saw it. My word, Andrew, she is so like you: her eyes, skin tone, hair color, and if that is not enough, she has many of your mannerisms."

Andrew stared at the old, wood floor, his heart pounding, and Mike studied him with compassion. But for the clock's steady tick, both men were aware of the silence.

"Does anyone else know?"

"Not that I am aware of."

With a relieved sigh, Andrew leaned back in the chair and for a long moment studied the ceiling. "Good…I am not ready for them to know. My real name, Pastor, is Wilkins, Jonathan Andrew Wilkins." Looking at Mike, Andrew smoothed his beard and shook his head back and forth. "I did not know if I could carry it off, but when Trudy did not recognize me…because of this," he said, indicating his beard and mustache, "I figured my secret was safe. But on Founders Day, I knew you realized who I was. You caught me watching Elizabeth, and I saw it in your eyes. I guess I am not very good at hiding my feelings."

Leaning forward, he rested his elbows on his knees and studied the floor. "You must think I am a pitiful excuse of a man to run out on my daughters the way I did."

"I think nothing of the kind. What I see is a man who loves his daughters very much."

Andrew shook his head and stared at the shelf behind Mike's desk, a faraway look in his eyes. "Ten years…I threw away ten years. You have no idea how I regretted that over and over again." Closing his eyes, he sighed deeply. "Mary died in childbirth. Part of me died with her, Pastor Mike. I do not remember much about the days following Elizabeth's birth. I cannot even tell you what she looked like or if…if I even held her. And little Caroline…she was only five."

Andrew's face was full of pain, and Mike wondered on the agony and turmoil he was experiencing. The next words came slowly and quietly, and Mike bent his head to catch them.

"Lord, how confused Caroline must have been, not understanding her mother's death and my leaving." Releasing a slow breath, he continued, "My brain and heart were numb to my daughters. All I felt was this incredible pain. Mary was my life…I loved her so, and suddenly she was gone. I don't know…I don't know why or how…I just woke up one morning and knew I could not stand another minute in the house without her. Thank God Trudy was there caring for the girls, because I was incapable."

Pausing a moment, his gaze held Mike's, and he stated flatly, "I thought of no one but myself. After a sleepless night, I threw a few belongings in a bag, and I…I left."

Moved at the heartwrenching pain in his eyes, Mike sat back and patiently waited for him to continue.

"I wandered around not doing much of anything for a good three years and finally ended up at Grandmother Baxter's...Wilkins rather. Baxter was her maiden name. She took me in, loved and comforted me, and helped me on my road to recovery."

A slight smile crossed his lips. "She was a wonderful Christian woman, Pastor Mike, and she revealed Christ's love to me in so many ways. I owe my coming to the Lord to her. I would give anything to have known him when Mary died, to experience his peace and comfort. Mary was a strong believer, but I...was not at the time. If I had been, things would have been so very different."

Andrew sat back and closed his eyes, relieved to finally share his heart. "I want to know my daughters, and I want them to know me so desperately. I cannot believe the love I feel for them. I did not expect it. Caroline was a small child when I left, and now she is a beautiful young girl, and Elizabeth...I never knew Elizabeth. She is so precious. How can you love someone you do not know? It is an incredible thing. But I do...They are a part of me. I want to tell them how much I loved their mother, what a wonderful person she was, and try to explain why I left, but I don't know. I just do not know."

He was silent a moment, and Mike said nothing, allowing him to continue at his own pace. "My coming here was the right thing to do. My daughters deserve the truth. I have no idea how Trudy and Henry explained my disappearance. But I need to own up to my responsibility, and I pray that the three of us might somehow come to share Mary's love."

Andrew crossed a leg and studied his shoe a long moment and then looked up. "I do not know the outcome of this journey, but one thing I do know...the Lord led me here, and I will accept whatever happens as his will for my life and my daughters' lives. The love I have for them is a great blessing, even if that love is never reciprocated. I am here. I want them to know who I am, but for the life of me, I do not know how to accomplish that."

Mike studied him a moment. "Continue loving them, Andrew, and be patient. You said the Lord led you here, and I do not doubt that in the least. With that said, we can hold to the promise that 'all things work together for good to them that love God, to them who are called according to His purpose.' All things, Andrew, every part of this, every life that is touched, every action, every decision, and every result will be according to his plan and purpose. He will work it out in a wonderful way. You have to hold on to that promise and know he is in control, and he is directing how and when the truth will be revealed."

Andrew nodded and smiled. "I know. You preached a sermon on that very subject shortly after my arrival. I never told you how much your words helped me that day and many times since. If not for his word and promises, I do not know what I would do."

"My friend, God's word and grace is all sufficient, no matter what happens. I know; I have been there," Mike said softly, his eyes traveling to a small photograph on his desk of him and Leah at a much younger age.

Leaning forward, he looked directly at Andrew. "I cannot tell you how this will turn out or what you are going to experience, but everything, and I mean everything, will work together to the end result." Holding his gaze, Mike spoke firmly but gently. "Andrew, there are many circumstances you need to consider. You must remember the girls have known no other parents than Trudy and Henry. Caroline may have a small memory of you and Mary, but I would say it is very little. Henry and Trudy have loved and provided a good home for them, and they will no doubt feel threatened. Legally, the girls belong to them, and that is something you must accept."

Mike observed the disheartened look. "I am not discouraging you. I cannot do that, knowing the Lord directed you here. I am simply laying the facts before you. You need to look at the whole picture and prepare yourself."

Mike's eyes traveled to the window, and he paid little attention to the swirling snowflakes. "There is a very, very strong probability, Andrew," he said quietly, "that Caroline and Elizabeth will resent you when they know the truth, and that will break your heart. But I have known them for ten years, and they are sweet girls. They will not harbor resentment…but it will take time. How much time do you have, Andrew?"

"I have as much time as it takes, Pastor Mike. I will not walk away again. I cannot, even if I wanted to. I may be wealthy, but, as far as I am concerned, my daughters are all I have in the world, and I will do whatever it takes for as long as it takes to establish a relationship with them."

Mike nodded and smiled. "Then I guess you are going to be in Oak Grove for quite some time."

"I am." Andrew folded his arms and stretched his legs in front of him. "I will be going home to Connecticut for Christmas. I need to take care of business and check on my household staff. And I have relatives with whom I spend the holiday, they will be expecting me."

"You are quite welcome to spend Christmas with us, Andrew. Leah and the children would love it."

"Thank you, and I appreciate that, but I think it would be best this Christmas if I went home. I will be back the first of the year, and at that time, I plan to look for a place where I will have more room. I am very comfortable at the hotel, but with the prospect of a long stay, I need to look for something to call home."

"Well, I am glad. My family and I have grown quite fond of you."

"And my feelings are the same. You have a wonderful family, Pastor; one I hope to have some day if the Lord is willing. You are wonderfully blessed."

"I am very well aware of that; indeed I am."

Rising to his feet, Andrew lifted his jacket from the back of the chair. "I feel much better. I don't know why I put off confiding in you as long as I did." Andrew chuckled and shook his head. "Miss Mattie told me to do that very thing the first Sunday I was here, even if she didn't know what was troubling me. She is a woman of exceptional insight."

"Most definitely," Mike agreed, coming around the side of his desk. "Nothing gets past Miss Mattie. She has been a great inspiration and help to me through the years."

"You have no idea what an inspiration and help you have been to me. Thank you for allowing the Lord to mold you as he has."

Humbled by his sincerity, Mike was much aware of God's ever-present grace. As natural as his next breath, Mike looked at Andrew, "Let's pray and thank God for all he is about to do."

Willy glanced through the window. Snow flurries had stopped, and he knew Melba would be disappointed. Retrieving six Champion spark plugs from the shelf, he grinned, remembering her excitement over the possibility of snow. Bending beneath the hood of Hank's '42 Plymouth, he stared unseeing at the motor, recalling warm, green eyes. He shook his head. It was becoming increasingly more difficult to concentrate on anything but her.

Melba had gotten to the very core of his soul, and he never imagined he could love anyone as much as he loved her. Replacing one of the spark plugs, he looked at the old one, tossed it in the trash barrel, and grabbed another. When finished, the car would run like new. Examining the plug in his hand, the thought struck that Melba was the spark that brought life and meaning to his lonely existence. What would she think of his comparing her to a spark plug? Chuckling, he bent beneath the hood again, whistling "Prisoner of Love" along with the radio. For the first time in his life, he knew what it was to wholeheartedly love someone, and he never wanted to disappoint her. He would do anything she asked.

"Ah reckon gettin' married is catchin' 'round here."

Looking up, Willy stared a moment at the tall black man standing in the doorway. Noah Cook was one of very few he considered a friend growing up.

"Noah," he said with a broad grin. Grabbing the extended hand, he shook it warmly. "It's good to see you, pal."

"Good ta see ya too," he replied, slapping Willy's shoulder. "It's been a long time. Yer lookin' fit. Ah guess that's what love does ta a fella."

Laughing, Willy pointed to a small step ladder. "Have a seat," he said, leaning against the car's fender. "So you know all the news, I guess."

"Ah shore do. They was all talkin' about youins, Uncle Ben, Mercy, and Ben and Lizzie. Sounds like things are goin' good for ya," Noah stated, taking a seat on the ladder and propping a foot on one of its rungs.

"My life is good, Noah. It really is."

"Ah'm proud ta hear it, Willy. Ah shore am sorry 'bout Mr. and Mrs. Stanton. They was good folks," Noah commented, shaking his head. "They always treated me real good."

Willy nodded and rubbed a hand along his right thigh. "They were pretty special and took good care of me."

"That the leg they got ya in?" Noah asked, watching him extend his right leg and move his foot back and forth.

"Yeah, it aggravates me when the weather changes."

"Ah heard ya 'bout lost it. Ah'm glad ya didn't. Now me, ah got it right in the shoulder here," Noah remarked, pointing to his left arm, "Salerno, September 9, 1943. Thought ah was goin' ta meet the good Lord right then and there."

Both men were quiet a long moment, lost in thought. Willy closed the hood of Hank's car and looked at Noah. "But we made it home, didn't we? So many of my buddies—"

"Ah know; ya don't have to say it." Noah shook his head and stared at Willy. "Sometimes ah still wake up at night in a cold sweat. Do ya do that too?"

"Occasionally. Would you like a bottle of pop?" Willy asked, wanting to change the subject and yet continue at the same time. Few men knew what he had gone through, and it was good to have a comrade that understood.

"No thank ya, Willy, ah cain't stay. Ah was on my way ta Mercy's. She's fixin' supper tonight, and ah was jest headin' over ta Reese's ta fetch a loaf o' bread. Ah jest wanted ta stop by a spell and see how ya was doin'."

"I am glad you did, Noah. How long will you be here?"

"Ah don't rightly know for shore." Shuffling a foot back and forth, he looked at Willy with a pained expression. "Ah lost my job at the tool company. They closed the place up."

"That's too bad. If you were staying in Oak Grove, you might get hired on at the lumber company, especially with Ben working there."

"Ah was thinkin' that very thing. Ah asked Ben 'bout it, but he thinks ah'm jest curious. Ah don't want none of 'em to know 'bout my job 'til after the weddin', so I'd appreciate it if ya didn't say anything."

"I won't, Noah," Willy replied. There was a short silence as the two looked at one another. They had experienced the horrors of war and understood the other completely.

"It really is good to see you, Noah. Be sure and drop by anytime so we can—"

"Yeah, ah know. We'll talk some more. Ya got a customer out there at the pump. Ah'll see ya, Willy."

Chapter 23

Moderate temperatures, clouds, and rain fairly ruled the first three weeks in November. An occasional drop in temperature produced enough snow flurries to tease children and the young at heart with the first good snowfall of the year.

Ben and Lizzie's wedding day was the exception with an unseasonably warm temperature, sunshine, and not a cloud in the sky. "A sign from the Lord, blessin' their marriage," Hannah told Miss Mattie.

Oak Grove Baptist Church was filled with family and friends, and Ben looked as if to pop the buttons off his suit coat when he saw Lizzie in her wedding gown. All went as planned; Noah fumbled only once getting the ring out of his pocket, Mercy cried throughout the ceremony, old Ben blew his nose, and Mike noted Leah dabbing her eyes. Showered with rice, the newlyweds drove away, tin cans rattling along behind Ben's car.

Explaining his work situation, Noah was convinced to stay in Oak Grove, and Ben promised to do his best to get him a job at the lumber company. Old Ben enjoyed his company, Willy welcomed their renewed friendship as well as his help at the gas pump, and Mercy . . . "Well," she said, "Noah is still as big a pest as ever, but ah'm happy he's stayin'."

Methodist and Baptist ladies, under the direction of Trudy and Mildred, busily gathered names of those in need, set up displays for collecting canned goods, and received contributions from White's Bakery, the Sweet Shop, and Reese's Market. "My soul," Trudy exclaimed to Mike at prayer meeting, "I do declare, this year's Thanksgiving baskets will be the most bountiful we have ever put together."

Colorful pictures of pilgrims, Indians, and turkeys hung on school windows; the Star Theatre advertised *Song of the South* coming November 26; and plans for the annual Thanksgiving dinner, hosted by the Baptists this year, promised to abound with food, fun, fellowship, and inspiration.

Lunch with Miss Tillie went well. Andrew found her delightful, was pleased with her interest in his art, and, fascinated with the infamous Tin Lizzie, accompanied her to the garage to take a look. Much impressed with the amount of information she managed to glean from the unsuspecting Andrew, Mike grinned when Andy, as she chose to address him, promised to visit again and go along with her to discover the thrill of a *real* automobile.

Miss Tillie was still hesitant over the idea of a house guest, and Mike didn't push the issue but continued to pray about it. "We will wait," he told Dr. Miller over coffee at the cafe. "The Lord will show us who he has in mind."

Much to Mike's astonishment, the old Myrtle was vanishing and a new emerging. Gay and giddy, her wardrobe was suddenly colorful. Drab navy, black, and brown dresses were replaced with softer colors and usually adorned with a scarf or gaudy pin of one sort or another. She smiled more, walked a little lighter, and, more often than not, did not hear a word he said. The change was pleasing, though the day she walked in with her hair cut and permed he almost fell out of his chair. And she didn't even ask if he liked it. Of course it hadn't taken him long to figure out who her *old friend* was and the reason for her transformation.

Clyde's cab was a familiar sight on the church parking lot. Often delivering packages for Ron since he was "going that way" or since he was "just driving by, he wondered if there was anything he could run to town and pick up for Mike." On one occasion, he shared his *calling* to provide Alice transportation back and forth to church on cleaning days; albeit a small ministry, he wanted to offer. Convenient and much appreciated by Alice and Cooley, it provided Clyde another opportunity to mill around the church and talk to Mike for five minutes and Myrtle thirty or forty. Attempting to ignore the love birds, Mike found it difficult with her office directly across the hall, and following one visit that displayed an extreme amount of guffawing on Clyde's part and gushing on Myrtle's, he considered turning his desk in another direction but decided he was too stubborn to give in to the temptation. In spite of it all, he had to admit he was getting a kick out of watching the courtship develop. Clyde suddenly sported a slicked-back hairdo and took to wearing a tie, and Myrtle was forever telling Cooley to mind his own business, all to no avail. The familiar rumble of coal in the chutes usually brought someone to the porch where he passed on the latest "goin's on twixt the two" to the delight of most everyone in town.

A familiar sight traveling up and down the streets in his dump truck, Cooley wore his usual red and black wool jacket with an elbow ripped out, pant legs tucked into black rubber boots, and a brown, leather cap with earflaps. Having the process down to perfection, he could back through a yard to the chute, elevate the truck's bed, and dump a load of coal into the coal bin quicker than a flash.

Taking a ribbing over the questionable need for coal in Ned's one mild day, he promptly retorted, "I'd like to see jest what youins would do if I didn't deliver any and ya found yerselves freezin' yer backsides off. Then I guarantee you'd be cryin' around for me to bring ya some. By jingees, let me tell ya, it might jest not be bad today, but cold weather's gonna set in any day now, ya mark my words."

A few days later, temperatures dropped, rain turned to flurries, and by evening, the ground was covered with white powdery snow.

"Look at it, Will. Isn't it beautiful?" Melba exclaimed, looking through the window at the snow-covered trees.

"It sure is," he agreed, peering over her shoulder. Placing both arms around her, he squeezed warmly. "Just think, next winter we will sit by the fire and watch it snow all night if we want. I won't have to leave and go home."

Leaning her head back against his chest, Melba smiled with pleasure. "That will be so wonderful, Will."

"Why should we wait, Mel? Why don't we get married now," Willy asked, turning her around to face him. "I hate going home in the evenings."

"I know," Melba sighed. "I do too."

"Then why should we wait, Mel? Why?"

Looking into his dark blue eyes, Melba wanted so badly to agree. She missed him every minute they were not together. "Oh, Will, I cannot wait until we are married, but—"

"But what?" he asked, in confusion. "Mel, are you not sure you love me?"

"Oh, no, Will, I love you with all my heart. How can you ask such a thing?"

"Then what is it? I don't understand."

Melba looked at the uncertainty on his face and reached for his hand. "Will, I love you. I never want you to ever doubt that." Walking to the sofa, she turned and looked at him. "You do believe that, don't you?"

Sitting next to her, he slid his arm along the back of the sofa and looked at her tenderly. "Yes, Mel, I do. I know you would never lie to me about anything, but I do not know why you are hesitating."

Melba laid her cheek against his arm. At times like this, her heart was so full of love it frightened her. "Marriage is such an important step," she commented softly. "I have no doubt that you are the man I want to spend the rest of my life with, and I know you feel the same. But, I want us to be ready and know exactly what we expect from one other."

Willy looked at her a long moment, not saying a word. Moving his hand to her hair, he lifted a curl and studied it. He never thought he would ever trust anyone. Melba was his life, and he knew she loved him. She would be a good wife and mother. He could depend on her to stand by his side, and he would never doubt her about anything. There was nothing more he wanted or expected from her. But what about him? What did she expect from him?

Dropping the curl, he reached down and took her hand in his. "Tell me, Mel. Tell me what I lack and what I can do about it. Tell me what you want and expect from me."

"Will, you lack nothing. I love you for who and what you are. I love you, William Stanton." Leaning across, she kissed him lightly on the lips and sat back, studying the handsome face. He was watching her expectantly, and Melba commented quietly and hesitantly. "It does trouble me, Will, that you never talk about your past. A husband and wife should have nothing they cannot discuss. I know you are very bitter over your mother."

Watching the unconscious stiffening of his body and the changed expression on his face as he clinched his jaw and stared across the room, she commented softly, "There; that is an example of what I am talking about. I can't stand to see you in pain. I want to help heal your hurt, Will. But I cannot, because you shut me out." Tears blurred her eyes as she noted the stubborn set to his jaw. "Would you not want to help me if I were hurting?"

Willy turned and looked at her. "Of course I would. You know that."

Releasing a long sigh, he stared at the floor and was silent for several minutes, and then he spoke, his words barely above a whisper. "At one time...my mother was beautiful."

Reaching for her hand, he looked at it a minute and then continued. "She had dark hair and blue eyes and a beautiful smile.

"I did not know my father. He was killed in the war when I was about a year old. We lived with my grandparents at the time, but I don't remember. My earliest memories were of a small place my mother and I lived in when I was about four."

He became very quiet, and Melba watched his expression soften. Twining her fingers with his, he looked at her. "She worked somewhere...I don't know what she did. A lady upstairs, Bertie, looked after me. When my mother came home...we ate and played silly games. She read to me every night. That was my fondest memory," Willy said, laying his head on the back of the sofa and closing his eyes. " She would get me ready for bed, and we would curl up together and look at books. She would exaggerate the words, and...she always smelled so nice," he said, his voice trailing off.

He was silent, and when he spoke again, there was an edge to his voice. "I guess around the time I was in second grade she began coming home later than usual, and she and Bertie argued about it. I remember one time she was crying and told Bertie she had to make a living somehow. I didn't understand what was going on. Then things got worse...she came home later and later. Bertie was aggravated, but she continued to feed me supper and then send me downstairs, where I would wait. When she did get home, most of the time she was tired and cranky, and...I thought it was my fault."

Tears filled Melba's eyes, and she scooted close, laying her head on his shoulder with her arm across his chest. "I am so sorry, Will," she whispered, feeling the rapid beat of his heart against her arm and the tenseness in his body.

"I heard Bertie tell her one night that if she didn't start coming home and taking care of me, she would call the authorities." Willy gave a short derisive laugh. "That's when I began meeting all of my...uncles," he stated flatly. "Some of them stayed a few weeks and others a night or two. They were not interested in a seven-year-old boy, and neither was my mother anymore."

His voice was bitter, and Melba felt his anger. "By the time I was in sixth grade, she was terribly thin, smoking and drinking heavily, and I heard the neighbors and other kids making fun of her. I realized then what she was. I started running the streets and hanging out with the worst kids in the neighborhood. I wouldn't go home until dark...I didn't want to. There was nothing there. She was usually drunk or well on the way, there was no supper, and more often than not, a strange man would be lying on the sofa."

Willy stood and began to pace. "I hated her for not loving me anymore, and I wanted to get even with her for hurting me. So I began stealing. I was hungry, and it was pretty easy to grab something off the shelf at the corner grocery."

Rubbing a hand across his forehead, Willy sighed. "I probably wasn't fooling anyone. Mr. Friedens...he owned the market, undoubtedly knew and felt sorry for me. At the time, I didn't care. I figured if I got caught it might embarrass her the way she embarrassed me." Willy ran a hand through his dark hair and then put his hands in his pockets and paused in front of the window.

"Then I began running with some tough guys who knew a whole lot more than I did, especially Tom. He taught me the ropes, and I got really good at...stealing most anything. Our gang hung out in an old abandoned building, and we stole everything—food, clothes, booze, anything we could sell, and anything we wanted or didn't want. We stole just for the fun of it."

Turning, he faced her, and Melba choked back tears at the anguish on his face. "Then one night...there was this man walking alone, and Tom said we should get him. They jumped him, and he fought back, but they...they beat him and stole his wallet. I was scared to death, and when they ran, I ran. I got a couple of blocks away and was afraid he might die, so I went back. He was unconscious, and while I was bending down looking at him, the police drove up. I froze...I couldn't move, and they cuffed me and took me in. A few days later, Uncle William showed up and brought me here."

Turning back to the window, he looked out at the darkening sky for several minutes and then turned and faced Melba, a look of defeat on his face. "There you have it," he said quietly. "By the age of twelve, I was a thief, a liar, a troublemaker, a drunk, a cheat, and a street bum. I don't expect God to love someone like me, and I wouldn't blame you if you didn't love me anymore either."

Tears streamed down Melba's face, and Willy knew he had just lost what he loved most in the world. The old, familiar dead weight of despair descended, and the silence in the room was deafening as he watched Melba rise slowly from the sofa, an expression of disbelief on her face. He wanted to stop his ears from the words he knew were coming. The next instant, she was in his arms, crying and clinging to him.

"Can't you understand?" Melba cried. "I love you. What you were is not who you are now, Will," she said, both hands gripping the front of his shirt. "And you are so wrong...God loves you much more than I do."

Willy stared in disbelief, and it hit him full force. She truly loved him. In spite of everything, she loved him. Grabbing her in his arms, he crushed her against him and held her, never wanting to let her go.

"Make yourselves comfortable," Abigail Cranston said, ushering Gloria and Andrew into the parlor. "Lottie will bring coffee and dessert, and we will enjoy it here in front of the fire. We often do that, don't we, Sam?"

"We surely do, especially on a night like this," he replied, nodding toward the window. "There's nothing more relaxing than a nice warm fire, sharing a hot cup of coffee with family and friends, and having something sweet and delicious to fill my belly," he said, taking a seat in one of the wing back chairs.

"This is one of my favorite memories," Milly remarked, perched on the piano stool. "I thought I was so grown up when Mama let us start coming in here for dessert and cocoa."

"Me too, though you were always spilling something," Molly remarked, glancing strangely at her mother as she took her arm and steered her toward the sofa.

"I was not."

"Yes, you were; on the floor, on the sofa, and remember the time you spilled cocoa all over the piano keys?" Molly replied, cackling.

"Oh shush, the both of you," Abigail remarked, sitting in the other wing back. "Now, Molly, you scoot down and make room for Andrew and Gloria." A pleased look on her face, Abigail sat back in the chair and patted Scooter, who jumped into her lap and made himself comfortable.

Gloria hesitantly sat on the sofa and wondered at Andrew's reaction to Mrs. Cranston's quite obvious seating arrangements. Maybe she should not have come along.

Closing the library, she had walked to the drugstore for some Anacin and Smith Brothers Cough Drops to ease her scratchy throat. Purchasing the items, she had stepped out on the sidewalk and stood for a moment watching the snow fall. The last light of day was fading, street lamps flickered on, and Hank was locking up the hardware store. Edna turned her open sign to closed, Cooley was lowering the flag, and most of the other shop owners appeared to have gone home. Glancing at her wristwatch, she saw it was ten minutes past five and felt guilty about detaining Gerald. The café was open until six o'clock, and she mulled over the idea of a nice, warm meal or going on home. Hopefully, the repairman would have her stove in working order tomorrow. She was tired of cold cuts.

At that moment, Andrew stepped out of Reese's Market and found her trying to decide what she would do.

"I am forever finding you walking in the dark," he said with a grin, strolling up to her with a loaf of bread in his hand.

"Hello, Andrew," she replied, flushing slightly. As always, when he was near, her heart raced and she felt herself becoming flustered.

"You know how I feel about ladies walking around alone at night," he commented, smiling, "and with it cold and snowing, it is unthinkable."

Gloria laughed and looked up at him. "In the first place, it is not dark yet. And in the second place, I am not out walking around. I was on my way to the café, and besides, I love walking in the snow."

Andrew studied her a moment. She was different than any woman he had ever met. Unless he was mistaken, she was headed to the café to eat alone, which did not bother her in the least. Women he knew would never admit to dining unaccompanied. Clear gray eyes looked directly at him, her cheeks were rosy from the cold, and her dark hair held flakes of snow.

"Are you meeting some tall, dark, handsome man for dinner?" he asked, tilting his head and grinning at the blush creeping up her neck and cheeks.

"No, I turned him down. He is such a pest," she replied, laughing softly.

"That is his loss," Andrew remarked, taking her arm and leading her along the sidewalk. "I am kidnapping you."

"What? Where are we going?" she asked in surprise as he led her across the street.

Andrew looked sideways and laughed. "My sweet, innocent Gloria, the kidnapping does not bother you, but the curiosity of where we are going does. I am taking you to the hotel. Lottie is always telling me to invite my friends to dinner, and she will be tickled pink to discover I returned from Reese's with not only the last loaf of bread but a pretty dinner guest as well."

"Oh, Andrew, I can't—"

"Of course you can. I don't want any excuses. Unless," he said, halting and staring at her, "you really do not wish to."

"Of course, I would love it...if you do not think I am imposing."

"Imposing?" Andrew said, opening the gate. "The Cranstons do not know the word."

Leading her up the steps, he opened the door, stepped back, and allowed her to enter, where she was warmly greeted by Abigail and a chattering Milly and Molly.

Now sitting contentedly on the sofa, she accepted the slice of cherry pie Lottie offered. Supper was delicious, the Cranstons warm and friendly, Lottie and Paul's bickering funny, and Milly and Molly delightful. And surprisingly, she had felt at ease sitting across the table from Andrew.

"Ya be careful now. It's still warm," Lottie stated, handing Andrew a generous slice and then serving Mr. and Mrs. Cranston. "Now the coffee is on the sideboard if ya want a refill. Gloria, it sure was nice ta have ya join us for dinner, and ya come back any time. Ah'm gonna have my dessert across the hall with Paul. Ah'll get my gown on, put my achin' feet up, and then ah—"

The fire whistle pierced the night air. Halting abruptly, Lottie turned with wide black eyes.

"Oh dear," Abigail exclaimed, looking at Sam.

Only two blocks down the street, it sounded to Gloria as if it were coming from the kitchen. Rising and falling, the whistle sounded strange and eerie. Her heart pounding, she rose from the sofa and looked at Andrew, who was headed to the foyer.

"My word," Molly said, standing to her feet, "that is the fire whistle."

"Surely it is not a tornado," Milly remarked, looking from one to the other.

"No!" Paul exclaimed, hurrying down the hall and jerking the front door wide, "It's a fire," he yelled, stepping out onto the porch.

"Lord have mercy," Lottie exclaimed, wringing her hands and following him.

Picking up and holding a whining Scooter, Abigail bustled along behind Gloria. "This is terrible, oh, dear. Sam, this is terrible. Where do you suppose it is?"

Gathered on the southwest end of the porch, they watched several cars speed by in the direction of the fire station, neighbors congregated on porches, and Gloria found herself trembling, not knowing if it was from the cold or the frightening sound of the fire whistle. In a matter of minutes, the fire truck sped past the hotel with lights flashing and sirens blaring.

"There," Sam exclaimed, pointing west in the direction of the library. "I see flames."

Above buildings and snow-covered tree tops, a yellow glow filled the night sky, and Gloria stood frozen, staring at the eerie sight.

"Why, Gloria," Abigail remarked, turning to her. "I believe the fire is in your neighborhood."

Turning, Andrew glanced at Gloria and then in the direction of the flames. Striding across the porch, he jerked the door open and grabbed their coats from the hall tree.

"Here," he said, throwing her coat around her shoulders. Slipping into his jacket, he grabbed her hand and hastily led her down the steps.

"Andrew, where ya goin'?" Lottie called anxiously, watching them hurry toward the car.

Gloria stopped dead in her tracks and stared at him, realizing what was running through his mind. "Andrew, you don't think—"

"I don't think anything, Gloria. We are going to drive over and see what is going on." Opening the door, he waited for her to slide in and then closed it and ran to the other side.

Bewildered and confused, she watched him get in, slam the door, and start the motor.

No, it couldn't be, Gloria thought, her heart pounding as a cold fear gripped her. Tears sprang to her eyes, and her whole body trembled.

Driving around the square, Andrew glanced over and noted her panic-stricken face. "Everything will be all right, Gloria," he said, patting her hand. "It is probably a shed in someone's backyard."

Heading down Oak Street, he turned left on Hunter and found he could go no farther. "We will walk from here," he said, pulling to the curb. Gloria was out of the car and hurrying along the street by the time Andrew got to the front of the car.

Catching up with her, he grabbed her arm and held it firmly, already knowing what they were going to find.

Turning the corner, they halted. Flames shot high in the air, and the fire truck was parked in the middle of the street, its loud motor rumbling, yellow lights flashing, and its hose sprawled atop the snow. Ned stood in the front yard spraying water on Gloria's roof, Jim Walker and several volunteers were attempting to gain entrance through a side window, and Sheriff Walker warned several frightened onlookers to stay clear.

Andrew heard Gloria's gasp. A cry escaped, and she jerked free. Hastily grabbing her, Andrew gripped her by both arms and turned her around.

"Let me go," she cried, looking over her shoulder. "Let me go."

"No!" Andrew said firmly, shaking her. "There is nothing you can do."

"I said let me go," she yelled, hitting him on the arm with a free hand.

Grabbing her with both hands, he pulled her into his arms and held her tight while she twisted and turned, trying to break free, and then finally gave way to sobs. One side of the house crumbled, and Andrew was thankful her head was buried in his chest and she did not see.

Jim Walker and the others stood back, evidently discussing their course of action, and Pastor Mike appeared a few feet away.

"What am I going to do?" Gloria cried, tears streaming down her cheeks as she watched flames engulf the rest of her house. "What will I do?"

Observing the anguish in her face, Andrew rested his arm across her shoulder and held her close to his side. "We will figure it out, Gloria. It will be all right."

"All right?" she questioned in astonishment. "Everything I have is gone...all of it," she choked out, bursting into fresh tears again.

"Gloria!" Ron exclaimed, rushing up and grabbing his sister. "Gloria, you are all right."

"Praise God," Pastor Mike said, striding up. Releasing a long breath, he placed a hand on Gloria's back as she wept in her brother's arms, and he looked over at Andrew.

"Everyone thought Gloria was at home. We thought you were inside, Gloria," Mike said, his hand still on her shoulder.

The words penetrated her brain, and Gloria looked up at the fear on her brother's face, glanced at Andrew and Pastor Mike, and then stared at what was left of her burning home. She would have...she would have been inside her burning home if she had not been with Andrew.

Chapter 24

"Burnt to the ground," James said, shaking his head. "Nothing left but the foundation."

Louis moved one of his checkers and then sat back and rubbed a hand across his chin. "It's a shame, a young girl losin' everything like that. Yes, suh, a cryin' shame."

The mood in the blacksmith shop was subdued this morning. Sitting on a stool next to Ben's worktable, Mike glanced around, the lack of normal chatter and arguing very apparent. Sitting on either side of the cracker barrel, James and Louis were attempting to play a half-hearted game of checkers, and old Ben, sitting in his rocker, puffed on his pipe and stared at the leafless maple tree beyond the window. Noah, whittling on a small piece of wood, glanced up as a car passed the shop and honked, and Phillip sat quietly in an old ladder-back chair drinking a cup of coffee.

The burning of Gloria's home shocked everyone. As in all small towns, each tree, house, and landmark held a memory, story, or some significant event, and a sudden, unexpected loss of that which was a part of their lives had a sobering effect.

"Did they ever find out what started it?" James asked, glancing up from the checker board.

"Ah ain't heard tell," old Ben replied, tapping the bowl of his pipe in the palm of his hand. "It was an old place, most likely the wirin' or somethin'. Gosh a mighty, now let me recollect," he said, smoothing his mustache with thumb and forefinger. "David Cranston built that house back in…seventy-one, ah believe. And he and Rose lived there till they passed on. Come ta think of it, the back porch burnt one other time. Everbody said two of the boys was playin' with matches and caught it a fire. All's ah remember is they got a good lickin' over it."

Chuckling, old Ben put his pipe in the pocket of his overalls and stretched his legs out in front of him. "They left the place ta Ruby, and when she and Paul Laughlin married, he jest moved in and that's where they stayed. They didn't have no youngins, and when they was gone, Gloria bought the place, about six years ago, as best as ah can recollect."

"Thank goodness she had insurance," Phillip commented, rising from his chair and walking toward the stove. "I expect that don't help her grief much. Some things just can't be replaced. She will have to start all over again now."

"Yes, she will, but Gloria will do just fine," Mike replied, looking at the faces turned toward him. "She's young and resilient and very grateful to be alive. You know Ron will make sure everything is taken care of properly."

"You bet; that's what families are for." Phillip lifted the white enameled coffee pot from the stove and filled his cup. Replacing it on the cook lid, he studied it a moment. The handle and top were trimmed in black, enamel was chipped in several places, and the bottom was dark from use. Ben had made coffee in that old pot for how many years now? *For as long as I can remember,* he thought, returning to his chair. He shook his head. Poor Gloria doesn't even have a coffee pot.

"My, how we take everything for granted," he commented. "Two years ago we were in the middle of the war, living one day at a time and now a year after war's end, we've gone back to taking everything for granted again. Have you noticed that? It takes something like last night to remind us again how quickly things can change."

"That's fer shore," Noah remarked, closing his pocketknife. "Ah made it through the war and come back home, got a job, and thought ah was doin' jest fine. Then the next thing ya know, ah don't have a job no more. Jest like that; went ta work one mornin', and they was closin' the place up."

"None of us know what tomorrow will bring," Mike said. Setting his coffee cup on the work table, he looked at Noah's disheartened expression. Work at the lumber company looked promising in the spring, but Mike knew he was worried about what to do until then. "God is good, Noah. He always takes care of his own."

His words reached every ear in the shop, and the men nodded at one another, knowing the preacher was right.

"The Lord gives, and he takes away, but there is always a blessing in what he does and in whatever circumstances we find ourselves. Why do you think you are back home in Oak Grove, Noah?" he asked, looking at him intently. "He guided you here for his own will and pleasure. He will reveal it to you and, in the meantime, supply all your needs."

Noah nodded in agreement and glanced at Uncle Ben rocking contentedly. Perhaps Uncle Ben was part of the reason God had brought him home.

"And now, let's think about Gloria," Mike continued. "The fire could have been a greater tragedy. It was a blessing she was not home at the time, and the houses on both sides of her did not catch fire and create more damage and heartache."

"Yes, suh, you are right about that, Preacher," old Ben remarked, nodding his head. "Ah've seen it time and time again. The Lord almighty never lets ya down, and now…well, suh, he's givin' us the opportunity ta help Gloria. That'll be a blessin' for us all."

The men sat in companionable silence for a few seconds; then Phillip grinned. Why had he not thought of this sooner? His son was the mayor, and he was certain he would agree. "How about the emergency fund? All the town council has to do is authorize some of it to help Gloria."

"I can't think of any better use," James agreed, hooking his thumbs in his suspenders. "That's what the money's for, now isn't it?"

The door opened, and a blast of cold air blew in.

"By jingees, but it's cold," Cooley exclaimed, standing in the doorway. "Didn't I tell ya it was gonna turn cold? We're gonna have a hard winter, now ya mark my words."

"Close the blamed door, Cooley. You're letting the heat out," James said loudly and then turned back to the checker board.

Shoving the door, Cooley glanced around and retorted, "*Some* of us has to be out there workin' in the cold instead of sittin' around in here by a nice warm fire like a bunch of women."

"Have a cup of coffee and warm yourself," old Ben said, chuckling, as he watched him remove his gloves and stuff them in his pocket.

"I hope youins got them chains on yer tires 'cause it's comin' down pretty good." Rubbing his hands together, he walked over and stood next to the stove for a minute and then retrieved his cup from a nail on the timber post and filled it with coffee. "Well do ya?"

"Do we what?" Louis asked, studying the checkerboard and wondering how James's checker managed to get where it was.

"Chains, ya got chains on yer tires?"

Mike watched in amusement as Cooley looked at Louis and shook his head in exasperation, his cap's ear flaps flopping back and forth.

"If you'd get cinders on the streets, we wouldn't need chains," Louis taunted.

"I have you know they's already cinders on the streets," Cooley retorted. "Course I don't suppose ya'd notice, not with that pea brain of yours concentratin' on that there checker game."

Ignoring his comment, James leaned back in his chair. "You know what I heard on the radio this morning? In Chicago you can go to the bank, and you don't even have to get out of your car."

"Why would a body go ta the bank and not get out of their car?" Louis asked confused. "That don't make no sense at all."

"It is what they call drive-up banking," James replied, jumping Louis's man and grinning. "They say you just drive up to the side of the bank to a little window and a teller takes care of your business right then and there."

"You don't say," Phillip said, shaking his head. "What will they think of next?"

"Folks is gettin' plumb lazy if ya ask me," Cooley remarked, dragging a stool next to the stove. "Drivin' up to a window so ya don't have to get out and walk to the door. And handin' yer money over to some stranger ain't fer me. I'd jest as soon keep it in a shoe box under my bed."

"What if your house catches fire like Gloria's?" James asked, wondering how much money Cooley had in his shoe box.

"Well, for cryin' out loud, a smart feller don't keep all of it in one spot. It's a good idea to take some out to the barn, then if'n the house did burn, ya wouldn't lose everything. I figured ya'd know that much." Cooley scratched an ear beneath the flap of his cap and sighed.

"O'course ever'time I get a little money saved up, it don't stay in that shoe box very long, 'cause I have to take it out and use it for somethin' *compulsory*. That there's my word of the week," he announced, looking about as smug as capable with his cap crooked on his head and an earflap practically covering one eye.

"Compulsory?" Louis asked, looking at him over the rim of his glasses, knowing if he didn't ask, he would keep repeating it until someone did.

"Yes sir, compulsory means somethin' that's needful or required." Crossing a leg, he looked around the shop proudly. "By jingees, it's a good thing I'm learnin' these words, or youins wouldn't know nothin'."

Mike watched him take a gulp of coffee and look around expectantly, waiting for someone to ask him to use the word in a sentence. "Come on, Cooley, you've told us what it means; now let's hear you use it."

"Well now, let me see," Cooley said, studying a beam of the ceiling. "By jingees, I got it. I expect it's compulsory we do somethin' for Gloria. Don't ya think?"

"Well, suh," old Ben commented, nodding his head. "Ah have ta agree with ya, Cooley. We was just talkin' 'bout that. That's a good idea. Yes, suh, ah'd say it's compulsory we do somethin' for her. Ah'll get a coffee can, and we'll jest put somethin' in it ever'day, and when it's full then, Preacher, we'll let you give it ta her. That be all right?"

"I would be happy to," Mike said, looking at each man. With all their varied personalities, strengths, weaknesses, and quirks, he couldn't think of another bunch of men he admired more.

Stepping onto the porch, Andrew pulled on his gloves and looked up at the morning sky. The sun was making a feeble attempt to break through the clouds, and a few flurries still swirled in the wind. Buttoning his jacket, he looked across the square. Approximately two inches of snow had fallen during the night, transforming it into a picture postcard. Smooth and as yet undisturbed but for the path Cooley had cleared, it lay in stark contrast to the trail of black cinders he had dumped on the street. Sidewalks were swept clean in front of the shops, and those who were out and about were bundled up.

His gaze traveled along the block to the library, and he knew it was closed; it was Tuesday. Wondering how Gloria was faring from last night's shock, he stood quietly for a moment, the memory of holding her still fresh in his mind. It had been a long time since he had done that for anyone, and he pondered how good it felt. *I will check on her later,* he thought, heading toward the drugstore.

Snow crunched underfoot, and he glanced up as Clyde honked and waved, the cab's tire chains crunching in the snow. Perhaps he should have Willy apply them to his vehicle, although Lottie adamantly announced at breakfast the snow wouldn't continue.

"It won't last through the day; it's too early fer a big snow," she declared, thumping a pan of hot biscuits on the table. "Ya ain't seen nothin' yet, jest wait 'til January and February get here."

Well she was correct. The snow is tapering off, he thought, crossing the street to the drugstore and stepping inside.

Gerald was coming from the pharmacy and handed a package to an elderly lady Andrew did not know, Sam, Sheriff Walker, Mayor Driscol, and Nelson White sat at the soda fountain, and Mildred Reese, tying her headscarf beneath her chin, was adamantly telling Trudy something. Straightening her black, wool hat and slipping her gloves on, Trudy replied with a loud humph, jerked her handbag from the table, and then smiled with pleasure when her eye caught his.

"Why Andrew," she exclaimed, putting her handbag across her arm, "you are just the person I hoped to see."

"Good morning, Trudy, Mildred."

"Gracious me, but I am so proud of you for saving Gloria's life," she remarked, patting his arm. "It was nothing but divine intervention that saved that poor girl."

"I will have to agree on the latter, Trudy. It was a wonderful blessing Gloria was not home at the time of the fire, but I am hardly a hero."

"Oh, Andrew, don't be so modest," Trudy exclaimed loudly. "My soul, but you are the reason she did not…my gracious I cannot say it," she said, placing a hand to her cheek. "We were just talking about that, weren't we, Mildred?"

"Yes indeedy, Mr. Baxter, we certainly were. I am so grateful Gloria was with you, otherwise—"

"Ladies," Andrew said, "I did nothing to warrant—"

"Oh, and by the way," Trudy interrupted, smiling like a fat feline with a cornered mouse, "I was not aware that you and Gloria…well, I must say, Mildred and I were just commenting on what an attractive couple you make."

Astonished, Andrew stared at her. Where did she get the idea there was anything between him and Gloria?

"I am afraid there is a misunderstanding. Gloria and I are—" he began, noting the amused grins from those at the soda fountain.

"Now, now"—Trudy giggled,—"you don't have to explain. That is personal, and I don't like to pry into other people's lives, but I am so happy for the both of you."

"Trudy," Henry exclaimed, rising from the stool and taking his wife by the arm, "you are right. That is personal, so don't be prying. Did you invite Andrew to supper?"

"Oh, good gracious, no. Land sakes, I don't know where my mind is these days. Well, yes I do, we are collecting for the Thanksgiving baskets and organizing the church dinner, and then, of course, we need to do something for Gloria, and Caroline has been begging for a new dress for Miss Mattie's Christmas party, and the school dance. My," Trudy sighed, "I cannot believe she is old enough to attend a *dance*, of all things. Of course it is a school function, and I don't—"

"Would you join us for supper Saturday evening?" Henry interjected, glancing at his watch.

"I am afraid I have plans," Andrew replied, knowing he had responded too quickly. An evening in the company of his daughters sounded wonderful, but how would he handle seeing them in the house they called home and interacting with the two they considered parents. He couldn't even...no, not just yet. "If we could make it another evening, I would love it."

"Why of course, we will plan on it," Trudy beamed. "I will check Henry's calendar and get back with you. And bring Gloria. We would love to have the both of you."

"I do not think Gloria will want to go anywhere. Last night was very traumatic. I think she will want to stay home with Ron and Betty, at least until she gets her feet beneath her."

"Nonsense. You can talk her into it, and it will be good for her." Smiling coyly, Trudy leaned over and patted his arm, commenting gleefully, "Do you really think Gloria could resist you, Andrew?"

"Trudy," Henry said, exasperated, "leave this poor man alone. We will get back with you and plan dinner soon, Andrew."

"Fine," Andrew replied, watching him steer Trudy toward the door. When would he be ready to step into the Driscol home?

"Bless my soul, General Longstreet, I do not know what is taking Jake so long to bring the carriage around. You will forgive the wait, won't you?"

"Don't worry about a thing, Miss Matilda," Mike replied, wondering why in the world she thought him to be General Longstreet. "Perhaps we could have a cup of tea?"

"Yes, of course. My gracious, where are my manners. Please have a seat by the fire, and I will return shortly."

Watching her bustle across the room and down the hall, Mike took a seat in one of the wingback chairs and looked up at Miss Tillie's portrait. The lovely, young woman was confident and vibrant, and he supposed Matilda Jane Compton in her younger years was charming and quite irresistible.

A small, gilded frame with a photograph of Miss Tillie and Harold sat on the side table, and Mike studied it a moment. Standing next to the infamous Tin Lizzie, the dignified gentleman was laughing at his wife, her head tilted at a haughty angle and a hand resting on the door handle. A smile crossed Mike's face, and he imagined Harold must have had his hands full with Miss Tillie. *Where had she gone?*

Making his weekly visit, he had hoped to approach the subject of a live-in guest, but the thought vanished when she greeted him. Dressed in a red, long-sleeved, two-pieced day dress from a bygone era, Miss Tillie was the epitome of a grand Southern lady, as she ushered him into the parlor. Turning to face him with a rustle of petticoats, he felt he had slipped into history.

The dress was actually rather charming, he thought, wondering how she managed to get around in such a voluminous skirt without tripping and falling. The blouse gathered at the waist, flared up the front, and was pleated at the shoulders. White lace trimmed a standup collar, sleeve edges, and several layers of the wrinkled skirt. Red slippers peeked beneath the folds of her gown, and a green and gold brooch completed her attire.

The tea kettle whistled in the kitchen, and he heard the clink of china. Staring into the fire, an uneasy thought flitted through his mind. Miss Tillie built this fire—something needed to be done and soon.

"Here you are, General," she commented, entering the room carrying her china tea set. Placing it on the tea table between them, she took a seat and poured a cup. "A tiny hint of mint and two teaspoons of sugar, just the way you like it."

Mike studied her curiously. Clearly confused, yet she remembered how he preferred his tea.

"Thank you, Miss Matilda," Mike replied, watching her daintily stir in a spoonful of sugar.

"I was not expecting you, General." She smiled and touched a strand of dark hair. Now streaked with gray, it was parted in the middle and pulled back into some sort of elaborate bun. "Papa will want to know you are here, just as sure as you're born, but I do not know where he is at present."

Rising, she walked to the window, glanced out, and then turned to look at him. "I will have Jake bring the carriage around, and we will take a drive. Would you like that?"

"Yes, but it is not necessary," Mike replied. "I would just as soon enjoy a cup of tea. It is very good, thank you."

"You are welcome. I wish Elizabeth and Isabelle were here. I would so like you to meet them."

Mike watched uncertainty cross her face, and she looked at him questioningly for a minute as though trying to figure something out.

Releasing a small sigh, she fingered the brooch and gazed across the room. "Now, where do you suppose those two have gone?"

"I suppose they will be here shortly," Mike replied, sipping from the small cup and wishing she would just once bring him the flavorful stuff in a nice big mug. It was uncommonly good, and he found having a cup of tea with Miss Tillie very relaxing.

"No," she replied, setting her cup and saucer on the table. Her brows furrowed, and she stared into the fire a moment and then looked at him. "Please forgive me, General, but Isabelle…why, that's right…Isabelle is no longer with us. Now how could I have forgotten that?"

"Miss Matilda—" Mike began, sitting forward.

"Oh, General Longstreet," she exclaimed with a sudden shift of mind, "I would like to show you something special."

Rising and moving to the tall, mahogany secretary, she removed the lid of an ornate dish and retrieved a key. Unlocking the side drawer, she glanced at him, smiled, and then pulled it open.

Mike knew she was looking for her box and prayed for the right words when she realized it was not there.

For a moment she stood very still and then pulled the drawer all the way out and bent to look inside. "It is not here," she exclaimed in alarm. "General Longstreet, it is not here. My box has disappeared. Someone has taken it."

Rising, Mike went to her and took her hands in his, speaking quietly, "Miss Tillie, your box is safe."

"But you do not understand. It is a beautiful, wooden box with my initials on it, and it is very valuable and contains—"

"Miss Tillie," Mike said gently, bending down and looking into her eyes, "I promise you, your box is safe. Trust me, I know it is."

"But, Pastor Mike, there are some important documents that...Pastor Mike?" Miss Tillie's eyes widened in recognition, and she stared at him.

"Yes. Pastor Mike. You forgot for a minute, but now you remember, don't you?"

"Oh dear," Miss Tillie replied, tears blurring her eyes. "Of course I do. I...for a while I—"

Glancing down at the front of her dress, she stared at it a moment and then rubbed her fingers along its sleeve. "Well now, I have gone and done it again, haven't I? How long was I..."

"I am not sure," Mike replied, watching in amazement as the feisty Miss Tillie emerged back into the present. "Leah was here the day before yesterday, and you were fine then."

"Hmmm, yes, I remember now. I was showing her Mama's needlepoint."

"That's right. She told me," Mike replied, gently taking her arm. "Now, let's sit down and finish our tea."

"Oh, now, don't start mollycoddling me. I am all right." Spinning around to return to her chair, her swirling skirts sent a teaspoon from the tea table onto the floor, and Charlotte, meowing loudly, jumped out of her way and leapt to the back of the chair.

Chuckling, Mike watched Miss Tillie take her seat, slap at her skirts, and shake her head in exasperation.

"When I was a young girl I loved these cussed garments, but thank goodness styles have changed. Women don't have to drag around in these skirts and petticoats anymore, and we are free of those infernal corsets that made you feel like a cat with fur that shrunk three sizes."

Mike threw his head back and laughed. "Miss Tillie, you do have a way with words. Welcome back to the present."

"Thank you. Now...I see we evidently were enjoying a cup of tea," she remarked, glancing at the cups. "I am sorry, Pastor Mike. You like a small amount of mint. Let me brew a fresh pot."

"No, no, Miss Tillie, as a matter of fact, you prepared it the way you always do."

"I did? Well, I'll declare. I wonder how I managed to do that."

"I wondered the same myself."

"What were we talking about?" Miss Tillie asked, sitting back in the chair. "And you tell me the truth, do you hear?"

"I will never lie to you, Miss Tillie. I told you that before." Crossing one leg over the other, he looked at her and answered honestly. "You mentioned Elizabeth and Isabelle. You wanted me to meet them."

"Lizzie and Isabelle," Miss Tillie murmured softly. "How I miss them. Hmmm, you know, I think that is why my spells do not frighten me, Pastor," she said with a small smile. "During those times, I am with them again. Does that make any sense to you at all?"

"I suppose it does, in a way. Were Elizabeth and Isabelle Christians, Miss Tillie?"

"Oh, yes. Thank God for that."

"What a comfort that must be, and what a glad reunion you will have one day."

"Indeed. I will see them all: Harold, Mama and Papa, and my sisters." Relaxing, Miss Tillie smiled and patted Charlotte who jumped from the back of the chair into her lap. "And may I ask, who did I think you were?"

Mike chuckled. "I was quite proud, Miss Tillie. I was General Longstreet."

"General Longstreet, forevermore! He did visit Edgewood once. It was several years after the war, and I was only about six. He spent the night, and I didn't care a whole lot for him. Of course, I did not really know the man. I am sure he was very nice. He was quite well known, very serious, and didn't talk much." Miss Mattie sighed. "I was a bit frightened of him, but I suppose I did not understand what the man had been through. I am certain the war took a heavy toll on him as it did everyone."

"I am sure it did."

"Why on God's green earth would I even associate you with General Longstreet?" Miss Tillie asked, looking at the man across from her. He was the complete opposite of what she remembered of General Longstreet. Pastor Mike was friendly, kind, genuine, and humorous, and, if she might add, quite a handsome man.

"I certainly do not have the answer for that."

"Ah well, I guess everything is all right. I am back to normal again."

"For now," Mike commented, looking directly at her, "but you must allow me to find someone to stay with you, Miss Tillie. I am serious. I cannot take no for an answer. I care too much for you well-being."

Sighing, she looked away and replied softly. "I know, but it is just so hard to admit that I...need nursing."

"Not nursing, Miss Tillie, only a companion that would be with you when you get confused. You by no means need a nurse."

"That is a relief to know. And who did you have in mind?"

"I do not have anyone in mind. I am waiting for the Lord to tell me who that might be."

"What about Andrew? I like my great-nephew, and he cannot live at the hotel the rest of his life or however long he plans to stay here."

"Andrew is looking to purchase a place of his own," Mike answered. "Therefore, I cannot see a reason for him to move from the hotel. He is already considering a couple of places."

"Then he is planning on staying?" Miss Tillie asked, delighted.

"I believe so, for a good while anyway."

Miss Tillie stopped petting Charlotte and raised a brow. "Now you tell me why a young man whose business is in New York and home in Connecticut would want to purchase property here? What are you not telling me, Pastor Mike?"

Pulling the hairbrush through her hair, Leah observed her husband's reflection in the mirror. He was propped against the pillows, one hand lying on the open pages of his Bible, and he was staring at the window. Unusually quiet at supper, she supposed him to be tired but now knew something was on his mind.

Laying the hairbrush on the vanity, Leah rose and walked to the bed. "What are you in such deep thought about?" she asked, removing her slippers and sliding in beside him. Brushing back the lock of hair that always fell across his forehead, she leaned forward and kissed his cheek.

Smiling, Mike caught her hand and lifted it to his lips.

"You were very quiet at supper."

"I know," he replied, adjusting the pillows behind his back. "I am concerned about Willy. I had the opportunity to speak with him this afternoon again, but...he is not ready."

Leah laid her head on his shoulder. She knew how burdened he was over Willy. They had been praying for his salvation for such a long time.

"He seems so close, Leah, and he has come so far, but he still will not let that barrier down. I know not to rush things, and the Lord knows Willy's heart and how and when his salvation will come about. But I am so burdened for him...and Melba also. This affects her too."

"She asked something that troubles me," Leah commented quietly, thinking of their conversation in the salon.

"What?"

"She asked how I knew marrying you was the right thing. I know she loves Willy. I don't doubt it. But there was a bit of reservation in her manner when she asked. I think she is hesitant about marrying him."

"Of course she is. Melba has strong convictions, and she wants a Christian husband." Rolling to his side, he propped his head on his arm and looked at her. "I talked with her after prayer meeting last week. She believes Willy is under conviction, and she is waiting for him to make that decision."

"How agonizing, praying and waiting for someone you love so much to come to faith," Leah replied softly.

"Trust, Leah, we have to trust the Lord to bring it about. Sometimes it is hard to wait. I know. I am waiting to see who he has in mind to live with Miss Tillie. That situation needs to be addressed fairly soon. And there is Gloria, of course, and Louise. I am praying this short visit with her aunt will help her."

"Do you still worry about Nathaniel?"

Lying quietly and looking at the ceiling, Mike thought of the young boy from the hills. In many ways, he had adjusted well. "Nathaniel is…doing well academically, but he doesn't make friends. I want him to be happy and carefree." Mike rubbed a hand along Leah's arm and chuckled. "See how I am? The boy lived in the hills away from society for fourteen years, knows nothing of city life, was thrust into a world foreign to him, and I want the Lord to change him yesterday. I am very impatient."

"Yes you are," Leah replied, smiling. "He has only been in Oak Grove three months. Not everyone can walk up to a total stranger and chat like old friends the way you do. Besides, Johnny said he has gotten to know some of the boys on the football team."

"That is true. I watched them practice the other evening, and he didn't appear to have any problems. And I suppose the fight he and Billy had over Lacy Bingham is forgotten."

"Sarah said the Binghams are attending services quite frequently," Leah remarked, laughing softly.

Mike opened a closed eye and looked at her. "What is so amusing about that?"

"Nothing, silly. I was thinking of her description of Lacy. 'That Lacy Bingham is a little vixen,'" she said, imitating Sarah Clark's sweet voice.

Mike smiled sleepily, "That is a harsh statement coming from Sarah. Lacy must be a handful, but then every church has one. We have Elizabeth."

"Yes we do, and we love her to death, don't we?" Kissing his forehead, she rolled to her side. "Good night."

"Good night, darlin'," he murmured, pulling her close.

Leah lay quietly, listening to Mike's breathing become slow and even. *Two little vixens,* she thought, smiling to herself. *I wonder if they will both be at the Thanksgiving dinner.*

Chapter 25

"Cranberry sauce?" Melba asked.

"I love the whole Thanksgiving meal," Willy exclaimed enthusiastically. "Turkey, stuffing, sweet potatoes, cranberries; you fix it, and I will eat it."

Rising from the kitchen chair, she took a seat on his lap and laughed as she placed both arms around his neck. "I bet when we get old you are going to be fat."

"Will you love me anyway?"

"Of course I will. What about you? Will you love me if I get...plump?"

"I will love you when you are fat, gray headed, wrinkled, and hard of hearing," Willy chuckled, kissing her lightly.

Sighing, Melba ran her fingers through his hair and smiled down into his eyes. "This will be our first Thanksgiving, Will."

Lifting her hand, he looked at her finger, longing to put a ring on it. "We could make this Thanksgiving extraordinary."

"How so?"

"We could have Pastor Mike marry us, and it would truly be our first Thanksgiving together."

Laying her forehead against his, she sighed, "Oh, Will, it will be so wonderful when we are finally married."

"Finally?" Willy asked, looking at her questioningly. "Do we have...obstacles?"

"No," Melba replied, standing up and pulling his hand. "Let's go into the living room where we will be more comfortable. I can finish the grocery list in the morning."

"Grocery list," Willy muttered, flipping off the light switch and following her from the kitchen.

Jack lay by the fire and raised his head, looked at them a minute, then laid it back on his paws.

Sitting on the sofa, Willy watched Melba cross the room to the radio. Nat King Cole's "I Love You for Sentimental Reasons" filled the room, and, adjusting the volume, she turned and looked at him. "This is such a beautiful song."

Relaxed, Willy stretched his legs out and rested his head on the back of the sofa. He stared at her intently, and Melba found it hard to breathe; she loved him so much.

Standing to his feet, he smiled and held out his hand. "It is. Dance with me."

Pulled closely into his arms, she laid her head against his shoulder and closed her eyes. Aware of his lips brushing her temple, she snuggled closer, and the smooth, mellow voice on the radio touched her heart.

I think of you every morning,
dream of you every night.
Darling, I'm never lonely
whenever you are in sight.

More content than she had ever been, Melba knew she would never be lonely as long as Will loved her. Moving slowly to the music, feeling his nearness and the sound of his voice in her ear, she was lost in a wonderful place.

Please give your loving heart to me
and say we'll never part.

Never part. Melba opened her eyes. A strange foreboding deep within began to spread through her. *What would I do without him? What if we parted?* Raising her head, she looked up at him.

"I love you, Will. No matter what happens...forever, I will love you."

Looking down into green eyes filled with emotion, Willy thought she had never looked so beautiful. "Mel...I will always love you too. Marry me...marry me soon. I love you so much."

Melba's heart ached at the longing in his eyes, and she laid her head against his chest, feeling his heart beat against her cheek. "I want to so badly, Will."

Placing both hands on her shoulders, he looked at her almost pleadingly. "Then let's do so, there is no reason for us to wait, Mel. I know you—"

"Yes, Will, there is," she replied, staring up at him, the words tumbling out. "I want a Christian marriage, and I want a Christian home for our children. I cannot marry you until I am sure of that."

Surprise crossed his face, and he shook his head. "Hon, why didn't you tell me this before? Is that...that is why you are hesitating?"

"Yes, Will. God has to be in our lives."

"I know, I know, hon, and I agree." Placing both arms around her waist, he smiled and hugged her. "I will talk to Pastor Mike about getting baptized. It is something I should have already done. Then nothing will stand in our way."

"Will," Melba replied, knowing he meant every word. "I do not want you to get baptized to please me so we can be married. You have to think about this."

"I have thought about it, Mel, and it is what I want," he said, pulling her into his arms. "It is the right thing to do. A family should be in church together. I know that now. I didn't before...with my mother and...my past. But now I want to do the right thing."

"Ron, did you see that box of cl . . ." Gloria asked with a look of surprise as her eyes met Andrew's.

Groaning, she wanted to run from the room. She wore no makeup, her hair was a mess, and Alice's slacks and Ron's overlarge shirt she wore did not even match, whereas Andrew looked incredibly handsome in a burgundy sweater and dark slacks.

"Good evening, Gloria. How are you?" Andrew asked, noting her flushed cheeks.

"I am okay, thank you," Gloria replied softly. Why did he have to catch her looking a fright?

"Can I get you a cup of coffee?" Ron asked. "I was going to have a cup."

"No thanks, Ron, I do not believe so."

"All right," he said, turning to Gloria, "how about you, sis?"

"None for me either."

"Then I will leave you to visit. Alice and I will be in the kitchen listening to Amos 'n Andy. It is good of you to stop by, Andrew," he said, smiling.

Heading for the kitchen, the smiled faded. He wished Andrew Baxter would soon complete whatever business he had in Oak Grove and be on his way. For the last several weeks, he had been aware that Gloria was much enamored with the man, and it was just as apparent that he was *not* of the same mind.

"I am sorry, Andrew," Gloria said, acutely aware of her stocking feet, "please, won't you have a seat."

Her heart pounding in her chest, she watched him sit on the sofa. The memory of his holding her close while they stood in the street watching her house burn was fresh in her mind, and his presence was unnerving.

Andrew glanced up questioningly. She looked very young and almost frightened as she hesitantly sat at the other end. Clearly she was still very upset.

"I know it is a little late to be visiting, but I was on my way home from Pastor Mike's. They invited me to celebrate Johnny's birthday with them, and I wanted to see how you were getting along. I worry about you, Gloria," Andrew said, noting her trembling hand as she brushed a dark strand of hair from her face.

Tears sprang to her eyes, and she glanced down. A longing to be held in his arms was so strong it almost frightened her, and she nervously clasped her hands together.

"Thank you, Andrew. That means a lot."

The softly spoken words stirred something within, and Andrew was once again struck by the smooth, velvet voice. He watched her nervously straighten a cuff of the shirt, and it suddenly dawned on him she was embarrassed by her appearance. What was it about women and their ideas of attractiveness? Although he found Gloria rather cute in stocking feet and an oversized shirt, he knew enough of women to keep quiet.

"Gloria," he commented, leaning toward her, "you have become one of my best friends, and I want you to know that I want to help any way I can."

He was looking intently at her, and she was aware of the cologne he wore. He was much too close. Stifling the urge to move away, she glanced down at her hands.

"Gloria, look at me." Andrew said gently. Lifting her chin, he gazed into the clear, gray eyes. "I am your friend. This is a troubling time, and I want to be here for you."

"Thank you," Gloria replied, accepting the handkerchief he offered. "I am sorry, Andrew. I am so emotional. I can't believe this has happened."

"Of course you are emotional. Anyone would be," he said, patting her hand. "I have experienced things I didn't understand and wondered why they happened, but now I can look back and see how God blessed me and made something good come from it. And you will too."

"I know. Pastor Mike said the same thing and that unbelievable blessings will come my way."

A small smile touched her lips, and she glanced away. "I am trying so hard to believe that, but…I am…I am afraid my faith is lacking at the moment."

"I want you to have this," Andrew said, reaching into a back pocket for his wallet. Removing a small card, he laid it on the coffee table and retrieved a ball point pen from a shirt pocket beneath his sweater. "I am leaving for Connecticut Monday morning for the Thanksgiving holiday and will be gone a week. I want you to call me if there is *anything* you need or if you just want to talk. This is my home number," he said, turning the card over and writing on it.

Handing the card to her, he sat back and crossed a leg. "Now, tell me what you are feeling. Nothing is worse than keeping everything bottled up. I know what it is like to go through a tragedy. It helps to talk."

Gloria studied the compassionate eyes. Never would she have thought Andrew had experienced a tragedy. He seemed so in control and confident. Sitting back, she pulled her legs beneath her and thought a minute.

"I am frightened…I…I could have died, Andrew. If I had not gone with you, I would have been home. And I know that was God's love and protection, but I…it is so frightening."

Andrew nodded, "I know. Keep dwelling on his love and protection, and the fear will disappear. Believe me, it will."

"I am also sad because there are things that cannot be replaced…things that held sentiment for me, and they are gone forever. My hopes and dreams are gone."

"Our hopes and dreams are never gone, Gloria," Andrew said, touching her hand. "They are just buried beneath other emotions right now. They will come back."

"I hope so, but it is hard to have hopes and dreams when you have nothing…clothes, a bed, or even a toothbrush," she said, shaking her head. "I feel like an orphan or charity case."

"Gloria," Andrew remarked firmly, "you are not a charity case. You happen to be a young woman who suffered a tragic loss. That is it. People in this community are here to help just as you would one of them. I have not lived here long, but I know that to be true."

"I know. I suppose I am feeling sorry for myself, but...Andrew, the fire was my fault."

"Why would you think that?"

"I was having trouble with my oven. It would not heat, so I didn't...I should have called the repairman sooner."

"Your stove did not start the fire. Old wiring was the cause."

Gloria looked up in surprise. "What makes you think that?"

"I talked to Jim Walker this afternoon at the cafe, and he said that was what they determined."

"Really?"

"Really. Now toss that feeling of guilt away. What do you think of that?" Andrew said, watching a grin cross her face. "That's better."

"I do feel better knowing that."

"I know," he replied, wishing there was more he could do. She was different from other women he knew, and for a reason he didn't quite understand, he was proud of that fact.

"I need to go and let you get back to what you were doing," he said, standing to his feet.

"Thank you, Andrew, for caring and listening. You are a very good friend."

Looking down at her a moment, Andrew rested a hand on her shoulder and spoke softly. "We have become very good friends, haven't we, Gloria?"

"Yes, we have, and I am very glad."

"Me too." Leaning down, he kissed her forehead and then straightened and pointed his finger. "Do not lose my business card, and call me any time, day or night." Slipping into his jacket, he smiled again. "Remember, I am only a phone call away."

"I will."

Following him to the door, she was aware of everything about him: the blue of his eyes and his olive skin, the darkness of his hair and beard, and his smile.

"Are you sure you are okay?" he asked, noting her strange expression.

"I am quite sure, thank you."

"Good night, Gloria."

"Good night, Andrew," she said quietly, watching him walk across the porch and down the steps. Closing the door, she crossed the room and picked up his business card. Turning it over, she read, "I am but a phone call away."

Chapter 26

"By jingees, Preacher, I never thought they'd be so many folks show up jest to eat," Cooley exclaimed, looking around at the crowd in the church basement. "I'd bet a dime to a hard biscuit some of 'em ain't been here since last Thanksgivin'."

"That is all right, Cooley. It is good to see their smiling faces. You never know who the Lord is dealing with, and all it might take is a word or smile of encouragement to touch their hearts," Mike replied, pleased with the unusually large turnout this year. "One never knows how our actions may affect someone."

"I expect yer right about that," Cooley agreed, scratching his ear. "If ya hadn't slammed that cell door and set yer backside down on the bunk next to me, I never would've give the Lord much thought, I guarantee ya that."

"It was nothing I did," Mike replied, recalling the day Cooley had had too much *hooch*, as he called it, and proceeded to entertain everyone on the square with his banjo and off-key singing. Sheriff Walker found his hands full when Cooley refused to leave and, not knowing what else to do, locked him up, called Mike, and as one thing led to another, he found his pastor in the cell with Cooley, proving the point they were both sinners in God's eyes. Much could be said of Sheriff and Jim Walker's patience that day. For the next two hours, they were subjected to a loud sing song of varied choruses, hymns, and questionable lyrics until Cooley finally sobered up.

"The Lord has brought you a long way, do you know that?" Mike asked, placing his hand on Cooley's shoulder. "You are a real blessing to me and a joy to him."

"Thank ya. I'm tryin', Preacher, and as long as I keep readin' God's Holy Bible, hittin' the hooch ain't one of my *aspirations* no more."

"Word of the week?"

"Yes, sir, me and Alice are writin' 'em down. We got ten new words so far. I'll soon be teachin' school," he exclaimed, guffawing and slapping his leg. "Ya know what I think I'll jest do?"

"What are you going to do, Cooley?" Mike asked, watching the wiry little man hook both thumbs in his suspenders.

"I believe I'll mosey on over and talk to ole man Batch. He looks like he was nursed on a lemon, did ya ever notice that? But he was right friendly last week when I delivered his coal."

"I think that is a great idea."

Mike watched Cooley weave his way in and out of the crowd in the direction of Cornelius Batchcum. Listening to the steady buzz of talk and laughter and the combined aromas of turkey and dressing, fresh baked bread, desserts, and coffee, he was reminded once again why this season was so special. From now until after Christmas, the community came together like no other time of year, and he loved it.

Sipping his coffee, his eyes roamed the crowd. Closely placed tables provided opportunity for visiting, and Trudy had several ladies' undivided attention. *What is she up to?* Mike wondered. Talking earnestly, she kept nodding her head, the black feathers on her brown suede hat moving in all directions. Teenagers and children, including his four, sat at tables along the back wall and were presently creating a lot of racket and laughter, Leah chatted with Melvin and Mary, and Myrtle, all gussied up in a red dress, sat next to Clyde and kept touching her curls and smiling. Would he ever get used to the new Myrtle?

His gaze rested on Andrew, whose attention was focused across the room on Caroline, and his heart went out to the man. *He is right,* Mike thought. *She looks exactly like her mother.* Scanning the room, he found Elizabeth in the dessert line. She looked so much like her father. How could he have fooled so many for so long? Trudy and Henry did not have a clue, and, although, it had been ten years, they should have recognized something about the man. Glancing back toward Andrew, Mike's attention was drawn across the table to Gloria. She was staring at him, and in an instant, Mike knew she was in love with him.

"I have missed these Thanksgiving dinners," Miss Tillie remarked, coming to stand beside him.

"And we have missed having you," Mike replied, noting how well she looked. "But you are here tonight, and that pleases me."

"I made up my mind to attend several days ago. Mattie said I was acting like an old fuddy-duddy, and I expect she was right. Besides, she would have gotten me here one way or the other."

"Miss Mattie can be very persuasive. I imagine she is extending very good advice to Melba and Willy right about now. And if she is in error about something, old Ben will correct her." He laughed, noting his old friend propped back in his chair across the table. Looking around the fellowship hall, he seemed preoccupied, but Mike knew he was not missing a word.

"I suppose Melba and Willy will be our next wedding?"

"We will see," Mike replied, noting a fleeting glimpse of sadness cross her face.

"Oh, Pastor Mike, I hope I have my senses about me then. I do so love weddings."

"Then we will pray to that end," he replied, patting her hand.

"Thank you. And speaking of my…condition, I have decided a companion is a splendid idea, and I also know who," she stated confidently.

"I am glad to hear that. Do you mind telling me?"

"Not in the least. It is that poor, young girl who just lost her home."

Tilting his head back, Mike looked at the ceiling, chuckled, and then grinned broadly at Miss Tillie. "I was planning on approaching you this week with that very suggestion. Looks like the Lord handpicked Gloria, didn't he?"

Relaxed, Andrew sat in the overstuffed chair in his sitting room. It was nice and cozy, and he glanced around the small quarters that had been home these last weeks. The French doors were closed against the cold, night air, and he studied his painting of the old mill. Done from memory, it reflected the peace he discovered there shortly after his arrival in Oak Grove. Several other paintings were propped against the bookcase, and he knew they would sell easily. Absentmindedly smoothing his beard, he pondered on that idea. They portrayed a new life, and a part of him wanted to keep them private.

The clock in the downstairs hall chimed the eleven o'clock hour, and he closed the book in his lap and rested his head on the back of the chair, giving way to his thoughts.

The evening before he was to leave for Connecticut could not have been better, and he realized tonight how much the people in this small town meant to him. Staring at the ceiling, faces and voices paraded through his mind.

Pastor Mike was one of the most unique Christian men he had ever met. At the age of thirty-eight, he possessed a wisdom some pastors never attained. Strong, committed, and affectionate, he and his family epitomized all that Andrew wanted in life. His thoughts turned fondly to the Cranstons, who treated him as one of the family, not proprietors. There was Miss Mattie, old Ben and the men at the blacksmith shop, and Gerald, dishing out advice with his ice cream. Alan waving him into the Chronicle, Sheriff and Jim Walker forever bantering back and forth, and Michael Madison who always went out of his way to be helpful every time he went in the bank.

A slight chuckle escaped as Miss Tillie came to mind. He didn't know who was more colorful, her or Cooley. Melba, red hair and glorious green eyes, *I have to paint her*, he thought, wondering how Willy would feel about that. He would be shocked if he knew how Andrew envied him, but he was genuinely happy for them. They had a wonderful future ahead.

Gray eyes and a husky voice drifted into his mind, and a slow smile crossed Andrew's face. Gloria warmed his heart. Young and innocent, occasionally moody, bold at times, curious, graceful, and unpretentious, she had displayed surprising courage the past several days, and he remembered holding her while she cried. He had given something of himself that night, and it felt good. He had not experienced that in a long time.

A suffocating feeling came over Andrew at the memory of Caroline approaching him and inquiring about his art work. "I enjoy it too, Mr. Baxter. I hope to paint like you someday." She had looked directly at him with a smile that tore at his heart, and for a brief instant, he was transported back in time and speaking with Mary.

He tried to remember his response, something about giving her tips and teaching her, but he was too captivated with how much she looked like her mother; the same heart-shaped face, straight nose, and blond hair. He stood with hands clasped behind him while they chatted, and he studied her; the small dimple in her chin, green eyes, and her mouth, curving up when she smiled. It was all Mary. She was tall for her age, and he realized that was the only trait of his she possessed.

The moment became only sweeter when Elizabeth rushed up and grabbed his arm. "They said you are going back to Connecticut. Don't you like Oak Grove, Mr. Baxter? We want you to stay, don't we, Laura?" she said, looking at her friend and then back up at him.

Taking her small hand in his, he looked down at her, acutely aware of the precious feel of his daughter's hand. A frown creased her brow, and she stood with her free hand on a hip, awaiting his answer. He smiled and bent to her level, his own eyes staring back at him. She was a beautiful child with dark hair and olive skin so like his own, but she was also full of spirit, and he again knew she would be the one he would have to contend with.

"Elizabeth, I am leaving for Connecticut in the morning, but I shall only be gone a week."

"Nifty," she commented, grinning broadly. "Because I have some other things I want you to draw for me."

"Elizabeth," Caroline exclaimed, "don't be rude. Mr. Baxter does not have time to draw pictures for you."

The precious moment ended as quickly as it began when a young girl called to Caroline, and Elizabeth, satisfied that he was returning, wished him a happy Thanksgiving and then rushed off across the room.

"I don't care how long it takes, Lord," he prayed silently, "please let my daughters come to know and love me."

"You have been awfully quiet," Melba commented, scooting across the sofa and laying her head against Willy's shoulder.

"Ummm."

"Is everything all right?"

Will had not been himself all evening. They had enjoyed the Thanksgiving dinner, the music, and the fellowship, but as the evening passed, he had become more reticent. *Perhaps Pastor Mike's sermon is on his mind,* she thought hopefully. He had presented the plan of salvation this morning in such a simple and appealing way, she could not imagine anyone coming away untouched.

"I don't know, Mel." Twining their fingers together, he rested his head on the back of the couch and sighed. "I'm confused."

"Confused about what, Will?"

Staring at the ceiling, he was silent a minute and then remarked, "Pastor Mike."

"Pastor Mike? Whatever for?"

Unconsciously massaging his injured thigh, Willy looked at her a long moment and then shook his head. "After church, I told him I would like to get baptized. He seemed pleased and said if I had time to wait we would discuss it. There was something about him that...I don't know."

Rubbing a hand across his forehead, he sighed. "I guess I should have stayed, but he was greeting everyone, and I knew what a busy afternoon it would be, getting all those tables set up for tonight. I figured we could talk about it later, so I didn't stay. He probably thinks I was not very serious."

"I am sure he did not think anything of the kind. He said to wait if you had time, didn't he? I am sure he will be by to see you tomorrow, you just wait and see."

"Why do we have to discuss it in the first place?" Willy asked, irritated. "I want to be baptized, and that's that. He could have just said okay."

Leaning forward, Melba looked at him closely. "Will, Pastor Mike talks to everyone before he baptizes them. It is an important decision, and he wants to make sure everyone understands what they are doing. He is not treating you any different than anyone else." Kissing him lightly, she smiled and touched his cheek. "I am so happy for you."

"Why, because the *great preacher* is going to meet with me?" Willy remarked, realizing how ridiculous he sounded, but he was angry. He was fond of Pastor Mike, but somehow it was his fault that...that what? He did not know, but somehow this confusion he felt had something to do with him. "Who does he think he is? How does he know more about what I want than me? I told him I want to be baptized, and that should be enough."

Surprised, Melba sat back and studied his clenched jaw. "Will, Pastor Mike respects your feelings. I know he does, and he cares a great deal for you. He only wants you to share what you are thinking and feeling."

"And then what...he decides if I should or should not get baptized? Is he the *ruler* of the church?" Willy impatiently ran a hand through his hair. No one was going to stand in his way of marrying Melba, no one.

"No, Will. Pastor Mike is not the ruler of the church. He...he shepherds us and cares for us...teaches and ministers to everyone, even those who are not members. He would never do anything to hinder your becoming a Christian or hurt your feelings in any way. You know him better than that."

"I guess," Willy replied, releasing a long breath and feeling guilty. "I was...afraid he was going to tell me no, and I know how important it is to you."

Melba sat transfixed, looking at the emotion in his face and attempting to ignore the same feeling of apprehension that had gripped her the other night. Panic seized her as the question formed in the back of her mind. *Please, God,* she prayed, her heart pounding as it loomed larger.

"Will?"

"What is it, hon? What is wrong?"

Placing trembling hands together, she took a deep breath. "I need to know... I... I want to know why you want to be baptized?"

Her manner troubled him, and concern crossed his face as he took her trembling hand in his. "What is this? I didn't mean to upset you, Mel."

Pulling her into his arms, he kissed her cheek. "I am sorry. I was not being fair to Pastor Mike. It is just that I love you, Mel. I love you more than life itself. And we will have a good Christian home. I promise."

Of his sincerity she had no doubt, but the question was there, and she had to know.

"Why, Will, why do you *really* want to get baptized?" she asked, suddenly knowing she did not want his answer.

"Because I know how happy it will make you, and I need to. It is the right thing," he answered, smiling reassuringly.

"Will," Melba said softly, moving out of his arms, "you should not get baptized to make me happy. That is the wrong reason."

Tilting his head in a manner so familiar, she watched confusion cross his face, and she prayed he would understand. "I want you to follow Christ in baptism because you know that he died for your sins, you have asked his forgiveness, and you want him to live in your heart. That has to happen first."

Staring at one another for a long, silent minute, Melba knew by the look in his eyes he had no understanding of what she was saying. "Will, Pastor Mike preached this morning about the man, Nicodemus, who came to him at night. Jesus told him that no one could see the kingdom of God unless he was born again. You must be born again, Will."

For a long moment Willy studied her face, taking in her every feature and knowing something critical was happening. An impulse to do something seized him, a desire to flee, to laugh, or take her in his arms and kiss her. He had to do something, anything, to stop this moment. What was happening? What was she saying? He hadn't understood it when Pastor Mike had said it this morning, and Willy knew that was why he was angry. Pastor Mike had spoken of something he did not comprehend, and Willy blamed him for his lack of understanding.

"Mel," Willy began, grabbing her hand. "I am trying. I really am, but I don't get it. I don't see how something that happened so long ago could... how does it happen?"

"It is like Jesus told Nicodemus, Will. You can hear and feel the wind, but you don't know where it comes from or where it is going, and that is how God's spirit is. You can feel and hear him. Jesus is God's Son. He came into this world so that all who believe in him would not perish but have everlasting life. You only have to believe that he died for your sins. He took our punishment for those sins so we would not have to."

Sitting forward with his head in his hands, he was quiet for several minutes and then looked back at her almost pleadingly. "Mel, I do believe Jesus died on a cross, I do. I would never lie to you. I read it in the Bible old Ben gave me."

With a relieved smile he sat back and faced her. "I know it is true. I wasn't there, but I believe it. I wasn't there when Thomas Jefferson wrote the Declaration of Independence, but I believe he did, and I wasn't there when Abraham Lincoln gave the Gettysburg Address, but it is history. You see? I do believe."

A terrible ache filled Melba's heart as the truth hit her. She saw it, but Willy did not. "Will," Melba said tenderly, a tear running down her cheek, "yes, you believe, but…you believe with your head…not your heart."

"Don't cry, Mel. Please don't cry," Willy said, pulling her into his arms. "I will figure it out. One of these days I will," he said, kissing her softly. "It will be all right. I will get all this head and heart business straightened out. It will just take time."

"I am praying so hard," Melba cried. "More than anything, I pray for your salvation. I pray for the both of us. It is so hard loving you as I do and knowing I cannot marry you unt—"

Abruptly releasing his hold, Willy looked at her strangely. "Until? Until what, Mel?"

"I know you are so close. God is working in your heart, and—"

"Wait a minute," Willy exclaimed, suddenly angry. "Until what? You said you wanted to be certain we would have a Christian home before we got married, and I understand that." Sitting back, he looked at her in astonishment. "I have done everything you wanted. I have been going to church, Sunday morning, and Sunday evening, I might add. I have been reading that little book, *God's Minute*, every day, as you asked, and I agreed to get baptized. Now you are telling me you won't marry me until I have this *mystical experience* or whatever?"

"Will, it is not a mystical experience…It is—"

Standing to his feet, Willy looked down at her. "Do you love me or not, Melba?"

"Of course I do. You know I do," she exclaimed, rising to her feet and grabbing his arm. "I love you with all my heart."

Staring at her, he only knew he never wanted to be without her. "If you love me, then marry me…now! I am tired of you putting it off."

"Will," Melba cried, tears streaming down both cheeks, "I know you are so close to becoming a Christian, and you said…you said you will figure this out. God will make it clear to you. He does to all that seek him, and more than anything—"

"No!" he exclaimed, jerking away. "I can't take this any longer. If you love me, then you will marry me with no strings attached. Do…you…understand?" he ground out, his eyes full of anger.

"I can't, Will. I can't," Melba cried, pleading for him to understand. "Not just yet."

"Yes! Yes, you can," Willy exclaimed, gripping both her arms. "You can marry me, and you know it. This is ridiculous…putting off our marriage because I do not measure up to your *biblical* standards."

"Willy, I am not asking you to measure up to anything or anyone. Please try to understand. I want what is best for both of us."

"And you think this is best?" Willy questioned, raising his voice. "Tormenting me is best?"

"I am not tormenting you," Melba retorted angrily. "You know I would never do that. I want to get married as much as you."

"You have a fine way of showing it. Maybe if I was a little more like the *charming Mr. Andrew Baxter*, you wouldn't be dragging your feet," he said through gritted teeth. "I mean, he is the *perfect Christian man*. In fact, he is the man you wish I was, isn't he?"

Melba's face turned red with anger. How could he think such a thing! "I refuse to comment on such a ludicrous remark. I love you, and you know it, and I am not marrying you at this time because it is what I have to do for the both of us."

Willy stopped cold and stared. *It is what I have to do for the both of us*, his mother's words, her exact words when he accused her of what she had become. A cold rage churned inside, and through the rage, he saw his mother. Melba was no different. He could not trust her either.

Crying silently, Melba watched the changing emotions cross his face. Fury blazed in his eyes, and he stepped back and stared at her. She watched anger drain away and a terrible sadness replace it. For an instant, he looked pleadingly at her and then stared unseeing at the wall across the room, a look of total bewilderment on his face. Shifting his gaze back to her, he opened his mouth to say something then closed it, his shoulders slumped, and he looked at the floor, shaking his head in denial.

Wanting to throw herself into his arms, Melba stood unmoving, watching him. Did he not know how much she loved him?

Slowly, he raised his head and stared at her, and she was taken aback by the look of disgust on his face. "You are no different than any other woman," he stated flatly. Turning abruptly, he grabbed his jacket and strode to the door. "You are all the same."

The quiet closing of the door was louder than if he had slammed it, and Melba stood in the middle of the room staring after him. *This did not happen*, she thought. *Oh, God, please don't let this happen.*

Chapter 27

Surprised when Noah appeared to fill his gas tank, Mike listened with a heavy heart, wondering what had happened from yesterday to this morning.

"Uncle Ben and ah was sound asleep when we heard poundin' on the door. Ah jest knew somethin' awful happened. There stands Willy lookin' madder than a ragin' bull." Noah shook his head, screwed the gas cap on, and replaced the nozzle on the pump.

"Uncle Ben tried ta get him ta come in, but he said he was through with ever'body in this town. He stood there starin', and ah thought he was goin' ta hit me. Then he asked if ah wanted a job, and ah said shore, and he said, 'Ya got one,' and tole me ta take care of the place and stomped off."

Handing Noah a dollar, Mike placed his wallet in his back pocket and leaned against the car, puzzled. "He didn't say where he was going?"

"No, suh, not a word. Uncle Ben walked over ta his house early this mornin', but it was locked up tight and no hide nor hair of him."

"Thank you, Noah. He will probably return in a couple of days. Until then, I know you will look after the place."

"Ah shore will, but, Pastor Mike, he was mad, real mad about somethin'. Ah don't know." Noah removed his ball cap and scratched his head. "Ah guess a man's gotta do what a man's gotta do, but...ah jest don't know."

Nodding, Mike got in the car and drove around the block. The shades at Willy's were drawn, the garage door closed, and Jack lay on the front porch looking forlorn. Stepping out of the car, Mike slapped his leg and called, but Jack only raised his head and laid it down again. Walking across the yard to the garage, he slid the wood door ajar and peered inside. Willy's Plymouth was gone.

Jack trotted up and followed him around the house. Noah was right; everything was closed and locked tight. "Where did he go, boy?" Mike asked, rubbing his ears. It was unlike Willy to leave Jack behind with no food or water.

Looking up into the gray, November sky, he mulled over yesterday's conversation. "I would like to be baptized," Willy said. Rejoicing, he had asked him to wait a bit so they could talk, but when everyone was gone, so was Willy. He and Melba seemed happy at the dinner last night, although, now that he thought about it, Willy had not circulated and visited with anyone much. He should have known something was wrong. That was not like him at all.

"Come on, Jack." Crossing the street to Ben's, he stepped up on the curb, turned, and looked back. Jack was once more lying on the porch. Troubled, Mike walked up the steps, opened the door, and stepped in. "Ben?"

"Ah'm back here, Preacher."

Walking the familiar hall, he found old Ben at the kitchen table with a cup of coffee and his open Bible in front of him.

"I'll get it." Motioning him to stay seated, Mike retrieved a cup from the cupboard, poured himself a cup of coffee, and sat down across the table. "I just spoke with Noah."

"Ah don't know what ta think. Gosh a mighty, but Willy was in a bad way. He woke us 'bout two thirty this mornin'." Ben shook his head and smoothed his white mustache with his thumb and forefinger. "Ah ain't never seen him like that. He was full of anger, and the look in his eyes was…hard. Ah ain't seen that in a man in a long time."

Ben pushed his cup back, sighed, and shook his head. "He wouldn't listen to me a'tal, not one bit. It was like ah was lookin' at a stranger, ah tell ya."

The two men sat silent for a minute, confused and wondering what changed Willy so drastically. Noting the misery in Old Ben's face, Mike knew he felt as bad as he did.

"I don't have any idea where he might have gone, do you?" Mike asked, racking his brain to remember if Willy had ever mentioned any friends or acquaintances.

"Ah cain't think of any place either. He didn't have no other family. The Stantons was the only kin he had left."

"Did he ever mention anyone from his past, Ben?"

"No, suh. Willy did everything he could ta forget his past. Do ya think Melba knows he's gone?"

Mike sighed and ran a hand across his forehead. "I don't know, but I suspect…something must have happened between them. I don't think anything else would have caused him to pack up and leave."

"What do ya think troubled the waters?"

Mike sat his coffee on the table and looked at his old friend. "Well, if I had to guess, I would say it had something to do with Willy's spiritual condition. Melba was concerned about that."

"Ah tole him as much. He was over here one night, and we was talkin' 'bout it," Ben said, absentmindedly stirring his coffee. "Ah know the Lord is dealin' with him."

Mike nodded. "I know. He told me yesterday he wanted to be baptized, and I thought…it just doesn't make any sense, Ben, unless—"

"Unless what?"

"I don't know. We should not judge anyone's behavior until we have all the facts."

Mike stared at the floor, his mind a blank. The clock in the living room chimed eight thirty, and he heard Ben release a breath and move his feet. Looking up at his old friend, he saw Ben was staring at the stove.

"Ah'd say it was a lover's quarrel, but…ah'm feared it's much worse than that. If you'd a seen the look on his face…no suh, it was much more'n a spat."

"I am afraid so too, Ben." Mike gazed through the window at Willy's house. "The Lord has definitely been working on him. We are going to have to trust him."

"Yes suh, yer right about that. Ah jest hope he don't do nothin' foolish. Ah guess we'll have ta depend on the Lord ta look after him, won't we?"

Mike nodded and took a drink of coffee.

"Ya got all them Thanksgivin' baskets ta deliver this mornin'?"

"Yes," Mike answered, glancing at his wristwatch. "We are meeting at the church at ten o'clock, but I think I will head home and see if perhaps Leah has heard anything from Melba. I imagine she will need someone to talk with."

"Ah expect ya better go then. Ah'll keep an eye on things across the street."

"Have prayer with me first, will you, Ben?"

It did not take long for news to spread that Willy had departed Oak Grove, leaving everyone to wonder why, where he had gone, and what about Melba? Concern was genuine, but all he could tell them was he did not know. Frustrated, Mike asked himself again why he had not seen it coming, or perhaps he did and failed to act. Either way, his heart was heavy. He knew exactly how Willy felt and what he was going through.

Mike laid his head along the back of the sofa and closed his eyes. He was tired. Today had been filled with a mixture of emotions. Hoping to catch Andrew before he left for Connecticut, he had stopped by the hotel, but Abigail said he had left early for the Chesterville Airport, and Melba, answering the door teary-eyed, preferred him and Leah to come back at a later time. Missing Gloria at Ron's, he went home, picked up Leah, and they headed to church to deliver Thanksgiving baskets.

Ignoring Myrtle's scrutiny and raised brow at his lack of a tie, she informed him Trudy was already downstairs organizing the whole shebang, and all the work she did getting addresses and typing the lists was for nothing.

The discussion in progress was more confusion than organization, debating over who was going to ride with whom, how many trips would have to be made, and if Baptists should deliver to Methodists and Methodists to Baptists.

Taking matters into hand, he announced everything was already planned and then proceeded to thank Trudy and Mildred for co-chairing committees, Myrtle for her work in the office, and everyone who showed up to help distribute the bounty. Reverend Clark led in a word of prayer, trunks were loaded, and they were on their way.

The rest of the afternoon blessed Mike's heart. Gratitude and happiness beamed from worried faces, and wide-eyed children rummaged through baskets, grinning happily when they found various flavored candy sticks from Milly and Molly. The elderly gripped his hand tightly while he prayed with them and offered their thanks over and over again, unable to show enough appreciation.

It had been a good day. The house was quiet now, his own children asleep in their beds, and he wondered on Willy's whereabouts.

"Are you tired?"

Opening his eyes, he saw Leah sitting on the footstool watching him. "Yes, come here," he said, extending his hand.

"There is nothing you can do about it, Mike."

A tender smile crossed his lips, and he squeezed her. "Reading my mind, are you?"

Stretching his legs, he ran his hand along her arm and murmured softly, "Where did he go? Why didn't I see—"

"Mike, there was nothing to see. Willy and Melba were happy. Whatever happened, there is nothing you could have done. It is between the two of them."

"I know, and I am fairly certain the problem is Willy's lack of faith. Melba spoke with me about it several times. She truly loves him, but as long as he runs from the Lord, neither will ever be happy. This may be what will bring him to his knees."

"I feel so badly for them. Surely they will work things out." Leah snuggled into the crook of his arm, enjoying the feel of his hand in her hair and the comfort of his nearness.

Lifting her hand, Mike looked at her wedding ring, remembering the day he slipped it on her finger and of the love they shared. "I don't know what I would do without you, darlin'."

"I know. I love you so, Mike. I wish everyone was as happy as we are. That is my prayer for Melba and Willy, and Andrew also. I feel so sorry for him. For all of his wealth, he is so terribly lonely."

"If he would just open his eyes and take note, he wouldn't have to be."

"What do you mean?"

A look of devilment in his eyes, Mike grinned. "You are not very observant."

Curious, she stared at him, "Observant about what?"

The grin still in place, he laid his head back against the sofa. "Gloria."

"Gloria?" Leah asked in wonder.

"Gloria. I watched her last night, and she couldn't take her eyes off him. Love was written all over her face."

"Gloria...she is so sweet. She is a little young, but wouldn't she be good for Andrew?" Raising a brow, she looked at Mike and shook her head in frustration. "And I suppose he does not even suspect."

"Not in the least." Recalling how often he heard Andrew speak of her, Mike grinned. "At least not at the present, but I would say there is a whole lot about to happen in that man's life that will send him into a tailspin, and I am going to enjoy every minute of it."

Chapter 28

"I don't know how things went so wrong," Melba said, wiping a tear. "We were talking and enjoying one another and then...I am sorry."

"Melba, it is all right," Leah said, patting her hand. "Cry if you need to."

Wiping her eyes, she quietly stared at her hands in her lap. Leah and Mike looked at one another, and Mike prayed for words of comfort as she looked at him and tears flowed freely again.

"I am sorry." Sitting up, Melba took a deep, trembly breath and looked at them apologetically.

Observing her anguish, Mike remembered the raw emotion he had once experienced. "Never be sorry for tears, Melba. Tears are evidence of one's great capacity for love. And we know how much you love Willy."

"The look on his face when I told him I could not marry him was...I tried to explain, but he became enraged and said I was no different than any other woman and I could not be trusted, and he...he looked at me like...I was disgusting or something. That hurt the most, I think," she said, beginning to cry again. "It hurts so much."

"I know it does," Mike said, rubbing her hand. "I know it does."

"No you don't!" she cried. "You can't know what I am feeling." Dropping her head, she began weeping again.

"Oh, but I do. I know exactly how you feel," Mike replied quietly, his gaze traveling to Leah. "For you see, Melba, I have been where you are now."

The soft tone of her pastor's voice touched her, and she looked up into his face.

"I know it hurts, for several years ago I fell in love with the most beautiful, wonderful girl I thought God ever created. She was everything I wanted, and I knew he made her just for me. She was the first thing I thought of every morning and the last thing I thought of at night. When I was not with her, she was all I thought about. She was my whole life, just as Willy is to you."

Amazed that her pastor would tell her something so personal, she listened in rapt attention, forgetting her own pain for a moment.

"I guess you could say my love for her consumed me, and the Lord made it clear I was to give her up. I was so angry with him. I am sure Willy feels much the same right now."

"What did you do?" Melba asked quietly.

"The hardest thing I ever did in my life," he said quietly, looking at Leah. "I was angry and confused, but I was also frightened. If I did not obey, God might take her from me. All manner of terrible things ran through my head: sickness, her loving another, even death. My father instructed me to trust God and follow his lead. It was not what I wanted to hear, and I was angry with him also."

Melba watched as he absentmindedly rubbed a thumb across Leah's hand. "And then began my despair. I was so lonely, I missed her so much it hurt physically, and I felt like a walking dead man. I was angry, confused, hurting beyond measure, and even wondered why I was living. But, Melba, when things could not get worse, God reached down, picked me up, and comforted me. I began to need him more than anything in this world. I studied his Word and prayed as I had never prayed before.

The Lord taught me more of myself during that time of testing, which I would otherwise have never known. He drew me to him and opened my heart to the fact that I had never put him first in my life. He helped me realize who I was and who I was not and revealed what he wanted from me. And after that...I knew as well as I knew all the truths he taught me that he was pleased, and he allowed me to make this girl I loved my wife."

"What a beautiful story," Melba remarked softly.

"I do not know what the Lord has in store for you and Willy. I cannot tell you this will end as it did for us. But I know God longs to comfort you. Postponing your marriage to Willy was the right thing to do; you can take comfort in that. I also know the Lord loves Willy. He has been convicting him for some time now, and no matter how far or how long Willy runs, he cannot hide from him forever."

"I know," Melba agreed. "It is just so hard."

"Of course it is. But he is here for you. Now is the time to allow him to work in your life. Let him comfort and sustain you. Turn loose of Willy and allow God to take care of him. You have to let go and trust him to do so."

"Please," Melba said imploringly, "pray that God will increase my faith and trust."

Moving to the arm of Mike's chair, Leah slipped her arm around his shoulder and watched him take Melba's hands. Closing her eyes, she bowed her head and listened to her husband petition the Lord for Melba that she might feel his strength and comfort and know his direction in her life, as well as for Willy's protection, confusion, heartache, and salvation.

Stomping snow from his boots, Mike stepped through the door of the blacksmith shop to mingled smells of burning wood, oil, coffee, pipe tobacco, and whatever Ben was cooking on the stove. Looking up from the anvil, Ben waved his hammer and nodded, and Phillip, pouring a cup of coffee, grabbed Mike's cup from the nail and filled it.

"Here's your coffee, Pastor."

"Thank you, Phillip," Mike replied, removing his jacket and hanging it on a peg along the wall. Taking a seat on the stool next to Ben's work table, he looked at Louis, who grinned and jumped the last two of James's men.

"What do you think you're doing? You can't do that!" James exclaimed, staring at the checkerboard with a frown and running a hand through his wiry red hair, causing it to stick out in yet another direction. "Just how and when did you manage to move your man there?"

"I expect you ain't watchin' close enough," Louis retorted. "You are the easiest man to beat. At least Phillip…and even Cooley give me a little competition."

"Well who won the most games Thursday?" James asked, standing to his feet.

"Nobody, Thursday was Thanksgiving."

"Dad blame it, then Wednesday."

"Don't rightly remember," Louis replied, stretching his stiff legs.

"Don't remember? Well now I've heard everything. Preacher, now he's taking up lying on top of everything else."

"You don't remember either."

Chuckling, Mike, sat his cup on the worktable and crossed both arms, watching the two old men go at it.

"Have you heard anything from Willy?" James asked, lifting the lid from the pot on the stove and peering inside. "How long is it going to be before this is done, Ben?"

"Pert near another hour," he replied, lighting his pipe. "I ain't heard nothin. Have you, Preacher?"

"No, no I haven't," Mike answered, wondering where he was and what he was doing.

"I guarantee you, Noah is doing a fine job at the garage, Ben," James commented, taking a seat on the bench next to the stove. "And when the chips were down, he came through. I don't know what would have happened if Noah hadn't stepped in to take care of the place."

"I expect," Old Ben said, puffing on his pipe, "and I'm right proud of him, but…it jest don't seem right to look out there and not see Willy."

All was quiet for a moment, heads nodding in agreement. "Where do ya suppose he's off ta?" Louis asked, looking at Mike.

"I don't know."

"Here I thought we would be having another wedding," Phillip commented, placing his men on the squares. "Now…well who knows. I wonder how Melba is doing. What do you suppose happened between the two of them?"

"It's not goin' ta do any good sittin' around tryin' ta figure out what went wrong," Ben said, his feet stuck out in front of him while he slowly rocked back and forth. "We could all throw out an idea, but we'd all more'n likely be wrong. It don't do no good ta speculate, no suh, no good."

"Yep," James agreed, nodding his head. "You just never know what is really going on in someone's life. Now you take that lady over in Chesterville, and I don't mean to spread gossip, Pastor, but I know this to be true. Miriam's sister lived right across the alley from her. It seems the poor old thing was sick and had to go away for treatment. Well, lo and behold, when the truth was known, she had run off with the Fuller Brush Man. And Miriam's sister said everyone thought she and her husband had the perfect marriage."

"Yeah, and I recollect here a few years back," Louis said, shaking his head, "over in Dexter it was tole that the Methodist preacher's wife got ta flirtin' so bad with the egg man, he was givin' her free eggs. When the townsfolk found out, they had ta up and move clean away. Who'd ever thought a preacher's wife would be a floosy."

About to choke on his coffee, Mike wiped his mouth with the back of his hand and burst into laughter. "The egg man?"

"The egg man."

Chapter 29

The cold air against Andrew's face was refreshing as he stood on the balcony outside his room, his eyes roaming across the square. The street lamps illuminated most of the area, and he allowed his gaze to wander along the now familiar shops. How he had missed this small town in the week he was gone. New York, teeming with activity, was a far cry from this. He had been busy the first couple of days finalizing business decisions, spent some time in his art gallery, and even managed to have dinner with friends, but it all rang of emptiness.

The rest of the week he spent in Connecticut. Even though the estate now belonged to him, he would always think of Wilkins Manor as Grandmother's home. The household staff was happy to see him, the home, stables and grounds well maintained, and Thanksgiving went as he instructed, continuing his grandmother's long-standing traditions. It was not the same without her. Most of the older generation had passed on, and those who chose to come felt much the same as he; Grandmother was the glue that had held the family together. Teenagers wandered the manor in awe, and curious to his travels and bachelor status, they thought it all quite glamorous. The little ones ran helter skelter enjoying themselves, and he found it refreshing.

He enjoyed the staff and Cletus more than anything, taking his meals in the kitchen with them and reminiscing over days long gone. Wandering around the place, he took advantage of the solitude to examine his own heart and soul, knowing his life would never be the same again.

Climbing the stairs one evening, he stepped into his grandmother's room and glanced around, her familiar scent still lingering after all this time. Strolling across the room to the fireplace, he looked at a photograph on the mantel. It was taken down by the stables, and he stood with his brothers and grandfather. He stared at the photograph for a long moment, guessing himself to be about seven or eight years of age. How in heaven's name had he been able to fool so many people? Elizabeth looked just like him. Replacing the photograph, he wondered what she was doing at this precise moment and grinned, probably something mischievous.

The latter part of the week, he spent much of his time in the stables grooming General, his own big bay presented to him by his grandmother on his thirtieth birthday. Snorting and pawing in recognition each morning when he approached, he would toss his head up and down and then stand patiently while Andrew saddled him. Racing across the fields at full gallop, Andrew discovered those mornings to be a balm for relinquishing long held regrets.

Feeling the cold, he stepped back into his room, closed the door, and glanced around the small sitting room. As much as he loved Wilkins Manor, the hold this small town had on him could not be denied. As long as his daughters were here, so was his heart, and after the holidays he would check on an old place outside of town that caught his attention. He needed a home that his daughters could one day visit.

Unusually content, he sat back in the large overstuffed chair and relaxed. He heard Scooter bark and Lottie tell him to hush, and he stared at the wall, thinking of his last night at Wilkins Manor. As was his habit, he went to his grandfather's den to read. Completing the passage he was studying, Andrew closed his Bible and looked across the room at Mary's portrait above the fireplace.

Beautiful, sweet Mary—how he had loved her. The thought jolted him. How he had *loved* her? He still loved her. Why had he expressed his feelings in the past tense? He would always love Mary. Transfixed, he examined her portrait, absorbing all her features; her eyes, nose, mouth, and chin. Where was she? He stared at her portrait. It was but an image on canvas. Thinking hard, Andrew tried to remember the sound of her voice and her laugh, and in astonishment realized he could not. Standing to his feet, he walked over and looked up, staring at her face in disbelief. How could he have forgotten? She was looking down at him, a sweet smile on her face, and truth dawned. Mary was part of his past, and she was becoming a distant memory. How could that be? Frustrated, he tried to recall the fragrance of her hair and the feel of her hand in his. Rooted to the spot in front of the fire, it all soaked in and spread through his heart and mind. Mary was gone, never to return. This, today, was the present, and he and their daughters a part of it. Mary would want them to be happy. *Caroline and Elizabeth must know how wonderful their mother was,* Andrew thought, staring at the crackling fire, *and I will make sure they do.*

Lifting his gaze, he stared up at the same heart shaped face and features Caroline possessed. "I am going back, Mary," he said softly. "I am going back to tell Caroline and Elizabeth I am their father, and our daughters will know how much I loved you."

"Now, my dear, this will be your private quarters if you so choose to accept my proposal," Miss Tillie said, stepping through the open door. "Come in and look around."

Standing in the middle of a spacious sitting room, Gloria looked around with pleasure. The colors were peach and cream, and a dark, rich green rug lay on the floor. A chair was positioned to look out into the back yard, and a peach damask settee sat in front of a fireplace.

Crossing the room and swinging the doors wide, Miss Tillie stepped back and allowed Gloria to step into the bedroom. A canopied bed sat predominantly in the middle of the room, its coverlet a rich, silk brocade of green, cream, and apricot. Large windows occupied one wall and at the opposite end a door stood ajar revealing a spacious bathing chamber.

"Miss Tillie, this is so very lovely."

"Thank you. I think you will be very comfortable here, and if there is anything you wish to bring along, please feel free to do so. I have plenty of room in this big old house."

"I am afraid that would not…well, I really do not have…I lost everything in the fire," she explained, disheartened.

"Of course, please forgive me," Miss Tillie replied, looping her arm through Gloria's and steering her toward the door. "I was not thinking. I am so very sorry. Shall we go back downstairs and have another cup of tea with Leah and Pastor Mike?"

Descending the steps, Gloria ran her hand along the rich wood banister. Miss Tillie's home was beautiful.

"There you two are," Leah said, watching Gloria and Miss Tillie enter the living room. Pouring each a cup of tea, she studied their faces and glanced at Mike.

"Miss Tillie has a beautiful home, doesn't she?" Mike asked, rising as the two women took their seats.

"Oh, yes. It is so very beautiful."

Mike smiled, pleased with Gloria's apparent satisfaction. "It is quite spacious and very comfortable. It is also very well built. I don't think they build homes like this any more."

"Now, Pastor Mike, don't you start giving me or Gloria a bunch of your gobbledygook. If this young lady wishes to take up residence here, I would be most happy. But don't you start trying to sway her opinion. This is entirely her decision."

Mike laughed and looked at the surprise on Gloria's face. "You might as well get used to Miss Tillie. She says exactly what she thinks."

"Yes, sir, I sure do. It makes life a whole lot simpler when everyone knows where you are coming from and who you are. Even when I get befuddled and forget who I am for a while, I hope I am the same."

"Yes, Miss Tillie, you don't have to worry about that," Mike answered, chuckling.

Gloria giggled and glanced at Leah.

"Miss Tillie, you are a treasure." Leah laughed.

"I shall get right to it, Gloria," Miss Tillie said, smiling. "I would love to have you stay with me, but I don't need any mollycoddling, so you might just as well forget it if this preacher has put that notion in your head. He thinks I need someone to keep an eye on me, even though I heartily disagree. I can take care of myself, even though he thinks I cannot."

Sipping her tea, she glanced over the rim of her cup at Mike. "But, alas, I fear I have run into someone as stubborn as myself, so I have given in to his wishes. So, my dear, if you do decide to accept my offer, all you will have to do is keep one eye on me when I slip back into the past. I must say I enjoy the spells. And who knows—you may too."

Grinning at Miss Tillie's forthright manner, Gloria found herself perfectly at ease.

"Miss Tillie, I don't believe I need to think about it any longer. Your offer is an answer to my prayer. I would be most happy living here."

Sighing, Melba laid her head against the sofa. Willy's handsome, rugged face loomed in her mind, and the familiar ache in her heart of the last two weeks brought fresh tears.

"Oh, Jack, where is he?" she asked, looking into the faithful brown eyes. "If he walked through the door right now, you would be all over him, wouldn't you?"

I would too, Melba thought, *I wouldn't care where he has been or what he has done. If he would just come home.*

She loved Will, and he loved her. But what if he chose not to accept Christ, what if harm came to him, what if he met someone else, and being so hurt and vulnerable, he—

"Stop it," Melba spoke aloud. Frustrated, she rose from the couch and made her way into the bedroom. Slipping out of her robe, she sat on the edge of the bed and watched Jack flop down in his spot on the rug, his new residence now that Willy was gone. Looking up at her, he tilted his head and then laid it on her knees as though sharing her grief.

Tears flowed freely, and Melba knew she had to get a grip on herself. But how? She missed Will so terribly. Switching off the bedside lamp, Melba lay back and wished for numbness. Would it ever come?

Pastor Mike's words echoed in her ears. *I missed Leah so much, it hurt physically.* Sighing, she rolled to her side and stared through the window. It had worked out for Pastor Mike and Leah, but that was God's will. Nevertheless, he hurt just as she did now. How did he get through it?

Trying to think of all he told her, Melba went over their visit in her mind.

I cannot tell you this will end as it did for Leah and me. You were right in postponing your marriage to Willy. You can take comfort in that.

"Comfort? Where is your comfort when I need you, God? I did what you wanted." Curling into a ball, Melba cried into her pillow. "Where are you?"

Shocked at her anger, Melba dashed the tears from her eyes. She should not be angry with God. Who did she think she was? Had Pastor Mike felt guilty? He had been angry too, he said so. What else had he said?

I do not know what the Lord has in store for you and Willy, but I know God loves you, and he loves Willy.

Melba released a long breath. Yes, that was true. She believed it with all her heart. And if he loved them both, wouldn't his will be that they have a good marriage?

Melba lay quietly, remembering. *God has been convicting Willy for some time now, and no matter how far or how long he runs, he cannot hide.*

She must pray for Willy. Melba sat up and stared at her shadow in the mirror, a shocked revelation dawning. All the times she had prayed for Will, she had prayed selfishly. She was praying for his salvation so they could be married. Melba sat dumbfounded, the realization of how selfish and wrong she had been washing over her. It had all been about her happiness, not Will's spiritual condition at all.

"Oh, God, I am so sorry. Please forgive my ignorance. What have I done?"

Fear gripped her. Will was lost. Gripping her trembling hands together, Melba shook her head back and forth. How could she have failed with the one she loved so desperately?

"Wherever he is God, please, please draw him to you. Open his heart and mind to understanding so that he might become a child of yours. Not for me, not for me, but that Will might have eternal life."

Curled into a ball, Melba lay silent for several minutes, her pounding heart gradually slowing to an even beat. Slowly and gently acceptance settled in her heart. She would always love Will, and if the love they shared was but this brief time, she was blessed and would always hold his love precious in her heart.

She lay still, listening to the clock ticking on the bureau. Jack moved on the floor by the bed, and a car passed on the street. Willy's smiling face floated into her mind, and the smallest hint of a smile touched her lips. A warm peace settled in her heart, and she knew it was the peace Pastor Mike spoke of.

The year 1947 would soon be here. It would be a new year and a new beginning, whether she shared it with Will or not. Regardless, it would come, and God would see them both through.

Epilogue
-December 14, 1946-

Chicago—Lower west side

Stepping out on the sidewalk, the man pulled his sock cap down over his ears, turned his collar up, and shoved ungloved hands into the pockets of his patched coat. He squinted in the heavily falling snow and turned back for a last glance at the old brick building. Except for a light in an upper window, it was dark, and he knew most of the homeless were sleeping.

Below-freezing temperatures and unrelenting snow forced more than the normal number of vagrants to seek shelter in the large, rundown building at the corner of West Washington and Morgan Streets. Mercy Mission provided warmth from the cold and a bowl of soup and bread to those who would otherwise starve or freeze to death. Wind whipped around windows and under doors, but at least the place afforded a dry place to sleep and a helping hand to those who had none.

Head bent, he labored along, snow almost to the top of his boots. Mary would have a fit that he walked home this late at night, especially in this weather.

"Lord, I do nah know why ye be wantin' me to go home tonight. Ye know the place is full to overflowin', all o' them wantin' a wee bit o' comfort. 'Tis a good opportunity ta tell them o' your love along with a warm blanket and fillin' their bellies, but I should've stayed. Charlie and Bill, they been there three nights in a row, and 'tis me turn."

Pausing at the corner, he stood in the light of the lamp post for a minute, took a couple of deep breaths, and looked around. It was impossible to tell where the street ended and the sidewalk began. Other than his own trodden path, there were no visible signs of anyone having been out and about for some time. Snow covered everything, erasing all traces of dirt, grime, sorrow, and sin that filled the lives of the hopeless on the streets and broken homes of Chicago's lower west side.

Patrick O'Keefe was a big, brawny, Irish man, thirty-five years old with red hair and brown eyes. His sheer size and powerful voice belied the tender heart beating within, and he stood now with a lump in his throat, aware of the beauty around him at this midnight hour.

Glancing back the three blocks he had come, he hesitated again, wondering if he ought to return, and then recalled Bill throwing his coat at him. *Now, Patrick, you know as well as Charlie and me, if the Lord is telling you to go on home, he's got his reasons. Now go on, get out of here.*

"Aye, he's right. 'Tis best I move along. I'm sure ye did nah send me on me way to lollygag around here at midnight, did ye?" Shoving his hands deeper in his pockets, he turned west. "Four blocks more is all 'tis."

Not walking more than a half a block, he raised a hand, brushed snow from his eyes, and the next instant was sprawled in the snow.

"Blast it all!" he exclaimed, rolling over and staring at a leg protruding from a mound of drifted snow. "Nay, not another dead one, Lord," he moaned, brushing the snow away and turning him over.

Tearing his gloves off, he lay his fingers against the man's cold neck and laid his head on his chest. Beneath his fingers, he felt the slight pulse. "Thank ye, Lord," he exclaimed, rising to his feet and pulling the man to a sitting position. The left arm hung at an awkward angle, and realizing there was nothing he could do about it, he removed his coat, wrapped it around the man and heaved him up over his shoulder.

"I got to get ye home 'fore ye freeze to death. If ye was conscious, I'd apologize for the pain, lad, but since ye ain't, I'll ask yer forgiveness later."

Trudging through the deep snow, unaware of the cold, he prayed for the man he carried. "Who might he be, Lord? Ye won't let him die will ye? Aye, 'tis clear now, he's the reason ye sent me home tonight. Right here in me path ye put him."

Stumbling under the man's dead weight, Patrick paused, took a deep breath, and continued. "We are almost there, lad, 'tis just another block."

Heart pounding in his chest, he labored slowly down the street, aware of a muffled groan from the man across his shoulder. Sighing with relief, he turned and made his way up the front steps. Lifting a foot to kick the door, he found it flung wide and Mary staring at him with round eyes.

"I saw you coming down the street." Shivering, Mary closed the door and scurried past her husband down the hall. The room at the back of the two-family flat was used frequently for many sick and wounded, and she threw the door open and flipped the light on. "What happened, Patrick?"

"Dunno. He was lyin' in the snow, and I tripped o'er him."

Quickly jerking the bed covers aside, Mary observed the fatigue and worry on her husband's face. "You undress him, and I will run upstairs for Doc."

Easing the man onto the bed, Patrick fearfully checked for a pulse and sighed with relief. He was still alive. Taking advantage of the man's unconscious state, he peeled away the ice- and snow-crusted shirt and trousers, throwing them to the floor. "Lord, 'tis even his shoes they made off with," he ground out, jerking his socks off.

"Doc will be right here," Mary exclaimed, appearing in the doorway. Red faced, she turned away from the near naked state of the man on the bed.

"More blankets, Mary. The lad's nigh froze."

Making her way down the hall, she closed Katie's door, listened for Doc's step in the hall, and then grabbed three blankets from the closet and rushed back to the room.

"Here," she said, draping an army blanket across the lifeless-looking man. "Oh, Patrick, will he live?"

"What do we have here?" Doctor Cole asked, appearing in the door in his night shirt and hastily donned trousers.

"Praise be to the Lord in heaven," Patrick exclaimed, moving away from the bed. "I stumbled o'er him on me way home. Bloody blokes beat and robbed the lad 'tis what happened."

Doctor Cole looked at the bruised and bloodied form of the man and sat his worn bag on the floor, glancing at Patrick. "Get out of those wet clothes, Patrick. I don't want to doctor two patients tonight. Mary, get him something warm to drink while I examine this chap."

Following Mary downstairs, Patrick sat at the kitchen table, exhausted.

"Here," Mary said, handing him his robe. "Get out of those clothes, and I will heat water for tea."

Removing his trousers and shirt, Patrick slipped into the warm robe and sat back at the table. "'Twas not me idea to come home tonight, Mary," he said quietly, looking at his wife in wonder. "'Tis the Spirit in here," he said, touching his chest. "He would nah leave me alone, and there was naught I could do to ignore him."

"It was divine intervention," Mary commented, her eyes wide and dark as she touched her husband's arm. "He woke me out of a dead sleep. I went to get a drink and saw you coming down the street. Our heavenly Father has great things in store for that man, Patrick. Wouldn't you say?"

Scratching his head, Patrick rose and ran a hand through his hair. "Aye, let's go see what Doc says about the lad."

Glancing up with a frown, Doc looked at Patrick and Mary. "Well you've brought home a good one this time. He is in bad shape. There's a gunshot wound below the right clavicle, and as best that I can tell, the left arm is broken and jerked out of socket. From the bruising, I am certain he has cracked ribs, and here," he commented, pointing to a bloody, swollen area along the left temple, "someone gave him a good blow to the head. That alone could have killed him. Whoever did this didn't have a conscience, if you ask me."

Standing to his feet, Doc studied the man on the bed and then turned to Patrick. "I will take the bullet out and patch him up as best I can, but let's pray pneumonia doesn't settle in." Shaking his head, he rubbed his chin with his forefinger, "As far as the blow to his head…I don't know. He might wake up tonight, tomorrow, or he might be unconscious for some time. Did he have any identification?"

"Ye know the bloody blokes would o' made off with his wallet," Patrick commented, lifting the wet trousers from the floor and rummaging through the pockets. "Aye, they did."

"He is not a vagrant. You can tell by his clothing. Does he look familiar?"

"Nay, I ne'er seen him 'round here, but 'tis hard to tell with his face bruised and swollen."

"Look. Look at this, Patrick," Mary said, retrieving a small photograph from the pocket of the shirt Patrick had thrown in the floor.

Studying the young man and woman in the photo, Patrick scrutinized the man on the bed.

"Do you think it's him?" she asked softly, glancing at the picture her husband held.

"'Tis hard to tell, Mary. He has the same build and dark hair. It could be. What do ye think, Doc?" Patrick asked, handing him the photograph.

Studying it a long moment, Doc looked at the man on the bed and then back at the photograph again. "I wouldn't say for sure, but it very well could be. Look at the forehead and chin, and you're right about the hair color and build."

"Aye, 'tis the same man."

"I agree, they look to be one and the same." Turning it over, Doc noted the writing. "I fear this is all we will know of him until he wakes up."

Patrick looked at the back of the photograph, glanced at Mary, and then read the handwritten words:

—Melba and Willy
July 4, 1946